THE GIRL WHO DARED TO DESCEND

THE GIRL WHO DARED TO THINK 3

BELLA FORREST

Before the Tower, history was riddled with stories about humanity defying the status quo. Regimes would come and go, nations would be united and then divided, treaties would be brokered and broken... The list went on and on, each generation inventing new ways to seize power, fight power, restructure power. The goal was always the same: change what you didn't like into something you did.

Before the End and the Tower, humanity fought against tyranny, battled their oppressors, and their tales and deeds became noteworthy enough to survive despite the history we lost —kept alive by people who didn't seem to want to fight anything anymore.

But I sure as hell did.

I swung helplessly between several sets of hands, unable to tell if there were only two people carrying me, or four, thanks to the black cloth bag covering my face and neck. The sound of

heavy boots on the metal floor of the halls I was being unceremoniously slung through told me there were too many to fight.

But that didn't mean I didn't want to.

I had been in the middle of trying to wrap my head around
the fact that my boyfriend was now being inhabited by the AI
predecessor to Scipio—the master AI that controlled most of the
day-to-day life of the Tower. My version of the AI—not that I
could claim ownership in any way—was one I had discovered in
a sealed office after narrowly avoiding death (or worse) at the
hands of Devon Alexander, Champion of the Knights. Who had
just been killed by Leo (my AI). Who was currently living inside
of Grey's (my boyfriend's) body.

It had been a busy day. Days. Weeks? Scipio kill me, had
this mess been going on for *months*?

It was hard to even remember at this point, so much had
happened. And was still happening.

I shifted and wriggled. My knees, hips, and shoulders were
all beginning to feel the strain of being dangled between people
like this.

"Be still," a male voice said.

"Then let me down to walk," I grunted, continuing to strug-
gle. "C'mon, Lacey, this is ridiculous. And it's starting to hurt."

I didn't use her honorific, although I should have: she was
the head of the Mechanics Department, which meant I should
refer to her as Engineer Green. And I knew she was there—only
a few seconds had passed since I heard her voice telling me to
calm down. Or at least I *thought* it had only been a few seconds.

To be honest, my head was still reeling from the fight that I'd just been a part of back in the Medica.

Devon had almost killed me. I shuddered, recalling the violent and angry look in his dual-colored eyes, and tried to steel my stomach against the creeping anxiety. My neck ached, and I knew I was going to have bruises there, imprints of his fingers that would remind me of how close I had come to death. Even after they faded, I knew the memory would continue to haunt me for a long time.

Scipio help me, I wanted nothing more than to curl up in Grey's arms and cry on his shoulder. He'd listen—he was good at that. I craved the warm feel of him against me.

But even that thought broke my heart. Devon had shorted out Grey's net in the fight, using his baton to fry the strands of silicon fibers that stretched over Grey's cerebral cortex. I'd seen the brain scan afterward—the black, cracked tissue that should have been a bright, shiny pink. It had looked like cracks radiating around the outside of a bowl. Cracks wide and cavernous enough that it seemed like it would never be reassembled.

Leo said that he could repair the damage, using the special net that Lionel Scipio—his creator, and founder of the Tower itself—had designed. He'd downloaded himself into Grey's net to help heal the damage to Grey's brain and recover his mind. He'd done it to save Grey, and I appreciated the gesture, especially since he'd potentially sentenced himself to death in the process—because if we couldn't find a place to put him once he was done healing Grey, he would die.

But that didn't mean I didn't wish that Grey were with me right now, instead of Leo wearing Grey's body.

"Lacey's gone," the voice said, and I blinked away the tears that had started to form. I had gotten caught up in my sadness and fear—and had forgotten that I was still in the middle of being kidnapped. There was a keen sense of disappointment, followed by irritation, both caused by the same thought: Lacey being gone did not help get any of my questions answered. Nor did it tell me where they were taking me—or what their plans were.

And why was she gone? What was she doing that necessitated her attention while her people were moving a known fugitive and murderer across the Tower?

"Just let me stand up and walk," I replied, recalling the thread of conversation. "And seriously, if this is all meant to help us, can we lose these black bags? We're enemies of the Tower. We're certainly not in a position to reveal your identities and have it be believable."

There were a few chuckles at my statement, and I smiled in response. If I could get these guys to laugh, then that meant they had a sense of humor. People with a sense of humor were good people, but rare in the Tower. The ones I knew from experience would generally see reason. I just hoped my hypothesis proved to be correct.

"Well, no. The bag is there to keep our identities from you entirely," the voice replied, still thick with wry humor. "If we have to follow you in the future, it's better you don't know our faces."

"I know your voice, now," I replied, bristling with impotent frustration at the fact that I was being forced to have this conversation while dangling between them. "Surely that won't help."

I was acting more confident than I felt. The fact that he was admitting to following us, or that he might need to in the future, made me afraid. I had been certain no one had followed us back to Sanctum after I had first met with Lacey and Praetor Strum, the head of Water Treatment. We'd been so cautious! But then, how had they found us? How had they known where we were—and where we were going to be?

And why would they need to follow me in the future?

I thought of Eric. They knew his face, because he'd gone with me to that first meeting. Had they followed him, too—and when he'd been with Zoe? What about Quess and Maddox—had they even made it out of the Medica in one piece? Leo had said as much, but now... how could I be certain, with how quickly they had found *me*?

There were too many unknowns, and my active imagination didn't help. My mind began to reel at all the possibilities, each one worse than the last. I was going to freak out before we ever got to where we were going—and that would make me useless.

I needed to focus and try to stay in the moment.

"Well, the next time I'm set to tail you, I'll do my best to refrain from speaking." The line was delivered dryly, and achieved more chuckles from the people around us. I fumed.

"Seriously, keep the bag on, but let me walk," I said. "This is ridiculous, and I—"

"Shut up," the voice ordered in a brusque whisper that was

low and thick with urgency. "We're nearing a public area, and we need to keep you hidden. The entire Tower has heard about what you've done: a second raid on the Medica, killing the Champion of the Knights. You need to remain quiet if we're going to help you through this without getting caught. We're almost there, and we have a ride for you. Lift her up, lads."

I felt myself rise, thanks to the increased pressure of their hands, and then a surge of vertigo hit me as they dropped me. I flailed, certain they were throwing me right into the plunge, but the fall was short, the landing soft. I had a second to sit up and start to feel around before my hands were roughly seized and yanked behind my back.

"Seriously?!" I demanded, struggling against the hands holding me firmly in place.

"The bag remains, and if you keep talking, I'll undo it enough to gag you. Now stop fighting us, and submit."

I sucked in a deep breath, trying to put a cap on my temper, and relented somewhat, although it stung my pride to do so. Still, it was better than enduring the humiliation of a gag, so I bit my tongue and waited. I could be compliant for now, but if they tried one thing...

They bound me quickly and efficiently—the knot not too tight, merely tight enough and high enough to elude my fingers no matter how much I twisted and turned them. I still had circulation, which told me that this was not their first abduction.

I was pushed onto my side, and then something landed on me with an "oof." I froze as what felt like an arm and a leg

shifted on top of me, sliding around and groping, and then wriggled as the hand grew too close to a private area.

"Grey?" I asked, my voice a harsh whisper.

There was a pause. "I'm not sure if I should respond to that."
I breathed a sigh of relief at the sound of Grey's voice, but then
remembered that it was Leo who was answering, and I could
hear the question in his hushed words.

"Yes," I said, pitching my voice low so we couldn't be heard.
"You absolutely should—if we start going around calling you
another name..."

I paused. Now that I thought about it, I supposed it didn't
really matter. No one would have any idea that Leo was inside
Grey—they'd have no reason to suspect anything, other than
someone who preferred a nickname. A damned odd one,
certainly, but nothing worth being alarmist over.

But then I thought of Devon, and the other two legacies who
had been with him in the room before we had attacked them. I
wasn't sure what had happened to them after our fight—I was
certain we hadn't killed them. What if one of them had been
conscious while Leo was downloading into Grey? What if they
had heard something about Leo?

Devon himself had asked about Leo, before Leo killed him.
He had heard me talking to him in the Medica. What had he
asked? Something about it being a sentient, or another dummy
replicate program? What did that even mean?

And if he had heard something, did that mean the other two
had? I wasn't sure, but now suddenly I was completely coming

around to the idea of making sure we called him by Grey's name.

"Liana?" his voice asked, and I realized that I had trailed off mid-sentence and fallen silent.

"I'm still here," I replied. "I was just thinking about those other two men who were in the room with us. They might've heard me use your name. We definitely have to be careful."

"I agree. So, um. Do you know what's happening to us?"

I opened my mouth to reply when suddenly things began to fall down onto us. I tensed at the first one—a heavy-feeling object that draped over my hip and legs. Then another fell, and another, until I was covered in them. When something fell on my hands, I immediately began to touch whatever it was, eager for some sense of what was happening to me.

It was microthread, with a texture that matched only one thing: a Tower-issued uniform. It was hard to tell which departments the uniforms belonged to—only the color and design would denote that. Then a smell, sour and pungent, invaded my nose. My hands felt further around as I stretched my legs out, touching the rough woven and plastic walls for any sort of opening. And then it hit me: we were in a laundry bin.

"Liana, what's happening?" Leo asked, a thread of fear and anger in his voice.

"It's okay," I whispered soothingly. "I know the people who grabbed us. They're using a laundry bin to move us and keep us hidden."

I was suddenly sad that Zoe, my best friend, wasn't there.

She was missing one of her favorite tropes in any fiction: laundry bins being used to smuggle the heroes to safety.

Of course, I didn't want Zoe anywhere near this. It was bad enough that Grey was—I hadn't told him or anyone else about the meeting I'd had with our abductors. We'd been so preoccupied with our attempt to save Maddox that I hadn't wanted to distract from it. That, and Lacey and Strum had made it abundantly clear that they didn't want any of my friends to know. Now I realized it was a mistake. I had kept them blind, and even if they were still free, they wouldn't even begin to know where to look for us or how to find us.

Even if they had been grabbed, I still should have told them. So, at the very least, they could have some idea of what was happening to them. I prayed Lacey and Strum had ignored them. They wanted their identities secret, didn't they? They wouldn't touch my friends, not unless they were willing to jeopardize their identities.

I tried to take solace in that. Tried to believe that Zoe and Eric had made it back to Sanctum after having broken Maddox's leg to get her sent to the Medica—where we could save her. That they were hidden, safe behind the paint Quess had created, with Tian, and hopefully Maddox and Quess as well.

And that they were trying to come up with some way of tracking us down and rescuing us. I hoped we didn't need to be rescued, but it would be nice to have a backup plan nonetheless.

We started to move, slowly at first, and then faster and faster, until the sound of the wheels on the corrugated floor became overwhelmingly loud, even through the layers of soiled uniforms over both of us. The hard surface beneath us began to rattle and shake, and my shoulder and hip began to ache where they rested against it, absorbing every impact.

"Where are they taking us?" Grey... Leo asked, pitching his voice high enough to be heard over the clatter and clank of the bin.

I shook my head on impulse, and then remembered he couldn't see me. "I don't know," I replied honestly. Somewhere safe, I hoped, but I couldn't be certain. In Lacey's eyes, I had completed the task she had set before me. Now we were going to find out if she was going to honor it, or get rid of any witnesses to her crime.

"Why did they grab us?"

I sighed. He was in this with me. He deserved an explanation. "The people who grabbed us contacted me the other day with a job—to kill Devon Alexander. I hadn't told anyone about it, because they had given me a week to decide, but they said they would take his death as an acceptance of their deal as well."

Leo was silent for a long second, and I wriggled around on the floor, trying to shift some of my weight off my hip and shoulder and onto my back.

"So when I killed him..."

"You apparently set off whatever contingency plans they had to find us and grab us. Which... I'm still wondering how they could've done, by the way."

"It is a mystery," he said a handful of seconds later. "Do you trust them?"

I hesitated, debating between telling him the truth or not,

and then opted for honesty. We'd come this far already. "I'm not sure."

"Shh," the voice from above said urgently, and the two of us grew very quiet, the conversation dying under the prospect of danger.

The cart rattled along, and soon I could hear the sound of voices carrying past me, too difficult to discern until someone drew close. Whenever I could hear a voice clearly, I stopped breathing, my heart pounding hard against my ribs as my mind conjured images of a Knight marching up and demanding to inspect the bin.

All they would have to do was slide a few uniforms aside, and bam—Tower enemy number one, and the girl who they assumed had just killed their leader. I wondered if they'd even let me make it to a trial, or if they would beat me to death in the halls. After thinking about it, I decided both options sucked.

If they came, I'd fight them, and hopefully Lacey's men would back me up.

It felt like forever slid by as I bounced along, the cart jolting and jerking against the grooves in the floor, and after a while, I realized I was hearing the noise of not one, but two carts. They were using more than one to add to the disguise. It made sense—most of the laundry was delivered in more than one batch. One traveling by itself might draw an eye, but a whole bunch of them? No one would think twice about it.

The thought reminded me of how alone we really were, and I began thinking of ways the others could find us. If Quess got a hold of Mercury, they could ping my new net and find my location easily enough, but it could be hours before they realized that we weren't staying away intentionally. A day, even, before they really got upset.

The sharp clatter of the cart jolted me out of my head space, and I realized we were picking up speed through... whatever common area in the Tower we were slipping past.

Odds were it was a market set up in front of one of the greeneries, judging by the occasional whiff of something delicious that got through the odor of dirty clothes enshrouding me, and the sheer volume of noise. They often sold pre-made food in exchange for ration credits in markets like that, and those who didn't have time to cook could always count on the food stalls. Which one it was, I couldn't tell—although from the smell, I guessed we were close to the Menagerie.

A chill went through my spine at the thought of them passing so close to our hideout, and suddenly I wondered again how Lacey had found us.

It didn't make any sense that she'd had her people follow us. I thought I had been so careful after my meeting with them. I'd waited until they'd left, even waited their required time of sixty seconds. Surely they wouldn't have stuck around just to follow me. And even if they had, I would've noticed, especially since Eric and I took the long way back.

So, then... *how* had they found us? Where had I screwed up?

It was far too late for it to be of any use at the moment, but still, the question refused to leave my mind. The bin continued to rattle and shake around me, bouncing me and Grey around and forcing me to slide heavily to one side as the person pushing it took a corner too fast, shoving Grey's body into mine for a few uncomfortable seconds. I then returned my thoughts to how we had been found. If Lacey had some other way of tracking us, I wanted to know about it—so I could avoid it in the future. I had learned to change clothes before returning home thanks to a lesson delivered by Devon and his radioactive material-coated lash ends. He had used the radiation signature to follow me back to Sanctum, and killed both Roark and Cali as a result.

I prayed that this time, my mistake didn't get anyone I cared about killed.

I tried to reassure myself that Lacey was doing this to honor our deal. Maybe she had grabbed Grey—Leo—and me in order to enact whatever cockamamie plan they had to hide us from the wrath of the Tower. Which was going to be severe, now that Devon was dead.

Considering they had wanted him dead in the first place, I could only hope that whatever plan they had in place was good. Damned good. As in, here's a secret room that no one knows about, kind of good. Because otherwise, it was going to take a miracle from on high to help us out of this situation.

Grey shifted slightly next to me, and then let out an irritated noise. "I have the most uncomfortable sensation on my nose, Liana. It's getting worse, and I have the urge to rub it, but can't with my hands bound."

For a second, his words filled me with a mild state of confusion, and then I remembered that it wasn't Grey, it was Leo. And he had never had an itchy nose before. For a second, I struggled with how to explain something as simple as scratching one's nose, the sheer oddity of it all. But he didn't know—how could he? He had never had a body of his own.

"Use your shoulder and the fabric of the bag. It's scratchy enough; it will help."

I waited patiently.

"Much better," Grey said after a few muffled movements.

I grated my teeth together and shook my head, reminding myself yet again that he was now Leo. I forced my brain to pair that name with his face, while coldly ignoring the way my heart cried out forlornly against such a treacherous act. It wasn't logical, but purely emotional—and useless to me right in that moment.

The bounce and jolt of the ride came to a sudden and unexpected stop, and I tensed at the silence that replaced it. The fabric on top of me began to shift and move, and I stiffened when a hand suddenly grabbed my upper arm, pulling me up.

"C'mon, you two," the voice said gruffly, as more hands grabbed me. "It's the end of the line."

2

I was hauled out before I could even begin to process the statement, and placed on my feet, my uniform bunched from where several hands had grasped it. I settled my nerves, understanding immediately what they wanted, and was then propelled gently forward, my captors giving me some time to regain my balance. I came to the conclusion that they weren't about to push me off the edge and into the plunge.

Then something creaked, and I was shoved forward more forcefully. I staggered and came to a stop, then stumbled forward again when something slammed into me from behind. I immediately stiffened, my head swiveling back and forth as I tried to identify the location of my attacker.

For several heartbeats, I could hear nothing except a grating sound that I immediately recognized as a handwheel being turned. The metallic grating stopped after a few seconds, and then someone in the darkness said, "Hello?"

My heart in my throat, I turned toward the sound, moving slowly. "Zoe?" I asked, immediately recognizing her voice in spite of the bag over my head.

There was a click and a hum, and then someone said, "Liana!"

What happened next was a sequence of events that were both noises and sensations: boots on a metallic floor, coming toward me, hands fiddling with ties on my wrists, other hands coming around my neck. I jerked away from the last, Devon's recent attack still a vivid memory in my mind—and then suddenly my hands were free.

I snatched off the hood and stood, staring at Zoe, who had her own hands outstretched, concern etched into the soft lines of her face. "Liana?" she asked, her blue eyes tracing over me and pausing at my neck. "What happened?"

My fingers found my neck, skimming over the raw and angry flesh there, and I snatched them back. "Devon," I said gravely. I immediately began looking around, and saw Eric, Quess, and Maddox. Leo had been shoved in as well, and Eric was helping him out of his ties.

I looked past all of it, intent on studying the room.

It was small—tighter than anything we'd ever been in—with barely enough room for us to sit down and stretch our legs out. Pipes made up the walls, barely an inch of space between them as they snaked in and out of the room. Our prison was well chosen: even the ceiling was a dense network of pipes, impossible to penetrate.

"We're in a water closet," Zoe informed me, a tad impatiently. "I'm guessing somewhere in Cogstown."

It made sense, considering Cogstown was under Lacey's jurisdiction. But how had the four of *them* wound up here? And where was Tian? We had left the youngest member of our group alone and undefended in Sanctum; if she wasn't here, did that mean they *hadn't* figured out where we lived?

"Liana, what happened with Devon?" Quess asked, and I looked over at where he was kneeling next to Maddox. The young man's face was lined with worry as he stood up and looked at Leo and me. "Where's Leo? Did he manage to find the formula for Paragon?"

I looked over at Leo, and the AI stared back, somehow keeping any expression from reaching Grey's face. I opened my mouth, prepared to tell them everything that had happened, when Maddox interrupted.

"To hell with all that," she growled, struggling to get up out of the seated position she was in. Her leg was wrapped in a thick plastic sheet filled with hexagonal shapes that provided supplements meant to accelerate the healing process, meaning it would be fixed in a day or so. Provided we were still alive at that point.

She heaved herself upright after a few seconds and stood, staring at me, one hand on her hip. "Liana, do you know where we are, and what's going on?"

Everyone looked at me, and my answers to Quess's questions flew apart under their solemn gazes. I gazed back at the four of them, and then ran a hand over my face.

Lacey had told me not to tell them anything, but if she had wanted me to keep her identity a secret, she should've let my friends go without bothering them. She hadn't, and in my mind, that meant she had forfeited the right to secrecy.

"I do," I told them. "The people who grabbed you are working for Lacey Green."

"*Engineer* Lacey Green?" Quess asked, his eyes rounding in shock. Then his brows drew together, and he frowned. "That doesn't make any sense. Why did she grab us? We didn't do anything to Cogstown. The Medica is well outside her jurisdiction."

"Shut up and let Liana finish," Eric said sharply. I shot him a concerned look, alarmed by the anger in his voice, and saw that my other best friend was not all right. Sweat dotted his forehead, and he kept looking up and around, as if he expected something to fall on him at any moment.

"Eric?" I asked, taking a step closer to him, one hand outstretched. He took a hurried step back, his eyes huge in alarm, and I froze.

"He'll be all right," Zoe said as she slid around me and over to him. He reached for her, like a man terrified that the world was falling out from under his feet, and I realized he was in the grip of a panic attack.

All of us were, in one way or another, but this was worse. Eric was actively beginning to exhibit signs.

"What's his problem?" Maddox asked as Zoe began to guide him down to the ground, one arm wrapped around his shoulder with the other over his chest. She pressed against one enlarged pectoral muscle and cupped it protectively, as if the action were shielding his very heart from harm.

"He's a Hand," Zoe reminded her. She kept her voice soft and gentle as she settled him on the floor, before sitting down next to him. "He was raised in a greenery. Tight spaces are not good for him, especially like this. Liana, explain things and see if that can't help him calm down."

"Right," I said, licking my lips. Zoe was now guiding Eric's head into her lap, her fingers already sliding through his brown hair and stroking the side of his face. Eric had one arm over Zoe's legs, hugging her close. His breathing came in sharp, tight gasps.

"I'll be fine," he said, nodding his head forcefully, but in a way that was so emphasized that I wondered whether he was trying to reassure himself more than us.

"Shush," Zoe said gently, her fingers drifting over his lips. "Let Liana talk, and just try to breathe, okay?"

He continued to nod, and a few seconds later, all attention was on me.

I exhaled and began. "Lacey Green and Praetor Strum are part of some sort of shadow group that is... I don't know... at war with other shadow groups over control of the master Scipio AI. They wanted me to assassinate Devon Alexander, which... I sort of did before we escaped the Medica."

"You killed the *Champion?*" Quess exclaimed.

"Bigger picture, Quess," Maddox said curtly. Her green eyes remained on me as she spoke, and she took a jerky step forward. "Liana, did you agree to this?"

I hesitated. "Not exactly. And I certainly didn't plan to do it today. They gave me a week to do it, and it was my intention to talk to everyone about it after we rescued you. As you'll all recall."

"I don't understand why you didn't just say no in the first place," Quess protested. "I mean, we are talking about two members of the *council* who are trying to institute a regime change in another department. And having the leaders of other departments assassinated for good measure. We should not be involved."

"I know that," I replied, with more patience than I felt. I glanced at Eric, but he was in no shape to back me up and confirm that I had been pretty upset after the meeting. "I did give this whole mess a lot of thought, even before it became a mess. Getting us involved in some sort of shadow war that seems to have been raging since the beginning—"

"The beginning?" Maddox asked, cocking one dark eyebrow. "What are you talking about?"

"You missed a lot, Maddox." It was Grey's voice, but I knew it was Leo speaking. "Apparently Devon is part of a family that has been working to subvert Scipio and take control of the Tower. He was allied with someone in the IT department—"

"We don't know that," I interjected softly, and he looked at me, brown eyes widening in surprise. "Just because those other two Inquisitors were part of IT doesn't mean that whoever they are working for is. If these are family units, starting from the beginning, it makes sense that they would plant future generations in other departments, as they needed to."

Silence met my statement, and I felt the weight of the truth I had been carrying for the past twenty-four hours settle in on them.

"Liana, what was the deal you made with them?" Zoe asked carefully.

"Supposedly, they'd be able to exonerate Le—" I caught myself, remembering that they weren't ready for that particular truth bomb yet, and continued on quickly, glossing over my mistake. "Grey and me, and integrate all of you back into the Tower."

"All of us?" Quess asked. "Back in the Tower? And what if we don't want to go?"

I looked at him and shook my head. "Again, I didn't plan to kill Devon today. I meant to ask you guys about everything first. It just—" I glanced at Leo and back at Quess, my fingers itching to touch my neck again, if only to confirm that Devon's fingers weren't still there. "—happened," I finished lamely. "They said they'd take his death as acceptance of their proposal, so I'm hoping all of this means that they're putting their plan in motion. Although, what concerns me more is how they knew to grab all of us. And whether Tian is okay..."

And whether Grey was okay, but that was a question I would ask Leo personally. And one that I was sure the AI would get sick of.

"We never made it back to Sanctum," Zoe said, indicating herself and Eric. "After we hurt Maddox, we were heading back, but were jumped from behind."

"I got one of them," Eric said quietly, and Zoe smiled down at where he was still lying, his head in her lap. He'd grown less panicked and calmer under her care, but I could tell he was still feeling the tight confines of the space, and empathized with him. "Not dead, but I definitely cleaned his clock."

"Good for you," I replied. "Quess? What happened with you and Maddox?"

"Well, Leo led me to a room, and I administered the counter drug to the sedative they had given Doxy. We made it out, and were just over the bridge and into the shell when they grabbed us. How did they know how to find us?"

"Or who we even were?" Maddox asked on the tail of Quess's question.

"I don't know," I replied honestly. I tried to recall whether they had touched me at all during that first meeting—perhaps they had slipped a locator on me without my knowing, or used some sort of radioactive isotope like Devon had. But there was nothing that stood out. "I suppose they could've followed us, but Eric and I were so careful..."

"What about Mercury?" Zoe asked, looking around. "He brokered the whole deal, after all. He certainly could've told them our new net IDs. If they knew who we were pretending to be, it would be a lot easier to track us."

I frowned. We'd only just gotten new nets—stolen directly from the IT department. Mercury, along with my brother, Alex, had been responsible for the plan to get us in. It seemed counter-productive of him to go to such great lengths, only to turn around and sell our net information to Lacey, but it was a theory. He had wanted me to make a deal with them, after all. He knew, better than we all did, that being integrated back into the Tower gave us a better chance of replicating Paragon—the only chance he had of hiding his failing rank and escaping the eye of the Tower. There was a very real chance he would've sold us out, if only to force my hand.

And if he had, they knew where Tian was, too.

An icy wash of fear and anger raced down my spine, and I balled my fists. If they harmed one hair on her head, I wouldn't wait for them to exonerate me. I'd be adding their murders on top of Devon's, and combining it with the laundry list of charges the Tower had likely stacked against me. Even though Lacey had told me in the hall she was upholding her end of the deal, I didn't like the idea of anyone going after Tian when she was alone and defenseless.

I realized I was being overprotective and emotional, but I didn't care; Tian was perhaps the brightest part of my life, next to Grey, and even though I had known her for only a short time, I'd come to care for her deeply. Couple that with the fact that she was a young girl, incredibly child-like and naïve, and add my protective instincts, and, well... it didn't matter how much I'd liked Lacey before.

"It's possible it was Mercury," I finally admitted, breaking out of my tangled web of thoughts and returning to the moment. "I hope not, but it is possible."

"Liana." I turned and looked at Leo, and found him standing

closer to me. "What happened right there? You seemed to experience several emotions at once."

Leo's question was based purely on curiosity, which was just like him, but I couldn't help but flinch and then massage my temples, knowing that everyone was going to pick up on that oddity.

"Grey, why are you acting so weird? Are you okay?" Quess's question was riddled with concern.

"Well, that's complicated," Leo began, and I put a hand on his arm, forestalling him. He glanced down at my hand, his face inquisitive at first, though that quickly morphed into delight, and I realized that he was still adjusting to what it was like to be inside a human body.

"Grey was injured in the altercation," I announced.

"I'll say. Why is he looking at you like a man who's never been touched before?" Eric asked, sitting up. "Is he going to be okay?"

"I'm working on it," Leo said, his hand reaching up to brush over the backs of my fingers. I snatched my hand away. It was impulsive, but the sensation of the calloused pads of Grey's fingers tracing over mine, plus the knowledge that it wasn't him, made the feeling distinctly uncomfortable and left me slightly nauseated, like I was somehow betraying Grey by letting someone else even touch me.

To say it was confusing was an understatement.

"What do you mean, you're working on it?" Maddox asked.

Leo was staring deep into my eyes now, his expression a mixture of hurt, concern, and alarm, but when I didn't explain myself, he turned to Maddox. "I'm Leo," he said simply, as if that explained anything.

Quess took a step closer, his brows coming together. "Okay, now I'm worried. Grey, you're not Leo, you're Grey. Liana, did he get hit on the head?"

"No," I said, my throat tightening around the words. "He's Leo. Grey's net got overloaded, and the damage was..." I swallowed, trying and failing to keep the image of Grey's brain from my mind. I sucked in a deep breath and plowed forward, not wanting to waste time breaking down on everyone. "The damage was extensive. Leo used the net to implant himself into Grey, with the hopes that he and the healing abilities of the net can restore him."

Silence met my statement, and I glanced at everyone to see how they were processing the news. The short version seemed to be: not well. Maddox and Eric were staring at Leo with a mixture of confusion and fear, while Zoe's eyes were on mine, brimming with concern and horror as she tried to imagine what I was going through. Quess was downright shocked, his eyes wide with awe. But there was nothing I could do about it, except face several more questions, many of which I doubted I would have the answers to.

The wheel squeaked suddenly behind us, and I turned quickly, alarm radiating down my spine.

"Liana?" Zoe asked, her voice harsh with fear and panic.

"It'll be okay," I said, trying to reassure her.

The wheel continued to turn, though, and then stopped,

hitting its limit with a dull clang. The door swung open, revealing first Praetor Strum, and then Lacey.

And between the two of them, hands clutched tightly in front of her, was Tian, her back hunched, her blue eyes wide and darting around.

3

The little girl shifted uncertainly as she stared at us gravely, her hands fidgeting in front of her. "There were a lot of them," she said tentatively, twisting to see if either Strum or Lacey was going to stop her from saying anything. When they didn't, she continued breathlessly, as if they could cut her off at any moment. "I tried to fight them off. I even managed to get one of them in the face with a lash bead, but they just kept coming. I..." She paused, her face starting to crack apart under the brunt of a great sorrow.

I was taking a step forward, ready to tug her behind me and get in Lacey and Strum's faces about the treatment of a little girl, when she produced a satchel from behind her back and dug into it, pulling out a large stuffed bear, and his smaller, now unattached arm. "They hurt Commander Cuddles!" she wailed, tears pouring down her face.

While her distress was quite palpable, I had to fight back a laugh, especially when she reached up and used Commander Cuddles's severed arm to wipe away her tears. I heard several other chortles from behind me, but managed not to break. Lacey couldn't keep the amusement off her face, though, while Strum couldn't seem to stop his eyes from rolling in their sockets.

The only one who was unaffected by our humor was Leo, who looked both concerned for Tian, and mortified that the rest of us were greeting the crying girl with smiles and laughter.

And he was right. While to us, the loss of Commander Cuddles's arm wasn't the end of the world, to Tian, it was. Laughing at her tears was probably the quickest way to upset her more, given her attachment to the bear, and the last thing we wanted to do was hurt her. Even if she was being unintentionally cute.

Luckily, Tian would never lack for rescuers. But the hero for today did surprise me a little.

"Hey, hey, hey, Tian Bo-bian," Eric said loudly, his voice booming in the small space. "Guess what? I'm a super-secret bear surgeon, and my official prognosis is: we can fix him."

Tian blinked back her tears and sniffed a few times. We all waited patiently for her to speak.

"Really?" she squeaked hopefully, her tears beginning to dry up. She took a few steps forward, perched on the tips of her toes, and then paused, clutching Commander Cuddles to her chest and resting her chin on his head.

"It's true," Zoe chimed in. "He's the best damned bear surgeon in the Tower. I give you my word of honor."

Tian looked at me for confirmation, and I gave her a confident nod, even though I had no idea what skill Eric possessed that could help her.

"Do you sew?" Lacey asked, echoing my thoughts.

Eric's smile faded as she addressed him directly, and just like that, the tiny spell that Tian had cast upon her arrival popped, and we all came back to reality. Current reality being that our potential captor was asking us a question after having us kidnapped, black bagged, and shoved in a tight water closet with no means of escape—and with no clue about what was coming next.

Tension crept up my spine as I nodded at Eric, signaling that it was okay to answer.

"I have one sister, four female cousins, and I'm the youngest," he replied carefully. He didn't say any more, and I didn't let her ask him anything else.

"Tian, there's one other person who's happy to see you."

Tian smiled, her eyes going misty. "I know," she whispered, her eyes already locked on Maddox. "My Doxy?"

Maddox smiled, tears coming to her own eyes, and she nodded. "My Tian," she replied, and within seconds the young girl had raced over to Maddox, leapt into her arms, and wrapped herself around the bigger girl.

I moved forward, worried about Maddox's leg, but she caught Tian easily and hugged her back. I watched them for a moment, relieved that I had been able to keep my promise to Tian and Maddox both, and then turned my back to them. Lacey had broken the rules of our engagement, and hurt my friends. This wasn't the time for sentimentality; it was the time for questions. Namely mine.

"How did you know where to find us?" I asked, stepping closer to Lacey and Strum and dropping my voice low. "And what gave you the right to go after my people? That wasn't part of the agreement."

Strum and Lacey exchanged looks, and to my surprise, Strum was the one who spoke first. "We never anticipated that you would move so quickly on this," he said, his voice still surprisingly deep for such a slender man. "I know we said if you did it within twenty-four hours we would take that as a yes, but you moved even faster than that. We assumed you would want more discussions, perhaps his schedule or routine and possible schematics first—but you didn't. I'm glad we had the foresight to have a failsafe in place. Otherwise, our plan might have been jeopardized. Considering we had to collect you all before anyone else found you."

He tried to hide it, but I could tell he was impressed. That told me a few things: for one thing, they thought this was our plan from the get-go. They believed that my team and myself were highly coordinated and fast acting, which had earned us a modicum of respect. It meant a more even playing field.

I considered that for a long moment, and decided to keep back the fact that Devon's murder had been completely accidental. I had no idea what they had in store yet, but if they thought we were that good, maybe it would make them think twice about trying to hurt us in any way. And maybe it would ensure that they held up their part of the deal.

"Well, I assumed you gave us all the relevant information at the first meeting. And if you had told me you needed everyone in one place for your plan to be effective, I would've just had us all meet you there," I replied sarcastically, giving him a withering glance that I hoped looked moderately annoyed. "But again, I ask: how did you know where to find us?"

Lacey coughed, and I saw a flash of a smile before it disappeared behind her hand. I studied her; she'd changed her hair since yesterday when we'd met, and it was now braided tightly against her scalp in tiny, narrow braids that twisted into an intricate pattern along the crown. The rest of her hair stood out around the back of her head, in a poof that seemed to ripple like water when her head moved. I eyed it enviously, my own hair feeling like grease and dirt had just gone ahead and decided to raise a family right there on my scalp.

I wouldn't say I would kill for a shower, but it would be tempting at this point.

"We infected you and your friend with a designer bacteria," she admitted. "We needed to be sure that we could grab you when you were ready to move."

"A *designer bacteria?*" I asked, my eyebrows drawing together. "Quess, you ever hear of a designer bacteria?"

"Oh yeah, we experimented with them all the time in the Medica," Quess called back. "Not all bacteria are bad, you see, and—"

"Thank you, Quess," I called, not wanting him to reveal too much of his backstory in front of Lacey and Strum. I didn't think they would use it against him, but the less they knew, the better.

"Tell me more about it later." I had broken eye contact with Lacey while I talked to Quess, and now that we were finished, I could sense that she was waiting. Impatiently. I turned back to her. "What is it? What does it do? How did you do it? And why do it in the first place? You asked me to help you, so why risk an already fragile trust by doing something so invasive?"

"Well..." Lacey paused and looked at Strum, who shrugged. "Designer bacteria can be used in all sorts of ways to help further medical studies or find health problems, but this one was designed specifically for us. Remember the bags over your heads before and after the meeting? They were laced with the cultures, and when you inhaled, you drew them into your body and infected yourselves. Don't be alarmed, though—it can't hurt you. All it does is raise your body temperature to a certain level so that we can track it through the nets."

What? I shook my head twice and wondered how the heck she could track body temperatures through the nets. I looked at them both and raised an eyebrow. "Quess—"

"No, wait." Lacey sighed and ran a hand over her face, and I realized right then that the woman was tired. She looked about as tired as I felt, only she wasn't riding the tension high like I was, so she felt it more. "Look, the nets take your temperatures up until the fifth point after the decimal. It's just a way to gather as much information as possible for Scipio to process and refine his algorithms. It's also used to study how fast nets are currently degrading, and so forth and so on. As you know, we all run a little hot as a side effect of the nets, but that temperature fluctuates naturally. The bacteria strain we have raises your body temperature to a specific point, designated by us, to the fifth decimal point. We have a backdoor into the thermal scanners, and we just had them scan for that exact temperature."

I frowned, thinking. There were tens of thousands of people inhabiting the Tower, and odds were likely that someone else could've been coincidently running the same temperature at that time. I opened my mouth to make that observation, but Lacey's approving smile stopped me.

"You're asking yourself how we picked yours over anyone else's that was, at that moment, the same?" I nodded, and her smile grew. "I knew you were smart; that's why I like you. In answer to your question... turn around."

I didn't, because I knew exactly what she wanted me to look at: my friends. "I transmitted it to them," I said with a groan. "You just had to see where the most people with the same number were concentrated."

"Indeed," Strum supplied. "Shared communal spaces, talking, kissing, sharing food... You infected the others. We never would've found you all otherwise—which would have meant we didn't follow through on our promise to you. Our people tell us the paint that you put up is quite effective at blocking net data. While you're in there, of course, Ms. Euan. As soon as you stepped outside, we picked you up. It wasn't hard to figure out where you were hiding after that."

He winked as he purposefully used the last name of the fake ID that I was hiding behind, but I just narrowed my eyes at him. "Let me make this clear to you: you came into our *home*," I said, stressing the word. "You had people go in there and scare a young girl. That wasn't part of the deal, and I say again: if you wanted me, you should've let me know to meet you somewhere."

I was being obstinate, but I wanted them to understand that this was serious to me. They needed to understand that I didn't take intrusion into my home, or the kidnapping of my people, lightly. By demanding an answer, no matter how good their intentions, I was showing them where my boundaries were—which would make them think twice before crossing them again.

"We didn't have a choice," Lacey replied. "I'm sorry, Liana, but we didn't. You're on everybody's radar now. Everyone in the Tower wants you. I had to risk six of my people for you and Mr. Farmless alone, and even then, we were damned lucky that you'd somehow overcome the lockdown procedures of the Medica and were able to get that elevator to take you to a higher floor. The Medica is one of the few places we can't seem to break into, so if you'd gotten trapped in there..." She trailed off and frowned. "Speaking of which, how were you able to do all that?"

"That's my secret," I replied, keeping my eyes on her. I had no intention of telling her about Leo, or about his residence inside of Grey—and if I looked at him, it would be noticeable. Not because they could ever guess that there was an AI actually inside of him, but because they might question him, and realize that a huge part of his memory was missing, like his designation number, and just... general knowledge about his life or the Tower itself. That was what Leo was working desperately to save, and I couldn't have them looking into his memory loss and discovering the damage. Or the net. "And I'm not sharing."

Strum looked ready to argue, but Lacey reached out and laid a hand on his forearm. "That's fair enough," she said with a nod. "You don't have to tell us anything you don't want to. I also want to assure you that your *home* is fine. We didn't take anything, except for maybe a few samples of that paint."

I considered her statement. "So you stole from us as well."

"Guilty, but as you can see, we aren't exactly on the right side of the law, either, and that paint could be useful to us."

"Then make a deal with us for it," I said flatly. Strum and Lacey exchanged surprised looks, but I didn't stop. "If there's one thing I've noticed about being part of the fringe community of the Tower, it's that we're going to have needs while we're in hiding. You now have a sample, and presumably it won't take you long to figure out how to make it. You took it, and now you owe us."

Lacey opened her mouth, paused, and then shook her head. "Fine," she said. "You're right, we shouldn't have even taken that. It was bad form on our part, and we'll try to think of some way to reciprocate."

"Deal," I replied, breathing out quietly. I actually wasn't sure where all of that had come from. I wasn't the type to think so materialistically, but there it was. A rationale I hadn't even considered before, but one that came spilling out as soon as Lacey admitted that she had taken something from us.

Truthfully, I was pleased with the way this conversation was going. If they were willing to strike a deal for something unknown in the future, then that meant we *had* a future. I just needed to know what that future was.

"So what's this plan?" I asked, deliberately changing the subject. "How do you plan to get me and my friends off the hook after we've committed murder and conspiracy?"

"Well, your two friends... um... him and the young one..."

I looked where Strum was pointing and realized he meant Quess and, of course, Tian, while he continued to speak.

"They were never really on the Tower's radar for this. We just grabbed them because they were with you. As such, they won't even be brought up."

"They will be cared for," Lacey added, before I could even ask. "New identities and nets, placement in whatever department they want and are qualified for. I give you my word."

I stared at my friends, thinking. Maddox and Eric were watching us closely from a few feet away, and I was certain both were ready to spring into action if things went wrong. Not that I thought they were going to anymore. Quess and Zoe, meanwhile, were distracting Tian right behind them, and Leo was standing the closest to me, watching our exchange in silence. I met his gaze, and then turned back to Lacey and Strum. If this could buy them some protection, and get the Knights off of us, it was worth it—if only so that we could hide in plain sight for a little while.

"What about Zoe and Eric?" I asked, nodding to them. "What's their role in all this?"

"Victims..." Lacey trailed off and pulled a pad from the front of her orange coveralls. "It's easier if you just read this. There isn't a lot of time, and we're about to be late for the council meeting."

She held it out to me, and I took it and stared at the rectangular square. "What council meeting?" I asked slowly.

"Well, less of a council meeting, more of a trial. Yours and Mr. Farmless's, to be exact."

"A trial?" I sputtered. I looked around again and saw my fears echoed on all of my friends' faces—except for Leo, who looked eerily delighted by the prospect—and turned back. "That's your *plan*?"

"It is," Strum said solemnly. "It'll be much easier if you just—"

"No, I'm sorry. I don't mean to be rude, but I have to stop you right there." I took a deep breath and tried to ease some of the panic that was threatening to make me come apart and really lose it. An official trial presided over by the council was complete and utter *lunacy*. Scipio had been tampered with—they both suspected as much, but I knew it to be true. Even with Devon gone, I knew for a fact that there was someone else working on... well, whatever their plan with Scipio was. All it would take was for Scipio to render a judgment of guilty—which, if he was being controlled by Devon's allies, he would! Surely, they didn't think that with Devon gone, Scipio would fall right back into line!

My thoughts jumbled together, and I quickly began to sort them in order from most important to least, to explain to them why this wouldn't work. But then Lacey looked at her wrist and shook her head.

"Whatever reservations you have, wait until you read the

talking points we gave you. I'm sure your concerns will be addressed. Now, we have to go."

And before I could really say anything, they turned to head out of the room.

"I hope you and Mr. Farmless are good liars," Strum called as the door began to swing closed. "If not, just try to be as emotionless as possible. And practice!"

I was staring dumbly at the door, unable to process how quickly everything was moving, when it all suddenly clicked.

"Wait!" I managed.

But I was too late. The wheel squeaked as it spun around, sealing us in.

I stared at the door, alarmed and confused by their hasty departure.

"What's on the pad?" Leo asked, his voice very close behind me. I practically leapt out of my skin and whipped around.

I gazed at him, while he looked at me expectantly. Then I reluctantly looked down at the pad in my hands, and exhaled.

"Right," I murmured.

I straightened my back and squared my shoulders before tapping the screen. It immediately came on, and I clicked the only icon on the homepage.

It was a text file, with several bulleted talking points. I skimmed them for a few seconds, and then did a mental double take, blinking my eyes several times to make sure they weren't playing tricks on me. I slowed down to read it again, my eyes gobbling up more and more of the words as their meaning and plan became clearer and clearer.

"What's it say?" Leo asked eagerly.

I looked up at him. "A lot," I replied dubiously, my eyes returning to the screen. I hoped they knew what the hell they were doing.

Because if they didn't, this mammoth of a lie was going to get us all killed.

4

Leo and I walked quickly across the Grounds at the bottom level of the Tower. Above us, the Core, the Medica, and the Citadel dangled, forming a triangle. It was hard not to lift my eyes upward and stare at them in awe. No one was allowed on this level unless they had business with the council, so I had never been able to see what they looked like from this angle before.

They were breathtaking, to say the least. The black and blue geometric steps of the cone-shaped Core glistened and gleamed as we moved under it, making it look like a bullseye against the roof of the Tower for an instant—until we stepped out from under its zenith several paces later.

I had to lower my eyes to follow the attendant who had come to fetch us not ten minutes ago. Both Leo and I were wearing shock shackles, which would shock us if we fell too far behind him, so we had to keep up—unless we wanted a particularly nasty jolt that would render us unconscious within seconds.

The attendant was already over a wooden bridge that crossed a small stream some ten feet ahead, and I paused as I stepped onto the wood, marveling at the shiny planks. We had trees, but harvesting them was strictly prohibited, as they played an integral part in the Tower's oxygen production. Most of them were also food-bearing trees, so cutting them down meant threatening the food supply—another big no-no in the Tower.

The Grounds, however, were covered with non-fruit-producing trees, running thick and wild across the floor. Paths similar to the one we were on cut through the vegetation, but everything else was devoted to plant life, aiding in oxygen production and providing lush scenery that replicated a world that no longer existed. I passed by a bench that overlooked a stream as it poured into a lake. Orange, white, and red fish, some as long as my arm, swam through the waters, occasionally breaking the surface in the pursuit of food.

I continued across the bridge, trying not to stare, but it was hard. I should have been mentally reviewing the talking points that Lacey had given us, but all that green, and the smell of wet earth and water, called to me, begging for my attention. After a few weeks of being cut off from a greenery (one that wasn't dedicated to animals, mind you), I had forgotten how much I loved it.

Let alone the feel of walking across something made of actual wood. It seemed so fantastical, a luxury that had to have been brought into the Tower long ago and preserved throughout the ages. And only the councilors could enjoy it, marvel at its age and wonder at its history. It seemed wrong, somehow, that such a quiet and serene place could be kept from the citizens. Didn't we all have the right to enjoy such a place?

The attendant waved a hand, then, and Leo and I quickened our pace in order to keep up, the threat of being shocked before we delivered our fabricated testimony lending speed to our wearied limbs.

"Are you sure you're going to remember everything?" Leo asked quietly. "I can take point if you think you aren't up to it."

I considered his question. It would be easier to let him do it; he had a photographic memory, apparently, so only one look and he'd had it memorized.

But I did, too. The words were too important for me to forget. The trick was making it believable, and for all of Leo's insistence that he could lie, and do it well, I couldn't risk all of our lives on his untested abilities. I, on the other hand, was a pretty good liar.

"I've got it." My eyes slid over to him. "H-How's Grey?"

The question had been burning inside me since we had gotten to the cell in which Lacey and Strum had held us captive. But I hadn't given it rein. I couldn't, because I bore the burden of responsibility, which meant making sure everyone else was safe, first.

Now that we were away from the others, I needed to know what was going on.

Ahead of us, the attendant turned a corner, disappearing behind a few trees, but I kept my pace the same, trusting that he wouldn't get too far ahead of us without stopping and waiting.

As much as I didn't want to get shocked, I also knew, after thinking about it logically, that Lacey or Strum would have told the attendant not to let that happen. Or at least, I hoped they had.

Beside me, Leo sighed, and I looked over at him.

"Liana, it's not a fast process," he said, looking at me with Grey's warm brown eyes. My heart clenched, and I looked away, uncomfortable at knowing that the person behind them was not the person I wanted it to be.

"I know that," I murmured. We turned the corner, and sure enough, the attendant was waiting for us to appear, standing next to another path that disappeared between two thick clusters of trees, which held deep, dark shadows. The path seemed to glow white between them. "But... it's Grey. I'm... I..."

I blinked back tears and sucked in a deep, cleansing breath, trying to soothe the stabbing pain that was threatening to pry my heart in half. "I shouldn't have brought it up," I said, once the pain had faded some. A glance at Leo told me he was confused, and I let it lie there, unwilling to dredge it up again.

He, however, was not so ready to let it go. "Liana..."

"It's okay," I said. "You told me it would take time, and you're right. I shouldn't pester you."

"No. I know that you care for Grey very much. So I promise, I will always give you an update whenever you ask." I looked up at him, and he smiled kindly. The dagger in my heart twisted deeper.

"Thank you," I managed hoarsely.

We turned the corner, and the path shot long and straight

through the murky woods. The attendant continued ahead, making for the dome-shaped building at the end: the Council Room. We all knew about it; I had seen it from above many times, as I dangled from the tip of the Citadel, studying the view below. Inside, the heads of five different departments would be waiting. I wasn't sure if Devon's second in command, Lieutenant Salvatore Zale, was going to be in attendance—I was unclear on the protocol for that—but even if he was, I doubted he would get an actual vote.

Still, I wasn't going to enjoy seeing him, one way or another. He was an intimidating man, through and through—one who grew quieter when he grew angrier, not louder, if my parents were to be believed. And he had been close friends with Devon Alexander.

I was about to go confess to that murder. I could only imagine what he would do to avenge that death.

I went over the talking points in my head as the white dome loomed closer, ignoring the growing impulse to try to make a run for it. Lacey and Strum were on my side. That was two, and without Devon, that only left three more to convince. I prayed that Lacey and Strum had a way of dealing with Scipio.

We broke through the trees into a wide space between the tree line and the white dome. Several fountains encircled the structure, feeding into a stream running around it. More fish swam lazily through the water, moving both upstream and down. Flat bridges, wide enough for just one person, spanned the gap over the stream, running between the fountains.

Across the bridges, steps rounded the outside of the building, leading up into the outer circle, which was lined by large white columns. A symbol for each department was carved into every column, facing out so everyone would know that this was a place for everyone.

A chill crept down my spine as the attendant moved forward, striding across one of the bridges and guiding us closer to what Lacey and Strum promised would be victory—but in which I could clearly see the possibility of defeat.

"It was all Devon's fault," Leo reminded me as each of us stepped onto a narrow bridge, and I nodded.

That was the lie, although it was more complicated than he was making it out to be. The plan essentially revolved around putting blame on Devon's shoulders, but there were a lot of details that I had to remember. I knew that whatever happened once we were in that building, the only thing that mattered was convincing everyone that we were telling the truth. It was the only way for us to get out of here. But it wasn't going to be easy.

I still had no idea what Lacey and Strum planned to do about Scipio, or how they were going to prevent him and whoever was controlling him from denying the accusations outright. But I had to trust that they knew what they were doing.

We climbed the steps side by side, moving between a pair of columns and up to a tall set of double doors carved out of wood. On the outside was an inscription: *For the good of the Tower, we do what we must, in order to survive.*

The words did not comfort me as the attendant pulled one of the doors open and waved us in. We moved inside, into a surprisingly small reception chamber with wooden chairs lining the walls. The ground was metal, like most of the floors in the Tower, but was missing the corrugation designed to provide maximum traction; instead, it was smooth and gleaming, dark whorls and swoops running through the metal, revealed only at certain angles under the bright lighting overhead. In the middle of the room sat a table with several glasses and a large pitcher of water, and I made for it immediately.

As I poured the crystal-clear liquid into a cup, I heard the murmur of voices drifting through the doors opposite the ones we had entered. I poured another cup for Leo, offering it to him. He accepted it with a delighted smile, and took a small, experimental sip of the liquid. I watched his excitement fade to disappointment, and felt vaguely upset that I didn't have something more delicious to offer him. Then I remembered that he was doing this in Grey's body, and the discomfort returned. I masked it by taking my glass and moving closer to the door, curious as to what the voices were saying.

The attendant made no move to stop me, so it wasn't against the rules. I took a sip of my water, wetting my mouth and slaking the sudden thirst I was feeling, and then grew very still, trying to discern the voices.

"—if I understand this." My ears picked out the voice, muffled though it was, and I marked it as female. That meant it was Executive Sadie Monroe, the head of the IT Department, as she was the only female on the council besides Lacey. "Liana Castell—the same one who broke into my department to steal nine of our nets—murdered Devon Alexander, the head of his own department, and you're trying to tell me that she reported to you and turned herself in right afterward? I have to say, Engineer Green, that's a bit of a stretch, especially coming from a Cog."

She practically spat the last word, and I frowned at the disdain in her voice. "Cog" was the nickname for those in the Mechanical Department, but we all had nicknames. As a Knight, I would've been a Shield. If Grey had been allowed to remain in the Farming Department, he would've been a Hand. Zoe was a Diver, and Quess had been born a Medic, although he had made several department changes in his life before finally becoming an undoc—a person living in hiding and self-exile within the Tower.

"Not entirely sure what you want me to say, Executive Monroe," Lacey replied smoothly. I took a step closer to the door, listening. "I've dutifully reported that she surrendered herself to me and requested a trial with Scipio present. She's on her way here, and will arrive any minute. Why don't you let her tell her story, and stop badgering me with questions I don't have the answers to?"

I had to admit, Lacey was a good liar. Everything she said sounded natural and unforced.

"I think we should just let Lieutenant Zale drag her down to the expulsion chambers in the Citadel," Executive Monroe replied haughtily. "What sort of precedent are we setting by agreeing to a terrorist's request for a trial? Have you considered that this could be some sort of trap? She could be walking through these doors with some kind of bomb meant to kill us all!"

"The scanners along the floor will detect and alert Scipio to any sort of threat long before she arrives." Strum's voice boomed out, easy to pick up, but the next masculine voice was harder to discern.

"Executive Monroe brings up several good points, however. You cannot deny that all of this is highly suspicious. What sort of criminal kills a council member, only to then surrender themselves to another council member?"

"Isn't that the sort of question you want answered?" Lacey exclaimed. "You're not wrong in that everything is suspicious, but doesn't that make you curious, too?"

"I will admit to some curiosity."

This voice was different than the other masculine one that had sounded earlier. There were only two possibilities for who it could be: the head of the Medica, Chief Surgeon Marcus Sage, or the head of the greeneries, Head Farmer Emmanuel Plancett. Having never heard either of their voices, it was hard for me to tell who was who.

"I myself have many questions I'd like to have answered. Besides, Executive Monroe, there's no use in complaining about it now. We already voted, and you lost."

"And I'm begging you to reconsider. This girl has a laundry list of charges against her. She sprang the other one, Grey Farmless, from the Citadel, and then murdered her mentor. She infiltrated the Medica to get a few more of her compatriots out, and seems to have teamed up with a merry band of undocs in order to steal nets and murder council members! This girl is flat-out guilty, and we should just let Lieutenant Zale take her before she even has a chance to speak. Who knows what sort of treacherous plan she has up her sleeve!"

"Enough!" thundered a new voice, and this one I did recognize. I'd only ever heard his voice through the net in my head, and only when he personally delivered orders, but it was the same. Recognizable in its cold arrogance, which always made me imagine a princely man on a throne made of ice. "These arguments are moot. The girl is here, and I would have her be heard before rendering any opinion on the matter. Data, esteemed council members, is always necessary. Open the doors and let us see what she has to say."

There was a murmur following the command of Scipio, the master AI that controlled most aspects of life inside the Tower, and then the doors began to swing open.

I watched, glass in hand, my heart suddenly in my throat, my brain screaming for me to run. This was the moment of reckoning that had been haunting me since I freed Grey from the Citadel. I was caught. Everyone in there, except for Strum and Lacey, hated me. They feared me. They probably wanted nothing more than to have me killed right then and there. And without Lacey and Strum's plan, I would easily be found guilty... and executed. But thanks to that plan, I had a chance—just one—to make sure that we *didn't* die in the chamber rooms in the Citadel.

It was time to do what I did best, and lie.

5

I stared dumbly at the wide gap left in the wake of the doors opening, a chasm of dread growing wide and deep in the pit of my stomach. The attendant who had been guiding us waved me forward, but I stood frozen, transfixed by the light spilling through the door, the dark floor and wooden walls, and the stand in the middle.

The attendant sighed and leaned toward me, grabbing me by the arm and pulling me forward. He plucked the glass of water from my fingers when he pushed me past him, and I almost stumbled as I was shoved through the doorway. The threshold was a tight hall, only a few feet deep, but I used the time to steel myself before I stepped into the light.

The room was circular, with high wooden walls that stretched up thirty feet to the ceiling above. The wooden panels were carved with a geometric design that seemed to have no beginning or end, but ran around the room in a rhythmic, slanted pattern, giving the entire cylinder the illusive appearance of spinning. The only places this was interrupted were where a large metal relief jutted out of the wood. There were seven in total, each one depicting the sigil for a different department. They were spread evenly apart, and stood high enough that I could probably reach up and touch the bottom of one with my fingertips, if I went to my toes.

At first, I thought the room empty—which was weird, considering the voices I had heard moments ago. But as my eyes continued to follow the lines and turn upward, I saw Strum sitting a few feet above the sigil for Water Treatment—a series of five pipes standing side by side, bound in the middle by a rod, a tear shape around it. He was wearing a bright blue uniform, which I could tell was reserved for more formal use rather than everyday work around the Tower, given the numerous insignias on his lapel and chest. His head gleamed under the bright light generated by a multi-tiered chandelier overhead, and the Diver's marks proclaiming his proficiencies, tattooed on his scalp, stood out in stark comparison. His face was carefully neutral when he met my eyes, but he did give a pointed look at the podium before turning his nose up.

"Liana Castell."

I paused and looked straight ahead, my eyes tracking up to see the spectral image of a holograph seated in a spot identical to Strum's, the mark of Scipio emblazoned just under him. It was my first time meeting the master AI, and I was surprised to see that his image bore a striking resemblance to Leo's. Only more detailed and, well, lifelike.

When I first met Leo, buried deep in Lionel Scipio's hidden office, he had emitted an aura that was almost too bright to allow for any details. But this projection was different, and hyperdetailed. Scipio's inky black hair was combed back and gathered at the nape of his neck in a tie. Blue eyes that had glowed white in the office watched me as I stopped and made a passable bow. I didn't want to, but it seemed... appropriate, given the lies I was about to tell.

"Lord Scipio," I said in greeting, pulling my eyes from him to the floor. "Esteemed members of the council."

It was all I could do to force the words out, but somehow I managed. And hey, my voice didn't sound at all like I was on the verge of wetting myself, so a point to me. Still, I could feel the weight of Scipio's eyes burning into me, and I was certain that he could see through the charade we were perpetrating.

"Please step onto the dais so we can get this over with," came the stiff feminine voice of Sadie Monroe, and I straightened, twisting up and around until I could see her. She was just to the right of Scipio, and wasn't at all what I expected. Then again, her election to the position had occurred around the time my ranking had dropped from a six to a five, and I had paid little attention to the series of debates that were recorded and transmitted to every citizen. I had been too preoccupied trying to drag up my rank.

Dark auburn hair spilled in tight curls around a heart-shaped face with skin so fair and pale I was momentarily startled by how unblemished it was. She was beautiful, yet there was a hardness about her that made me wary.

Especially with those dark blue eyes, so strange a hue that they almost seemed violet.

I gaped at her for a second, and then nodded, intimidated to hell and back at the coldness and open disdain there.

Next to me, Leo had straightened as well, but his gaze was on Scipio, his eyes wide and staring with open curiosity at the thing that had been built partially *from* him.

I could only imagine what he must be feeling in that moment. Especially after all we had learned. Legacy groups, like Lacey and Strum's, had been attacking Scipio since the beginning of the Tower, unable to accept his role in shaping humanity's destiny. Each generation would make headway and then pass their skills and knowledge down to the next, and on and on, so that one day, generations later, people like me and my friends would be used by one side or the other in a war that, as far as I could tell, was only destroying the Tower.

The thought filled me with anger, and I used it to add steel to my spine. This was the only way forward—the only way for us to survive this clearly corrupted system.

I looked at Leo and realized he was still staring at Scipio, and had been for long enough now that I was certain someone was going to ask what his problem was. He was clearly shocked and fascinated by the holographic projection, and if he continued, it was liable to draw attention. I wasn't sure if Scipio had a way of scanning him that would reveal the net—but I did know that the only way to prevent that was to act like nothing was amiss.

I reached out and touched his shoulder, breaking his attention, and he looked at me.

"Let's get this over with," I said carefully, and he nodded once, visibly relaxing some.

I moved onto the dais, my boots thudding against the solid chunk of wood. Leo stepped up beside me, and I looked around the room. Strum, Lacey, and now Sadie, I knew. But this was my first time seeing Head Farmer Plancett and Chief Surgeon Sage.

Head Farmer Plancett had dark, swarthy skin, a deep black beard, and black hair that hung wild and shaggy around his head. His green coveralls were not dressed up in any way, and he had streaks of dirt and grime on his arms and hands. He watched us with hooded eyes.

Chief Surgeon Sage was the oldest member of the council at nearly a hundred and twenty years of age. Although he didn't look any older than seventy, certain signs of his age were apparent, from the slight tremor in his limbs to the thick spectacles placed over his eyes. He certainly wasn't practicing medicine anymore, but he didn't need to, either. His expertise was what made him Chief Surgeon, not his physical abilities.

In truth, I figured even the Medics were perplexed at why the man had lived so long, his aging process clearly moving slower than that of everyone around him. Rumor was they'd gone over his genes with a fine-toothed comb, and found no genetic anomalies, not even dormant ones. Quess had mentioned once that there was even a prize for anyone who could crack his genome for the secret to his prolonged life. One that offered instant promotion to his personal staff, and unlimited prestige.

The man watched with twinkling blue eyes and a crooked grin on his face, as if he knew some secret joke that the rest of us did not.

I turned my gaze from him to the only empty seat—the one where Devon would've been were he still alive. Lieutenant Zale was absent, thankfully. I was sure that if he were there, I wouldn't have made it across the floor before he came down to finish the job Devon had started.

My fingers twitched to touch my neck again, but I resisted and looked around the room, carefully putting my words into what I hoped was a formal and earnest, yet confident, tone.

"First, I want to thank you for meeting with us. I understand that some of my actions in recent weeks must have caused you great fear, and I apologize for my role in the situation, but you must understand that what I did was necessary."

"*Necessary?*" Sadie spat, leaning forward and peering down at us with penetrating eyes. "It was *necessary* for you to break that man out of the Citadel—a known criminal, I might add— and then run amok inside the Medica, and the *Core*, before *killing* the Champion of the Knights? Please excuse me if I'm having a hard time with that story."

I stared at her, doing everything possible to keep myself calm. "Perhaps if you'd let me tell you more about what happened, you'll have an easier time understanding," I said carefully.

She narrowed her eyes at me, and then waved a dismissive hand, gesturing for me to proceed.

"Some time ago—I'd have to think carefully to recall the exact date—I was with my mentor, Gerome Nobilis, when Scipio contacted me directly with a mission." I paused theatrically and turned slightly, so I could look at the councilors behind me. "To uncover Devon Alexander's plan to subvert the master Scipio AI."

Silence met my statement, followed by: "That's not possible."

I turned toward Sadie. "Apparently it is, and it has happened. I was as shocked as you when I found out, but here I am, telling you that this was what I uncovered during my investigation into Devon Alexander."

I recited the points Lacey and Strum had given me, explaining that Devon Alexander had managed to force Scipio to vote with him on the resolution to execute ones, instead of restructuring them, as the procedure had been in the past. I told them about how Grey became my point of contact to meet Roark, and through him, Cali. In this narrative, however, Cali had possessed evidence of what Devon had done—evidence that I needed. I had been in the process of arranging a meeting when Gerome arrived. He revealed that the Champion ordered him to watch me, and after we subdued him, I realized Devon was onto me—and ran.

"Later, when I found out Gerome had been killed and myself and Grey framed for the crime, I realized that Devon was using his position to paint me as the villain. Even though I was acting on Scipio's behalf."

I went on to explain that I had insisted that we still meet with Cali. From there, she had shown me the evidence that proved Devon had influenced Scipio's vote that day during the council.

"Then I learned that the laws regarding ranks had changed once again, and that somehow, my friends had gotten caught up in it. But it was a trap; Devon used my friends to try to lure me into a confrontation, and silence me altogether. I escaped, but he tracked me down, killed Cali and Roark, and then destroyed the evidence. After that, I felt I had no choice. Devon's guilt was proven, but as an enemy of the Tower, I knew my words would carry no weight. I had no other options. I was honor bound to act, to protect Scipio, and through him, the Tower."

They listened as I wove the story, telling them how we fled. I maintained an appropriate level of embarrassment as I explained our attack on the Core, to steal clean nets so we could hide from Devon, rationalized as a girl trying to fulfill her duty to Scipio, a girl who didn't know whom to trust or how to avoid Devon long enough to even report the information to anyone in the council.

Lacey and Strum had done a good job with the story, making my exploits around the Tower look heroic, if a little naïve. It was eerie how much they knew, and I had plans to ask them about it. The part about Cali was a big question mark in my mind, as I had no idea how they'd even known about her in the first place, but the rest of it... Well, it was public knowledge that I had been in most of those places. Public opinion was that I was there as a full-blown anarchist, trying to destroy the system, and that had labeled me a criminal. But that was all based on Devon's word. And my story openly called it into question.

Now that the council was presented with an alternative narrative, one that painted me as a desperate and unlikely hero, both struggling to survive and performing an essential service to the Tower, they were forced to reevaluate their assessment of me.

Of course, some were faster than others at making character judgments, and from the bland look of utter disbelief on Sadie's face, I could tell she was going to be the first to launch the inquiry.

"You paint a very noble picture of yourself, Squire Castell," she began, leaning forward on her elbows. "But your actions have thrown this entire Tower into chaos, and while I am unsurprised that you lack a certain amount of finesse, I find it very hard to believe that our great and wise Scipio would task someone as inexperienced and green as yourself with a mission against a seasoned veteran like Devon Alexander. And the fact that the so-called evidence incriminating him was destroyed before we could take a look at it? Preposterous."

Her hands gripped the edge of the wall that also served as her table, and she shook her head at me, her face a mask of contempt. "And to try to sully Devon Alexander's name in order to preserve yours? I find it highly suspicious."

"Squire Castell's story is true," Leo said flatly. "I was there."

"Mm-hm. And how was it that you two were able to break into one of the most secure levels of the Core? Neither you, nor those two friends you fled the Medica with the first time, have any skills in coding. But you got into the Core, which means someone hacked the system. So who helped you? Where is the girl my Inquisitors captured during your escape? According to the tests, that girl was not Zoe Elphesian, so who was she? Her blood tells us Devon was her father and Cali was her mother, so how do we know you weren't part of a plot started by Cali to murder Devon for getting her pregnant and refusing to marry her?"

"If you'd ever met Cali Kerrin, then you wouldn't consider her capable of such an action," Sage said, his voice a wet rattle. "She had more honor and integrity than anyone in this Tower. Murder was not her way."

"Then maybe it was her daughter! She was raised outside the system—a true undoc, for all those not paying attention. How many others are there down there? How many did Cali steal from the Tower—and how many is Ms. Castell now protecting? And for what reasons?"

Eyes returned to me, and I shifted. Lacey and Strum's notes hadn't addressed questions of that nature, so I needed to think of something—and quickly—before I looked guilty of anything.

"Cali was taking care of several individuals when I met her," I admitted. "And yes, in their grief over losing Cali, they wanted justice. So, I took their help. But I promised them that in exchange I would not reveal who they were to the council, and I'll honor that promise. I know they are a threat to the Tower, but..." I trailed off and fidgeted, trying to look appropriately torn up over this imaginary decision I'd made. "I honestly didn't know what else I could do at the time. I needed their expertise, and they had skills I could use. They had resources, and food, and most importantly, they were willing to aid me. So, I will honor their request, and keep their number, and their identities, a secret."

I didn't care if they bought it. I had no intention of revealing the identities of my friends. Nobody needed to know about them. The fewer people who knew, the safer they were.

"That's not good enough, Squire Castell. You come in here with your boyfriend and some story about how you and your friends, an unknown number of them undocs, broke into several areas around the Tower and murdered the Champion, all on the orders of Scipio? Are we just supposed to accept your word?"

"Why don't we just ask Scipio?" Strum asked, leaning forward. Sadie turned toward him, an angry scowl on her face, but he raised his eyebrows and met her gaze head on. "I'm not your enemy, Executive Monroe, so I'll thank you kindly to keep your ire to yourself. Squire Castell's story is, as you say, a pretty one, but one that we can confirm very easily. At least, we can confirm her claims that this was a mission, and not an act of anarchy. Lord Scipio?"

There was a rustle of movement as everyone shifted in their seats to turn toward where Scipio was watching the proceedings unfold. He hadn't moved, not once—just sat still as a statue, listening and watching, blue eyes glittering.

Now that he was being addressed, however, he looked up at the other councilors, and then up farther, toward the dome, growing distant and vacant. "I am downloading Liana Castell's service file now," he informed them. "Accessing... Ah, yes. Squire Castell is correct: I *did* task her with following Devon Alexander and learning his true loyalties. It seems that during one of my normal self-scans, I noticed a discrepancy, one that proved to be over twenty years old. I did an in-depth analysis, and while I had no proof, I began to suspect that Champion Alexander had played a critical part in something. But because he was the Champion, I realized that any investigation meant I would be asking a Knight to turn on his commander, and decided I couldn't trust that Devon wouldn't find out and attempt to do something more drastic. So I tasked Squire Castell here to do so, instead."

He paused, frowning. "It would appear that an aspect of my code has indeed been subverted."

My eyes widened as he spoke, my heart beating harder and harder as every word coming from the speakers continued to confirm my story. I looked at Leo, whose carefully neutral features were beginning to grow alarmed, and reached out to grab his forearm, squeezing it. We couldn't afford to show our surprise—or any other reaction to what we were supposed to already know as the truth.

He glanced over and quickly relaxed his face, and I exhaled, but I was far from feeling at ease. The tension that had been gripping my spine had suddenly twisted, so much so that it felt like my nerves were on fire. I glanced over at Lacey and saw her smiling a small, secretive smile, her eyes already watching me, studying my reaction. I brought my brows together, and she nodded, infinitesimally, before the smile melted and horror spread across her face.

But that little nod was the only thing I needed. It was the thing I focused on as I realized that Lacey and Strum *also* had a way of controlling Scipio. That changed my feelings toward them drastically, because if they could do something like this, then there was no telling how much more they could do. That level of control... To falsify a memory or program his response... How were they even doing it, and what did it mean for us, for Scipio, and for the Tower? My eyes flew back to Scipio. He looked devoid of any reaction save the frown.

"Dear God," Sadie said, her features sliding from righteous fury to absolute horror. "That's not possible! If... If people were to learn about this..."

"Relax, Executive Monroe," Scipio said, holding up a hand. "A scan of the code and the decision he affected twenty years ago shows me that it only happened the one time, and it seems that all it affected was my mood for the day. But your techs are updating my firewalls millions of times a day, so it seems likely it was a random fluke. I doubt that any such code could touch me again, although I couldn't be sure until I questioned Devon. It's unfortunate that he was killed—I was curious to know how he got in. In any case, it seems he got lucky and found a weak point at the right time, but was never able to replicate the results. I'll need you and your team to go over my coding as soon as possible, but I do believe I am intact."

He didn't know. Or maybe he *couldn't* know—I couldn't tell. How many changes had been made to him over the years? How many lines of his code had been slowly whittled away or subverted by his enemies, until only this unaware shell remained? Stiff, expressionless, pensive... but no sign of joy or life or curiosity. Nothing like his predecessor, whose simple, inquisitive nature and attempts to be more human had drawn me into a friendship I'd never thought I'd have. The two of them were so different, so drastically different, that it was apparent to me that Scipio was now just a puppet, robbed of any aspect of the life that had once made him a marvel.

How had that happened? How had so much damage been done to him?

It was strange, but suddenly I didn't feel afraid of the great machine. I felt *sorry* for him. Who knew what changes had been made over the centuries? It must have been a slow and deliberate death, with small doses of poison over a long period of time. And in my eyes, the great machine no longer looked indifferent. He looked weary.

I made a note to have Alex do a little digging, and returned my focus to the matter at hand.

"Then that means Squire Castell is a hero," Head Farmer Plancett declared, breaking through my dark thoughts. "She punished a man who violated Scipio and threatened our very existence in the Tower."

Well, not your existence, but certainly mine and my friends', I thought as I folded my hands in front of me. Although, Devon had admitted to doing *something* to Scipio, so perhaps Plancett was right.

Except that one of the two Inquisition agents with him had

referred to someone else—their own leader, presumably—who was working with Devon. That meant someone *else* was pulling the strings. And whoever they were, they certainly weren't going to fall for Lacey and Strum's trick, if they had as much control over the system as the two councilors claimed. They would know it was a lie, a fabricated memory.

Unless Lacey and Strum were the leaders Devon had been answering to, and they had done all of this to eliminate Devon and keep whatever code he and his family had developed over the years for themselves.

But none of that mattered right now, and I certainly couldn't ask right then and there without blowing everything to smithereens. So I kept my mouth shut and my head down, and waited to see what would happen—whether Lacey and Strum's efforts would work.

"Yes, but we'll have to go back and review every decision made in the past twenty years to be sure," Monroe said, folding her arms across her chest and tossing her wild mane of hair to one side. "This is a nightmare. What are we going to do?"

"Not talk about it while Squire Castell and Citizen Farmless are in the room," announced Lacey. "Thank you for your testimony, but you two are dismissed. Please follow the attendant back, and wait for one of us to come to explain what happens next."

"Yes, and keep your mouth shut about all of this," Sadie demanded.

Our dismissal was delivered suddenly, and with such a note

of finality that I had little choice but to leave, with the vague impression that... maybe things had gone well?

That note of hope didn't seem right given our present situation, and as we left the dome, I realized why: I hadn't actually expected this plan to work.

And even as we walked out, I still wasn't sure that it had.

6

My eyes snapped open at the sound of the handwheel turning, and I pulled my cheek off Zoe's shoulder and scrambled to my feet. Leo was already upright, and looked like he hadn't slept at all, given the dark shadows under Grey's eyes.

It had been hours since we had been brought back, and after filling everyone in on what had happened, I had ordered us all to sleep. It was the fastest way I knew to pass the time, and the best way to avoid repeating questions that no one in the room could answer.

Now the door pulled open, revealing a person who *could* answer those questions, and I stared blearily as Lacey stepped in.

"What happened?" I demanded, moving up to her. "What's going to happen now?"

"Relax," she said, holding up her hands, palms out, before

bringing them together in front of her. "Everything went according to plan, thanks to Scipio corroborating your story."

"You mean *your* story," I stated flatly. "And speaking of which, how you did that is just one of the many questions I have for you. Are you and Strum now in control of Scipio?"

She arched an eyebrow and looked over my head toward the group pressing in just behind me, easily able to hear every word. "You do realize, of course, that not a word of that can be breathed outside of this room, or go beyond any of the people present, correct?"

"You mean, do we realize that we can't go running around the Tower screaming about how council members are manipulating the entity practically worshipped by everyone in the Tower as some sort of electronic god, in an attempt to have complete and total autonomy so they can do whatever the hell they want? You mean, we shouldn't do that?"

Lacey blinked several times and then shook her head. "You made your point, although it was a bit on the sarcastic side for my tastes."

"Well, I'm sorry," I replied. "But I'm tired, sore, scared, angry, and worried about all of the people behind me. I also have a bajillion and a half questions for you, regarding what in the heck you did to Scipio, and how I can trust that you won't go back on your word now that the deed is done."

"Well, for one thing, you and Mr. Farmless are going to be celebrated as heroes, and you're all to be integrated back into the Tower. We have a net for each of you, with your identity and the identities of Mr. Farmless, Mr. MacGillus, and Ms. Elphesian restored, while your undocumented friends will receive new identities. Except for you, young lady." She turned and speared Maddox with a pointed look. "If it's not known throughout the Tower that you're Devon Alexander and Cali Kerrin's daughter yet, then it will be soon. Some things are too juicy for us to keep quiet, and it'll add to the rumor mill, and keep people away from the knowledge that Scipio was manipulated."

Maddox blinked in surprise, a hot flash of anger coming over her face. She had taken the news about Devon with some... understandably mixed emotions, but we'd all been there for her, and she was keeping it together. I could only imagine how she felt, and in truth none of us would ever know what it was like finding out your long-lost father had killed your mother and tried to abduct you as well, but all we could do was be there for her. "Do I get to choose which surname I use? I don't want to have my father's."

I hadn't even considered her dilemma, and I realized that I hadn't put any thought into what would happen after the council meeting. To be honest, I never thought it would go well in the first place, so the fact that there was even an "after" to consider left me a little disoriented.

But hey, everything had been happening pretty quickly, all things considered, so I assumed this was just how life was going to go from here on out.

"Of course you may," Lacey replied, slightly aghast. "I can only imagine what you went through in all of this."

"Yeah, about that," I said. "How did you know about Cali?"

Lacey crossed her arms and smiled. "How did you and your friends break into the Core? Or gain that much access to the Medica?"

The answers were Mercury, my twin brother, and Leo, in that order, but there was no way I was telling her that. And she knew it—which was why she had countered my questions with her own. Questions I wouldn't answer in exchange for questions *she* wouldn't answer.

I sighed and ran a hand along my face. Lacey's sometimes enigmatic, sometimes direct communication style was a little frustrating, but honestly, I kind of liked her. I just wished I knew what she and Strum were up to, and that what she had done to Scipio had been to help us rather than exert more control over him to hurt people.

I had so many questions for her about what she and Strum had done, who they were, what their plans were, and what they wanted from me. Who their enemies were, and whether they would be after us now. How long it would be before we could disappear again—and resume our mission to escape this twisted place.

Or use Leo to replace Scipio, a prospect made seemingly impossible by the fact that we lacked the other AI fragments that had been used to fabricate the full Scipio unit. Unfortunately, their original codes had been destroyed by the council. Weirdly, I had discovered Jasper, a computer program that I met in the Medica, before I had learned any of this, and it turned out that he was one of the fragments needed to help grow Leo's program

—whatever the hell that meant. Yet with his existence, we now had reason to question whether the other AIs were still around—which meant the plan, however insane it seemed, was still on the table.

In short, we hadn't decided on which plan we were actually following, outside of trying to rediscover Roark's formula for Paragon, the pill that would mask our ranks and keep us from dropping to ones. Keep us—and those under our care—safe in the Tower, at least for a while.

There were too many thoughts rattling around my skull, but I was finally able to settle on one. One question above all the others that stood out in my mind, and it wasn't even something I had heard from Lacey, but rather Devon. Still, I was certain Lacey had to know.

"Lacey, what is a legacy net?"

Her eyes widened and then narrowed, and she took a step closer. "Where did you hear about those?"

I hesitated, and then realized that there was no harm in telling her. "One of the Inquisitors who was talking to Devon mentioned that they had recovered one from Cali's body."

"Cali was a *legacy*?" Lacey's gaze grew distant, presumably as she became lost in thought, and then snapped back to me. "Legacy nets are... were... at one point readily available to everyone in the Tower. Then the IT department notified everyone that there was a lack of the material needed to make them, and that criminal elements in the Tower were harvesting them to implant new IDs and avoid authorities. They voted a change to the models still being issued today—

models that did not have the vast storage space of the legacy nets, or the knowledge they contained of the world before. Only a few of the original nets survived removal, and the legacies now use them to pass information and knowledge to the next generations, namely all the coding changes each previous generation has done to alter Scipio... or to fight his attackers. Cali... My group discovered that she had tried to expose Devon's actions for months after she disappeared, and I always wondered about that. But we couldn't find any evidence that her family line was ever a legacy, which is what it's become, most nets being passed down from parents to their children. So I'm baffled as to how she managed to get her hands on one."

I looked at Leo, who nodded, confirming that she was at least telling some truth about the nets. "Thank you. So, what happens next for us?"

"Well, the only thing that's left is for your team to pick what departments they want to be in. Save for you, of course. We need you to stay in the Knights, for now."

I narrowed my eyes. "What do you mean, need? We're done."

Lacey looked slightly guilty. "I'm sorry, but we're not. We need you, Liana."

"For what?" I asked. "We held up our end of the bargain, and yours was our freedom and reintegration. You can't go back on it now."

"We can and we will," Lacey said firmly. "Removing Devon was only the first step in our plan. Now we need to replace him.

Now, we have a candidate who is a part of our network of legacies, and he's certainly skilled enough to take the title, but..."

"But the Tourney is dangerous," I finished for her. "And you need human meat shields like me out there to keep your candidate safe."

"Exactly," Lacey exclaimed with a smile. "And you're in a position and have the skills necessary to help him to survive."

I glared at her, annoyed that she had so glibly ignored my dry humor. "And yet, I am still not inclined to help you."

She gave me a long, hard look and then looked away. "I'm really sorry, Liana, but I was hoping that you would be more agreeable. After all, I thought you would want to help the Tower. We need to put someone into the Champion seat, and we need to make sure our candidate gets out of the Tourney alive. We don't have a lot of active agents in the Knights. In fact, the Knights are likely filled with more of our enemies than allies. So, if you won't help us willingly, then we move on to threats—something I would prefer not to do, as it puts strain on our fledgling relationship."

I stared at her, studying her closely. She seemed earnest about what she was saying, but I had heard her lie during the council meeting. She could be convincing when she wanted to be.

"What is the threat?" I asked, needing to know exactly what she was promising to do.

"That you fabricated the memory inside Scipio to help clear your own name and get away with murder. Your friends' undoc statuses will be revealed, and everyone will be arrested by the

Knights." She said the words as if they made her angry, and her body language reflected the same emotion—coiled tightly and ready to spring.

If she was acting, it was masterfully done, but I was inclined to believe that she was reluctant to do this. In fact, she seemed puzzled and confused by my desire to refuse, and I could understand why. She had no idea that we were considering washing our hands of the Tower and escaping. It was unfathomable to most, as we'd all been taught that life couldn't be sustained outside the Tower. So to her, we were just acting selfishly. Which she couldn't understand.

"I see." I folded my arms across my chest and thought about what she was asking me to do. With Devon dead, the Knights needed to select a new Champion—something they did through the Tourney, a series of events that took a week. The events were designed to test a candidate's ability to command, respond, and protect the citizens and the Tower. Knights were eliminated until only one remained.

The last one had happened only a few years before I was born, and in truth, I hadn't expected to see one for at least another twenty to thirty years. Let alone *participate* in one.

And now I was going to have to, if I wanted to keep everyone safe from being exposed and arrested. Fan-freaking-tastic.

"Excuse me? Engineer Green?" I turned, and followed Lacey's gaze toward Quess, who was helping to support Maddox by letting her lean on him. I looked at him quizzically, but he didn't meet my gaze, and instead held hers. "I feel like I speak for all of us when I say we know what department we want to join *now*."

"You do?" Lacey looked back to me, and then to him. "All of you?"

"Well, obviously," Zoe said. "We go where Liana goes. We'll be joining the Knights as well."

"Zoe," I said, shaking my head. "Everyone, you don't have to do that. I'm sure I can handle keeping one Knight safe. And the Tourney is dangerous—it's not worth all of you risking your lives. Besides, I know there are departments some of you have always dreamed of joining. Now is your chance."

I gave Zoe a pointed look, knowing that it had always been her dream to join the Cogs, but she just smiled.

"That's very noble of you," Lacey began, but Maddox cut her off.

"It's more than that," she said softly. "We're a family, and we're not going to let you tear us apart in whatever mad little scheme you have for the Tourney. We watch each other's backs, which means we'll work together to make sure your guy makes it through."

Everyone behind her nodded, and I felt a rush of both gratitude and love for them all.

"Well... you heard them," I said to Lacey, and after a moment's hesitation, she nodded.

"Very well. I can certainly do that for the young man over there, Ms. Kerrin, of course, and Grey, since he was in my department to begin with. But Ms. Elphesian and Mr. MacGillus must go back to their original departments, as it would be too noticeable for them to be in a different department within a few hours of their exoneration. We can fabricate transfers later on, but for now you must proceed as if everything has returned to normal. The youngest one will need a guardian—probably one of your undoc friends—and she will be expected to go to school with all the other children. Your undoc friends will be placed as out-of-department recruits, but, Liana, your parents are Knights. You'll have to stay with them until you're twenty-one."

My heart sank into the pit of my stomach, so deep that I was quite certain it had plummeted down the remaining thirty stories to the bottom of the Tower, where it was currently trying to find the smallest, tightest, and darkest hiding place.

"My parents?" I managed, trying not to sound too terrified. Someone grabbed my hand—Zoe, was my guess—and squeezed it, offering me unwavering support and sympathy. But I could barely feel it.

I hadn't considered that coming back into the Tower meant having to deal with my parents again.

And now that I knew... well, I wasn't exactly excited to see the people who had conceived me and raised me for the past twenty years.

Especially since I was guessing they wouldn't be too pleased to be saddled with me again. Because hero or not, I was still their screw-up of a daughter, and an embarrassment to the Castell name. They had flat-out told my twin brother to refuse any contact with me after Gerome was found murdered and I was blamed for it. Because they thought I had done it.

And now I got to move back in with them for a whole... I realized I had no idea what the date was, but my birthday had been six or seven weeks away when I went into the Medica for rank intervention treatment. It had to be close, though—maybe even a few days. Hopefully no more than three or four.

Piece of cake.

7

"I 'll let you all have a few minutes to talk things out. When I return, I'll have new nets and uniforms for all of you, as well as some food."

Zoe murmured something—I wasn't sure what—and then Lacey left, a once-again closed door replacing her in a matter of seconds.

Several more seconds passed, and then everyone began talking at once.

"Did you hear what she said about—"

"How do you think—"

"Why does she—"

"What's a Tourney?"

The last one was asked by Tian, and it was the easiest of them to answer.

"The Tourney is a competition," I told her. "Meant to test an applicant's abilities as a leader in order to find out who will make the best Champion."

"And Lacey wants you to protect her friend during the Tourney?" she asked, her features muddled with confusion. I nodded, but her frown only deepened. "Why does she want you to protect her friend? Is the Tourney dangerous?"

"It's very dangerous, Tian," Quess answered for me. "An average of four percent of contestants have died, while an additional two percent lose a limb of some sort. But you're missing the point, kiddo: we have to do this."

And get someone we didn't know through it without getting them killed, and win enough challenges to qualify them for the position. Just winning wasn't enough; they'd added bodyguard services on top of it.

"Oh." Tian fidgeted again, and then craned her neck around. "Why do we have to do this? I can find us a new Sanctum."

There was a pause, and then all gazes shifted to me, questions lurking in their eyes, all echoing Tian's inquiry in some variation or another. Why were we entertaining this? Why didn't we just try to run? What could doing this now mean for our plans? The list of questions was about as long as my arm.

"Liana, what *is* our plan here? Like Tian said, we *could* just find a new Sanctum. We could run." Quess gave me an earnest look as he asked the question.

I shook my head, already dismissing that idea. That meant playing along for a short time and then trying to escape before we fulfilled the job that Lacey was blackmailing us to do. But I had no doubt that she would have her people following us at all times, as well as having our nets monitored for location and transmissions. "Guys, we're talking about a group that has a designer bacteria with which they are able to track us. I don't think it's wise to turn around and try to run. At least not immediately. We will need a new Sanctum, but the council is going to be watching us."

"Not to mention, you'll be on every other legacy watch list," Maddox added. "At least those that were allied with Devon. They'll figure out something was done to Scipio to back your story up, and if any of Devon's legacy family is still around... you know they'll be gunning for you."

"I think you're all that remains of Devon's family on that front," I told her softly, and she blinked in surprise a moment before her face went hard and flat with anger.

"That man was not my father," she spat. "And I'm glad he's dead."

I nodded. Her reaction made sense. Maddox and her mother Cali had been close, and Devon had taken that from her. I knew that Devon had wanted to try to teach Maddox about his legacy family—I had heard it from his own mouth. Even then, though, I had known that there was no way Maddox would go along with that. Now I was just grateful that she didn't have to.

"That's nice, Doxy," Quess replied congenially. "But that doesn't help us figure out what we're going to do. I mean, what is the plan, Liana? What are we going to do about Jasper, the Paragon, the people relying on Paragon, leaving, staying, the Tourney..."

Once again, everyone was looking at me, and I sucked in a deep breath, thinking. The first thing that stood out was that Maddox was right: we knew for a fact that there were other legacy families in the Tower. And according to Lacey and Strum, one of them was in control of Scipio. Now, whether or not they knew Lacey and Strum had also had access, and had tampered with Scipio during my trial, was an unknown, but for safety's sake, I had to assume they knew something was done.

Furthermore, we had to assume they would be watching me and my friends to try to figure out if it had been us, or someone else. As soon as we stepped back into our lives in the Tower, most of us would be under surveillance by whatever legacy group currently had control of Scipio, and probably by Lacey and Strum's people as well, but the latter was beside the point.

We did have a few aces up our sleeve—namely that Quess and Tian would be off their radar for now, as their names hadn't been mentioned at the trial once. No one knew who they were to me, and they would be hidden from everyone except Lacey's group, especially if they used disguises. We could use that to our advantage and have them run a few side missions, but even that could be dangerous if they were to be spotted. They'd be on their own, without any backup or support to reach them in time to feasibly do something. I hated risking either one of them, although I was certain they would both insist that they didn't mind.

And on top of all those problems, we still hadn't solved our big picture problem. Mostly because we didn't *have* a big picture beyond this.

"Okay, guys," I said, realizing that was the starting place. "Before I can decide anything, we need to finally decide what we are going to do. Are we staying or are we going?"

There was a pause, then Eric said, "Wait, you want to have a discussion about our master plan right *now*?"

"Yes," I replied honestly, looking around at my friends. "Guys, we are going to be watched from here on out, make no mistake about it. We have to be more careful than we ever were in Sanctum, because there are some thirty-nine thousand humans on the other side of that door, and all of them are potential enemies. We can't use nets to communicate with each other, not until Quess, Mercury, Alex, or Zoe creates a way to do so without anyone else hearing. And we can't go out alone—we need to make sure we always have someone with us, in case anyone tries to jump us or attack us, or is even following us. Eric, Zoe, that means you two have to stay as close to your families as possible."

"So do you," Zoe said pointedly, and I suppressed the feeling of dread that thought created, and shook my head.

"I know—my movements are going to be watched most of all. Mine and Leo's, I'm sure."

"Yeah, about that," Quess said, scratching his jaw. "Um... How is this going to work with... with Leo in... in Grey?"

I looked over at Leo, who was standing by, watching. The AI had been unusually quiet since we were grabbed in the halls, and I was concerned. Leo loved a good conversation, and was bound to have strong feelings about what had occurred today. But he'd been strangely mute.

"What do you mean?" I asked. "We call him Grey in public, Leo in private."

"No, I mean..." Quess looked at Grey and dropped his voice an octave lower. "What about his terminal, when he's finished? He only set up a few fail-safes before he left it, and isn't there a possibility that the virus has shorted the entire thing out? Or that Lacey and her crew found it and... I don't know, decided to smash it up or something?"

The terminal Quess was referring to was the terminal Leo had been living in for the past two hundred plus years, buried in Lionel Scipio's secret office. In an attempt to murder Leo, it had been infected with a virus placed there by Ezekial Pine, the founder of the Knights. Leo had held it back over the years, and had left it in a state of stasis to come help me. But that was temporary. If the terminal went out, we wouldn't have anywhere to put him when he was finished healing Grey.

Which meant we would have to figure something out for him, too.

"I can hear you," Leo said. "And Liana's answer will be that she doesn't know. Although I doubt they found it. Liana only found me because I was talking to myself."

"Well, actually, my answer was going to be to have Quess and Tian go check it out together," I informed them both. I went over everything that needed to be done, the biggest thing being finding out what Lacey and Strum had done to Sanctum, and from there, beginning preparations for finding a new hideout.

Suddenly, I knew what I was going to do. I was going to get Lacey's candidate through the Tourney, but after that, I wanted everything in place so that we could disappear in the resulting chaos the event was bound to cause.

"Tomorrow. And I'm sorry to put this on you both, but you'll need to start packing our things in preparation of a move. I'd have other people join you, but..."

"But no one knows who we are," Quess said dryly. "Which makes us your little spies."

The thought had crossed my mind, but I still hated asking it. Spying required delicacy, and was dangerous, especially if you got caught. But the fact was, I was going to need their anonymity as a weapon, to act as our eyes and ears when necessary, or to track down things we might need so we didn't draw too much attention to ourselves. I was sure Quess and Tian were more than willing to help, possibly bordering on downright eager, but it didn't mean I had to be comfortable with it.

"In a word, yes. But, I don't want either of you to actively follow anyone unless we decide you absolutely have to. Keeping your relationship with us a secret is going to be hard enough as is, so I want you both to be extra careful no matter what you are up to. And try not to go out alone, until we can figure out a way to mask our net transmissions to each other."

"I have to go alone," Tian said, and I looked down at her in confusion. "If you still want me to find a new Sanctum."

She added the last piece as if it explained everything, but in truth, I had only known Tian for a short time compared to Maddox and Quess. Which meant I found myself turning to them for help interpreting what she meant.

"Tian's always gone off on her own to find new safe places,"

Maddox stated begrudgingly. "We've tried to keep up with her in the past, but she's so small that she can slip in and out of places that we can't."

"It's my super power," Tian said, beaming. "But I promise I'll be safe. I'm fast, and really, really good at hiding."

I hesitated, and then looked up at Maddox and Quess again. "I want to say no," I told them flatly.

"We also want you to say no," Quess replied. "But I sense a 'but' in you, so..."

I licked my lips and looked around. "Honestly, guys, I don't see any way of getting out of here until after the Tourney finishes. Not just because Lacey and Strum have their hooks in us, but because people will be *expecting* us to run right away. Which means that any chance we have at running means finding a place to go *before* we plan to run. Which means letting Tian do what she does best. I might not be able to convince Lacey to pull her people from us, but I will make her understand Tian is off limits."

"Do you think she will honor that?" Maddox asked.

I nodded in response, because I did think she would. Lacey didn't like the idea of leveraging us, so I was betting she doubly didn't like the idea of stalking a young girl. Strum and Lacey had done nothing to hurt Tian so far, and they probably believed that she was just a child. Which she was—but she was also capable, and clever.

While I hated the idea of letting Tian go off by herself, I had to believe that she could take care of herself.

I had to trust that they *all* could, I realized. Quess, Maddox, and Leo were going to be Squires, like me, but I was not going to be staying in the barracks with them. I was going to be with my parents. And my friends were going to be *without* me more than we were going to be together, especially since they were going to have classes, tests, and training. I struggled to remember whether the Academy was canceled during the Tourney, because I was going to need them desperately, but decided to address that later.

"Please, Doxy," Tian begged as Maddox continued to brood over the decision. Doxy's eyes slid over to Tian's bright blue ones, and softened slightly.

"Okay," she relented with a nod. "But here are the rules: every time you leave, you have to net in every hour, on the hour, and let us know that you are safe."

"But Liana said no netting!" Tian exclaimed, looking at me.

"In this case, it will be okay. I'm pretty sure that one of us will be listed as your official guardian, since you are underage," Quess replied. "And it will have to be me, because Maddox is known. It would make sense for her to call me to check in. Just check in, though; the reports on places can be delivered in person."

I nodded in approval of the idea, and felt some of the weight on my shoulders lift.

"Okay, so I'll handle old Sanctum, and Tian will handle finding the new location. Once we find it, then what?" Quess asked the question casually, looking around.

"We'll start transferring stuff over—discreetly, of course. That will come later. Lacey might be watching it, but again, I think I can convince her to back off some. And during the Tourney is when she's going to be most distracted, so that would be the best time to get the bulk of it moved." I sucked in a deep breath, thinking. "I'm going to tap Alex and Mercury to see if they can find Jasper, and the formula for Paragon. We also need to get the Paragon from Sanctum up here as soon as possible. I do not want Lacey's people finding it and getting curious about what it is."

"I'll grab it tomorrow," Quess replied. "Or today, rather. As soon as we get out of here."

"Good," I said, reaching out and grabbing his hand to squeeze it. "Thank you."

He nodded. "Of course. But what are we going to do? Leave or stay?"

"If I may?" I looked over in surprise to see Leo watching us, an expectant expression on his face. I realized he wanted to say something that was just a little longer than a question, and stepped back, allowing him to have the floor, so to speak. "I want to make a case for staying here and helping me," he said carefully. "And it starts and ends with this: if all of the legacies have been tampering with Scipio for generations, then it won't be long before the Tower itself fails. So I want your help tracking down the other AI fragments, so that I can incorporate them into my code and become the new Master AI."

I had been waiting for him to bring this up, and I was surprised it had taken him this long. The six of us shared various uncomfortable looks, mine fueled by the suspicion that he wasn't going to get the response he wanted, but it was Zoe who spoke.

"How bad do you think the damage to Scipio is?"

"Bad," Leo replied without hesitation, his face and voice grave. "For Lacey and Strum to have overridden a memory like that... Those are deeply embedded in our code, which means there must be serious damage to the system. That's the only thing that would've allowed them access to do what they did. I'm not sure how bad it could be, but..."

"But what?" Quess asked, a tremor of fear in his voice. "We weren't able to recover Jasper, and as you said, there were four other AIs besides him that completed the final AI. According to the video you showed us, they were destroyed." He left it unspoken, but all of us were thinking it: without them, it was a doomed cause. Lionel Scipio had somehow used all of the fragments, and Scipio himself, to create the master AI, and without them, Leo was too small to run the Tower.

"Yes, but if Jasper is still around, then maybe they weren't," Leo replied. "They could've fought, like I did!"

"But you said they weren't full AIs like you were," I said carefully. I could already tell how the others felt about this, and that was beyond reluctant. While I sympathized with Leo, I also understood their fear about what he was suggesting. It meant staying longer, more chance of exposure, and planning an attack on the Core itself—something we had barely managed to survive the first time around. If it was between an unknown future escaping the Tower to find a new place to live, and trying to take on the Tower, and the Core itself, then outside won, hands down.

Still, if I was really honest with myself, I didn't like it. Leaving seemed cold and indifferent to the people inside the Tower, who were living their lives with no idea of how close catastrophe was. We had all grown up among them, Tian and Maddox excluded. Most people bought into the dream and lie of the Tower with an almost fanatical attitude that made it impossible for them to see reason.

But how could the seven of us stand a chance against that many people? People who were made our enemies specifically by their belief in Scipio and his infallibility? Even now, the council was going to brush Devon's supposed manipulation of Scipio under the table, so that people never learned he had been tampered with. Just his word was good enough for them.

What sort of fairness could be achieved when the system itself was no longer impartial?

The answer was none, which made it hard to even consider standing up and fixing it.

No, leaving was the only option for them, for us, because we all knew that staying on the inside would only get us killed faster. If not from our ranks dropping to a one, then from the unknown enemies we were rapidly acquiring.

They were good people. We all were. But that didn't mean we wanted to die in a mad attempt to save the Tower.

"This is hard for me to say, because I'm very close with my family, but... I know that if they were here, they wouldn't want me to have any part in trying to fix the Tower. They'd urge me to leave before they'd ever let me do that." Eric looked around and shifted. "They'd tell me to do whatever I could to keep myself and the people I cared about safe. That plan doesn't seem safe to me."

Zoe reached out and took his hand, and I smiled in spite of the somberness of the conversation. The love between them seemed to chase away the dark fear lurking in both their eyes, if only for just a moment.

Leo, however, looked crestfallen as he swiveled his head around. "And the rest of you?"

"I'm sorry, Leo," Maddox said, her eyes down. She was holding Tian's hand, her thumb stroking Tian's smaller fingers. "I can't risk the people I love. It's bad enough we're thinking about escape, but that's... that's easier than what you're asking. And less dangerous."

"I see." His eyes crossed the room and settled on me. "Liana?"

I took a long moment to consider, even though I could sense his impatience for an answer. "I'm not voting this time," I finally announced softly. "I can't. I see the merits of doing either, as well as the cons, and... I don't care, as long as we do it together. That's what's important to me."

Zoe's arm slid around my shoulder as I met Leo's recriminating stare with an apologetic one. I knew he wanted me to back him up, and a part of me really wanted to. I certainly didn't like the idea of turning my back on anyone in the Tower, but I recognized that the fight for the Tower was harder than the fight to leave, and I wouldn't try to argue for the more dangerous mission if my friends didn't want to do it in the first place.

"I'm sorry, Leo, I'm out as well," Quess said, folding his arms over his chest. "You forget, I've lived inside the Core. The fact that we managed to get in and out once was a fluke, and even then, they got Maddox in the process. Couple that with the fact that Lionel Scipio didn't leave a manual called 'How to Replace Scipio,' or a list of locations where we could find the other AIs, and I just don't think it's going to be possible."

"I see." Leo gazed around and then nodded. "Well then, will you at least agree to help me look while you are still here?"

"Of course," I said quickly, forestalling everyone else. "Maybe once we learn more about Lacey and her group, and determine that they actually are working to prevent attacks on Scipio, we can arrange to leave you with her when we go. And if not her, then someone else willing to take up your cause. I owe you at least that much, for what you're doing for Grey."

He inclined his head toward me, and then took a step back, but I could feel the disappointment radiating from him. I wanted to say something, to explain it better, in a way that he could understand, but Quess stopped me by asking another question.

"Hey, since Lacey is bringing us nets, how are we going to explain Leo's net? Or the fact that Tian has an adult one, and not one meant for a child?"

I blinked. I had to remind myself that I was tired, and had had a very long and challenging day, because that was an observation I should've made long ago. All residents were implanted with a net from the age of two for security purposes, but the net for children was only used to prohibit movement inside the Tower and monitor emotional growth. This was to establish a baseline for Scipio to use to create one's rank during the second implantation that occurred at the age of fifteen—the age one started their apprenticeship to a department.

Tian wasn't old enough for an adult net, but a child's version would restrict her movement, sounding an alarm whenever she crossed into an area she wasn't allowed in. Because she was using an adult one, however, her lack of emotional maturity would play havoc with her ranking, so we needed to keep her on a strict regimen of Paragon to make sure she wouldn't get caught.

I ran a hand over my face, and thought about how we could accomplish that.

"We tell Lacey that you're going to do the implantations," I finally said. "You'll have to figure out a way to transfer Grey's net ID credentials into the net Leo is in, so as not to raise any suspicions, and then give Tian the one meant for Grey. Is it possible?"

I looked between Grey and Leo, and Leo was the one who nodded. "It is possible to download the ID into the net. Quess will have to help me, but just in placing the net they provide on the back of Grey's neck. I can download his data and permissions without hurting myself."

I nodded. That meant he could remain hidden in the eyes of the Tower. Scanners were everywhere, searching for ones or those without a net, and if they discovered him and what he actually was, who knew what would happen? The fact that it was possible to put the credentials into the net was a relief, as it meant we could continue to hide Leo while he worked on restoring Grey's mind.

"As for Tian, well, we can use the net meant for Grey. If they give us the IDs and nets separately—which they should, as pre-programming chips is the fastest way to make sure that you don't put the wrong net in the skull—then I can just tweak the permissions before I put it in. It won't be hard."

I nodded. "I'm sure Lacey won't give us too much push-back," I said.

Still, everything laid out in front of us was based on more what ifs than I thought any of us were comfortable with. One "no" from Lacey, and the jig was up.

I looked around the room. Everyone was tired, and afraid, and on the verge of becoming demoralized. Even though we now had a plan of action, the lingering threat of the unknown still loomed over us. I needed to say something to them, to fill them with confidence.

"Guys, I know you're scared. I'm scared, too. But we have managed to do some impossible things in our short time together. I know that being separated is going to be hard, but we're still going to make this work. We need to be patient, and watchful, but we're going to get through this. I promised you all I would do everything in my power to keep you safe, and I intend to carry through on that promise. Whatever obstacles are in our way, we will overcome them. I have no doubt that together, we can do anything."

I still had reservations about being the leader, but in that moment, during my speech, I could see my words rekindling the spark of determination in my small, bedraggled group, and for a moment, those misgivings faded away and all I could feel was pride. We were scared, outnumbered, and had been through a lot.

But we weren't done. Not by a long shot.

8

I swallowed, worked more moisture into my mouth... and swallowed again.

It was just a door. It shouldn't have represented any problems in terms of opening, but for the past two minutes, I had been standing outside it, wrestling with exactly *how* I should open it.

A knock was polite, but incredibly formal. Knocking followed by opening it was more like what a really close neighbor would do. Just opening it was something someone accepted as family would do.

With my parents, however, I existed in some sort of nebulous area between all of those things. I wasn't unknown to them; I had lived with them all my life, the last six weeks not withstanding. But then again, we weren't exactly close—especially considering I knew they had been willing to write me off.

And now I had to head back inside and face the music. Oh, I

was more than afraid—I was terrified. I was also angry, hurt, sad, and a whole range of other emotions that all added together to make me jumpy and anxious. It was only a week, but I dreaded any more interactions with them. They had spent my entire life making me feel inferior, and I couldn't see a future in which they did anything but that.

So... to knock, or not to knock. Of all my problems, this was the only one I couldn't seem to make any headway on. I had gotten Lacey to agree to let Quess install our new nets, and then given her the description of the two Inquisition agents who had been in the room with Devon, as well as a breakdown of what they talked about. I had even assigned Zoe and Eric the point position on Paragon distribution for the twenty-nine people who had been recruited by Roark, so high five to me for still having the wherewithal to process what needed to be done.

But this friggin' door...

I sighed and shook my head. I was overthinking things. They would've already been notified that I was returning to them. Granted, it would've been at most two hours ago, but that announcement also would've included information exonerating me... so they couldn't be angry, right? I had finally done a service for the Tower, both in their eyes (I hoped) and mine, so... maybe they would finally accept me?

My stomach roiled at the possibility, and I swallowed again, my nervousness doubling. I could take their anger, or disappointment, or flat-out negativity. But what if they *praised* me?

It had only ever happened once, to my recollection, and that was after I woke from my Medica-induced fugue state to find

that some sort of Tower-friendly version of me had comman-
deered my life for a week. I'd called her Prim and hated her, but
my parents... Well, they had *loved* Prim.

I glared at the door, the memory making me angry. They had
accepted that drugged, bland version of me, and even welcomed
her in a way that they had never welcomed me. I tried to remind
myself that I was only here until I turned twenty-one. After that,
it was private housing—just as soon as I was promoted, which
Lacey assured me would happen tomorrow, considering my
celebrity-hero status. And because Scipio had automatically
gifted us each with a rank of ten for our service, that meant I was
probably going to jump right to Knight Elite, possibly even
Knight Commander.

Glancing down at my wrist, I suppressed an irritated sigh
and turned the indicator away, hiding the bright blue glow of the
double digits. I was about to step back into a life where all social
interaction was decided by those stupid numbers: how you were
treated, how you were expected to act, and how you were
supposed to treat others. And with a ten, I would have to
conduct myself flawlessly.

Which in the language of the Tower meant being a jerk to
everyone lower than myself.

Oh, and of course, the ten wasn't permanent—it would drop
with bad behavior, just like before. Just like it always had. My
emotions were being scrutinized, my service being monitored.
Scipio's eyes were back on me, always watching, always judging.

In that moment, I suddenly wanted to cry. All of this felt like
one gigantic step backward. Lacey's addition to our deal was

incredibly frustrating on so many levels, because while I was sure that her little power play was for the benefit of the Tower, it didn't change the fact that I didn't want to be here. I had fulfilled my end of the bargain. Lacey should've upheld hers and just let us go!

I clenched my hands into fists and rolled my neck back and forth, forcing myself to calm down.

"You're tired," I whispered to myself. "The last forty-eight hours have been an emotional rollercoaster. Just open the door, get this crap over with, and then you can sleep until tomorrow."

Even with my pep talk, though, it took me a few seconds to reach out and open the door. I hated the fact that my hands were shaking.

The door slid open, and I automatically stepped back when my father was just... *there*. Inches from the other side, his hand reaching for the button on the inside to open it, his cheeks and forehead as red as the bright crimson uniform he was wearing.

I looked past his shoulder and saw my mother pacing back and forth in the common area, gnawing on her thumbnail. Both of them looked tired—but my father looked angry, while my mother looked worried.

My dad sucked in a sharp breath when his gaze finally sharpened on me, and I grew very still, my heart pounding. I waited for him to say something, but when he just stared, I lifted my chin and summoned up enough courage for two words.

"Hi, Dad."

He continued to stare at me, his mouth a flat line under his beard. "I'm late for my shift," he finally said, giving me a pointed look.

My stomach sank, but his response actually steadied me some. This was... normal, for lack of a better word. My parents' thousand little cruelties toward me over the years were really par for the course.

Only this time was different. This time, *I* was different. So much had happened in the short time I'd been away from him, and I found myself neither afraid of him nor hurt by his words.

And when I really thought about it, I realized it was because I was no longer living my life for their approval. Their entire way of thinking was based on a lie, and I knew them well enough to know that it would take Scipio himself to convince them that the entire Tower was falling apart. I'd never be able to get past "Scipio is broken" before my father or mother would strike me, call me a liar, send me to my room without a meal, report my behavior to my supervisor... The list was endless.

But to my own surprise, in that moment, I suddenly realized that they didn't hold any real power over me. And they wouldn't, unless I let them.

I stepped to one side and pasted a congenial smile on my lips. "My apologies. Don't want to stand in your way."

His brows came together, and he regarded me with no small amount of suspicion. "What's going on, here?"

I smiled more deeply. "Nothing," I said. "Have a nice shift."

He stepped slowly out into the hall, as if he were afraid I was going to strike him down right then and there. I waited, patiently, and then slipped by him and headed inside, not even bothering with any additional platitudes.

My mother had stopped her pacing when she heard my voice, and now she was watching me walk toward her. Her face was pale and drawn, and tufts of her normally pristine black hair —same color as mine was once again, thanks to Lacey—were sprouting uncharacteristically, in every direction possible.

"Mom," I said, coming to a stop in front of her. I looked past her toward my room, and then back to her. "I see Dad's glad I'm back."

Her mouth worked, and I could see her struggling with the words.

"Don't worry," I said. "I'm only here until I'm twenty-one, which I'm pretty sure is close, although I'm still not entirely certain what the date is."

"March third," my mother replied automatically, and I was pleased to see that she still had command of her voice.

The math was incredibly easy, considering I was born March tenth. We always celebrated it on Alex's birthday, though, which was technically March ninth, since she had delivered him pre-midnight while I was delivered post. But Zoe had always made sure to celebrate mine with me in private.

"You see?" I said with a grin, ignoring the disappointment that resulted from her announcement. I had hoped the time back with my parents would only last for a few short days, but I could endure. "A week is easy. We don't even have to talk to each other if you don't want to."

"I..." She faltered, and then shook her head. "Well, I mean...

It's going to be an adjustment having you back, is all. I mean, now you're a hero, when before you were..."

"A criminal?" I supplied helpfully. "Yeah—much easier to believe than hero. Don't worry, Mom. I promise to revert back to my criminal ways soon enough. Wouldn't want your expectations of me to grow too high."

My mother gaped, before she finally realized that I was being openly sarcastic with her, and then the anger flitted in. "How dare you speak to me that way! I am your mother, Liana Castell. You will treat me with respect."

I nodded at her, and then shook my head. "You know what? No. I came to this realization, y'know, when I was in the process of running and fighting for my life and the lives of my friends, that respect should only be given when it is earned. I talked to Alex, and he told me how you two reacted when I was implicated in Gerome's murder."

My mother's eyes widened, and she had the good grace to look moderately guilty. "What else could I do? Scipio tells us that—"

"When your own daughter is accused of murder that you just go along with it? Warn your son not to have contact with her ever again? I mean, did you ever once consider that I might not be guilty?"

"How could I have known that all of this was on Scipio's orders?" my mother exploded, finally fed up with my blasé behavior. "I mean, you're a Squire, and your rank at the time was positively abysmal. Why would Scipio ever choose *you* for a mission like that?"

The answer, of course, was that he hadn't. But that didn't change the fact that my mother was missing the point.

And I wasn't inclined to spell it out for her. So I chose the path of pettiness, and I took an inordinate amount of pleasure in it. "Careful, Mother. That sounds suspiciously like you're questioning Scipio's decisions. Are you trying to tell me that the great, infallible Scipio might be flawed?"

Okay, I *might* have layered the sarcasm on a bit thick at the end, but I couldn't help it. My entire life, my mother and father had followed Scipio's laws and edicts to the letter, reminding me constantly that we had to put our trust and faith in him. But now that their daughter was being openly hailed as a hero for revealing and removing a corrupt councilor, on the orders of the great machine himself... well, that apparently was a deal breaker.

And yeah, it hurt and it made me angry.

My mother's hand flew out to slap me for my insolence, and for the first time in my life, I lifted my arm and blocked the blow. Her anger faded some as she took a step back, and I pressed forward.

"You never get to hit me again," I growled. "You never get to *touch* me again. In fact, after this, we are going to embrace that not-talking plan, and I'll petition my new supervisor to expedite the process so I can get out of here. But you and me? We're done. We were done the second you chose the Tower over me. Which pretty much was the second I was born, so... sorry it took me twenty years to figure it out."

I stopped and sucked a deep breath in while my mother

stared at me, literally speechless. I took one final look at her and announced, "I'm going to bed. I'll stay out of your way until my birthday or the transfer—whichever comes first."

And then I left her there. Walked to my room and closed the door.

As I rested my back against the door, I let my eyes drift closed... and then broke down. The tears came fast and fierce, and within moments it was like a combination of bitter anger and crushing despair had reached up and wrapped a colossal hand around my lungs and throat, silencing any cries except for the wheezing.

I hated that I was crying, but I couldn't help it. Even though I had managed to keep it together, keep my wits about me, and finally stand up to my mother... couldn't she have at least pretended to care about what I had been through the last three weeks? Even buying into the lie, I couldn't wrap my head around what kind of parent would behave so coldly to their child after finding out what I had supposedly been up to. All I wanted, more than anything in the world, was for them to love and accept me—but now that I had shot my mouth off to my mom, I realized that there wasn't going to be any going back. Ever.

So I cried in mourning for both a relationship that could never be, and for the death of the one that was, and with it came everything else. Roark's death. Cali's death. Losing Maddox. Grey. Fear. Pain. Grief. Everything that had been burning a hole inside me, kept as tightly under wraps as I could possibly keep it, exploded out, right there on my bedroom floor.

It took a while, but I managed to cry all of the pain away, biting my hand at times to keep from making too much noise. Once it had passed, I looked around my room numbly, suddenly tired beyond all words. All of my belongings were now in cartons, even the bedding, and stacked on top of my desk and bed.

My parents hadn't bothered to unpack my stuff, and as I started opening boxes, I found myself wondering how long it had taken them before they packed it up in the first place. Had it remained for the short time they thought I was dead, or had they done it immediately after I'd left?

Ultimately, it didn't matter. It wasn't even a question I really cared to know the answer to. But I still wondered.

I found a blanket and stopped looking. The exhaustion that I hadn't been allowing myself to feel had crept in with the tears, sapping the last of my energy. I had just enough left to strip down, and then I found a small spot of open mattress not lined with boxes, made a pillow out of my arm, and curled up.

It didn't take long for sleep to find me.

9

A hard rap on the door startled me from my sleep, and I sat up so quickly that one of the stuffed cartons fell off the end of my bed, landing with a hard crash and scattering objects all over the floor. I clutched the blanket to my chest and looked around, my heart pounding hard in my chest. It took me a second to even remember where I was—and what had happened over the last two days.

"Liana, Knight Elite Ambrose Klein is here to collect you for duty," my mother's voice said through the door separating us. I detected an uncertainty there, but ignored it, focusing only on the name. I couldn't recall for the life of me who Knight Elite Klein was supposed to be.

And then I remembered Lacey mentioning it in passing before we left to drop everyone off at their new quarters (or old, in the cases of Zoe and Eric). He was the man we were supposed to protect—Lacey and Strum's legacy candidate, whom they had chosen to fill the position of Champion.

I stretched out my arms with a groan, my muscles now stiff from having fought with Devon and then sleeping for so long. Because according to my watch, I had been asleep since eleven a.m. yesterday.

Crap. I checked my indicator and noticed two things immediately. First, that it was eight a.m., which meant I was running late. Secondly, I had missed two net transmissions from Alex. I needed to talk to him and ask him to look into Jasper and Paragon. I also needed him to reach out to Mercury and...

My skull started to ache, my stomach protesting the lack of food. My last meal had been hours before we even went into the Medica, so I was beyond hungry. In fact, I was prepared to burn through a day's worth of rations just to appease myself right now.

My mother rapped on the door again. "Liana? Are you... okay?"

My brows came together, and I quickly slid out from between the boxes I had slept behind and got up. The floor was chilly, but not too cold under my bare feet, and I padded to the door and opened it.

My mother took a step back, alarm and discomfort fluttering over her features, and I stared at her, the ire from yesterday returning. "Excuse me," I said, nodding to the bathroom just behind her.

She moved back a few more feet, and I grabbed the uniform Lacey had provided from where I had left it crumpled on the floor yesterday. My mother stared at me the entire time, seemingly transfixed, but I ignored it. I knew she was already disapproving of the fact that my bed wasn't made, that I was going to wear a crinkled uniform, and that I wasn't even ready on time. I also knew that it shouldn't bother me—not after my declaration to her last night. But in truth, it did.

Uniform in hand, I turned, ready to ignore the familiar look, and then paused. My mother's eyes weren't even on my room or uniform. They were on *me*, and as I followed her line of sight, I realized she was staring at all the bruises on my arms and legs. The shift I wore under my uniform was white, so the ones on my torso shone brightly through the partially sheer material, bright red fading into purple. Her eyes moved up over my arms, and then to my neck, where they paused, sliding over the distinct marks left by Devon's fingers when they had dug into my flesh, trying to choke the life out of me.

I stood there for a long moment, confused by the look on her face. There was a hardness there, and a horror, and I didn't understand it. She'd never looked at me like that before, and I had no idea how to interpret it. Was it concern? Anger at the man who would leave such marks on her daughter?

Or approval that I had taken so many hits and kept fighting?

She finally met my eyes, and I waited, uncertain what was going to happen. But to my surprise, she didn't say anything. Just nodded and disappeared into the front room. I frowned, wondering if my words last night had affected her more than I thought possible, and then shrugged and continued my journey to the bathroom, deciding that it didn't matter.

One self-indulgent shower later, with extra hot water and about half the soap in the Tower, I began to feel more like myself. I knew Ambrose was waiting, but after the past seventy-two hours, he could stand to wait a few minutes more, couldn't he? I actually had no idea, but he was going to.

I was in the process of toweling off when my mother knocked on the bathroom door. I exhaled in frustration and checked my indicator for the time, swiping through the water droplets that had accrued there while I was bathing. It was 8:09.

"I'm almost ready," I announced.

Then there was a beep, and the door slid open. A check of the screen next to it showed me that my mother had overridden the lock, and I took a step back and pulled the towel around my nude body, allowing her entry.

"Mom, what are you—"

My mother moved into the room and stared at me, then took a step forward and placed something down on the metal sink. It was a small green tube.

"I got banged up a while ago, and still have some of the cream the Medica gave me for my bruises and aching muscles. I thought..." She trailed off, and then shook her head. "Anyway, if those are causing you pain, you should use it."

I blinked in surprise and looked at the tube. "Um, thanks," I finally supplied. There was so much more that I wanted to ask, to say, but after years of her treating me like an unfortunate accident, the rift between us was so wide that it seemed impossible to bridge.

She nodded stiffly and then left, closing the door behind her. I locked it again, even though she could override it, and stared at the tube. Everything about it left me feeling uncertain, like maybe I had spoken out of turn last night. Maybe my mother wasn't as bad as I had always made her out to be. Maybe my talk with her last night had forced her to reconsider?

Or maybe she just wanted to make sure that I was going to be at my best for the Tower. Either way, using the cream didn't cost me a thing, and I began putting it on. It tingled slightly, but greatly reduced the pain and soreness. From there, I got dressed, ran a brush through my hair, and then took a moment to braid it and pin it up and out of the way. Knight School 101: long hair could get caught on objects or be a liability in a fight, so tying it up was just prudent.

I checked my reflection in the mirror, and paused when I saw the circles under my eyes and the paleness of my skin. My oddly amber-colored eyes seemed dull next to the dark shadows, giving me a tired and almost glazed look, but after a moment, I decided it didn't matter. I didn't have to look good for anyone anyway, and everyone else could go to hell with the way I was feeling.

Suddenly I thought of Grey, and wondered what it was like for him right now. Did he know what was happening, or was it just like he was asleep? Did he dream? Was he able to hear us, hear me?

I leaned forward onto the sink and sucked in a deep breath,

reminding myself that Leo was going to do everything he could to save Grey. Which meant I needed to do everything I could to make sure I secured Leo a new home. If it was even possible.

A scary thought occurred to me on the heels of that one: what if I couldn't find a place to put Leo? What happened to him then? Would we have to pass him to someone else and just hope they didn't kill him?

Or what happened if Leo couldn't recover the other fragments? Would he just... come with us when we escaped? Could he come with us?

I sighed. The problem with Leo was going to be a daunting task in its own right. I wasn't sure what the status of his terminal was, but if we didn't find a place to put him once he was finished healing Grey, he'd be trapped inside him forever. The net he was in was fine for now, powered through Grey's body temperature for as long as he was alive. But once we pulled him out, he was on the clock—the net's tiny battery source only capable of keeping him alive for a little over twenty hours. If it went out while he was inside, then he'd be lost forever.

Yet none of that scared him. All he wanted to do was stay and save the Tower. A noble pursuit, to be certain, but how far would he take it? I trusted that he would keep Grey safe while he pursued his goals, but there were a thousand things he didn't know about current Tower life—things that could get him hurt, or worse. I would have to keep a careful eye on him, and keep him informed of my concerns. Talking to him about it was the best way to assuage any fears I had, while simultaneously being a friend and giving him any support and help he needed.

I added that to my already daunting list, although to be honest, I had probably included it yesterday at some point. I just couldn't remember. It would come back to me either way, and it was ultimately not important to the task at hand.

It was time to meet Ambrose, and get a feel for whatever his plan was to win the Tourney.

I opened the door and stepped out, looking down the hall toward the door. A handsome man with dark skin and blue eyes gazed back, hands clasped behind his back. I walked toward him.

"You must be Knight Elite Klein," I said. "Nice to meet you."

Ambrose raked his eyes over me, a small frown on his face. "You're in the incorrect uniform," he informed me. He had a deep, rich voice that would've been beautiful, were there not a wall of ice behind it.

I glanced down at my uniform and then back up to him. "I take it I'm no longer a Squire?" I asked, and he nodded once, curtly.

"You'll receive your new uniforms and insignia in Armament, along with your lashes and baton. As a Knight Elite, you will also be issued a light shield."

I registered my new rank, but it didn't fill me with pride or joy. If anything, I was a little disappointed that I didn't have the clout of a Knight Commander—but considering Ambrose was supposed to act as my supervisor, Lacey had probably done something to intercede, and blocked the larger promotion. Which was too bad, really, because I would've taken some petty pleasure in the rank, if only to rub my parents' noses in it.

No, it was Ambrose's speech that caught my attention. It was laced with arrogance and disdain. On top of that, he had known that I didn't have my new uniform assigned yet, so his comment about me being in the wrong uniform was petty, and honestly didn't bode well for our future relationship.

I couldn't help but feel that he thought he was better than me in some way. I looked him over closely. Everything about him screamed regulation. His uniform was pressed, and fitted him well. His insignia gleamed brightly, like it had just been polished, matching the gleam on his black boots. He was well groomed, with clean fingernails, and smelled vaguely of lemon.

Of course, none of that made him better than me—just neater. I looked back up at him and found him watching, one dark eyebrow raised.

"Do I pass your inspection?" he asked curtly.

I cocked my head at him and raised an eyebrow of my own. "That depends. Is being a jackass your normal setting, or am I just meeting you on a bad day?"

There was a flash of something in his blue eyes, but it disappeared before I could really recognize what it was. He exhaled once, sharply, and then turned. "We should go. We're late as it is."

I heard the blame in his voice, condemning me for being late, and rolled my eyes behind his back. So far, my impression of Ambrose Klein was not favorable. He reminded me of the many instructors from the Academy: smug, arrogant, and prone to making an example of the first Squire who made a mistake. I'd been made an example of a time or two before, so I was intimately familiar with the behavior.

And I hated it.

The door slid open, and he stepped out first, followed by me. Once the door was closed, I expected we would proceed forward, but we didn't. Instead, he looked down the hallway in both directions, to check to see if the coast was clear. Once he had confirmed that it was, he rounded on me, raising up to his impressive height—at minimum, six feet.

"Lacey has faith in your skills. I, however, do not. I also do not believe that I need a babysitter, especially one who is actually a criminal."

A surge of anger flashed through me, and I bit back a caustic response, struggling to remember that *Lacey* had demanded that I do this, not Ambrose. But reminding him of that wouldn't necessarily help us get along. If anything, I risked creating more disdain in him, which would make my job even harder.

No, I needed to react differently than that, and spell things out for him in a way that he would listen to. Hopefully force him to respect me a little more.

"Well, that is too bad, Ambrose," I replied, folding my arms across my chest. "Because I'm here, and I have a deal with Lacey to keep you alive. I might be a criminal, but I always try to keep my word whenever I give it, and that means that when it comes to your life, I am in charge. Now, how is this going to work? I assume that I'm going to be entered into the Tourney as one of your teammates?"

He frowned as I spoke, a small furrow forming over his nose, his brows drawing even closer together. "Yes. You are also responsible for finding me the other two members to round out the team. I have some personnel files for you here..." He began to pull out a pad, but I held up a hand, forestalling him.

"No. If we need more people on the team, I want those people to be mine."

"You mean the other criminals?" he fired back bitterly.

I didn't give him the satisfaction of a response, but nodded, my face serious. "Yes. I trust their loyalty, because their loyalty is to me. Everyone else in the Tower is a potential threat."

"Says the criminal," he retorted.

I let out an irritated sound as I struggled to keep a lid on my temper. I wasn't sure where Lacey and Strum had dug this guy up, but he was really beginning to grate on my nerves. Also, how unoriginal was it to just call someone a criminal repeatedly? The guy needed a damn thesaurus.

"Yes, I am a criminal! Can you please get over it and get with the program? We don't have to like each other, but you do need to let this go so we can move on."

"I don't need to do anything," he retorted. "I'm the one actually trying to become Champion, and that means that during the Tourney, you have to follow my orders. It seems to me you're unable to do so."

He had a point, at least about the Tourney, which was designed to test intelligence, intuition, cunning, improvisation, and physical prowess. But ultimately, it was about leadership, which was why at the start of the Tourney, qualified candidates were put into groups to see who among them would emerge as the leader. Typically, groups were already formed beforehand, but if you applied alone, you'd get lumped in with strangers. Regardless, those who didn't emerge as leadership material were eliminated, until only the best remained. If *I* got into the arena and began shouting orders, and my friends followed them without hesitating, *his* chances of winning would disintegrate.

"I follow orders that make sense, are safe, and don't get my people hurt—or worse," I said. "But in the Tourney, you're in charge. Outside, you have to follow my rules to the letter. All right?"

Ambrose laughed, a full, rich sound that came off as genuine, and I bit my lip, shifting uncomfortably. There hadn't been anything funny about what I'd just said, so his response was alarming.

"Why are you laughing?" I demanded.

"Because you're only here as a security precaution! Lacey and Strum are just being paranoid. I can take care of myself, and... now that you've eliminated Devon, any threat within the Knights has died with him. Even if he had recruits, they wouldn't know what to do with their leader gone. So really, you're unnecessary." He paused and took a minute to smooth down the already impeccable lines of his uniform. "Now, we're running drastically late, so, if you don't mind?"

He didn't wait for a response, just turned around and began moving away, toward the elevator. I watched him go, trying to decide if I should yell at him, strangle him, or not even bother, and decided on the latter. He had deemed me unnecessary, had even laughed at me for taking all of it seriously, but the truth was, I didn't work for him. I was working for Lacey, and that meant I was going to do my job.

Getting down to Armament and then to the training floor was bound to be more productive than that conversation could ever be. I just had to hope that he would remain blissfully quiet on the way down. Otherwise, *I* would be the one he'd need saving from.

10

The Salles—a large, open space that took up three whole floors—sat in the uppermost levels of the Citadel. Normally, it would have been filled with squads of Squires and Knights training in the various weapons available to the Knights. Now, however, it was a hubbub of a whole different sort of activity, most of it in preparation for the Tourney.

Half of the room had been completely blocked off by tall walls that descended from the ceiling, preventing anyone from seeing what was happening on the other side. Just outside of this barrier, several Knight Commanders stood watch, making sure that no one tried to sneak a peek inside at the challenges being constructed behind the veil. No one was allowed in—not until the Tourney started.

To the right, I saw several rings set up for sparring practice, some of which had thicker groups of people standing around, watching whatever fight was happening inside. On the left, there was a throng of people, all lined up to register. My eyes widened when I saw the line.

"Looks like registering is going to be a hassle," I commented to Ambrose.

He glanced over at me as we exited the elevator. "We won't be registering until the last day," he said. "Lacey wants me to keep the fact that I intend to compete a secret for as long as possible. Which is a waste of time, if you ask me, but hopefully by that time, all of this will have died off. Speaking of which, your team who came with you. Aren't they Squires?"

"They are," I said carefully, puzzled by his continued dismissive attitude toward Lacey's orders. Why was he being so glib? Did Lacey know that he found her orders to be more of an annoyance than something to listen to and consider? If so, why had she even selected him? Was it all based on his heritage—the fact that he was a legacy? If that was the case, then they really needed to spend more time grooming him. His attitude and demeanor, in my mind, did not make for a good leader, let alone a representative on the council.

If she didn't know, I wasn't breaking it to her; she needed to handle her own problems.

"I figured you could talk to... you-know-who and get them promoted."

He shot me an irritated look. "You clearly think her power is all reaching if you think she can affect the department that much."

"She got my friends into this department," I pointed out. "Seems like she's got more power than you think."

He stopped and turned so that he was blocking my path. "It doesn't work like that," he informed me irritably. "A department transfer is different than an internal promotion. So I ask again, how do you propose to get them qualified in time?"

"Well, we've got three days, correct?"

"Yes."

"Then I'll just have to get them ready to test out." I said it as if it were as simple as that, but testing out was not easy. It meant a minimum of twenty-four hours of tests and physical activities, and was a way for a Squire to skip the Academy, so to speak, if the department felt they were ready. Luckily, my friends were qualified for it, thanks to their ranks of ten.

Unluckily, I would have to get them up to speed on over two hundred years of the history of the department and vast amounts of protocol, and make sure they could at least hold their own for the physical part of the test.

Okay, it was daunting, no lie. But I had faith in my friends, and I was going to need them to complete Ambrose's team. I knew them, knew their loyalties, whereas having a stranger on the team opened up a potential security risk that I just did not want to deal with. But you had to be a full Knight before you could compete in the Tourney—which meant I had to get them through. Before we registered.

By the look on Ambrose's face, however, he did not agree. "We'll see," he said simply. "Now, let's get to the ring to see if you're actually *skilled* enough to qualify for the Tourney."

He spun away and moved through the throngs of people toward one of the Quartermasters—the Knights who were too disabled after years of service to perform their full duties, and became responsible for the training level—to put our names on the waiting list. I watched him for a second, the dull, angry fire that had sparked in my belly at our meeting flaring up in the wake of his attitude. I had barely known him an hour, and already he was threatening to grind on my very last nerve.

I didn't let him get too far away, however. I might not have liked him, but he was literally my responsibility, thanks to Lacey, and I had promised to keep him alive.

So.

I slipped through the crowds of people, keeping my eyes on Ambrose's head, but not following him directly. I watched those around him, eyeing them for any potential signs of threat as he moved. I paused when he got to the desk to the right of the rings, and kept one eye on him, and the other on the commotion coming out of the rings themselves.

They were encircled by a static fence that would shock the contestants inside if they ventured too close. Nothing harmful, certainly, but half of sparring was about staying within the ring. Which was stupid, now that I thought about it, as fights were not always contained to such a small and confined space.

Still, I supposed it taught us to be brave and face our attacker, rather than flee, so that was something.

Most of the rings were filled, but only a few had drawn attention. I could hear the clack, clack, clack of batons striking each other, followed by cheers and shouts, and after checking to make sure Ambrose was all right, I drifted a little closer, trying to get a peek inside.

"Hello, Liana."

A husky voice brought me up short, and I turned my head, my eyes widening to see Theo standing there. Theo had been my first girlhood crush, one that I had developed during our shared time at the Academy. I'd liked that he'd been like me, and we had often shared jokes about the ranking system. And then I'd met him more recently, and he'd completely changed— thanks to the drugs from the Medica.

My eyes dropped to his wrist, and I saw the eight that he'd had last time holding strong.

"Theo," I said carefully. "How are you?"

"Well. Although, I'm surprised to see you here. I would have assumed you'd want to keep a low profile after what happened."

I cocked my head at him, frowning. "What? Why would I do that?"

He gave me a confused look, and then looked around the room. I followed his gaze, and realized that people were staring at me. Some were looking at me with fear. Others with awe. I shifted, suddenly aware of the scrutiny I was under.

It hadn't even occurred to me that people would react like that. Now that I was standing there, under all of those eyes, I became aware of it, like it was a live wire running right under my skin. I was the girl chosen by Scipio. I was the girl who had killed Devon Alexander.

Theo looked back at me expectantly, and caught between my discomfort and the lie, I smiled embarrassedly. "I was feeling cooped up inside my room, and wanted to observe the chaos I had created." I meant it as a joke, but Theo's answering look was nervous, and I realized it was probably too soon for me to be making references to killing the Champion. I looked around, checking on Ambrose, and then took a step closer. "So, who's the competition?" I asked. "Are you applying?"

"Me?" He shook his head. "No, I'm not competing. I just came down here for some training after my shift."

"What? Don't think you're cut out to be the Champion?"

He blinked and then shook his head again. "Even an eight is unworthy of such a position of esteem. It is unfortunate that the Medica has taken me as far as they can."

I frowned at the disappointment in his voice, disgusted by his attitude. I knew I shouldn't be; his behavior was common among the citizens of the Tower. Self-worth was dependent on those stupid little indicators tethered around our wrists, always a reflection of social standing.

"Well, that's too bad, Theo. I think you'd make a great Champion."

I was surprised by the smile my words caused. Normally those under Medica treatment tended to emote very little, their entire demeanor monotone, so my statement had to have really touched something deep inside for that reaction.

Uncomfortable with the thread of the conversation, I paused to check once again on Ambrose, and saw that he was in the middle of a conversation with three other Knights, all males. A warning signal went up my spine, but Ambrose started laughing at something one of them said, and I realized that they were probably some of his friends. There was a familiarity to their interaction. I watched him gesture toward an empty ring, and the four of them headed over to it.

"So, have you seen Dylan Chase yet?" Theo asked, and I shifted my gaze back to him.

"Dylan Chase?"

"Dylan's probably one of the best contenders signed up thus far. Although some of my friends think it's going to be Frederick Hamilton. They're in those two arenas, doing King of the Hill Rules."

I arched an impressed eyebrow and looked to where he was now pointing. King of the Hill was no easy task: one person stood their ground against any number of assailants, and remained there until their opponents were gone, or until they fell and someone could take their place. They were the same rings as before, but the number of people around them had increased in the short time we'd been talking. I could barely see the blue sheen of the static fence along the perimeter, the people stood so deep. I heard the sounds of fighting, but couldn't make heads or tails of what was going on inside.

And making my way through that crowd would've been nigh impossible. I wanted to see some of what Ambrose and I were going to face inside the Tourney, but that way wasn't going to work.

"You got your lashes on you?" I asked, looking up.

"Of course I do. Why do you ask?"

I pulled my lash bead out and grinned. "Because I want to get a better view of the two in the ring," I replied. "And you seem to know who these people are, so I want to pick your brain about them."

"Why?" he asked, confused. A moment later, his face shifted to a look of alarm, and he looked around before taking a step closer. "You're not still working for Scipio, are you?"

"What?" I stared at him, then shook my head. "Of course not. Look, yes, I executed Devon. Yes, he was the Champion. But, he was also a dissident, and was using his position of power to hurt the Tower. I did what I did for the Tower, and I would've done it without Scipio's backing if I had found out about it on my own."

Ahhh... just enough truth mixed with lies to get things truly muddled. It occurred to me then that I was going to have my work cut out for me in keeping up with this charade.

Theo stared at me for a beat, and then pulled out his own lash. "Shall we?"

There was an obstacle course comprised of metal beams jutting out of the wall some twenty feet up, used exclusively for training new recruits on how to work a lash. We called them baby bars, and it didn't take long before they got boring. Most recruits started avoiding them after the first week of training.

Which meant no one thought of them as useful—which was perfect. I threw my lash, angling for the closest overhead beam. I needed momentum, however, if I was going to swing, so I got a running start first, reeling in the slack as I went, and then threw myself into the air, surrendering to the feeling of weightlessness. I used the controls on my hand and the gears in the harness to pull myself up several feet, creating a swing for myself, and now emphasized it by leaning in and out of the arc. Then I threw my second lash to the next beam. When it attached, I disconnected the first line and glided forward, defying gravity in the upswing.

I disconnected the second line at the apex, and spread my arms and flew for several feet, angling for the next beam. I reached out and grabbed the edge just before gravity began to re-exert its force. Most women had a difficult time with pull-ups, but I didn't, and I flexed my arms and chest and pulled myself up and onto it, straddling the girder.

Theo joined me a second later, although he did it the boring way, attaching his lash to the beam and slowly reeling himself up. I checked yet again on Ambrose, and took a few moments to watch him sparring with his friends. He was fast, but his move-ments were a tad sloppy. He used the length of the baton to compensate for his sloppiness, but it was still there. It was fine against his current opponent—but that was just because he had significantly less skill than Ambrose did. It certainly wasn't a fair fight.

But there were skilled individuals throughout the Tower, and if he expected to qualify, he was going to have to be more tactical and less wild. All it would take was someone with more skill, patience, and cunning, and he'd be out before the Tourney even began.

Once Theo was seated, I looked at him expectantly.

"That's Frederick Hamilton," he said, pointing to the ring closest to us. From our vantage point, I could see three men inside—but it was easy to discern who Frederick was, as the other two were attacking him flat out. He was a tall and exceptionally lanky man, with thick, short black hair and blue eyes so bright I could make them out from here. He wielded two batons and moved with lightening quickness, spinning them around his body in a cyclone of movement. It didn't take long for him to dispatch both of the others, his batons striking them both multiple times before knocking them down. The crowd cheered as he helped them up, and then two more replaced them.

"He's really fast," I said, impressed by his reaction time.

"And really noble, if some of the rumors are true," Theo commented. "But I don't think he's got the stuff. Not compared to Dylan. Look."

He pointed to the second ring, where a woman and man were sparring one on one. As I watched, the woman planted a mule kick to the man's chest and shoved him back several feet, until he stumbled and fell.

"I think your Dylan might be in trouble," I said.

He laughed. "Dylan's the girl, Liana."

"Oh." I turned my gaze back to the woman and watched as she stalked forward across the floor toward her opponent in a slow predator's gait. Her hair was so blond it might as well have been white, cut short and styled artfully in an asymmetrical bob, the longest bit curving around her round face. Her skin was bronze, and she was a strange combination of curvy but fit.

The man picked himself up off the ground and rose to meet her, but within three moves she had disarmed him, struck him, and then tripped him. She planted one foot on his chest and held the baton out, pointing it at his face. His hands went up automatically, and she smiled a feline smile, then reached down to help him up.

"She's pretty good," I commented.

"I know. She was my supervisor after I graduated the Academy. I'd follow her into the Wastes, if she asked me to."

I gave him an incredulous look, trying to figure out whether he was serious or not. The Wastes weren't anything to joke about; they surrounded the Tower in a sea of sand for hundreds of miles, and were highly irradiated. For him to say something like that, he had to be joking or insane. No one deserved that much blind devotion. No one was *that* inspiring.

But as people screamed and cheered around both arenas, I began to have doubts. Both candidates were popular, and seemed to have the skill to back themselves up. They could make a serious play for Champion. I would need to have them researched to find out if they were actually a threat. I'd also probably need to have them followed—which meant tapping Quess, as he and Tian were the only ones who weren't known by everyone, and wouldn't be so easily followed.

Even as all those ideas were added to my never-ending to-do list, I paused and looked back at Dylan and Frederick. Both of them were impressive and, as long as they weren't legacies within the opposite group, already seemed like much better candidates than Ambrose did. I knew what Lacey wanted me to do, but for the first time I found myself wondering if I even should.

I knew why Lacey and Strum were pushing for it—they needed more seats on the council to vote down whatever laws or decisions they didn't agree with, supposedly for the good of the Tower. While that remained to be seen, their choice of replacement was just unsuitable, and chances were, wouldn't win even with our assistance.

Which meant I was robbing someone else of a chance, someone who actually deserved to be in the seat. Someone who could make a difference and could stand apart from these shadow games. Didn't the people deserve a chance to at least have someone impartial sitting on the council?

My stomach churned at this newfound moral dilemma, and for a second, I teetered on the edge of calling this all off and taking my chances on the run. Then I remembered that everyone was relying on me to do this to keep them safe. This was the plan, morality aside. I couldn't deviate from it.

It helped, but it didn't solve my dilemma. It remained, like a little itch in the back of my mind. One I was choosing to ignore.

For now.

My gaze slid back over to Ambrose, and I saw him looking out into the crowd, his head moving back and forth. It took me a second to realize that he was looking for me, but once I did, I stood up on the bar.

"I've got to go, Theo," I informed him. "Thank you for the information, though."

"Anytime," he said with a nod.

I quickly threw my lashes and lowered myself to the floor before disengaging the lines and moving toward the ring, intent on showing Ambrose what sloppiness could lead to, while my mind considered Frederick and Dylan. Both were good in their own ways, and would create some stiff competition. I was going to need to know as much as I could about them, and anyone else who would be true competition.

Odds were that those individuals would be the most likely to want to assassinate Ambrose, especially if he became any sort of a threat to their plans. Especially if any one of them was working for another legacy family.

11

I squared my shoulders and exhaled slowly, trying to let go of the frustration that had accumulated over the past few hours, and relax. It had been a long day, and even though I had slept for a record twenty-one hours before it started, I was mentally and physically exhausted.

And there were still miles to go before I found sleep again.

Opening my eyes, I reached out and pressed the buzzer on the door I was standing in front of.

"*Caller?*" a rich male voice asked.

"Knight Elite Liana Castel for Squire Grey Farmless," I informed the door. I looked down the hall, confirming it was still empty. Most Squires were studying or eating right now, but Leo and I had arranged to meet at this time today, so I was certain he was in.

A moment later the door slid open, and Leo was there. He looked moderately disheveled, his eyelids heavy and hair in disarray. Even his uniform was wrinkled, like he'd slept in it. Then I realized that he *had* been sleeping, and I had woken him up.

"Liana?" he asked, blinking slowly and smoothing wild wisps of hair back from his forehead. "Oh dear. Am I late?" He lifted his wrist and stared at it for a second, and then shook his head and swiped his fingers across the lens, looking at the time. "So sorry," he said, his voice cracking as he yawned. "I am still adjusting to the concept of sleep."

I watched all of this, both fascinated and uncomfortable. As soon as he had opened the door, all I could see was Grey, and my initial instinct had been to throw myself in his arms and let him hug all of my irritation, fear, and loneliness away. Maybe even give me one of those hard, hungry kisses that left me feeling fluttery in my stomach. I'd done my best not to think about him all day, but now that he was standing in front of me...

I pushed the daydream aside and focused on what Leo was saying. "Why are you so tired?"

"Well, after everyone fell asleep yesterday, I accessed the history and protocols of the Knights, learned that you could test out of the Academy, and spent several hours memorizing the course materials. I then went to my advisor's office and declared my intention to test out. He offered me several dates, but I indicated that I wanted to start today, so he obliged me. I took all the tests first. I think he was impressed by my scores."

He moved back into his apartment as he spoke, giving me space to enter, and I did. The room was small, with Spartan-style furniture inside. Four twin-sized beds, one in each corner of the room, each flanked by an identical nightstand in a flat, gray color. At the foot of the beds were matching chests with digital keypads on the front. There was a row of narrow, locker-style doors on one side of the entry hall, and a door on the other side that led to the washroom. The kitchen and dining area took up the center of the small room, and was efficiency sized: one small sink, one refrigeration unit, one cooking element, and a handful of cabinets.

I had never gotten the opportunity to stay in the apartments shared by transfers, because I had a home with my parents, which was more efficient. But as I looked around, I found myself wishing I had. Maybe it would've made me more of a people person.

I returned my focus to Leo and saw him standing in front of the mirror, combing Grey's dirty blond hair. My brows came together—that look was decidedly *not* Grey—but then I decided that it was okay. Maybe even better. It would help me remember that he *wasn't* Grey. At least right now.

"So that was a lot to unpack," I said slowly. "I trust you're being cautious and not testing too well?"

"Of course. I kept my grades varied. Still within the top 10 percent, of course." He beamed at me through the mirror, and I hesitated. It was good he was performing well, but I had to make sure he only achieved the rank of Knight Elite or below, just like Ambrose.

"Your physical trials will be tomorrow?" I asked, and he nodded. "How do you think you'll fare?" I knew Leo could fight; he had demonstrated as much when we were fleeing the

Medica. But Leo had to be having some difficulties adjusting to being inside a real body, right?

"Oh, very well, I assume," he said with a pleased smile as he looked down at his body. "Grey took remarkable care of his body, and his strength and agility are great boons. With my mental acumen and reflexes, as well as several different styles of martial arts that I've studied, I think we should succeed with flying colors."

Disconcerted by how he referred to Grey both as an individual and as a part of *him*, I blinked—then tried to block it out and focus on the vein of the conversation itself. "What time?" I asked, stalling for a follow-up thought.

"Eight a.m. Right around the time when Maddox will be taking her tests."

My eyes bulged in surprise, and then I smiled. "You guys got to this before I could even tell you about it. I'm glad; it turns out I'm going to need you to round out the team for the Tourney. Is Quess also at the physical trial?"

Leo shook his head and ran a hand over his jaw, inspecting Grey's face in the mirror. The sight threw me off, and I looked away, still finding it difficult to reconcile that he was Leo, and not Grey. It turned out that it still made me uncomfortable when he acted *less* like Grey. Something I was going to have to work desperately hard to get the heck over.

"No, Quess has declined that route," he finally said. "I believe he intends to do just enough here to get by, while dedicating himself to... other tasks."

He refrained from saying what task he was referring to, but I knew: Quess was making sure that Sanctum was getting packed up so that we could move our supplies as soon as Tian found us a new home. I owed him bigtime for it, and planned to let him know that. Soon.

"How was your first day with Knight Elite Klein?" Leo asked, turning to me. He now looked presentable, but I barely noticed it, thanks to the irritated sigh that exploded from me before I could stop it. He cocked his head at me, his curiosity now spreading into concern, and I rolled my eyes.

"Yeah, it was great," I said. I didn't want to rant, but it had been building up inside of me all. Damn. Day. Which meant Leo was about to experience his first human bitch-fest. Whee. "I had to spend thirteen hours with him, and he drove me insane. First at sparring practice, where he wouldn't pay *any* heed to *any* of the things I pointed out unless I hit him over the head a hundred times. Which, admittedly, helped me feel a little better, but doesn't change the fact that it wasted most of the time we had to actually practice. I mean, what kind of imbecile doesn't listen to someone when they are trying to help them get better? An arrogant one, that's what. And that's what he is, Leo, a big, arrogant buffoon!

"Oh, and then we went on patrol, and he made us stop so he could harass a group of kids for playing in the halls. He lectured them about every citizen's responsibility to the Tower. *'Halls aren't for playing, children, they are for workers, and by impeding the workers, you are threatening the very safety of the Tower.'* I dropped my voice at the last bit, mimicking his voice, but repeating his actual words. I had been so livid, I had almost throttled him when one particularly small girl began to cry. "I managed to give the kids a chance to get out of there by yelling at him to shut up, but when I turned around to tell him where to stuff it, the smug, arrogant jerk had the nerve to look me in the eye and warn me not to undermine a superior in public, lest I get demoted."

I took a deep breath, and looked at Leo. His eyebrows were up and his mouth slightly open, his neck swiveling to follow me as I paced across the room. I realized that I *was* pacing, and stopped, let out an irritated breath, and tried to calm myself down again.

"Sorry," I said after my pulse rate had dropped a few notches. "That was a lot."

Leo smiled kindly, his eyes sparkling. "Lionel used to rant, although the experience is quite different now, under the circumstances. Did you know, my heart rate increased, and I felt this kind of tightness under my skin? This is tension, correct?" I nodded, and his smile deepened. "Fascinating. I am sorry to hear about your difficulties with Ambrose, though. Have you tried talking them out? Making these observations to him directly?"

"Oh, believe me, I tried that," I said, shaking out my arms to try to ease some of the stress. "I've learned that he doesn't really excel at listening."

"That's too bad. That will make your task much harder."

I chuckled, his matter-of-fact tone, laced with a thread of regret, amusing to me. He said it as if it weren't the understatement of the year. The smile helped break some of the discomfort I was feeling, and I relaxed a little more.

"Yeah, well, I'm glad you realized you could test out. I was going to ask you and the others to start working on it now. With Ambrose's behavior and attitude in general, I'm going to need all the help I can get. I can't trust a stranger as a teammate, so if you and Maddox can test out so I can get you on the team, then that's one less thing I have to worry about."

Leo blinked and smiled tremulously. "You want me to be part of your team for the Tourney?" A moment later, his face fell. "But that means I have to score a seventy-four percent on the physical side so that I don't get promoted directly to Knight Commander." He looked up at me with rueful eyes. "I wanted to set a record."

His words were disquieting, and my immediate response was: it wouldn't be you who would get the recognition. And that was a firm reminder that Grey wasn't here. How would he feel when he woke up and found out Leo had set a record on his behalf?

Luckily, I knew exactly how it felt. I had woken up to that— and recovered. And I would help him through it, as soon as he came back to me.

Speaking of which...

"Leo, how is Grey?" I asked, heart in my throat. "Any change yet?"

"Not yet, I'm afraid," he said. "I haven't started working on the connections to his long-term memory; there's too much tissue to heal and regenerate first."

I shifted, his answer as disappointing as it was unsurprising. I knew I was expecting too much, but I just wanted to know that somewhere, under all of that damage, he was still there.

"I don't suppose there's a way we could speed up the process, is there?" I asked, half bitter statement, half rueful joke.

"Well, copious amounts of proteins and fats are needed to help me replicate neural tissue faster, but the ration cards restrict—"

I jerked my head up at him and smiled. "I haven't eaten dinner today, and I know a place in the Lion's Den that'll give anyone ranked ten a little bit extra. My parents used to take me there. We can both get one, and I'll give you mine. Shall we?"

"If you didn't eat breakfast today, then shouldn't you—"

"I'm fine," I said, ignoring my stomach's indignant yowl. I just wanted to know Grey was all right, and if skipping a meal here or there meant finding out faster, then I was more than happy to go hungry.

Besides, the Lion's Den was perfect for why we were really meeting, which was to net Alex and fill him in on Leo and Jasper, and ask him to take a look through Scipio's code for Jasper. I was worried about the AI, first and foremost. But also, we needed him. Grey and I had given him Paragon to analyze, and now that we had lost Roark's notes, Jasper was the only one with the formula.

But Leo needed him as well—because he was probably one of the other five fragment AIs that were used to make Scipio.

It was a conversation that would require privacy and security. The noise within the Lion's Den would provide better cover than even the most secure room in the Tower. Anyone following us would have to be inches away to hear us, and as long as we kept moving, we avoided long-range listening devices.

Leo hesitated a second or two more, though, and then nodded, a smile coming to his face. "After you," he said cordially. I turned and led the way.

One elevator, a bridge, several turns through the twisting market stalls, and a short wait for our food, and Leo and I were walking and eating. Leo was picking apart grilled concoctions held in conical shapes by recyclable microfiber napkins. It was funny watching him trying to go back and forth between both cones, trying to decide which one tasted better.

As we walked, he told me about the test, his first time sleeping, and his disappointment about the lack of dreams. He also let me know that Tian had slipped out earlier to begin her hunt for a new Sanctum. I hoped she was all right, but trusted Quess to net us if she failed to check in.

Once he had finished his food, we took a moment to discuss how our net transmission was going to go down with Alex (just so Leo wouldn't jump the gun and join in early), and then I started the call, ordering my net to put me in contact with my twin.

The net buzzed on the inside of my skull as it connected, making me feel like my teeth would fall free, and a moment later, my brother's voice filled my ear.

Well, well, well, if it isn't the hero of the Tower, the one and only Liana Castell. As I live and breathe.

"Hardy har har har, you big doofus. I'm fine, thanks for asking, by the way. The parents would say hello, except I initiated a gag order on them, and then caught a twenty-one-hour nap, followed by readjustment to life inside the Tower. Is this line clean?"

Of course it is, my brother's voice informed me indignantly. *I would never jeopardize your safety, you know that! And I'm sorry I didn't ask how you were. I heard about the trial, so I assumed you were fine. Are you okay?*

I looked over at Leo and debated the safest possible answer. I was beaten and bruised from the fight in the Medica, emotionally drained from both my frustration with Ambrose and my concern over Grey, and mentally exhausted from trying to keep on top of so many different things.

"I'm okay," I told him, hoping my small fib would reassure him. I couldn't afford for him to get worried now, not when I had so much more to talk about. "Listen, Alex, I have something important to tell you, and this is super top secret. You can't even tell Mercury, all right?"

All right, my brother replied instantly. *You can tell me anything; you know that.*

I did know that. It was why I was okay with saying this at all. "Well, hold onto your hat, brother, because this one is a doozy." I spoke in hushed tones as we walked through the market, knowing the implanted microphone would still pick it up, and told him about Lionel Scipio's private office under Greenery 1. Then I told him about Jasper, and Leo now being inside my boyfriend.

Alex was, by nature, a quiet person, and he remained silent

as I talked, listening closely. When I was finished, several heart-beats of silence filled up the transmission.

That is a hell of a lot to take in, Liana. I mean, I almost want to call you a liar, that's how farfetched it sounds.

"But…" I said, stopping there and knowing he would finish the sentence himself.

But nothing. You sound like a loony toon. I laughed, and Leo gave me a curious look, but I just shook my head and waved it off. Alex waited until I stopped laughing before continuing. *Unfortunately, I have no choice but to believe you. I mean, you're crazy, but you're not that level of insane, which means you are telling me the truth. Which is… wow.*

"Process faster, Alex," I said, starting to feel paranoid. "We need your help. We need to find Jasper."

We? Wait, so you want to help Leo and recreate Scipio? I take it back: you are that level of insane.

"Alex, shut up and listen for a moment. Jasper has the formula for Paragon, and we need that. But now that you mention it, Leo has his own reasons for finding Jasper, and a request of his own, which I'll let him explain to you." I met Leo's eyes and gave him a little nod, so he could start calling Alex. "Leo is going to net you. Combine the lines, please and thank you."

My net paused for only one second, and then suddenly it was rattling around against the inside of my skull again, hard enough to make me grit my teeth.

"Greetings, Alex Castell," Leo said beside me. "And thank you for accepting my call."

Um, hello. My brother's voice was hesitant and wary. *You're welcome. You have a request for me?*

"Indeed I do," Leo said. "And do not worry, your sister and her friends also share your fears, and do not wish to join me in this task. Nor should they. But Liana promised to help me while she could, and I am taking advantage of that, and through her, you. I apologize for the clumsiness of our introduction."

I smiled. Leo was the only individual I knew who could make the most formulaic speech sound posh and charmingly natural. I wondered how my brother was handling it, and found myself eager for his response.

That's quite all right, he replied, and then paused. *Dear god, did I just say "quite" unironically? Liana, where did you dig this guy up?*

"I already told you that," I replied tartly. "Leo? Why don't you just ask my brother?"

"Very well. I am transmitting you a sample of the code we recovered from the Medica, one that is from the fragment known as Jasper. I've sent with it the timestamp of the data transfer, and the IP address of the terminal used. I would like you to track him down and let me know where he is being held."

Why? my brother asked. *What do you plan to do with that information?*

"We plan to rescue him," I informed my brother.

"After Liana and her friends have the formula for their Paragon, she will give his program to me so that I can find out what he knows about himself and the others."

Okay, now I think you're *crazy.*

"Alex, please. Leo thinks the problems with Scipio are much worse than even you suspect. Finding Jasper could be critical to his mission. And, aren't you just the least bit curious?"

My brother sighed, the sound a tonal cascade of descending and ascending harmonics. *Yes, damn it. But this is going to take some time. I'm under a lot of scrutiny from the department—apparently the Executive has a real hate on for you, so I've been getting nothing but scut work for the past few days. I will have to be careful.*

"By all means," Leo said immediately, concern thick in his voice. "I would never ask you to endanger yourself for my sake, and I am sure your twin feels the same way. So please, only do it if and when you are safe. I want to know, but that cost is far too high for my tastes."

My heart softened a little bit, and for a moment, in my mind, I heard the words as if they had been spoken by Grey. He was every bit as noble and kind as Leo in this way, his concern for others always taking precedence over his own goals. I don't know why, but it helped, and I found myself smiling at Leo, though he didn't notice.

Okay, Liana. I think I like this guy. I'll look into it as soon as I feel it is safe.

"Thank you, Alex," I replied. "Now listen, we've been on this call for a long time, and while I know you're covering your tracks, I—"

Have to go, I know. Look, you still owe me the full story on what happened at that trial. I also want to meet Leo and examine his net and terminal. I want to see exactly what we're dealing with here.

"Okay," I agreed. "I'll net you tomorrow with a day, and we can have lunch, okay?"

Sounds good. In the meantime, be careful, twerp. I am not designed for vengeance, so don't make me die trying.

I smiled. My brother always had the best ways of saying "I love you," even if he could be a jerk about it sometimes. "I love you, too."

We ended the call, and I looked at Leo, who was smiling crookedly. "Thank you," he said, and then on impulse, threw his arms around me, hugging me close. For a second, I just... slipped into the embrace, my hands, eyes, and nose all telling me that this was Grey. But my senses snapped back before I could fully get into it, and I held the hug for a moment or two for politeness, then stepped away quickly, smoothing my hands over my uniform to cover my discomfort.

"We should get back," I said hurriedly, flashing him a smile before turning. I didn't wait to see if he would catch up, but moved back down the aisles that wrapped around and through food stands. He'd gotten what he wanted—help from my brother —and he'd agreed to aid me during the Tourney.

And I was going to chalk it up as a success, if only because I needed the win.

I spotted my friends already sitting at one of the picnic-style tables outside the designated food stall, and moved through the early morning traffic to reach them, trying not to yawn.

I'd woken up two hours before I was supposed to meet Ambrose again for another riveting round of sparring, followed by another patrol, because I needed to see the team and find out how they were faring.

I approached them, and Quess noticed me first, smiling and waving a hand at me to come sit down next to him, even scooting a few feet down the bench to make more room for me. For a moment, I was taken aback by his appearance—he had changed his hair color to a deep auburn, and was now sporting a pair of contacts that turned his eyes a bright shade of green. The planes of his face had also been altered somewhat, and I realized he had used makeup to soften the strong lines, giving him a round-faced appearance.

I dropped down next to him, seating myself across from Zoe, Tian, and Eric. I smiled when I saw Commander Cuddles, arm now reattached, sitting upright in Tian's lap. Tian herself was looking up at Eric like he moved the stars in the sky, and I was relieved to see that the teddy bear surgery had gone well.

"Hey, guys," I said. "Sorry for the early hour, but it couldn't be helped. You look good, Quess. I hardly recognized you."

"Thank you—although it was a total pain getting the hair shade just right. Hold on a second." Quess held up a finger while his other hand began patting down his suit, clearly searching for something. He produced an object the size of a small bowl, but flat and smooth, with a big gray button on the top. He sat it down and pressed it, and a moment later the noise of the food stalls disappeared. "Noise-canceling generator. It'll prevent anyone from listening in unless they come within a five-foot radius."

I smiled, nodding my head approvingly. "How long have you had that for?" I asked.

"Oh, I got distracted last night during packing and decided we might need one for the meeting today, so I made one."

"It's clever," Zoe said, lifting the object up and inspecting the undercarriage. "It's a little heavy, though."

"Well, it's a prototype, darling. And just because she's heavy doesn't mean there's anything wrong with her."

Zoe rolled her eyes and leaned into Eric's shoulder, a smile playing on her face. She'd definitely relaxed some in her interactions with Quess, and was no longer responding to his flirtatious comments. Which was good, because it had been on the verge of becoming downright toxic before they managed to work it out.

"All right, let's keep it short, guys," I said. "I need status updates, and to talk about the next few days."

"Well, I'll just get the bad news out of the way." Quess turned to me, his normal smile absent behind his grim mask. "I already told Leo this morning before he went off to do his physical trials, but... the terminal is gone. The data crystals have been fried, and several of the smaller parts melted when the virus shut the coolant off. The only thing that's salvageable is the screen."

That meant we definitely had to find or make something to house Leo after he finished with Grey. I had anticipated as much, but wasn't pleased, as it was yet another daunting process ahead of us. "Thanks for letting me know. Any chance we can build a new one?"

Even as I said it, I found myself wanting to withdraw the question. Consigning Leo to a terminal again would leave him at the mercy of anyone who came along. I supposed we could find someone who was willing to fight for his cause, but how could we ever truly trust their motivations, especially if we were leaving him defenseless against them?

It would be one thing if Leo had some sort of autonomy, but... The thought of leaving him inside the terminal left me cold.

Quess scratched his chin, considering the question. "Probably, but I'll need Leo's help."

His words brought me back to the present, and after dwelling on his answer, I realized that we didn't actually have a lot of options. Besides, we would need the terminal sooner rather than later, for after Grey woke up. If nothing else, we could make it a temporary fix only, to be used until we figured out something better.

"Let me know if there's anything you're going to need to make it work," I said. "How did packing go?"

"I got the hydroponics packed up, as well as our hammocks and a few other odds and ends. The workroom is a bit of a mess, but I plan to tackle that next."

Crap. We had to get Sanctum packed up quickly, but with the Tourney looming and the possible threat it bore, I needed Quess, along with his anonymity and computer skills, helping out. I was going to have to shift a few jobs around to free him up for it, while keeping the goal of getting Sanctum packed up as a top priority.

"Hold off on that for now. There are a few people I want information on. They're the stiffest competition in the Tourney thus far, and I want to know more. I want you to get in contact with Mercury and get me some personnel files on Frederick Hamilton and Dylan Chase."

"Do you need them followed?" Zoe asked, leaning forward. "Eric and I can dye our hair, and could probably get our hands on a Knight's uniform or two."

I thought about it for a heartbeat, and then shook my head. It had only been three days since our trial; the last thing Zoe, Eric, or the rest of us needed was for one of us to get caught breaking the rules. "It's too risky for that right now," I told her. "Besides, I need you to take over Quess's duties and finish packing up Sanctum."

Zoe gave me a wry grin. "I knew not getting to be in the Knights with you was going to pay off with super-fun missions," she said, a dimple appearing in one cheek.

"How's it going with Ambrose?" Eric asked, sitting forward. "What do you think about the future Champion?"

I rolled my eyes and leaned back. "Might be easier to ask Leo. I'm pretty sure he can summarize it better and more quickly than I can."

Zoe arched an eyebrow and tossed her hair over her shoulder before leaning forward. "That bad, huh?" I nodded, and she frowned. "Devon Alexander bad?"

I considered the question. I didn't think he was cruel, just arrogant and pretentious. And while those two characteristics did not make for a great leader, that didn't mean they equaled a bad person, either.

"No," I told her. "Not that bad. And if he's Lacey and Strum's choice, presumably they can get him to tone it down some once he's in office. If we even get him that far. The guy is being a real bonehead when it comes to his personal safety."

"It's because you're a woman," Zoe scoffed angrily, her fist thumping down on the table. "He's clearly threatened by you."

"Nah," Quess chimed in, a congenial smile on his face. "It's because she murdered the last Champion. He's intimidated."

"He's already in love with her," Eric said around a mouthful of food.

"Or it's that he seems to think that Lacey's concerns for his safety are unnecessary," I said back, not even bothering to address Eric's comment past the dry look I gave him. "I think he genuinely believes that now that Devon's dead, he's going to be fine, although I'm not entirely sure why. And I don't know, maybe he's right. So far, I haven't noticed anything out of the ordinary. Then again, we haven't registered yet, so quiet is to be expected." I sighed and began massaging my eyebrow with my finger, trying to soothe my anger away. "I don't know. I just wish that—"

"Liana, look behind you. What are they doing?"

Zoe's voice held a note of deep concern, and I immediately turned around, scanning the aisle and food carts beyond. Quess pointed it out a second later, and my eyes zeroed in on three black-clad figures behind a juicing stall on the other side of the aisle. One had his hands knotted in the vendor's shirt and was shoving him away violently, but the other two stood on either side of the five-foot-wide stall, their arms held straight out from their bodies, pointed toward the back of the stall.

I immediately realized they were holding pulse shields, the weapons used by the Inquisitors, which fired a burst of kinetic energy. They were aiming them so that the stall would come slamming across the aisle and directly into us—but whether it was meant as a distraction, or was an attempt to kill us, I didn't know.

All I knew was that if they were trying to do the latter, it could work. The cart had to weigh three hundred pounds at least; if it hit us with the amount of force I knew those pulse shields could generate, we were going to be just as liquid as the contents of the blenders in the stall.

"The table," I cried, my mind working fast. I leapt over it just as I heard a loud, metallic tearing sound, Quess seconds behind me. Eric and Zoe scrambled out of our way, with Zoe hauling Tian up by her arms to move the girl away from danger. I turned immediately and grabbed the edge of the table, watching as the cart shot toward us at a dizzying speed. People began screaming as it tore through the crowd, but I couldn't do anything about that. I heaved the table up onto its side, and then immediately ducked down behind it.

"BRACE!" I shouted, and felt and saw my friends dive in next to me, placing their shoulders and hands and backs against the underside of the table.

Barely a second later, it slammed into us, violently enough to make it feel like I had been kicked in the back so hard I couldn't breathe, and then we were sliding across the floor, propelled backward by the cart's velocity and weight. The floor scraped under my uniform, the grooves stinging against my flesh as they slid under us. My boots scrambled for traction as I glanced ahead.

There was another stall looming right in front of us. We were going to be crushed between them.

"BRACE!" I shouted again, shoving my feet straight in front of me and trying to slow us down. I glanced over and saw my friends doing similar things, and as we gained more traction, the cart continued to slow... until we came to a rattling stop, just feet away from the second cart.

My heart was pounding in my chest, and I could taste copper in my mouth. I looked around, doing a quick check to make sure everyone was all right, and then stood up, sliding my baton out of my belt and pressing the button to charge the electrical node. My eyes surveyed the carnage the food stall had caused: several people were lying on the ground, moaning, while others helped them, and even more stood around gaping in horror at what they had just witnessed. My eyes traversed the fruit-lined path of destruction, searching for the dark figures. But there was no sign of them—or the vendor they had been holding back.

I came around the table and raced over to where I had last seen them, Quess and Eric flanking me. We quickly found the vendor unconscious behind a neighboring stall, and the two men began checking him over to make sure his injuries weren't life threatening. I ignored them, my eyes on the dark shadows created by the other stalls, and a tiny, narrow aisle that ran between them. There was no sign of movement, but I didn't let down my guard as I moved closer, searching.

"They're gone," Quess said softly, after I had watched for longer than I should have. I looked up at him, and then nodded.

"Liana." Eric came up behind me, and I turned, immediately noting the pad cradled between his two large hands. He had already turned it on, revealing one sentence: *If Ambrose Klein competes, your friends are the ones who will suffer.*

"What did you find?" Zoe asked, somewhat breathlessly. I turned to see her cradling Tian, the young girl's arms wrapped tightly around my best friend, and realized Zoe'd had to carry Tian all the way over to us.

"Oh, nothing. Just a big 'I told you so' that I get to have the joy of rubbing into Ambrose's face later," I replied dryly as I turned the pad around to face her. She read the words, her eyes narrowing, and looked up at me.

"Screw these guys," she said, looking around at the damage they had done. "You get Ambrose to start listening to you, all right? I'll figure out a way to keep Eric and myself safe, but you have got to get us some weapons so we can defend ourselves."

I agreed. "I'll see what I can do. But you're right. I'm going to get Ambrose to reach out to Lacey as well. Quess, I hate to add more to your plate, but once I'm done showing this to Ambrose, I'm going to need you to—"

"See if I can figure out who it belongs to, and try to track down whoever is targeting us?" He raised an arrogant eyebrow and grinned. "Of course, although... I might tap Mercury to help me with it. He's probably got better tools and programs for this than I do. Is that okay?"

I nodded. Quess was the most ideal for this job, given his time in IT, but if he needed Mercury's help, I wasn't going to discourage him. I had to assume that the pad would lead nowhere; our assailants were clearly from the IT Department, or working with them—how else would they have gotten their hands on pulse shields? And that meant they would have covered their tracks with the pad. But we needed to know who was after us, and we needed to know quickly. So I didn't care if it meant going to Scipio himself—I was determined to find out who they were.

Until then, however... "I want everyone to have their guard up," I said. "Let Leo and Maddox know as soon as they finish their tests, or the first chance you get. Quess, can you also use Mercury's anchor program and modify it so we can have shielded conversations through the nets? I think we need to avoid meetings in the future, whenever we can."

"Sounds good," Zoe replied.

"Says you," scoffed Quess, his hand going up to his hair and touching it lightly. "Now I have to change my hair again—and I was just beginning to like this look."

Zoe rolled her eyes at him, and then shifted to one side, straining under Tian's weight. I walked around her to get a good look at Tian's face, and realized the little girl had dozed off. I was baffled by her ability to fall asleep right then and there, but ultimately chalked it up as another Tianism—one of the little quirks that were just her—and moved on.

"All right, guys," I said. "Let's get out of here. We've lingered long enough."

Especially considering Knights were beginning to push through the crowds to find out what had happened. We hadn't done anything wrong—but it was better if they didn't know we were involved at all.

There seemed to be too many eyes on us as it was.

13

I knocked impatiently on Ambrose's door and looked both ways down the hall, checking for any sign of movement or possible attack. I felt exposed in the hall like this, but after the event in the Lion's Den, I needed to get to Ambrose and make sure he was safe. The attack could have been meant as a distraction.

I doubted it, but I still needed to get into his apartment. Somehow, they had known Ambrose was planning to register for the Tourney, and I wanted to know how. I was betting they had installed some sort of listening device in his apartment, and I was going to toss the place until I found it.

I knocked again, and was inputting my code, ready to put my override privileges to use, when the door slid open with a pneumatic hiss. Ambrose stood on the other side, his face angry and his mouth already open to chastise me. I pushed past him and into the living space, looking around. The room was configured almost exactly like the Knight Commanders' apartments, with the exception that it had a small dinette, instead of a whole separate room for dining. But my family's apartment was just that: one designed for a family with two children. These were designed for two Knights who were single.

"You better have a damn good reason for this," Ambrose growled behind me.

I ignored him. "Which one is your room?" I demanded, pointing to the hall ahead of me, which led to the bedrooms and shared bathroom. "Is your roommate here?"

"I don't have a roommate currently, and you still need to explain what you're doing here!"

I glanced back at him. "What I'm doing here is making sure you're safe," I informed him coolly. "Once I do that, I will explain. Now, close the door and help me look around. And for Scipio's sake, get your baton."

Ambrose glared at me for several seconds, and then opened the closet by the door and pulled his baton out. I watched the procedure with no small amount of alarm, because the closet was the least handy place to keep a baton. If I had been an enemy, I would've had him on the ground long before he could have gotten to the closet.

I added it to my list of things to yell at him about later, but ignored it for now. I wanted to make sure no one was lying in wait for him first. I went down the hall and opened up the extra room, as the other door was open and clearly in use. The room was empty, with no signs of life, but I went in anyway. I pulled my hand light from my pocket and checked under the small twin bed opposite the door first, clearing it. Standing up, I shone the light around, and then moved over to the closet unit on the wall, pulling open the various doors and checking them for signs of life.

Ambrose watched me from the doorway, his eyes narrowed suspiciously. "Nobody's there," he said once I had opened up the last closet.

I glared at him, then climbed onto the desk to inspect the vents.

"Oh, c'mon, seriously?!" he exclaimed. "You really think an attacker is going to come through the vents?"

"You clearly haven't spent enough time with criminals," I said as I pulled off the grate. "This is our favorite method of transportation." Ambrose scoffed behind me, but I continued to ignore him as I set the grate down on the desk. He still wasn't taking me seriously—but that didn't mean I was going to stop. Whoever had attacked us knew that Ambrose was planning to enroll, and that meant they had access to him in some way. I wasn't sure how, yet, but making sure his apartment was clear was the first step to figuring it out.

I held up my hand light and shone it inside the shaft, checking the duct. The long, tight space seemed to stretch on for eternity, the shadows fighting the light as I swept it around. But it was clear. I hopped down, not bothering to put the grate back on, and moved to the doorway.

"Your room is next," I said. "Let me pass."

Ambrose scowled at me before moving to the side—at a ponderously slow speed. I managed to hold back an eye roll, and instead pulled out the pad that our assailants in the market had left behind. I pushed it into his chest as I walked by, and entered his room.

His room had an identical layout to the room across the hall, and was exactly what I'd expected: pristine, with everything in its place, and not a thing out of order. Only the bedding was mussed, presumably because I'd woken him up and he hadn't had time to make the bed.

The closet seemed the least invasive as a first place to search, so I made a beeline for it, threw it open, and looked around.

"What is this?" Ambrose asked from the hall, his tone bewildered. "How did you get this?"

I pushed aside his extra uniforms and moved the hand light around, checking the back for any sign of a device—or anything else that didn't belong. "From some people who tried to crush me and my friends in the market earlier. They got away, but they left that behind." I paused in my search and turned, studying him to see what his reaction would be.

He met my gaze, and I saw a flash of real fear there, but then it was gone, his face carefully reforming into an expression of nonchalance and bemusement. "This is a prank—"

"Scipio help me, it is *not* a *prank!*" I shouted in disbelief. Why wasn't he freaking out about this? Someone had found out about his plan to register, despite his attempts to keep it secret. That meant they had resources. And they clearly had people as well, which meant coordination and planning.

This wasn't a time for him to be blasé. It was the time for him to wake up and pay attention.

I squared off with him and let him see my anger and frustration. "They nearly killed me and my friends, and they injured several other people in the process! And the note they left behind? That is not something we take lightly."

Ambrose's bemusement faded, and the anger returned. "You do not get to come in here, push me around, tear apart my house, and then expect me to blindly agree with you based on an attack on you and a pad with a vague threat! You do understand that Lacey is keeping an eye on everything, right? And that if there were a real threat, she would've *notified* me?"

I balled my fist up and bit back a growl. He was relying heavily on Lacey's ability to see everything, but the fact that she hadn't notified us about this threat only proved that she couldn't handle that particular responsibility alone. Which was probably the reason she wanted me and my friends on the ground with him. Ambrose couldn't seem to get that, and now we were in danger because of him. And there was a good chance he was in danger too.

But I wouldn't be able to protect him if he wasn't going to *listen* to me, and trying to get it through his thick skull would only be a waste of breath. I needed to find a way to make him listen—and the only thing I could think of was Lacey. I wasn't supposed to reach out to her directly, but I was certain Ambrose had a way to do it.

"No, I'm here because Lacey is blackmailing me to help *you*. Net her."

Ambrose's brows came together, and he folded his arms

across his chest. "No, I'm not going to do that. I'm not supposed to until after the Tourney is done."

I ran a hand across my face, trying for calm. I was sure there was a good reason for that, but it seemed moot at this point. If I couldn't get the person I was trying to protect to work with me, then I was definitely going to fail in protecting him. Lacey was the only way I could get him to see reason, mostly because she, herself, was *reasonable*. And if she couldn't do it, then I was quitting this stupid job.

"I don't care," I informed him. "You call her now and tell her I need to talk to her."

But he was already shaking his head. "I told you, I can't do that until—"

"Damn it, you arrogant jerk! You get her in a net conversation right now, or I'll spare your enemies the work and just kill you myself!"

He reared back, surprise and shock on his face. "You wouldn't dare," he bellowed, once he realized I was threatening him. "Once Lacey hears of this, her plans be—"

I grabbed him and shoved him up against the doorframe, hard, giving him a good shake while I was at it. "You don't get it. Your continued obstinate and arrogant behavior is making my job harder, and threatening to put my friends at risk. Now, so that you understand me, protecting my friends is the only thing I care about. So if it's between you and them, I will kill you to keep them safe. Get. Lacey. Now."

He stared at me, and I glared right back, daring him to test me. In truth, I had no intention of killing him, but he didn't know that. And I needed him to believe that I would—if only so I could get a hold of Lacey and get her to make him listen to me.

He glared at me, and then jerked free of my grasp. "All right," he said harshly. "I'll get it set up. Why don't you just finish doing whatever you're doing and then join me in the living room when you're ready." He tugged his shirt smooth as he spoke, rolling his shoulders.

"Fine," I replied, turning back and facing the room. I was fairly certain there wasn't anything inside, but I still had to check. If only for my peace of mind.

Also, it gave me a better understanding of the layout of the Knight Elite's quarters, and where the possible ingress points were, in case anyone tried to get to him while he was sleeping and vulnerable. There was only the front door and the vent on the opposite side of the room, but that was a lot. Too much for us just to check once a day.

No, it was becoming clearer that if we wanted to keep Ambrose perfectly safe, we needed to have eyes on him at all times, whether he liked it or not. Whether *I* liked it or not.

I finished my search quickly and efficiently, and then walked back into the common room and turned right into the living room. Ambrose was already seated, two pads—one of them being the one I had given him—placed on the table in front of him.

"I trust there were no assassins hiding in my laundry hamper?" he said smugly, arching an eyebrow.

I didn't rise to the bait. "Did you get a hold of Lacey?" I asked.

He hesitated. "I passed a message off through one of our contacts. He'll make sure she gets it, but it might take a few minutes. I still think this is pointless, for the record."

"Noted and ignored," I replied, giving him a withering glance. I looked around the room and dropped into a seat opposite him. We stared at each other for a few seconds, his look one of study, while mine was more sullen and irritated.

I could only imagine what he was thinking about me, but I was honestly beyond caring. The scrape in the market had shaken me more than I cared to admit, and I wasn't messing around anymore. Ambrose needed to start taking me seriously.

Not to mention, I needed information and support. Clearly, Lacey wasn't able to keep up with everything, but if she could help me pinpoint possible targets—or find out who had attacked us—that would help me keep Ambrose and my friends safe.

"I'm going to make a cup of tea," Ambrose announced after the silence between us grew long and strained. He stood up and moved around the table, into the kitchen. A moment later I heard him rattling around in the cupboards.

I sat in silence as the noise behind me continued, thinking. Something was bothering me about everything that had just gone down, but I still couldn't quite figure it out. I hadn't found any listening devices in the room... so how could they have found out that Ambrose was even registering in the first place? Because the message had been very specific about that. Ambrose had told me himself that he was waiting until the last day of registration to put his name on the list—so how had they known?

I looked at Ambrose's pad, still dark with inactivity, and

after a moment of debate, I reached out and grabbed it before standing up. There was only one way to find out.

I crossed the living room and moved into the conjoined kitchen and dining room. Ambrose was in the process of pouring hot water from an electric kettle into a teacup, his back to me. I watched him for a second, and then cleared my throat.

He jerked around, startled, and then hissed when hot water dropped into his hand. "What?" he snapped, bristling as he turned to run his hand under the faucet.

"Something's been bugging me," I told him, and he flashed an irritated look over his shoulder.

"What now?" he demanded, whirling back toward me to grab a towel from the island and wrapping it around his hand.

"How did they know?" I asked him, voicing my question out loud. He gave me a quizzical look, and I took a step closer, placing the pad on the counter between us. "How did they know you were planning to sign up for the Tourney? You told me your-self that you were keeping your intentions secret until the last minute. So I ask again, how did they know?"

He stared at me for a long, hard moment, and then looked away, his jaw clenched. "I registered last night," he finally admit-ted, his eyes coming back up to mine to see how I would react.

Anger, hot and thick, surged over me. This had been *Lacey's* plan, one that was meant to help *him*, and he couldn't even seem to follow that! Did he just not care that he had completely undermined her? And why had he done so? What purpose could he possibly have for signing up early, other than to brag or boast about it to his friends?

On the tail of all that, I had one additional question—one that I asked out loud.

"With who on your team?" I asked carefully, maintaining my eye contact with him.

Ambrose glared at me for a long moment, and then exploded. "There was no way you were going to get your friends to test out! So I took matters into my own hands and—"

"AND WHAT?!" I exploded, my temper finally getting the better of me. "This was Lacey's plan to begin with, and you couldn't follow it! Why did you even register now? What possible purpose could you have for doing it early?"

Ambrose shifted, suddenly distinctly uncomfortable. "When I was with my friends, they—"

I groaned loudly, amazed by his stupidity. I had known it almost as soon as he said that he had registered early—and even now, I still couldn't believe it. "You did *not* do this just to show your stupid friends you were serious about it, did you? How immature *are* you?"

"You want to talk about being immature? Your little teammates aren't going to be able to test out in time for the Tourney! But you wouldn't look at the personnel files I gave you, so like I said, I took matters into my own hands. If I hadn't, my friends would've been grabbed by another team! We should consider ourselves lucky they came to me before they went looking for someone else."

They came to him? And he didn't see that as suspicious at all?

"Sure," I said sarcastically, nodding my head. "And what if

they did that to make you choose right then and there to have them because they're secretly planning to kill you, hm? What is it going to take for you to realize that I have actually thought about this stuff, and am trying to help you stay alive?"

"You don't get it," Ambrose sneered. "You have no place giving me orders, threatening me, or anything! You're just a pawn, recruited by Lacey because she's overcautious like that. You aren't even a Knight, not really. You just got the position because of the lies Lacey told, so for you to march in here and start giving *me* orders? You don't have the slightest idea what we're trying to protect, trying to do, but you have the audacity to—"

A sharp buzz on the counter cut him off, and I immediately saw that the screen was lit orange. I looked back up at Ambrose, who was now smiling, his eyes on it.

"Good," he said smugly, taking a step toward it. "Now I can just tell Lacey that we don't need you, and finish this once and for all."

I watched him reach for it, his words burning an angry hole inside of me. For a second, I was tempted to let him tell her whatever he wanted, and walk away. The only thing keeping me from doing that was Lacey's threat of turning us over for tampering with Scipio's memory to get away with Devon's murder.

Well, that... and I really wanted to spite Ambrose. If using Lacey to get him to fall in line worked, it would go a long way toward fulfilling my petty desire.

He tapped a few things on the pad, and then Lacey's voice

filled the air, emitted by the pad itself. My eyes widened—I didn't even know something like that was possible!

"Ambrose, I assume Liana is there?" she asked, her voice tiny through the speakers.

"Yes, she is," Ambrose began. "Lacey, you need to get her out of here. She's a nuisance!"

"Then she's doing her job," Lacey said archly. "Liana, what's the problem?"

Ambrose shot me a sullen look. "Lacey, I—"

"Ambrose, you gave your contact more than an earful, and believe me, he got your complaints down and to me. Now I want to hear Liana's side of it."

Ambrose fumed, but said nothing. I listened to their exchange, and the firm way she handled him, and thought back on Ambrose's words from earlier, puzzling over them, trying to find the right angle. And suddenly I had an idea. And a clever one, at that. One that would help me, and satisfy my curiosity about something else.

I leaned on my hands on the counter and smiled sweetly at Ambrose. "Ambrose doesn't respect me," I announced. He snorted, but I ignored it and barreled on. "As a result, he's putting his life, mine, and the lives of my friends at great risk. But I think I have a solution."

"Oh?" Lacey asked, her tone a mixture of amusement and curiosity. "So quickly?"

"Well, I don't like to waste time, so yes. That quickly."

"I see. And what is this solution?" she asked, and I grinned.

"You're gonna give me a legacy net, and then give me whatever internal rank you use, so that I am higher than Ambrose."

I could actually care less about the rank, but Ambrose had made a lot of fuss about me not understanding what he was fighting for, and getting a legacy net and seeing what they were all about might help me convince him that I actually wanted to help his cause. I didn't, but he didn't need to know that.

And getting the legacy net was also important for a completely separate reason: Leo. With his terminal gone, we didn't have a lot of options for where to put him. But maybe one of these nets had the potential to hold him—or maybe he could be transferred back and forth between the one I was asking for and the one in Grey's head in some way, so that one could charge while the other kept him alive.

I didn't know, but it was worth asking Quess to take a look at.

"No, she will not!" Ambrose sputtered a second or two later. "Lacey, you cannot seriously be thinking—"

"Shut up, Ambrose," Lacey said, cutting him off. "Liana, you can't possibly expect me to give you something like that. The nets are... precious to us, and dangerous to possess. I don't even wear mine all the time, for fear of getting caught with it. And neither does Ambrose."

"That is really good to know," I said. "Still, you owe me for those paint samples you took from our home, and this is the price. And you're going to do it if you actually want me to keep Ambrose alive. It's the only way to get him to listen to me."

Ambrose gave me a confused look, and then looked at the

pad and back up to me. After several seconds, Lacey said, "Very well. Meet us in C-19 in Cogstown in thirty minutes, and I will give you one. Bring Ambrose. I want to know more about what's been going on with the two of you."

I opened my mouth to tell her I would, but the pad went off abruptly, the transmission clearly terminated.

Ambrose stared at me, a frown on his face. "Why?" he asked.

I licked my lips. "You said it earlier: I have no idea what you're fighting for. Maybe with that net, I can figure out what it is, and then you'll believe that I'm here to help you. That, and it's clear that you are a stickler for hierarchy, given how quickly you shut up when Lacey told you to. So if I get Lacey to put me over you, it will mean you listen to what I have to say."

"You have no guarantee of that," he pointed out.

"Yeah, well. Let's see what Lacey has to say about that. Get dressed. We're running late already."

For a second, it looked like he was going to act petulant and stand there glaring at me, but eventually he straightened up and headed back into his room to change. I watched him go, and then picked up his untouched cup of tea and took a sip, thinking.

I had never even considered asking for a legacy net, but once the idea had hit me, I had just gone for it. I hoped it would earn me at least a smidge of respect from Ambrose—and at the very least, it would give Quess something to study... and hopefully modify to help Leo.

And I could finally figure out what the heck was on them.

14

To my surprise, more boxes and belongings had been added to Roark's former apartment. I stared at them, confused by their presence. When I had met Lacey and Strum here for the first time, they had assured me that the room was for my group and myself as a peace offering. Lacey had even taken pains to leave it relatively untouched, though it had been missing the quintessential touch that Roark brought to it.

Scipio help me, I missed him terribly.

I pushed aside the pain and focused, heading deeper into the common space. Lacey was already there, as was another person I didn't recognize. Lacey was inspecting a beaker left unbroken after my fight with Gerome and our subsequent escape, but she turned when she heard Ambrose and me enter, and the man opposite her looked up from a medical kit he had been tinkering with.

"Liana," she said, a slight smile coming to her lips. "Glad you could come so quickly. I have a full schedule for the rest of the day." She arched an eyebrow at Ambrose. "Sorry for the circumstances. What's been going on?"

Ambrose's mouth tightened, and I could sense he wanted to defend himself, but was managing to resist. The level of control was impressive, but I was surprised to see that he was capable of it. It only reaffirmed my belief that my request, no matter how symbolic it was, would go a long way in getting Ambrose to listen to me.

"Nothing that this won't fix," I replied. "Ambrose just needs to understand that I take my blackmail-enforced jobs very seriously."

Lacey chuckled and sat the beaker back down on the table with a sharp click. "He's been pushing back?"

"Yes, and that's going to change. It has to change, now that he's officially registered in the Tourney. With people I haven't even vetted for it yet. As a result, my friends and I were attacked in the Lion's Den yesterday, and they sent a clear message to us." I produced the pad and turned it on, opening it to the note and setting it down on the table. It was a risky move, exposing to Lacey what Ambrose had done like that, but I needed her to know that I was taking this seriously, so she would, in turn, continue to take *me* seriously.

It was also good to show her how I handled problems—and would send a clear message that I wasn't going to let her hold me responsible for his mistakes.

Her head snapped up, her brows drawing together. "You

registered for the Tourney two days early?" she hissed. "I told you specifically—"

"I have been training for this day my entire life," Ambrose bit out angrily, his eyes flashing. "So I registered a few days early, so what! You sent this criminal into my life against my wishes, and now you expect me to sit by and take orders from her during what was supposed to be my moment! I am a man. I will not be babysat."

Lacey's face might as well have been comprised of stone. "I see. Liana, how do you want to handle this?"

"Well, for one thing, he is going to get me emancipated from my parents and moved into the apartment across the hall, along with Maddox. He's also going to move Grey in as his roommate. I don't want him going anywhere without one of us, which includes the bathroom and showers. Then he's going to fill out a change of team form to replace his two friends with Grey and Maddox."

"You have no idea if your friends are even going to pass the tests!" he exclaimed hotly. "How the hell are they going to be able to—"

I unzipped a pocket on my thigh and pulled out the thin plastic sheet I had received from Armament the first day I met Ambrose—part of the standard Knight equipment. It allowed us to search for citizens by name or ID number. "Maddox Kerrin and Grey Farmless," I commanded, and the screen lit up. There was a slight pause, and then both their images were floating there. "Display current test results."

The tests weren't finished, but their results were posted

hourly. I hadn't checked them yet, but I wasn't concerned. Leo was confident in his abilities, and I knew Maddox's physical evaluation would come back all right. And I was guessing that Maddox had learned a lot about the Knights from the technical manuals that Cali owned before they had been confiscated, so I felt reasonably confident displaying their standings.

A second later, four graphs showed on the screen: two physical and two mental. Leo's mental graph was finished—with him at ninety-three percent. Maddox's physical was also finished—at ninety-five percent, which was impressive. Their other graphs were incomplete, but were already showing results in the high eighties, with a little over half the tests already completed. I turned it around and smiled smugly at Ambrose.

"Grey is in the eightieth percentile; Maddox in the low nineties," I informed him. "My people are good at what they do, and you need to stop underestimating them. They are reliable, trustworthy, and best of all, being blackmailed as well. So change the damn team roster."

"He'll do it," Lacey announced softly, and Ambrose looked up at her, his eyes wide and horrified.

"Lacey, you can't!"

"I can and I will," she said, her voice thundering angrily. "I told you that this was what was going to happen, and I expected you to go along with it. You didn't, so now I have to step in and make you do it. I expected you to be a professional, Ambrose. We're trying to make you the damn Champion, for Scipio's sake. So when Liana says jump, you better damn well ask her how high." She marched up to him while she spoke, one muscular arm snapping up to grip him tightly by the chin and pull his head down until he was looking her in the eye. "Now tell me you understand me," she growled.

He jerked his head, but Lacey held on, her fingers gripping him so tightly that his dark skin grew pale under the force of them, the area around them becoming white.

"Yes, ma'am," he finally said. "I understand."

I watched their interaction with no small amount of curiosity. Their relationship was more familiar than I had originally thought it would be. It was an assumption on my part, but given what I'd seen of Lacey, I didn't think she was the type to get physical with any of her people. With him, however, there was an annoyance that seemed to grip her more tightly. They were of similar ages, too—perhaps they had been in a relationship at one point?

I wasn't sure, but it was something to note and possibly exploit in the future. Depending on how much pushback Ambrose gave me after this.

"Good," Lacey said, releasing him and taking a step back. "Lucas?" The man sitting at the table had been staring down at it, avoiding the confrontation completely, and looked up at her now, his expression attentive. "Please get started on Liana, if you don't mind."

Lucas nodded and waved me over, patting the stool next to him.

I sighed and unzipped the front of my suit, pulling it off to the waist. The procedure to change out nets was a common one, but there was still some blood, and I didn't want any of it getting on my uniform. I smoothed down the black, sleeveless top I was wearing underneath, and then moved over to Lucas, dropping onto the stool and presenting him with the back of my neck.

I tensed when I heard the sound of the aerosol blast, followed by the hair-raising feeling of cold droplets on my neck, numbing the area.

"Once you've explored it some, I suggest you pull it out until after the Tourney," Lacey said, and I looked at her, trying not to think about what Lucas was doing back there. "Don't take this the wrong way, but I'd rather lose you than it. The data on there is beyond priceless."

I started to nod and then caught myself. It made sense, but it was still quite invasive—I'd have to keep the net Lucas took out and then have Quess ready to change it out whenever I was worried about getting caught doing something wrong. Luckily, the regular nets lasted for two years when they weren't implanted, so as long as I didn't keep it out for very long, it would be fine. "Very well," I said. "How does it work?"

Lucas's gloved fingers pressed against the side of my neck, and I felt a dull pressure, indicating that he was now cutting the skin open and exposing the implanted net that he was about to remove. I clenched my jaw and quickly decided not to think about it.

"It has the same capabilities as a normal net: reading brain-waves and sending net transmissions. Only this one has data stored on it, and delivers the information directly into your mind," Lacey replied. "It takes a bit of getting used to, though, so fair warning."

I winced as the tendrils that draped across my brain began to withdraw, the sensation more nauseating than painful, and gritted my teeth, trying not to imagine them dragging along my cerebral cortex like vines that weren't willing to be uprooted.

It felt like forever before the sensation ended, and I exhaled sharply, instantly relieved. I heard the sharp *tink* of my net dropping into something metallic, and then braced myself, the momentary reprieve about to come to an end.

Seconds later, Lucas's fingers returned, and I felt pressure at the back of my neck again. I waited in expectation of the filaments pushing back in, and the teeth-clenching pressure they caused, but to my surprise, nothing came. I continued to wait, even as Lucas smeared dermal bond onto the incision point to seal it closed.

"I'm not sure this is working," I said. "I don't think the filaments extended. Are you sure this one is still good?"

"The filaments on these nets are... 'gentler' is the only word I can think of," Lacey said, rubbing the back of her neck. "They are about half the size of the ones we get now."

My eyebrows lifted. "That's amazing. And it can still do everything a regular net can?"

"Yup. You can net as usual, but you'll find the vibrations to be greatly diminished as well." That didn't surprise me—Leo had linked with my net once, and the vibrations while he spoke were greatly reduced. Still, from how Lacey had put it, I wondered if the vibrations on normal nets were always the same —which would mean that Leo had managed to alter them. Was there something else that made them rattle so hard—something that could be fixed? And if so, what was it, and why hadn't anyone done anything to fix it?

"Are you ready to give it a whirl?" Lacey suddenly asked.

I blinked in surprise and took a moment to recall what was happening. "How do I do it?"

"You have to focus your mind," Ambrose said. "Think about something specific, like... Think about the End, or something."

"Whoa," Lacey said, her hand shooting out in a universal symbol for "stop." "That's a bit... heavy for a first try. Let's start with something a little simpler. Liana, have you ever heard of a car?"

"Of course I have," I lied. "I read about them in a book once." It was almost true—I had read about a truck once. Leo had been the first to show me a car, so I did have an idea of what one looked like through his projector, but I wasn't about to tell her that.

In any case, I had just admitted to a crime—owning, let alone reading, anything other than a technical manual or school-book was illegal—but to her credit, Lacey only smiled. "Give it a shot," she said encouragingly.

I stared at them, and then closed my eyes, focusing, picturing the image that Leo had shown me. They were rectangular boxes of metal with four wheels. They had radios and windshield wipers and seemed prone to their tires going flat.

I was letting the details roll over my mind, trying to imagine what it really looked like, when the fuzzy edges of it snapped into focus. Details I had *never even known existed* sprang into focus. I suddenly knew the name of every part: exhaust, carburetor, air filter, oil tank... Things that Leo's image hadn't shown, and that I hadn't read about in a book, but could now understand. I focused on the image, wondering what it felt like to be inside of one, and then suddenly I wasn't just seeing the car, I was *driving* the car.

My foot pressed down as a feeling of elation, as wild and carefree as the wind whipping through my hair, rushed over me, making my limbs tingle. The car surged forward, the expanse of gray road rushing by beneath me. There was nothing overhead —it was a convertible, *something I now understood was different but the same—and the warm morning sun was shining down on me, warming my skin even as the wind cooled it. I turned my face toward it, smiling, laughing, just enjoying being alive...*

My eyes snapped open, and suddenly I was back in the Tower. I took a deep breath, and another, the experience so real that my hands were trembling in my lap. I balled them into fists and looked up at Lacey, who was watching me intently.

"What was that?" I asked. "At first, I could see it. I could understand it. But then something happened, and it was like I was—"

"There?" she supplied, and I nodded. "It's a tangent memory. When these were passed out among the first generation of survivors, Lionel Scipio wanted a way to preserve memories as well as history, so that later generations could feel connected with their ancestors, and the world before."

"Wait, that was someone's actual *memory*?" I asked. Lacey nodded, and I blinked a few times, trying to process how I felt about that. On the one hand, cool. On the other hand, it felt a little intrusive. "Doesn't that freak you out at all?"

"No," Lacey replied with a smile. "It makes me feel connected. Now, is there anything else you need?"

"Yes, actually," I said, putting my thoughts about the legacy nets to one side and focusing on the matter at hand. The net was just part of my plan, but I needed something else, too. And I needed Lacey's considerable resources to work for me, for once, to get it. "Dylan Chase and Frederick Hamilton. They are the strongest competitors signed up thus far, and I want their backgrounds, as well as knowledge about whether they are working with anyone."

"You think they might be from another legacy group?" Lacey asked. "What makes you think that?"

I smiled at her. "Perfectly justified paranoia."

"Look, we can't just focus on one individual," Lacey said. "I know you're trying to be thorough, but there are going to be a lot more competitors coming through. We can't waste time on each one."

"I'm not asking you to," I replied. "I'm asking you to do two. My people are doing their best, but we don't have the access and resources you do, and we're spread pretty thin. We need information."

"Yes, I am aware," Lacey said with a grin. "Your friend Ms. Elphesian is transferring into the Cogs with her boyfriend, and requested Roark's apartment. Those boxes are the ones they managed to get down here in their first trip."

I frowned, processing what she said. "Wait, what?" Why

were Zoe and Eric moving boxes here? What was she doing? We hadn't discussed anything about her and Eric coming down here. Just what was she thinking?

"I will let Zoe explain it to you," Lacey said. "And I will have someone look into these people, as you asked. Ambrose, I trust you'll be more tolerable to Liana in the future? As far as I'm concerned, she outranks you. So I trust you'll follow her orders when it comes to your safety."

Ambrose rolled his eyes, but nodded sharply, only once.

Lacey beamed. "Good. Now, please take care of my cousin, Liana. He can be a little jerk at times, but he's not all bad." They were related? That... explained a lot, actually.

But it killed any questions I had about Zoe, and the pointed look she gave me ensured that they didn't return. I swallowed hard, her message received loud and clear: I was to keep her cousin alive, or else.

15

I sat a carton down on the counter and exhaled, lifting my arms and clasping my hands over my head to stretch the aching muscles in my back while I looked around my new living quarters. My very first apartment.

I couldn't help but smile, pleased at the prospect of having my own home, free of my parents. I supposed, in a way, that Sanctum had been like that. But this was different. It had furniture.

I permitted myself a childish moment, and fell face-first onto the sofa in the shared living room, sinking into the cushions. I luxuriated in it, imagining what it would feel like to take a nap there once the Tourney was over and I could breathe a little bit more. Maybe curled up with a good book from Zoe's stash, letting my eyelids grow heavy as the words blurred together...

Hands shook me roughly as a male voice whispered "Mom"

in a low, urgent voice that called to some instinct deep inside, ripping me from a peaceful slumber.

I opened my eyes and saw my son kneeling next to the couch. I had dozed off again, for the umpteenth time today. Old age was getting harder and harder to resist, but I kept holding on—there was so much more to be done.

"What's wrong?" I asked, grabbing my son's hands and holding them tightly between my own. He was agitated, tears in his eyes.

"He's dead," he whispered. "Lionel's dead."

My head spun with the news, but I didn't let the shock rule me. I had already lost so many on the path here. Mourning would come later.

"How?"

"In his sleep," my son replied. "They found him in his quarters."

"Scipio 1.0?" I asked. We were supposed to have an emergency vote on that tomorrow, to finalize or reverse the decision to destroy him.

"The records show he was deleted," he replied. "We can't find any trace of the program."

"No napping until we're moved in," Maddox announced, jolting me out of the memory I had just gotten caught in, and my eyes snapped open to find her emerging from the hallway.

There was a moment of disorientation as the memory broke, but I breathed through it. These tangent memories had been happening since I'd received the legacy net, and I still wasn't used to it. Especially this time; the emotions that came with this one were more powerful than any of the generalized sensations I had experienced before.

I sat up, put my feet on the floor, and flexed my neck. The memory was interesting, but also irrelevant—I'd already known that Lionel Scipio had been murdered, and that nobody had been able to find Scipio 1.0. Until I had stumbled onto him by pure dumb luck. But now I knew why they hadn't searched: everyone had believed he'd been deleted.

What was interesting about it, though, was that the memory had belonged to someone who was there at the beginning of the Tower. I just didn't know *who*, only that they had been impor-tant in some way. And elderly.

I shook the memory and the resulting emotions off, and returned my focus to Maddox, who was now crossing over into the kitchen. She was wearing her new uniform, having passed her tests with scores high enough to be promoted to Knight Elite. Ambrose was now officially listed as her supervisor—and Leo's. Leo himself was in the process of moving in next door, although his move involved only one box, which was filled with his spare uniforms.

"I have a few more boxes to grab," I informed her. "But Quess and Tian are due at any second, and we're having that powwow with Ambrose while they do their inspection, and then our meeting right after that!"

Two meetings back to back was not ideal, but with the opening of the Tourney happening tomorrow, I needed to make sure we knew how we were going to keep Ambrose safe, as well as what was going on with the Paragon, new Sanctum, and whatever else was on my seemingly never-ending checklist. Call me a micro-manager, but I had a lot of balls in the air.

She gave me a look as she opened up a cabinet. "Need any help with those boxes?"

I laughed and shook my head. "Gee, thanks. That's what you offer some help on? And no, you do not have to come with me to my parents'. I couldn't subject you to something so inhuman. Maybe Ambrose, but you? I like you."

She blinked in surprise before a pleased smile blossomed on her face. And though she turned away to hide it, I felt a smile of my own tugging at my lips. Maddox wasn't prone to shyness, but she hadn't had many friends growing up, let alone any friends who were girls, so her vulnerability was understandable. She'd always wanted a female friend.

And in my mind, she *was* my friend. Which in my experience meant the person was even better family than the one you were born with.

She began pulling out coffee cups and setting them on the counter, busily preparing tea for everyone. Only Zoe and Eric would be missing from this meeting—partially because they didn't need to be involved in these particular discussions, and partially because they were settling into Roark's old apartment in Cogstown.

It hadn't taken much convincing for me to agree to their sudden transfer into the Mechanics Department, once Zoe pointed out the pros to me, the big one being that she and Eric would be safer if they were closer to Lacey. It would also give her more space and equipment for figuring out the formula for

Paragon—in case we never recovered Jasper. And it might even allow her and Eric to find out what Lacey and her legacy group were all about.

Besides, it meant she and Eric could take care of each other.

There was a buzz on the door, jolting me from my thoughts, and I stood up, waving Maddox back. I checked the peephole first, smiled when I saw who was on the other side, pressed the button, and stepped back to make room for Leo, Ambrose, Quess, and Tian.

"Liana!" Tian shouted, wrapping her arms around me in a tight hug. I started to hug her back, but she pushed away quickly and raced over to Maddox. Quess and I exchanged an amused look as he went by. Quess had changed his look again, and now had frost-white hair that rivaled even Tian's, and brown contacts. He'd done something to make himself appear younger, and I felt a little bemused at the boyish look he'd affected.

I stopped marveling at his skill with makeup long enough to give Leo a friendly smile and nodded to Ambrose as they both entered the apartment and I shut the door behind them. I pushed through the wall the three men had formed in the threshold, reminding them to spread out.

"Congratulations!" Tian cried, her arms already wrapped around her surrogate sister. "You look amazing!"

Maddox beamed and dropped a kiss on Tian's forehead. "Thank you, Tian. Want some hot chocolate? Liana and I made sure to get some packets for you when we were at the market."

Tian's blue eyes grew large, and she started bobbing her head emphatically.

"Nuh-uh, Tian," Quess said from next to me. "We've got to sweep this room and the bedrooms for listening devices, which means I need my tiniest helper focused. Hot chocolate will have to wait until afterward."

"Awwwww..." Tian pouted and remained where she was, staring up at Quess with eyes as large and luminescent as the moon. "I just finished Ambrose and Grey's apartment, though!"

The four of us shared a smile, while Ambrose's face reflected a hint of disapproval. I ignored it and focused on Tian. We did need the apartment checked, but Quess had developed that noise-canceling device, so there wasn't a huge rush for her to do this room first.

I shifted my eyes over to him and smiled when I saw him already pulling it out of his satchel, one thick eyebrow up in question. I gave him an approving nod, and then returned my eyes to Tian. We were about to strike a deal.

"All right," I said. I paused for a second—long enough for her face to light up in excitement—then added, "but..." She froze, and gazed at me with wide eyes. "You have to check the bedrooms first, while Grey, Maddox, Ambrose, and I have our meeting. Then you can have hot chocolate during our meeting, and check the front room last. Okay?"

Tian gave me a suspicious look. "Promise?" she asked, raising one blond eyebrow.

"Cross my heart," I replied solemnly.

She stared at me for a moment or two longer, reminding me of a cat who hadn't quite decided if the food I'd just offered it was poisoned, and then nodded her head and stuck out one thin hand.

"Shake on it." I smiled and took her hand, giving it a gentle shake. She nodded again, all business, and took her hand back, placing it behind her back. "Come along, Quessian," she said primly, marching toward the hall. "We have a deal to honor."

"Yes, of course, milady," Quess replied congenially with an elaborate bow, before straightening and sauntering toward the hall. "Ladies," he said in greeting, handing me his noise-canceling device and tipping an invisible hat to us before disappearing into the back after Tian.

I watched them go, both bemused and lighthearted at their antics. In just seconds, they'd managed to make this place feel more like a home than Maddox and I had done in five minutes. I hoped that Tian wound up staying here a few nights; having her around helped me forget about some of the things that were plaguing me.

The biggest one was that I missed Grey terribly. I tried to hide it, tried to not think about it, but it was always there, lurking on the edges. Keeping busy helped. Focusing on other worries that I could do something about did as well. But in the moments in between—like right before I fell asleep, or when I was sitting down to eat—it would suddenly hit me, how lonely I felt, and that highlighted his absence even more, making me heartsick.

"So, are we having this meeting or what?" Ambrose asked gruffly.

My joy faded some, and I turned to him and nodded, looking

down at the gray box I was now holding. "Please take a seat," I said, holding it out to him.

He accepted it gingerly and moved into the living room, taking a moment to look around the still-bare surroundings before picking one of the two solitary chairs opposite the sofa. He set the device down with a click, and I turned back to Leo, who was waiting patiently.

"Hello, Liana," he said formally. "I'm afraid I did not get to say hello due to Tian's entrance."

I chuckled. "It's okay. How's your new room?"

"Quite nice," he replied. "Although a bit dusty in the wake of Tian and Quess's investigation."

"Oh?" I asked, smiling politely.

"They apparently felt it was necessary to pull my uniforms out and toss them on the floor," Ambrose announced from the other room, his tone a grumble of disapproval.

I didn't hold back my smile, but didn't say anything other than, "I'm sure they were just being thorough."

Maddox moved past me, a tray of steaming mugs balanced between her hands as she crossed into the living area. Leo and I followed, and within moments we were all seated and she was handing out mugs of tea to everyone. I accepted mine, and then reached out to hit the round, black button on Quess's device.

I hadn't noticed a lot of noise before, but as I hit it, an impossibly deafening silence seemed to blanket us, making my ears feel slightly pressurized.

"Your friend made this?" Ambrose asked, his voice slightly awed.

"Quess is a whizz with tech," Maddox said softly, before blowing over the surface of her tea, trying to cool it. My mug was also warm, bordering on hot, and I hurriedly put it back down and leaned back in my chair.

"All right, guys, the qualifiers are tomorrow. All three events are going to be held in one day, so we'll need to be up and ready by seven thirty. I'm going to have Quess in the crowd to keep an eye out for anyone suspicious, but our priority is Ambrose at all times."

Ambrose frowned pensively and leaned forward, resting his elbows on his knees. "Look, I know you were attacked, and I'm sorry for that, but I'm still fairly certain that was just a prank. You're overreacting."

I opened my mouth to object, but when he gave me a surprisingly plaintive look, I reconsidered, and decided to hear him out.

"You said they were using pulse shields, right?" I nodded, and he continued. "Then it stands to reason that they were members of the IT Department and not Knights. I honestly think that any legacy presence within the Knights died with Devon, so you don't have to worry about me during the actual events."

I licked my lips. I wanted to give him this, because it would go a long way toward us finally getting on the same page, but I couldn't. There were a dozen reasons our assailants could have had pulse shields, and the list started with robbery and ended with working for another legacy within the IT department. Perhaps there were even other legacy groups backing candidates of their own, just like Lacey was doing with her cousin.

If there were, it was reasonable to assume that if they were willing to back a Knight to try to gain control over a department head, they would also be willing to kill to ensure that their candidate won.

"I'm sorry," I said earnestly. "I hear what you're saying, but I can't risk your safety."

He stared at me, his jaw clenched tightly shut. I waited for him to snap, or get angry, but instead he sat back. "Fine. But inside the ring, you will follow my orders."

"Wait, we have to follow his orders?" Maddox asked, blinking. "Why?"

"Because part of the competition is performance, but most of it is focused on the deeds you perform during the challenges," I explained, leaning forward. "Robotic drones will be covering each match, and projecting the feed to the Tower and all the department servers. They only choose the most exciting matches to display and transmit, and if a person or team *really* impresses them, they'll have a deed named for them. Like Devon was the Defender of Six Bells."

"Ah." Maddox took a sip of her tea and then sat it down. "And how will him giving us orders help him achieve a deed name?"

"Because they need to see that I'm in command!" Ambrose sputtered. "Tactical leadership is rewarded just as much as physical prowess."

Maddox arched an eyebrow at him. "And what makes you think you can actually lead us?"

"How dare you speak to me like that!" Ambrose declared after a momentary loss of speech. "I am the one who is going to be the Champion, and I'm your supervisor within the Knights themselves! You have to listen to me."

"Oh, man. That is so weak," Maddox said, setting her mug down and narrowing her bright green eyes at him.

Confusion radiated across Ambrose's face. "E-Excuse me?"

Maddox scrutinized him, then wrinkled her nose. "I said, that is so weak. But if you want to know what I mean, allow me to explain: a leader, a true leader, doesn't run around hiding behind the shield of a title. A leader doesn't need to. They do what needs to be done, and people follow them. You may be the next Champion, but if that's how you choose to lead, then you'll lose your Knights' loyalty faster than you can blink." She snapped her fingers suddenly, but to Ambrose's credit, he didn't flinch.

He started to open his mouth, but I cut him off before he could begin. "Maddox," I said, and the raven-haired girl turned and looked at me. I gave her a warning look and turned to Ambrose. "We'll go train together in the Salles later," I said. "That way we can practice together. We will do our best to try to follow your commands, and make you look good."

For a second, Ambrose looked unconvinced. But after several agonizing heartbeats, he finally nodded, and sat back in the chair. He was fuming, but he had chosen valor over fighting, and I appreciated that.

"We're here to talk about Ambrose's security," I continued, hauling the conversation back on course. I peered over my shoulder to see if Quess and Tian were done yet, and then turned back to the group. I didn't want them walking in unnoticed while we talked, and their presence would be a signal that it was time to end the meeting with Ambrose, so I wanted to make sure we went over anything.

Leo was the first to break the silence. "Liana, the crowds are going to be thick tomorrow. How are we going to get him from event to event without exposing him too much?"

I had actually given this some thought, and had come up with what I hoped was a workable plan. "We're going to limit our exposure in the Salles," I said. "We have to stop by the registration table tomorrow to pick up our schedule, but once we know our times, we'll either stay down there or come back up here to wait for our next event. I don't want us where we're supposed to be until fifteen minutes beforehand."

"That's cutting it a bit short," Ambrose said, his voice holding a note of worry.

"I know that," I said. "It sucks, but the less time you're out on the floors with a thick crowd of people, the better. To that effect, any time we're moving, you're in between the three of us. One of us is to be with you at all times, and if you have to pee, Grey is going with you."

"I've gotten better with zippers," Leo said cheerfully, giving Ambrose what I could only assume he thought was a congenial smile. I froze for a second, worried about how Ambrose would react—it was a bit of an odd statement.

There was an awkward moment in which the three of us who weren't Leo looked anywhere but at him, and after a few seconds, he sighed. "I apologize. I seem to have made everyone uncomfortable."

"My new roommate, everyone," Ambrose said dryly, and a surprised smile formed on my face. Ambrose had made a joke. What was better, he'd just overlooked the oddity of the statement as some sort of personality quirk. Leo wouldn't be the first odd person in the world, and he certainly wouldn't be the last.

He caught me smiling at him, and frowned in surprise. Then he cleared his throat and looked around. "If that is what you want to do to keep me safe, then I will trust you and follow your lead," he said, fixing me with a pointed look.

"Thank you."

He scanned everyone again and sighed. "Was there anything else you wanted to discuss about my personal safety?"

I shook my head. There wasn't at the moment—at least, not for him to concern himself with—but there was another piece of business that needed handling before he left. "No, but has Lacey sent you any information on Dylan or Frederick?"

"Actually, yes," Ambrose said, leaning back and feeling around on his abdomen for the zipper that opened a pocket designed specifically for a pad. "She sent me a data burst this morning at about three. The details are on the pad—just download them and return the pad to me after you're done with the other meeting."

He finally managed to get the pocket open and the pad out, and sat it down on the table next to the noise-canceling device.

"She wanted to know if you found out anything about the pad you recovered at the Lion's Den yesterday."

"I'm not sure," I replied. "Quess hasn't given me an update. But I'll let you know after the meeting."

Ambrose nodded, just once, and then stood up. "Well, in that case, I'll be leaving," he said politely. "Who will be coming with me?"

"I'll go," Maddox said, setting her now-empty mug down on the table and rising in a fluid motion.

I shot her a grateful smile, and watched as she and Ambrose left. For a moment, I worried about Leo and me being left alone, but then Quess and Tian emerged from the hall, with Tian bearing several dark smudges on her arms and face, but beaming happily.

I watched them approach, and then quickly leaned forward to hit the button on the table, dropping the noise-canceling device. The strange underwater feeling in my eardrums suddenly released, and I took a moment to adjust as the ambient sounds returned. I had never realized how much noise was in the Tower, but I was suddenly aware of it all—the slight rattle of pipes behind the walls and of metal expanding and contracting. It wasn't obtrusive, but it was still there.

Quess smiled as he opted to sit down on the floor next to my chair. "You don't have to do that," he said, picking up the still-warm mug containing water from the tray with one hand, setting it in front of Tian, and then emptying the silver foil packet of hot chocolate into the mug. "The device won't hurt us if we pass through."

I thought about it, realized that Maddox and Ambrose had just exited without any problem, and felt slightly embarrassed. Reaching out, I reactivated the device and leaned back, sighing.

"How'd it go with Ambrose?" Tian asked sweetly. I smiled at her, but she missed it, her eyes trained solely on the brown powder Quess was mixing into the liquid inside her mug.

"Actually, pretty well," I said, still feeling stunned by the exchange. It seemed that something had worked, because today he had been the most civil I had ever seen him. "But there are a few more things we need to go over before we can talk about that. Quess, what did you discover on that pad?"

I was referring to the pad our assailants had dropped in the market, and luckily, he understood.

"Not much," he replied as he spooned some sugar into his own mug. "The whole thing was wiped clean. There was a serial number on it, which I passed on to Mercury, but it was also a bust—decommissioned and supposedly recycled six months ago."

I wasn't surprised, but it was still a tad disappointing to have discovered nothing. "What about the anchor program for scrambling our net transmissions? Where are you on that?"

Quess took a long sip of his tea and leaned back heavily on one hand. "I passed it over to Zoe," he said finally. "I got a good start on it, but it got too difficult to keep on top of, so I had to delegate."

I frowned, and realized I had been leaning a lot on Quess recently. I'd been leaning on *all* of them a lot, asking them to see to the things that I should really have been helping with in the first place.

"Good," I said, giving him an approving nod. "And I'm sorry for putting so much on you."

"It's okay," he announced with a modest shrug. "Thankfully, all the cadet courses are canceled for the remainder of the Tourney, so I have a lot more free time to get more done."

I winced. Even though I needed our other objectives met, I needed Quess tomorrow, and for the rest of the Tourney, to keep an eye out and search for anyone who seemed to be overly interested in us. If we could identify them, I hoped we could identify whether they were working for someone—and who.

Quess noticed my expression, and sighed theatrically. "What do you need me to do?"

I gave him an apologetic look. "I'm going to need you in the crowds tomorrow during the qualifiers. More specifically, I want you up in the rafters. Keep an eye out for anyone who keeps showing up where we are, or seems like they're following us. If you see anyone suspicious, take their picture and we'll give it to Ambrose later, to send to Lacey."

He considered it for a second, and then nodded. "All right."

"What about me?" Tian chirped, wiping chocolate off her face with the back of her arm. "Am I in the crowd as the smallest super spy ever? Or... S.S.S., as I like to call it." She hissed the sound "ssssss", making me smile.

"You're letting a child be a spy?" Leo asked, cocking his head at me and spearing me with a curious look. "Fascinating, but not altogether unprecedented."

"I'm actually not," I corrected him with a laugh. "Tian, you have your own super-secret mission, remember?"

She sighed, her shoulders slumping. "I know, but every place I go, nothing is speaking to me! Cogstown and Water Treatment are both being quiet, and I don't know why. Although, I might have heard some humming by the hydro turbines yesterday. Maybe there's something tucked up underneath—"

"Absolutely not," Quess said, setting his mug down with a *thunk*. "Sorry, Tian, but you stay away from the hydro turbines. Promise me, right now."

Tian immediately looked contrite. "I promise," she said, sounding two parts mystified and one part scared.

"Thank you," Quess breathed, sounding clearly relieved, and I couldn't blame him. Even my own heart had lurched sideways at the thought of Tian doing something as dangerous as trying to navigate the hydro turbines. The massive machines sucked in hundreds of gallons of water from the river outside, and had thousands of working parts that she could get caught in or fall from... There was no way any of us were letting her take that risk.

Luckily, Quess was proving to be an excellent guardian for her, so I didn't need to be overly concerned.

"Well, keep looking, Tian," I said gently. "I'm sure you'll find us a really good place for our new home, but just remember —Quess and Grey aren't the best lashers."

She seemed to think about that for a long moment. "Right," she breathed. "That changes things. Hm."

I could see the gears in her head whirling, but didn't pry. Quess and Maddox both had faith in Tian's ability to find tucked away and hidden rooms around the Tower, and I trusted them—and her.

"Okay, well, I think that pretty much takes care of everything," I said. "We should use whatever time we can to train."

Quess nodded and hit the button on his device, shutting off the field it was generating. Leo and I stood, bade quick goodbyes to Tian and Quess, and then stepped into the hall to leave them to finish their check. They were also going to babysit both apartments, to make sure no one tried to access them while we were gone.

Outside, I started to cross the hall toward Ambrose's apartment, but Leo reached out and grabbed my forearm in a firm grip. I looked over my shoulder at him and then pivoted. "What is it?" I asked.

"Has there been any word from your brother yet about Scipio?" he asked.

He looked at me with hopeful eyes, and I felt bad that I didn't have anything for him, but there hadn't been a peep from Alex.

"Nothing yet," I said softly, and immediately put a hand on his shoulder when he seemed to droop. "I'm sure it's just taking some time because Alex is being cautious," I said, in an attempt to soothe him. "And don't forget—I want to find Jasper, too."

"For your Paragon?" he asked, and there was a touch of bitterness in his voice.

"No," I said, shaking my head. It was more than that. Jasper had saved my life, and helped me save my best friend from a fate that was literally death, and I owed him for that. "He's my friend," I finally explained, and Leo shot me a tremulous smile.

We stood there for a second or two, not talking, and when it started to border on awkward, I cleared my throat and pointed to Ambrose's door.

"Shall we?" I asked. "It's time for us to go train with Ambrose and Maddox."

Leo looked at it with a slightly haunted expression, and then nodded. "Let's go," he replied.

16

A yawn cracked my face, causing me to shut my eyes as it overtook me. It felt like forever before it passed, and once it did, my eyes were watering slightly from the force of it. I shook my head, trying to knock the morning's residual sleepiness out of my skull, and looked around.

It was early, but there was already a steady stream of people moving from the halls into the entrances of the Salles. We stood just beyond the lines, back behind a mobile partition that had the words *Competitors Only* on the side.

I was leaning against the wall, Maddox beside me, watching Ambrose and Leo. They were at the official's desk, seated just below one of the many statues that lined the high walls of the hallway. Metal sconces ran between the statues, emitting warm yellow light that reached all the way up to the ceiling, illuminating all of the figures.

I kept my eyes on Ambrose and Leo, though, watching as the

woman behind the desk handed Ambrose a plastic sheet. The two men moved a few feet away, and I tapped Maddox on the wrist and pointed over at them.

She nodded, and together we began to push through the crowds of people waiting in line to receive their schedules. Through the door just behind them, I could already hear cheering and the sounds of battle, but I had no idea what was happening to elicit such an excited response.

Maddox and I came to a stop right in front of where the two men were waiting, just on one side of the door.

"What's our schedule?" I asked, nodding at the plastic film, which displayed a digital readout of the times and places we were to report to. Ambrose held it firmly between two fingers and studied the digital display for a second, his eyes going over the glowing letters.

"Hand-to-hand is first," he said. He checked the clock on his indicator and narrowed his eyes. "We need to be at ring twenty-one in fifteen minutes."

"There's plenty of time," I said, noting the urgency in his voice. "Relax. We're right on time for the plan anyway, remember?"

That seemed to settle him some, and he handed the film off to me and headed for the door. We all moved into position around him, but I lagged a few steps behind, going over the details for our events. After hand-to-hand, we had to report immediately to the baton qualifiers. On the one hand, that was good—it meant we got two events over and done, and saved ourselves traveling time. But it also meant more time out in the arena... which meant more exposure to anyone working against us.

With that thought, I picked up my pace and tucked in closer behind Ambrose.

The wide oval doors spread open as we passed, and I looked around to see what had changed since yesterday. Stadium-style seating that folded into the walls was now fully drawn out, creating a half circle around the arena. Several people in different-colored uniforms were sitting on the seats, watching the events. Some were grouped together, some sat by themselves—but they were all watching the space below, or the screen on the wall behind it.

The area around the bleachers had been cleared of all equipment, and now contained several fighting rings, which were laid out in a grid. Five rows of five rings, all separated by walking spaces in between. Over each ring, robotic drones recorded and transmitted the fights, which were broadcast on the screen that took up a large portion of the recently erected wall that cut the arena itself in half. Over half now, in fact; the space had been reduced even further to accommodate whatever construction was happening on the other side. By tomorrow, the rings would be gone, the remaining space used for whatever the first challenge was.

A fight was being displayed on the biggest screen now, and to my surprise, I saw it was Dylan's hand-to-hand qualifier. The curvy young woman was in the process of flipping another Knight neatly over her back and unceremoniously onto his. She snapped a quick punch to his face before mule kicking another opponent rushing her from behind. He went flying backward, offscreen, and she straightened, taking a moment to brush her hair back. The drone grew close, and her face became larger on the screen. She was in the process of scanning the arena when she saw it watching her. She grinned, an attractive dimple forming in her cheek, and gave a two-fingered salute before running offscreen. The camera changed right afterward, to another fight in another ring, and I looked away.

Dylan had seemed so self-assured and confident, even when she smiled and saluted the camera. For me, the prospect of being recorded and displayed for everyone to see was slightly unnerving, but being shown on the screen was a way of garnering supporters, as it meant you were worth paying attention to.

And clearly, Dylan was worth paying attention to. The file Lacey had gotten with Dylan's records painted an interesting picture. Apparently, her parents had died—first her mother, of Whispers, when she was young, and then her father later, in some sort of electrical fire. She was Cog-bred, but after her father died, she was cared for by her closest living relative—her aunt. Her aunt was Cog-bred, but had transferred to the Knights when she was fifteen, and had earned retirement after her hand was smashed in an unfortunate accident in the plunge.

Dylan and her aunt still lived together, with Dylan now caring for her, which was rare. Most Knights who suffered some sort of functional disfigurement chose to transfer departments, because they felt ashamed that they were unable to serve the Tower. If they weren't able to transfer, or to find some new purpose helping the Tower, they eventually began dropping in rank, until they were forced to receive the Medica's intervention services. Family would typically abandon them long before that point, so the fact that Dylan was still residing with her aunt, and had been for several years, spoke a great deal to her character, in my mind.

Everything else in Lacey's report showed that she was, at the very least, a good Knight. Her record was exemplary, and her instructor reviews practically glowed with adulation for her bravery and dutiful nature to the Tower. Lacey's search had gone deep, but there was no evidence of her being a legacy—or ever working with a legacy.

I thought about Dylan as we wound our way down the ramp that led into the open space of the arena and through the aisles, and watched the numbers displayed on the blue-static walls of the fence keeping fighters inside. Her nebulous legacy status aside, all signs pointed to the fact that she would make a good Champion, and I once again felt a moment of doubt about what we were doing.

We came to a stop just as I was reminding myself that we had no choice, and I looked up to see the number twenty-one floating on a static shield around a ring. The fence was much taller than normal, the four metal posts that generated it standing at least ten feet high from where they slid out of the floor.

In the ring, a team was in the process of pummeling each other with their fists. It was clear by the complete and utter pandemonium inside the ring that the style randomly selected for them was Last Man Standing.

For all of the hand-to-hand matches, there would be a style or objective picked by a program for the candidates to ensure that they were able to adapt to all challenges they might face. Last Man Standing was literally that: they fought until only one person remained, using a three-hit elimination system. Others, like King of the Hill, were a time trial, where you had to oust your opponent from their position, and then hold it for a certain period of time, defending your own position against the other team. Protect the Specialist was the one I most dreaded, as it came with the biggest liability in one of the team events—one person acting as the target while the others tried to keep them safe.

"You okay?" I looked over to see Maddox giving me a curious look, but there wasn't any time to respond. The match that had been taking place inside the ring suddenly finished, with the participants leaving the field through an open slot in the static field, and we were being ushered through another opening opposite theirs.

Ambrose was waving at me, while four tall men streamed by him, entering the ring. They were clearly our opponents, and according to the film in my hand, their leader was a man by the name of Kody Tellerman. I clicked his name, and his information appeared, displaying a picture of a sandy-haired man with olive eyes and a crooked grin. His rank was a lowly Knight, but he was two years older than me. His test rankings were displayed next to his picture, along with a list of deeds that culminated in leading a fire response team to a fire that happened on Greenery 11.

I tucked the film away and followed Maddox into the ring, the shield dropping in place behind me with a sharp *zzt* sound that made the skin at the nape of my neck crawl. I shook it off and eyed Kody as we walked up, taking him in. Truthfully, I wasn't intimidated by his records or test scores—but I wasn't about to let my guard down, either. He was lean, with limbs that seemed slightly too long for his torso, but he held himself confidently.

Both he and Ambrose stepped forward to meet the official in the center of the ring. He was holding something in the palm of his hand, and as they approached, he gave them a slow nod, indicating that they should do something. I couldn't see what they did, but words began to scroll from top to bottom on the blue surface of the static fence. At first, they were too fast to read, but then they gradually slowed, coming to a stop and settling on one: Protect the Specialist.

I suppressed a groan. One player on each team was designated the specialist, while the remaining three were the escorts. The escorts' job was to protect the specialist. Each escort was eliminated if they sustained three direct blows to the torso, but if the specialist was hit once, the entire game was over.

Like I said, huge liability.

Luckily, we'd taken a good portion of yesterday training for this, and we had a plan in place.

"Who will be the specialist for your team?" the official asked Ambrose.

Ambrose gave a heavy sigh. "I will be," he announced.

I knew that was hard for him to say. He hadn't been happy

about it yesterday, either, but he had agreed to it. Still, I was glad he had kept his word, and I recognized the gesture he was making by means of the sacrifice. The specialist was not who you wanted to be if you wanted to shine for the masses, but it was the safest place for him.

The official gave him a look of surprise, and then handed him a white patch, which Ambrose pressed down over his heart, marking himself as the specialist. "And you, Knight Tellerman?"

Kody studied Ambrose for a second, a bemused smile on his lips. "Same," he announced arrogantly. This only made the official more confused—and had a similar effect on me.

"What's wrong?" Maddox asked, leaning closer to me.

I stared at Kody for a second more as he pressed his own blue patch on, wondering why he had chosen the position. It was the least desirable spot on a team if you wanted any sort of glory.

"I'm not sure, but keep your guard up," I replied, trusting my instincts, which said that he was up to something.

There was a huff beside me, and I turned to find Leo rolling his eyes, a dry smile on his face. I blinked, surprised by his reaction, and then cocked my head.

"When did you start doing that?" I asked.

"I..." Leo frowned. "I think that was the first time." He looked at me excitedly, his expression boy-like. "I was trying to express my feelings on how silly your statement was, as this is a fight, and our guards will inevitably be up. Did I do it right?"

I faltered, uncertain how to answer his question. "Yes?" I said, looking at Maddox. She gave me a wary and alarmed look, and I got the sense she didn't want to touch this either. "Sorry, Leo, I'm not sure how to render judgment on an eye roll." I hesitated, going over his words in my head for another second, and then added, "I will say that it was a lot to unpack with just one expression, so maybe try a sarcastic statement? There was a lot of nuance there that was lost."

He accepted my answer with a smile, his pleasure at this new learning experience obvious. I found myself smiling as well, taking part in his simple joy at learning how to express more complex behaviors. It was amazing how fast he was learning and changing.

Amazing and a little endearing. And concerning. What happened if Leo *liked* feeling things like this? What if he liked having a body? What would I do then? What *could* I do then?

I shook off the line of questions, and with it the deep pit of anxiety that had started churning in my stomach, and returned my mind to the matter at hand. Ambrose was now standing next to us again, while the official in the ring gave us the traditional speech of what was and wasn't permissible. I glanced over at Ambrose, who was wedged between Leo and me.

"Thank you," I said softly. "I know this isn't where you want to be."

"Let's just try to end it quickly," he breathed, tugging on his sleeves and staring straight ahead. "And if you can, leave their specialist for me."

I sucked in a deep breath, digging for patience. A part of me wanted to remind him that wasn't a good idea, especially with Kody acting so confident while taking the specialist position, but

I held back. This was my compromise to him, and I had to show him I was going to have his back.

"Of course."

The official wrapped up his speech with a nod and wishes of good luck to both teams, and my eyes turned to the opposite team. All four of the men on the team had similar smiles on their faces, as if they shared some secret that we didn't know about. I sucked in a deep breath, trying to calm my nerves.

"Form up," I said, taking a step forward. The buzzer hadn't gone off yet, but I wasn't attacking, and there was nothing in the rules to prevent us from getting into position. I heard everyone moving to flank me while Ambrose shifted behind me, but kept my eyes on the opposite team. A clock appeared on the wall behind them and started to count down from ten, but still they didn't move.

10... 9... 8...

I waited, watching the clock tick down and studying them. They were all standing in a straight line, with Kody in the middle. It wasn't the safest position, or the smartest, but they continued to stand there as the clock wound down.

6... 5... 4...

Overhead, I heard the whir of the drones, and I was momentarily distracted by two of them hovering a few feet apart on either side of the ring, their round bases swiveling around to rotate the camera views. A quick glance at the screen showed them locked in on me, and I realized that my presence on Ambrose's team alone was enough to broadcast.

Everyone wanted to see me in action.

A sudden scrambling sound across from me jolted me from the screen, and I quickly looked back to see the other team already moving, even though the clock was still at two. I tensed for their charge, knowing that they would be on us when the clock turned to zero.

2... 1... 0...

It took me those precious seconds to realize they weren't attacking, which only baffled me more, and I remained rooted to the spot, trying to understand what they were doing.

One was on his hands and knees in front of Kody, forming a table, the second settling into a low squat in front of him. The third was just stepping into place in front of him, guided by some unknown signal, and giving me a broad and open smile.

I gaped at their strange line, alarm making my spine tingle. I had never seen anything like this before, and I couldn't fathom what—

"They're making steps," Leo said from my right, and I realized that he was right.

I had a split second to make a decision, and I turned and charged at Ambrose, shoving him back several feet when I reached him. A shadow loomed behind me, and I twisted around just in time for Kody's hands to hit my shoulder, grabbing me hard and pushing me to the ground.

I managed to get one of my legs up and plant a foot on his thigh, my muscles working from memory and instinct alone, and I dropped my hips lower, surrendering to the momentum of his impact. My rear hit the ground, and I pushed with my leg, heaving him over my head.

He pulled me along with him, his grip on my uniform and my own momentum in the throw working for me. I landed, straddling his hips, and drew back my fist. I had a moment to register his brows drawing together in confusion before I hit him, a sharp rap across the jaw, and I stood up, barely even winded. I stared at him, and then looked back up at his friends, my brows drawn together.

Tension flooded my senses as the adrenaline began to hit me, and it took me a moment to realize that I had just ended the fight. It was surreal how quickly it had happened. I felt certain that this was a trick, that they had changed patches, or that I was missing something—but nobody on his team moved.

"Is that... Is that it?" I asked, looking down at Kody.

He coughed and sat up, looking rather chagrined. "We thought you wouldn't expect it if our specialist went after your specialist first," he admitted. I cocked my head at him, and then held out my hand, offering to help him up.

He accepted, and I pulled him to his feet. "No offense, but that was a dumb plan," I told him.

Kody gave me a smile and a nod, taking a moment to shake my hand before dropping it. "I think I've come to realize that," he said with a laugh.

He moved off to rejoin his team, and I shook my head. "That was anti-climactic," Maddox huffed. "I didn't even get to hit anyone."

"No," Ambrose said, his voice tight. I looked at him, saw him struggling to hold back some anger, and immediately felt bad when I realized he felt robbed of the opportunity to prove himself.

He looked away, and his expression grew even darker when he looked up at the screens. Heart in my throat, I looked up, and winced when I saw the video replaying my quick and easy defeat of Kody. The words that were scrolling underneath only worsened it.

Liana "Honorbound" Castell faces off with team leader Ambrose Klein with a stunning ten-second knockout. Could she be making a play for Champion?

I returned my gaze to Ambrose, who was shaking his head, his mouth a hard, angry slash across his lips.

"Ambrose, I'm sorry," I started, hating that I'd thrown our agreement into jeopardy. "I didn't mean to—"

"We should go," he said, cutting me off smoothly. "We don't want to be late for the next match."

I watched him go, my explanation dying on my lips.

"It was an accident," Maddox said a heartbeat later, her hand reaching up to pat my shoulder. "He'll get over it."

I shook my head and gave a heavy sigh, extremely doubtful that he would. This peace between us had been hard enough to establish, and we'd barely maintained it for twenty-four hours.

And in just under ten seconds, I might have smashed it all to pieces—which didn't bode well for the next two qualifiers.

Fan-freaking-tastic.

"Let's go," I muttered, deciding that if I wanted to fix it, I was going to have to make it up to him in one of the other matches.

Maddox, Leo, and I had to jog to catch up with Ambrose's stiff march, and when we did, I once again settled in the rear, giving Ambrose a little space to cool off.

Even though it was morning, lines were already beginning to form around the rings, and I cringed as a few groups lounging on the sides gave me congratulatory smiles and thumbs-up signs. A few of them offered a respectful nod, accompanied by a murmured, "Honorbound," and I suddenly wished I could melt through the floor. Or find the person who thought calling me Honorbound was clever. It wasn't. I hated it.

The scrutiny and attention was uncomfortable, both person-ally and for Ambrose's sake, and I was half tempted to break off from the group and pick another route to the next ring. I didn't, though, unwilling to risk Ambrose's safety in exchange for his ego, and instead just kept my head down, trying to ignore it.

We arrived at the ring in short order, and Ambrose checked

in with the official while we stood off to one side, waiting. I could hear the *clack-clack-zzt* sounds of the batons, but they were mostly lost among the noise as I simmered, wondering how I could make the previous challenge up to Ambrose.

He rejoined us long before I came to an answer. "We're next," he announced gruffly.

He led us over to the official, and we stood peering through the blue fence, watching the match inside. Nobody spoke.

A part of me felt like I should try to say something, to explain that I really hadn't meant for any of that to happen, that I'd just reacted, but it wasn't the time or the place, so I remained mute, staring blankly at the match inside.

"So how do those silver eggs work?" Maddox asked suddenly after some time had passed, and I blinked, looking at her.

The silver eggs she was referring to were unique to the baton qualifier. Unlike hand-to-hand, there was only one objective in this contest: hit your opponent more times than they hit you. The egg you held was a tool to measure the impact of the electrical current delivered to your body.

The reasoning behind it was simple: with batons, it wasn't just about hitting your opponent, but also delivering as much charge as possible. It was actually much easier to miss than one might think—only a ring about one inch wide at the top of the baton delivered the charge. If it didn't fully connect when you hit, it didn't deliver the full charge.

Baton qualification focused on precision with your hits, which was where the eggs came in.

I opened my mouth to answer her question, but to my

surprise, Ambrose beat me to it. "Your body conducts electricity when you are hit, and the egg absorbs it through you, to measure how much of the voltage actually hit you. The electricity is used to turn the small gears inside, which 'hatches' the egg, giving you a visual aid to show you how close you are to being eliminated. Once the chick cheeps, you have absorbed the maximum amount of electricity you can safely absorb, and are eliminated."

"I knew that last part," Maddox grumbled, folding her arms across her chest. "But thank you for explaining about the egg."

He nodded, just once, his eyes never leaving the fighting in the ring.

I stared at him for a second. I had been worried about how his anger at me was going to affect our teamwork in the next qualifier. Instead, he impressed me—even though he was angry about the last match, he had put it aside for the good of the team. It was the first genuine act of leadership I had seen from him.

My eyes returned to the fight in the ring in time to see it end with one man displaying the silver chick cupped in his hand to his opponent, signaling his defeat.

Ambrose turned and moved over to the official, and we all followed. One by one, the official handed us our batons and eggs. This was designed to prevent any tampering. The voltage for the batons was adjustable, and for the qualifier, they were adjusted so that we could actually make an exhibition of skills. Typically, when we used them in the field, we set them to render a target unconscious. Officials programmed them for a match with a set number, but there were a lot of them floating around, so it was always good to double check.

So I performed a quick test on them anyway, sliding each baton into the sleek black voltage analyzer available just for this reason, and expending a charge. The voltage was immediately displayed in cool blue numbers, and I nodded when it matched the number listed on the stat screen on the wall behind the official.

The team that had just been defeated was now filing out through a gap in the screen, and when I looked through it, I noticed an identical opening on the other side. Apparently they had set up two check-in points on the baton qualifiers, to make it easier to hand out equipment.

We waited for the team to pass and then moved inside, following the official. In the middle, the official went over the rules and safety speech, reiterating multiple times that solid baton contact should not last longer than three seconds, as it would result in the scores being docked, and that dropping the egg meant instant elimination. I tuned him out at a certain point, my eyes assessing the other team.

There were two men and two women, none of them people I recognized. They were all fit, like most Knights, and held their batons with an easy grace that gave me the impression that they knew how to use them.

I tightened my grip on my egg, tensing as the official left the ring. The countdown popped up on the blue fence, starting from ten, and I looked back to make sure everyone was ready before returning my eyes to the group in front of me.

"Stay close together," I reminded everyone softly, referencing our practice yesterday. We hadn't had time to formulate any sort of a strategy, so we were relying heavily on keeping our enemies close around us, so that we could help each other if needed. It wasn't much of a plan, but going over all of the hand-to-hand qualifier rules had taken a good portion of the time we had.

Nobody said anything, but then again, nobody had to; I knew they had heard me.

3... 2... 1... The buzzer sounded, and I tensed, waiting.

Our opponents didn't race toward us, but spread out, approaching us in a slow, cautious walk. I held my ground, watching as two of them drew nearer, eyeing me.

I waited until they were just outside of my swing, and then took a confident step forward and angled toward the one on the left. His eyes widened a fraction in surprise when I didn't even attempt to hit him with the baton. Instead, I went low and slammed my shoulder into his chest, spreading my legs wide to absorb the force of the impact and knocking him back a few feet.

I didn't even watch to see if he fell. Instead, I turned my focus to the girl who had been standing next to him and jumped back far enough to avoid her baton swing. I brought the tip of my own baton up, under her arms, and tagged her in the stomach. It was a glancing blow, barely even a second, but I heard clicks coming from her hand as she stumbled away, signaling that I had at least started the process of "hatching" her egg.

A shadow passed over my vision, then, and I stepped back and ducked right—just under the arm of the man I had hit first. Apparently he hadn't fallen, and was anticipating my evasive maneuver, because he snuck his baton up under my guard and jammed it hard against my ribcage as I attempted to pivot away.

Pain snaked out from the spot, like tongues of fire lashing against the skin, and my breath exploded from my lungs. My muscles involuntarily locked in place as the current held me fast. In my hand, the hard, smooth surface of the egg began to slide and move, but I couldn't even look at it. I was rooted to the spot.

A second later the current shut off and I sagged, panting slightly. I quickly looked up, anticipating another attack, but to my surprise, I saw that Ambrose had pushed the guy off me and was now fighting with him. Their batons crackled and threw sparks as they impacted each other, and I winced at the bright flares.

A quick check around me told me I was free, for the moment, but Maddox was in trouble, with two of the other team's members on her, and I quickly moved over to her, slipping around where Ambrose and the other man were deflecting each other's blows in an attempt to flank at least one of her attackers.

I kept an eye on her as I crept, watching as she deflected their blows with efficient speed, waiting for an opportunity. It came a second later, when the one I was standing behind landed a hit on Maddox's shoulder—and everyone froze.

I charged, my legs pumping and my breath coming in pants, and drove my baton into Maddox's attacker, stepping around him and using my other arm to knock his arm away from Maddox.

Maddox stumbled back, shaking her head, and lifted her

baton to block the incoming blow from the second attacker. I turned my back on them for a second to break the contact with my opponent, remembering that I was only supposed to hold it there for three seconds, and took a step back to allow him to regain his feet.

He took a moment to get situated and check his egg, which was now showing a simple crack. I stopped to check mine as well, and frowned when I realized that the crack on my egg was double the size of his. The top of my egg was split wide open, revealing the head of the chick inside.

I took a step back and looked up at Maddox, focusing on the egg in her hand. Hers was like mine—spread wide open—while her opponent's only had a thin crack, similar to the one his teammate had.

The voltage on their batons was set too high, I realized. It had to be, for our eggs to have registered so much damage already. I looked back at my opponent. There must have been a mistake. One of the officials had just calibrated their batons incorrectly. They would signal the referee so we could restart the match and...

The man opposite me looked down at the egg in my hand, a satisfied smile splitting his lips wide open, and he whirled the baton once in his hand, his expression eager. I realized immediately that he *knew* something was off—and that he had no intention of doing the honorable thing. He was going to try to end it.

But surely he would predict that we would contest the results and request an inquiry after the match was finished. That would cast a shadow over his team's victory, especially if the inquiry revealed that they had been dishonest. It could even result in their elimination.

So why were they taking such a risk? What was going on here?

The man across from me continued to smile, swinging his baton around and eyeing me speculatively, and I tensed, waiting for some sort of attack. But for several seconds, he didn't move, just stood there waiting. I took a hesitant step toward him, trying to figure out what sort of game he was playing, and to my surprise, he took a step back to match me. Frowning, I moved forward another pace, and again he dropped back, this time glancing up.

I paused, puzzled by his actions, and followed his gaze—and immediately saw a drone floating just feet away, watching us. Beyond it, a second drone hovered over Maddox, projecting the action between her and her competitor overhead. She kept pressing her attack, but the girl she was up against moved like water, easily deflecting Maddox's blows.

I turned back to him to find the man watching me, and narrowed my eyes. Something was going on here, and I couldn't quite figure out what it was. My opponent was waiting for something—and it had something to do with the drones that were watching us.

I glanced at the egg in my hand, and suddenly it came to me: they were waiting for the drones to focus somewhere else so they could hit us with their super-charged batons and hatch the eggs faster. The officials couldn't see the eggs, cupped in our hands as they were, and relied on the drones to make sure that all participants were behaving honorably. But there were only so many drones to go around. So they waited for the drones to move to something more interesting—while trying to pull us away from our teammates, scattering any chance we had of helping each other.

Instinctively, I took a step back. My opponent immediately frowned and took a step forward. I stopped moving for a second and watched him, my heartbeat pounding hard against my ribs.

And then, without any warning or second thought, I shouted, "Form up on me," and began jogging backward, away from my opponent. He lunged, but I was ready for it, and I brought my baton up and stepped to the side, letting him rush past me, and then turned and brought my baton neatly down on his other wrist.

There was a sharp crack, followed by his cry of pain, and the egg he was cradling dropped to the ground with a click as he fell to the other side, clutching his now-broken wrist to his chest. A ding went off, signaling that he had been eliminated.

I ignored it all, but latched onto the idea and the opportunity it presented: namely, a way of winning. The *only* way of winning, with those batons they were using.

I moved over to Maddox, who was trying to disengage from her opponent. The woman was now viciously pressing forward in her attack, openly trying to land a hit.

"Knock the eggs out of their hands!" I shouted, and Maddox did just that, parrying two blows and then using her baton to sweep the egg right out of the girl's palm.

It clattered to the floor, and I turned, my eyes seeking

Ambrose and Leo. To my surprise, Ambrose was still standing, and fighting hard to keep his opponent off of him. Next to him, Leo was using his leg to push his assailant back, and then landed a hit to his opponent's thigh.

There was a repetitive cheeping sound, and Leo immediately withdrew the baton. His opponent sagged, and opened his hand to reveal the now-hatched chick moving jerkily in his hand, fluttering its little wings in slow, exaggerated motions. Leo's egg, held flat in the palm of his hand, was completely untouched, smooth and perfect. He still hadn't even been hit.

I focused on Ambrose's opponent, but grabbed Maddox, holding her back. "Wait," I said, holding my hand up to stop Leo. "Ambrose, the egg! Go for the egg!"

If Ambrose heard me, I didn't know; his focus was completely on the fight in front of him, which was admirable. His strength, however, was fading fast. I looked at his cupped hand, trying to see how many blows he had left. By deciding to knock their eggs out of their hands, I had also gambled with our chances of qualifying, as baton scoring was about the number of blows you managed to make against an enemy team, both accurately and efficiently. While knocking the eggs from their hands was a viable strategy, and eliminated them, it would only rank us highly in accuracy. If we could knock them all out with our team intact, however, we would be awarded special points at the end of the match.

My conflict evaporated under that thought, and I rushed to help Ambrose, even though I knew he didn't want it. A moment later he *did* need it, as his opponent caught a wild blow delivered by Ambrose, and then pivoted and brought both his baton and Ambrose's down, slamming them both into Ambrose's thigh.

As the current ripped through him, his hand flattened some, displaying the egg. I caught the fine details of the silver chick's feathers as I surged forward, and a shout erupted from my throat, drawing our opponent's attention.

As I hoped, he quickly broke off and moved back a few steps, his gaze wary. I came up beside Ambrose and offered him a hand to help him up. To my surprise, he took it.

As I pulled him up, I stepped in close and said, "Tell Maddox and Leo to press the attack, and then use the distraction they provide to knock his egg out of his hand, okay?"

Ambrose took a step back, his eyebrows drawing together in reflection of his surprise, but I just nodded at the fight and pushed him toward it.

I fell in behind him, baton at the ready, hiding my smile as he took my advice.

"Maddox! Leo!" he shouted, and my two friends immediately threw themselves forward, their batons flying. The man opposite them valiantly held his own for a second, but then Ambrose was there, his baton smacking down hard on his left hand.

The silver egg fell to the floor with a sharp, metallic ting. I heard cheers start and exhaled, relaxing slightly—but not entirely.

My eyes returned to the man who had been trying to lure me away, finding the baton still gripped loosely in his hand. Then he and his teammates hurried away, and I watched as they traded in their weapons and disappeared into the crowd, leaving me to wonder.

Were they leaving so quickly because they were embarrassed that they couldn't win, even with more powerful batons? Or was it because they had somehow found a way to cheat—and didn't want to be questioned about it?

I wasn't certain, but I had to assume the latter until I knew otherwise. Which meant... either one of them was a legacy, or they were working with someone who was.

We exited the ring and walked down the open aisles, heading for the ramp that led to the halls. Everyone was in high spirits after our victory, Ambrose especially, but I couldn't join in, the problem with the batons weighing heavily in my mind. A part of me wanted to report the infraction, but since we won, there was a risk the move would backfire on us with the crowds—something I was sure Ambrose desperately wanted to avoid.

And the more I thought about it, the more reporting them seemed like a bad idea. For one thing, if they were working with anyone, then shining a light on them would only cause whoever they were working with to go even deeper into the shadows.

And I *was* fairly sure that they were working with someone, based on what I had witnessed with the batons, and the fact that more than one of them had been set to a higher voltage—something that shouldn't have been possible.

Batons were handled by officials, and handed out randomly. Every hour, they were exchanged for new ones, drawn at random from a sack. The officials were changed out just as often, their new rings determined by a randomization program. Trying to set up any sort of swap for a more powerful baton would have been extremely difficult with all of those moving parts in play.

Which meant a conspiracy, and a well-coordinated one at that.

A chill raced over my spine as I suddenly felt both vulnerable and exposed, and I picked up the pace, closing the distance that had grown between myself and the others while I had been deep in thought. Whoever it was had been working to eliminate us, and now that the plan had failed, they were going to try again.

My mind spun, trying to think. If I wanted to keep Ambrose safe, then finding out who was working against us was the fastest way to do that. If I reported the other team to the officials, I could lose that chance, possibly forever. Now that I hadn't, they might assume I just chalked it up to a team desperately trying to win no matter what. Which meant there was a chance that team could lead us back to whoever was pulling their strings.

Quess was the best way of accomplishing that. Now that our match was over, he was going to be waiting for us by the door out of the arena, specifically for something like this. I began to walk even faster, spurred by the idea of sending him after the enemy team we had been up against as soon as possible.

Maddox and Leo both made surprised sounds when I brushed by them, but I didn't want to waste time explaining.

Ambrose, who was ahead of them, looked back and saw me approaching him, and for some inexplicable reason, turned around and blocked my path, bringing me to a halt.

"Excuse me," I said, angling to pass him. I wasn't sure what he wanted, and I was too focused on finding Quess and his white-blond hair to pay any attention.

"Liana." He reached out and grabbed my arm, and I stopped. Twisting around, I saw his pensive gaze, and realized that he wanted to thank me for helping him look good for the cameras. But I just didn't have the patience right then.

"Look, can it wait?" I asked. "I need to go grab Quess to see if he can track down the team we just fought. I think they might have been cheating, and I want to see if they are working for anybody."

"Cheating?" he said, his brows drawing together. "What do you mean?"

I pulled my arm from his hand and righted myself. "Look, I don't want to have to explain it twice, all right? So let's just get to Quess."

He gave me a dubious look, but nodded and fell in line, letting me take point. I felt a small amount of relief that he was at least talking to me again, and then put it aside, focused on reaching Quess.

We emerged from the final row of rings and quickly angled ourselves for the ramp that led to the exit. Several people were milling around, and someone I recognized as one of Ambrose's friends shouted his name and waved him over.

"Hey, do you mind if I..." Ambrose trailed off when I looked at him sharply, a flash of self-doubt flickering across his face.

"No," I said immediately, realizing that my stress was beginning to affect me more and more. I hadn't meant to look at him like that. "I'm sorry. Of course I don't mind. Just take Maddox or Leo with you."

I glanced over my shoulder at Maddox and Leo with pleading eyes.

"I got it," Maddox volunteered graciously. I shot her a grateful look. She turned and ran to keep up, and then I turned my gaze around, searching for Quess.

I spotted him standing to one side with his back to the wall, his hands shoved in his pockets, his head down. I angled for him, but moved slowly, looking more toward Ambrose than at Quess, and taking a few minutes to meander through the crowds before casually moving over to the wall a few feet from Quess and leaning my back on it.

"Pretend like you're talking to me," I told Leo, angling my head toward him. "Quess, can you hear me okay?"

"Yes, ma'am," he replied. "I didn't notice anyone following you, but what was up with those batons?"

"You noticed?" I asked, smiling at Leo.

"I did. I've been watching the matches for hours, and I had the eagle's eye view from up top. I saw that your eggs were hatching much faster than the others."

"Do you think they increased the voltage?" Leo asked, his face quizzical. "I thought there were precautionary measures in place to prevent that."

"There are," I replied. "But at least three out of four of their batons were all on higher settings, which isn't coincidence. The only reason I don't know about the fourth is because the guy you were fighting never hit you. They found a way to cheat the system."

"Why not report it to an official?" Quess asked from behind me. It was hard not to turn around and look at him, but I was trying to preserve his anonymity. It was vital to keeping him off the radar that had zeroed in on Maddox, Leo, Ambrose, and me. And it kept both him and Tian safe, and gave him a little more leeway for helping us. The disguises were helping, but I didn't want him to find a new one unless absolutely necessary.

"Because we won, for one thing, and sometimes these complaints can come off as wasting time or trying to draw attention to yourself in an attempt to bolster your popularity," I told him. "It's better not to risk that, for Ambrose's sake. But there's also the added fact that if they are part of a conspiracy, I don't want to tip anyone off that we're onto them or suspect anything other than they were just desperate to win. That gives us time to find out what their motives were."

"So you want me to follow them and see who, if anyone, they are working for?" Quess asked, and I nodded once before I realized he couldn't see me, since our backs were to each other.

"Yes, please."

I heard him moving behind me. "I'm on it, but before I go, your brother reached out to me. He's heading to your apartment right now, and he wants you to take Leo there for a meeting."

I absorbed the information with some surprise—and alarm.

My brother hadn't reached out to me since I'd contacted him with Leo a few days ago. Now he was reaching out to me through Quess? I wasn't sure what it meant, but I knew that we couldn't keep him waiting. Especially not with the eager look that was now gracing Grey's face, thanks to Leo's enthusiasm.

I hesitated and looked over at where Maddox was with Ambrose, standing just behind him. We were supposed to return to the apartment to have lunch now and wait for the next event, but with Alex heading there, clearly needing to talk to me about something important, and most likely Scipio related, plans had to change. We needed to be able to speak freely, and I couldn't do that while Ambrose was there.

But I couldn't leave him completely unprotected, either. My suspicions about the team we just faced were too fresh for me to even consider that. I'd have to come up with some explanation for the change of plans on the fly.

"Thanks, Quess," I said, genuinely grateful. "Be careful."

"Oh, believe me, I will," he replied.

I waited for more, but after a moment, Leo said, "He's gone."

I nodded and pushed off the wall, moving toward Maddox and Ambrose, a dozen or so excuses playing out in my mind to explain why we were deviating from the plan.

"Liana," Ambrose called as I drew within earshot range. I looked up to where he was standing with his friends, and was surprised to find them all looking at me. "My friends are insisting that I have to go to lunch with them, even though I told them I have plans."

All of my excuses died on my lips, and I took a moment to

consider the one that Ambrose had offered up on a silver platter. On the one hand, if they were going out to lunch, that
meant more exposure for Ambrose, increasing the danger. On
the other hand, if I handled it correctly, there would be zero
suspicion.

"Oh," I said, looking a little hesitant and giving myself a few
moments to find a suitable lie. "Look, I didn't want to say
anything, but one of the guys in the last fight got me good, and I
wanted to go to Medica to get it checked out before lunch." I
fidgeted slightly, and then sighed, making it seem like I was torn.
"Can Maddox go with you? She didn't eat breakfast this morning, and I know you want to make sure we're all at the top of our
game." I gave him a pointed look as I said this, and he flashed me
a genuine smile, catching on immediately.

"Of course she can," he said, and I exhaled slowly, glad he
hadn't fought me. "Just make sure you get patched up before
lashes. We need you at full strength."

I smiled back, pleased that he seemed to be coming around,
and watched him turn back to his friends. There was a rustle
beside me, and I looked over to see Maddox leaning toward me.

"You actually hurt, or did something come up?"

"It's Alex," I told her. "He's on his way to meet Leo and me
at our quarters right now."

"Is everything okay?" she asked, immediately concerned.

"I don't know," I replied honestly. "Do you think you can
watch Ambrose by yourself? I hate to ask, but if Alex has news
about Jasper..."

"I got him," she said with a smile. "Get out of here."

She didn't have to waste any more breath convincing me. I turned and left, Leo following close behind.

It took us only five minutes to get back to my apartment, and I could see Alex waiting for us by the door as we approached.

"Alex?" I said, concern radiating through me as I took in his appearance. His uniform was slightly wrinkled, his hair disheveled, and a beard was beginning to grace his face. "Are you okay?"

He gave me a look that said, *of course I'm not,* and then nodded toward the door, and I quickly activated the scanner and opened it, ushering him and Leo inside and then following before sealing us in.

"Okay, we're inside, and Quess and Tian tore this place apart looking for bugs yesterday," I said. "What's wrong?"

Alex gave me a withering look from the other side of the room, and then ran a hand through his hair. "In a word, everything! Everything is wrong, and nobody knows it!"

I frowned, my alarm growing as I realized he was on the edge of panic. I took a step closer to him, moving slowly so as not to startle him, and placed my hands on his shoulders.

"It's okay," I said soothingly. "Just tell me what's going on. Maybe I can help you."

He made an irritated sound and stepped away. "That's the *thing,* Liana. I don't think anyone can help us. Scipio isn't just being manipulated. He's *dying.*"

Dying? My eyes bulged, and I immediately looked at Leo to find him standing close, watching us. His jaw tightened and his eyes flashed, and he took a step closer.

"What do you mean?" he demanded, and my brother glanced at him, his eyes growing wide as he remembered that Leo was now inside of Grey, whom he'd only ever met once before.

"You're Leo?" he asked, his voice hushed and carrying a note of awe in it.

"And you are Alex Castell, and you've come here with information for us," Leo replied, his voice barely containing his impatience. "Now, what did you find out, and where is Jasper?"

My brother's face fell, and he ran a hand over it, looking suddenly very tired. "I found out that Executive Monroe downloaded Jasper's program onto her terminal," he replied after a pause. "I'm not sure what happened to him after that, but since the download, he has not been uploaded again. So there is a chance he is still on her terminal."

Onto Executive Monroe's terminal? I absorbed that information with no small amount of confusion. Why would she be interested in Jasper's program? Was it curiosity on her part, or did she recognize what he was? If it was the latter, what were her intentions toward him? What was she doing with him even now? The questions swirled around, but without any more information to go on, any guess would be purely speculative, and that was a waste of time.

Leo looked pensive as he absorbed the information. "I

imagine getting to it would be incredibly difficult?" he asked, turning to me, and I nodded, albeit reluctantly.

"It would right now," I replied. "With the Tourney, I mean. But afterward... we can look into it."

We had to do more than look into it. Jasper was the only one with the formula for Paragon—something we were going to need sooner rather than later. He was also my friend, and the fact that he was trapped on Sadie Monroe's terminal made me even more concerned for him. The woman did not have the sunniest of dispositions.

Even with my resolution to see it through, though, I wasn't completely blind to the danger going after him represented. If the Core was a fortress, then Executive Monroe's office had to be a safe—and one that I was guessing remained heavily guarded, given her proximity to Scipio. That meant a lot of obstacles to navigate, which wasn't going to be easy.

My answer seemed to satisfy Leo, however. "Very well. Now, what news is distressing you so, Mr. Castell?"

"'Mr. Castell'?" Alex grinned and shot me a look. "Maybe if he'd called me that before, I wouldn't have given you such a hard time about dating him," he said impishly.

I knew he didn't mean it, but I immediately looked away as my heart began to ache, reminding me all over again that Grey was gone.

"That was insensitive!" Leo bristled behind me, cutting through the pain and giving me pause. I turned to find him standing even closer to Alex, his face angry. "This isn't easy for Liana, and as her brother, you should recognize and be cognizant of that. Pointing out my differences from Grey, even in a joke, is in poor taste, and I think you should apologize to your sister."

"It's okay," I lied, trying to defuse the situation. "It really is. I know Alex didn't mean anything by it."

"No, but it still hurt you," Alex said sadly, and I gave him a tentative look.

"It's okay," I said firmly. My brother knew me well enough not to press, but I could tell that he wasn't satisfied with my response, and was now beginning to feel guilty. I scrambled to regain our conversation from before, not wanting Alex's innocent mistake to get in the way of his other news. "Now, what were you talking about earlier? How is Scipio dying?"

"It's worse than that," he said, agitated. "We all have these screens that are displayed on our computers at all times, showing Scipio's emotional state using these circles. But once I started digging into the code to find Jasper's AI, I realized that the entire screen was a lie. It's a dummy program that displays whatever the controller wants us to see! It isn't a reflection of Scipio's moods at all!"

He looked at us both as if we would understand what that meant, and while I wasn't certain about Leo, I was confident that *I* had no clue. "Okay," I said. "But I don't understand what that means."

"It means that someone has been hiding everything that's been done to him. And, Liana, it's a lot. Entire sections of his code have been completely cut away, replaced with ghost coding that fell apart with any sort of digging. Other parts of his code have been cannibalized, and from what I can tell from scans taken of him in the past, this new code is being used against him to strip away everything that makes him who and what he is! And now, the broken bits of code are acting like a cancer, and degrading his processes even more."

I blinked. This was a lot to wrap my head around, enough to make my head spin. "Alex, how do you know for certain? Could you be mistaken?"

He licked his lips and ran a hand through his hair. "Look, when you asked me to look into Scipio, I started digging, and at first it seemed like there was nothing wrong with him. His moods were within the right margins; his coding seemed clean. I kept searching for some sign of foreign coding, programming glitches, the works, and came up with absolutely nothing. It wasn't until I started examining the coding that made up the displays that I realized the truth: the displays themselves are lying. It's a ghost program meant to simulate that Scipio is functioning correctly. Once I figured out that it was the display program, I hacked through it and a few other firewalls protecting it, and discovered the truth."

He didn't say any more, because he didn't have to. His eyes told me the truth.

Scipio was dying. His code had been attacked, undermined, viciously removed. New coding was running rampant against his own, trying to destroy him, slowly tearing away at him like a cancer from the inside.

If something wasn't done, he'd die, and with him, the Tower itself.

It was a lot to take in, and even more to accept, but I had no reason to doubt my brother's word or analysis. He was ridiculously smart, and had been studying Scipio his entire life. If he said it was true, then it was.

But what did that all mean? Why had anyone stolen chunks of his code—and what were they doing with them? How had they even done that? Just taken chunks of code like a Hand would pick an apple from a tree... Why hadn't anyone noticed that? How long did we have before Scipio started to fail, and the machines rumbling in the depths of the Tower below went still and silent, unable to run without his control?

"Alex, how bad is this?" I finally asked.

He exhaled shakily, and looked down at the floor. "His core processes are intact, and he's still maintaining the machines, but we don't know how long he'll be able to sustain them. I'm sorry, I tapped Mercury on this because he's been working with Scipio for much longer. Don't worry, I didn't tell him anything beyond, 'So I was poking around in Scipio's code the other day...'"

"Thank you," I said, relieved that my brother was being smart. I took another look at him and realized that he'd probably been working night and day on this, trying to solve this mystery, and I felt myself appreciate him even more for taking the risk. I just hoped he was being safe enough; I couldn't bear it if anything happened to him.

"You're welcome. Anyway, he's running projection models to find out how long we have, as well as seeing if he can figure out what was taken and what was left behind, but it's a lot of code. It's going to take some time."

"Time we might not have," Leo replied. "But thank you for sharing this with us."

"No problem," Alex said. He paused. "Well, some problems, but I knew what I was getting into. Well, no, I didn't even realize what I was getting into, but now that I know, I'd do it again in a heartbeat, so..." He smiled kindly at Leo. "Now, can I take a look at that net? And maybe a peek at your code, if you don't mind? I'm just ever so curious."

"Of course," Leo said. "I assume you brought—"

"The necessary tools?" Alex asked with a grin, pulling a flat, black zippered case from his pocket. "Never leave home without them."

The two men moved into the kitchen, Alex already asking Leo technical questions that made it sound like they were speaking a foreign language. I half listened to him, but my mind was far away, wrestling with the information that Alex had just shared with us, and what it could mean for our plans.

Nothing good, of that much I was certain.

19

The walk back to the Salles was quiet, both Leo and I deep in thought. I could tell my companion was sad—though he'd grown better at masking his emotions since he'd gained control of Grey's body, there was a haunted look on his face, his eyes distant.

I wanted to comfort him, but what could I say? It wasn't every day that you found out a computer program that was basically made up of pieces of you was dying. What was that even like? How could I possibly relate? Were they brothers, or did Leo feel some sort of paternal impulse toward the other AI? Maybe if I thought about them like family, I could find the words to offer him some peace of mind.

But they never came, and as we walked into the arena, I realized my chance to offer at least something had come and gone. There was no way we could talk about it in such an open space.

I sighed and checked the clock on my indicator. It was two

thirty. Our next event wasn't until four, so we had some time to kill. I looked around at the crowd, searching for Quess, and to my surprise found him chatting with Zoe and Eric.

Both Zoe and Eric were wearing the Cogs' orange overalls, and Zoe looked like she had just come off a shift, her hands and arms streaked with black grease, a smudge on her cheek. Eric also had some grease on his face—residue from where Zoe had no doubt kissed him when she saw him. The two were holding hands, their fingers interlocked.

I looked over at Leo and tried very hard not to think of Grey. "Zoe and Eric are over there talking to Quess," I said, pointing the group out.

His brown eyes flicked over to them and back to me. "Are you worried about revealing Quess if we're all seen together at the same time?"

"Pretty much." But I hesitated and then shook my head. I had to remember that I could trust my friends to stick to the plan. They were responsible people, and would've thought of something. "Actually, I'm being overly concerned. I'm sure Zoe's got a cover story all worked out to explain why they're talking."

"You're probably right," Leo replied distractedly. I looked over at him, wishing that I could say something to comfort him. Maybe something simple, like an "I'm sorry" would be enough? I wouldn't have to go into detail—I was certain he'd understand at least that. Before I could say anything, however, he began making his way over to them, moving seamlessly through the crowds of people.

I sighed and followed, feeling crappier by the second.

Of course, how could I help *him* process Scipio's inevitable death if *I* couldn't even process it? Besides, if it was years away, that was one thing—but what if it was mere weeks, days, or even hours away? What would happen if he shut down for good?

I knew what would happen. First, the machines that he operated would stop working. No more water drawn from the river; no more machines cleaning and circulating our air; no more sun for the plants in the greeneries. We would suffocate long before we would starve, though, and turn on each other long before any of that happened, first over supplies, then in self-defense. Those who didn't want to fight would opt for escape instead, spilling out onto the irradiated sands—and they wouldn't get far before the Wastes swallowed them whole.

It sort of blew a big hole into the getting-out-of-here plan. If Scipio was failing, then there wasn't enough time for us to find a way of escaping the Tower safely.

It blew a big hole into a *lot* of plans.

So when I approached the group, I couldn't help but feel like all of this was a little pointless. What did it matter if Ambrose was the Champion, if we were all going to die soon? Wouldn't our time be better suited to...

To *what*? Even if I wanted to fix something, we were in no position to do anything about it right then. Lacey had us under her thumb, and if we tried to focus on replacing Scipio, odds were she'd back her threat up and we'd find ourselves labeled as criminals again in no time. And it would be almost impossible to try to fix Scipio with the Knights and half the Tower hunting us down.

I just had to work on helping Leo when we could fit it in around the Tourney. And pray that Scipio wasn't going to die before it was finished.

I reached the group just as Leo was saying hello to Zoe and Eric. "Who's your new friend?" he asked, sliding his eyes over toward Quess and imposing a mask of curiosity on his features.

"Just a guy who got a great job," Quess said with a grin. "And couldn't wait to share it with the first people I met. I am really sorry for bumping into you again, miss."

"I'm sure you are," Zoe said with a smile. "But congratulations on your new job. I'll be looking forward to seeing your handiwork as the Tourney progresses."

Job? I swiveled my head back from Zoe to Quess and gave him a dubious look. "You're a Squire and you were hired for something?" I asked, arching an eyebrow. That was hard to believe; Squires were rarely trusted with any responsibility outside of stocking shelves and cleaning rooms.

"Well, they needed more people to help with drones," Quess said, a touch smugly. I noted the gleam in his eyes, and realized that he had put some very careful thought into whatever he was up to. "I have some experience with electronics, and they are shorthanded until after the qualifiers, but generally, nobody wants this particular job. So I should be able to keep it until the end of the Tourney."

"Oh?" I smiled at him kindly. "That's great."

"I know," he drawled confidently. "Now I'll get to watch all the fights up close and personal."

And be able to keep a better eye on you during the Tourney. It was unspoken, but still there, and I immediately grinned. I had known Quess was up to something, and was glad he was on our side. I never would've even considered trying to get him on the drone control team, but it was perfect for him.

"Well, good for you, Squire," I said. "I wish you the best fortune, and hope you enjoy seeing me and my team in action."

"You mean Honorbound and Untouchable?" he grinned, nodding toward Grey. I glanced at Grey, and then back to Quess.

"'Untouchable'?" Leo asked, before I had a chance to. "Do you mean... Is that my deed name?"

"Mm-hm," Quess said with a grin. "Because in both fights you've been in, no one has been able to land a blow."

Leo frowned. "That doesn't make any sense. The first match shouldn't even count! The other team used that inane tactic, and Liana ended the match before any of us could fight!"

I smiled at how indignant he sounded, and then sighed heavily. Ambrose wasn't going to like hearing that Leo had gotten a deed name before he did. We had to do something to bolster his image, and fast, or things were definitely going to revert back into hostile territory.

"I don't think you can protest a deed name," Zoe said lightly, a smile on her face. "You'll just have to live with it—or make sure you get hit in the future."

Leo immediately looked repulsed by the idea. "No, thank you," he said with a sigh. "I suppose it will have to stay, then."

I was curious as to why he had such an aversion to getting hit, but placed it aside for more important things—namely getting Quess out of there. He had been standing with us for much longer than polite small talk would dictate, and it would draw notice if it continued on for much longer.

"Well, it was nice meeting you," I told him brightly. "We have to be going, though."

"Of course!" Quess stammered, his eyes wide. His acting wasn't quite convincing, though, as he couldn't quite wipe the smirk off his face. "Anyway, I'll be rooting for you! Now if you'll excuse me, I've got some drones to pilot!"

He threw us a final wave and then turned and left, disappearing into the crowds. I immediately looked at Zoe.

"He was filling us in for you," she said, releasing Eric's hand to come close and give me a hug. "He lost track of the guys you wanted him to follow, but managed to make friends with one of the Knights who was trying to handle the drones, but having problems with manpower and experience."

"It's smart," I said, pulling away from her. I was disappointed by the lack of information on the men I had wanted him to follow, but hoped that he managed to find them using the drones. Maybe then he could even find out what they were up to, and help us get ahead of them somehow. But that would have to wait until after we found them.

I gave Zoe a onceover and smiled. "You look good in orange."

She posed, one hand going to a curvy hip that even the overalls couldn't hide, the other going to the nape of her neck. "I know, right?"

"It's the grease that does it for me," Eric said dreamily.

"Oh, ugh," I said with a wincing laugh. "I do not need any

details about your new life living together." Zoe gave me a look, and I smiled. "Okay, fine! I do need to know the details, because I love you both and I am very happy for you."

I *was* happy for them... but watching them was hard, and I had to look away. All I wanted to do was reach out and take Grey's hand and hold it as a reminder that I wasn't alone. But I was.

I swallowed back my self-pity and put it aside. This wasn't about me. It was about them, and I needed to remember that.

Eric beamed and reached out to snag Zoe's hand, bringing it to his lips for a kiss. "Me, too," he said, and Zoe flushed prettily, unable to mask the pure love and adoration radiating out of her.

"Fascinating," Leo whispered next to me, and I turned to watch him observing the two of them with rapt attention on his face. I softened some, seeing the delight on his features—and, to my utmost surprise, saw a smidge of envy there as well.

I was stunned by it, but realized then that this must have been something Leo had thought about. Kissing someone. Smiling with them, laughing, touching... All the intimate little moments that happened between people in love.

For a second, I wondered if I should encourage him to maybe go give it a try, just for the experience. Then I realized that while it would be Leo doing the driving, it would be Grey's body doing the touching. The kissing. The laughing.

And I was one hundred percent *not* comfortable with that.

Then I considered offering to let him try with me. Not even a heartbeat later I was slamming a mental door in front of that idea, then nailing it shut, tossing chains over it, and sitting on it for good measure.

There was no way. Nope. Nuh-uh.

I quickly latched onto anything that would pull my mind away from the black hole that had suddenly opened up in my head. I mean, I was close to Leo, sure. We were friends. And watching him grow the last few days had been endearing and fascinating in unexpected ways. But I couldn't—*wouldn't*—even consider that. Grey was still in there, and I was not giving up hope that Leo would heal him.

"Well, we don't have lashes until—" I was starting to say, about to ask them if they had eaten lunch yet.

Then a loud shout of "Liana!" went up back toward the doors.

I turned around, my muscles already tensing, but stopped when I saw Maddox racing toward us, her face flushed and red as if she had been running for some time. It took me a moment to realize that she was alone—and I instantly became concerned that something had happened to Ambrose.

"What's wrong?" I asked as she came to a stop in front of us.

Maddox was breathing heavily, but not winded. "They moved up our time," she said angrily. "They're saying we'll be disqualified if I don't get you and Leo up to the lashway entrance in the next five minutes."

They moved up our time? Alarm raced through me at the unexpected news. They wouldn't have done that without giving us ample notice, and Ambrose hadn't said anything. Which meant either that he had intentionally not told us, which made no sense whatsoever, or the notification had never been sent out.

They also hadn't buzzed us to alert us that we needed to report anywhere.

I supposed it could be coincidence, but after the illegally super-charged batons, I wasn't as certain. At this point, all signs pointed toward someone trying to push us out of the competition—by any means necessary.

And I wasn't going to let that happen. If only to spite whoever it was who was making my life difficult.

I turned back to Zoe and Eric and nodded for them to keep up as Maddox, Leo, and I began to move back toward the doors, not wanting to spare a second. "Get a message to Quess," I told Zoe quietly. "Somehow."

"That'll be easy," Zoe said furtively. "That was one of the things I wanted to tell you: I cracked a problem Quess was having with getting our net communications secured, and now have a system in place. I've already got his net synced up to it, but the rest of you..."

Whatever relief I might have felt at finally having a secure way to communicate with each other through our nets was lost in the wave of anxiety shouting for me to start running. "It'll have to wait. Besides, contestants' net transmissions are blocked during the Tourney."

We walked quickly through the doors, turning right down the hall toward the elevator bay. More and more people were streaming into the area, and moving against them was like trying to swim against a very strong current.

"Okay," Zoe said. "Then come and meet me at our house later. I still need to update you on some other things."

I realized she was probably talking about Paragon, as it was one of the only jobs Zoe had, and nodded, filing it away for later. "As soon as this qualifier is over and Ambrose is tucked in safely," I promised.

"Liana. Please be careful, okay?"

I waited for Leo and Maddox to get in the elevator and shot her my most confident smile, in spite of the scanners causing the net to rattle around in my skull. "It's lashes," I said blandly, but her frown only deepened.

Maddox murmured the floor number to the computer, and we slid away, Zoe and Eric disappearing behind us as I exhaled nervously. I hadn't mentioned my suspicions to them, because there hadn't been any reason to. Besides, if this was another setup of some kind, it was too late for them to do anything to stop it.

But that didn't mean I wasn't going to tell Leo and Maddox to be on their guard.

20

Ambrose was arguing with the official when we hurried down the hall toward him. He glanced over his shoulder, his brows pulled tight together, and then stepped to one side to let the official see us coming.

The man was portly and in his late forties, with round cheeks and wet, beady eyes that glistened angrily as we ran up. "Late is late," he was already barking, crossing his arms over his chest. "You only have two minutes to put on your harnesses, and that's not enough time."

I was already kicking off my boots. "Nonsense," I said with a smile, unzipping my uniform with a long, confident zip. I heard Maddox and Leo join me seconds later, and my smile broadened as I quickly slipped my shoulders out, shucking the material down off my hips and to the ground.

"You forget, sir, that we all had to spend some time at the Academy." I stepped over the pile I had just created on the floor and grabbed a harness off of the table he was standing behind, holding it out behind me to the others. "At four a.m., the instructors used to come in banging pots and ordering us to get geared up in under a minute. If we didn't, the whole company had to lash around the Citadel before breakfast!"

He smiled as I passed another harness back, the second grabbed as quickly as the first. The third was in my hands moments later, and I was stepping into it, still talking. "Boy, you never saw so many cadets move at the same time. And we all did it, too, except for this one kid, Billy."

I clipped the harness across my chest and cinched it tight before hurrying back to my suit, sitting down, and shoving my legs through the legs of the uniform. I stood up, yanking the uniform up as I went, tucking my underclothes and excess straps under the edges. I slid my arms into the sleeves, and then took precious seconds pulling the cables out of the harness and attaching them to the weights that dragged the lines through my suit. I felt the lines shift as I set the lashes to come out next to my wrists, and then quickly attached the beads. Pulling the zipper up to my neck, I finished the look, and took a moment to check on Maddox and Leo, both of whom were ready to go.

"Luckily," I said brightly, if a bit breathlessly, "no one on this team is a Billy."

The official laughed, and Ambrose, who had been watching my display with a combination of growing horror and rapt fascination, looked at him with shock and surprise.

"Get along with ya, girl," the official said, casting a thumb toward the open hole in the wall just behind him.

That was the lashway, one of many open doorways that led directly to the outer walls of the Citadel. They were used as ways to move quickly between floors without having to wait for elevators, as well as training grounds for Squires and Knights alike to practice their lashing. Beyond the opening were the black, gleaming, high-vaulted arches and buttresses that lined the walls, growing from the bottoms of the levels above, and creating a maze of sorts—which Knights practiced on daily.

I had grown up inside the Citadel, and these arches were as familiar to me as breathing. I had no concern about my skills during this competition. Well, one concern.

My eyes slid over to Ambrose, and I sighed. I had to remember to tone it down for the other members of the team.

Especially *that* one.

Because lashes were my specialty, and he wasn't going to be able to keep up with me—which would end up making him look bad. Again.

"I will be in the lead," Ambrose said as we walked past the official toward the lashway a few feet behind him. "Maddox, you're behind me, and Grey will be behind you. Liana, I want you to stay in the rear. We're going to be hitting the inner walls, so make sure you keep an eye on the Knightsmarks."

The lashes qualifier was nothing but a straight-up time trial. The outside architecture had been separated into three paths around the Tower, each path with different qualifying times attached to it. Ambrose wanted to take the inner walls, arguably the most dangerous place for lashes, thanks to the density of the architecture, and that gave us only three and a half minutes to race around at breakneck speeds, while using the Knightsmarks —symbols painted on the walls themselves to guide us through dangerous terrain—to navigate.

For this competition, fast reflexes and correct interpretation of the marks were going to be critical.

Yet I knew why he was willing to risk it: he wanted to impress people and earn some prestige among the other Knights. And lashing along the inner walls would do exactly that.

It was risky—lashes were where most of the teams got eliminated—but I had to trust that he knew what he was doing. I had promised to do that much, at least.

In truth, I was eager for this; I lived for the thrill and rush of lashing, and this was an excuse to do it very quickly, as it was not only a trial for precision, but for speed as well. Knights had to be quick to respond, so the future Champion had to at least have mastered lashes.

This test would determine that.

Wind caught my hair as we came to a stop next to the lashway, and I took a moment to peer off the edge, looking down. The feeling never failed to elate me, and I felt my skin begin to tingle in anticipation for the qualifier.

"Candidates will prepare their lashes," a prim, digitized voice announced. "You may start when the buzzer sounds, in fifteen seconds."

I tugged on the small bead at the end of the lash line, pulling a few feet of it out to create slack, and took a few steps back, since I was going last. Then I perched on the tips of my toes, waiting, as a series of electronic beeps began to sound, counting down the remaining seconds.

Just over Maddox's head, a white drone dropped down, the tiny blades whirring as the camera fixated on us. I didn't know if Quess was operating it or not, but given how the last team had waited for the cameras to be *off* of us before they fought dirty, its presence gave me some reassurance. With it here, I was certain anyone wanting to try anything would be held off, unless they were willing to risk exposure.

Still, better to avoid it. It was within the rules to fight with other teams that were on the course, but most didn't, as it wasn't deemed honorable. The risk of an accident was too high.

The pitch of the beeping suddenly became higher, and within the span of a heartbeat, Ambrose had thrown himself through the opening. I dropped the bead and excess slack from my hand and began to whirl it around, using the action to soothe myself as I waited for the others to go. The beads used the static they absorbed through friction with the air particles, but what I was doing was completely unnecessary. Just a way to make myself feel more prepared.

Maddox followed Ambrose, and as soon as Leo's lash end hit and he stepped off the ledge as well, I was running, racing toward the hole with my lash still spinning. I leapt without even casting the line, loving the sensation of weightlessness just before gravity began to exert its pull.

I savored it for the split second it was there, and then threw my line, kicking my legs forward and shifting my hips to the right to adjust my weight and the angle of the arc so it would take me out and around. I knew this lashway entrance well, and there was a giant buttress of gargoyles jutting out of the side, hung upside down for added confusion.

But I knew every line of them, and had even created names for a few of them when I was younger, and lonely. But that was a different story.

I cast my second line, following the bright pink Knightsmark instruction painted on the side of the most prominent gargoyle's face, which gave him a tattoo in the form of a hole with a slash through it. The bead hit an arch five feet below and ten feet away, and I quickly disengaged and fell, the wind rushing past my ears. I saw Leo disappear under the arch as I dropped, his hand already throwing the next bead, and I quickly readied mine, my eyes already looking for another bright mark.

I saw it moments later, halfway down the arch, and I quickly began reeling myself in with the connected line, my hand casting a line immediately to my left, to hit one of the posts.

We were in a corridor comprised of them now, the columns set fifteen feet apart. I was certain the test designers wouldn't leave us here for long—it was a straight shot with no difficulty.

Then I noticed Ambrose a few columns ahead, weaving left across Maddox's path, while she swung right in front of Leo's, and I realized that they were weaving around the arches. A glance at the Knightsmark ahead showed why: they expected us to weave around each arch, rather than moving in a straight line.

I immediately cast my next lash, following the mark and swinging around the first column, then across the path to the next one... and then the next one. I drew my lines tighter, needing to be closer to the objects to generate enough momentum through each turn, then lashing diagonally through the gap before swinging around the opposite column of the next arch.

I smiled, elated as I took yet another turn, and then saw Ambrose drop another fifteen feet ahead, down through a gap between the final two arches. He was in complete freefall, with no lash attached, and my heart leapt in my throat. But a moment later I saw him throw his lash, connecting with the top of the final arch and swinging forward, both legs extended, and I relaxed.

I swung around the next column and then lashed directly to the center before disconnecting and dropping. Once again, gravity claimed me, and I surrendered willingly. I dove instead of going feet first, unable to resist it, and then twisted and cast my line, giving myself a little more slack so I would fall longer and gain more momentum.

The line connected with a ting and I leaned into it, trying to get more weight into the swing. Then there was a sharp, groaning sound, and a second later, I was in freefall.

My limbs flailed for a second as my mind tried to fathom what had just happened, my eyes seeing only the fishponds and forests of thick green trees below. Then it occurred to me that I was about to see them in a very permanent and final way, and my left arm quickly threw out a line, acting purely on reflex.

I must've noticed something to connect to even before the fall, because to my surprise, the line caught immediately, bringing me to a jerking halt that jostled me violently as the harness bit into my flesh.

My hands immediately went to the line, and I could feel a tension radiating from it. It practically vibrated, and I quickly jerked my hands away, afraid to even touch it before it had settled, afraid that it too would give before I could get my first lash connected again.

Wait. That other lash had *hit* before—had been holding my weight, even. So why had it disconnected? Had it simply lost a charge for some reason? Or had I made a false connection? My heart thudded in my chest, and I realized the line was still dangling free from the hole in my sleeve.

I quickly hit the button to reel it in, letting the smooth material glide by under my fingers as I dangled from one arm. I looked around, searching for any sign of my friends, but they had disappeared. It was likely that they hadn't even noticed I was missing. I had to get back up on the course so they could see me. Surely someone would be coming back—if even one of us didn't make the time, none of us did.

I slowed the line as it drew in, and immediately saw why it had failed. The bead had fallen off. It happened occasionally, but still... it was odd.

And bad. Without a second lash, I was going to be stuck until my team came back for me. Unfortunately, there were no exceptions made for broken lashes, as ingenuity must always be tested. It was up to my teammates to figure it out and come for me—before we got eliminated.

I clenched my teeth, angered by my predicament, and began

reeling myself in again, hoping that I could at least climb up and get back to a place closer to the marked course so they could find me more quickly.

The line continued to tremble as the gyros in my harness worked to drag me up, and I shook, knowing that all that stood between me and death was the single line anchoring me in place. If it disconnected or broke, I wouldn't have time to reel it in and cast it again. I would've fallen too far away from the Tower by that point. So I had to be careful.

"Liana!"

Hearing my name being cried out startled me, but I managed to not jerk around too much, twisting instead to find Leo racing toward me, his lashes flying. I stopped the gears in my suit, and moments later he was close to me, his entire body radiating his concern.

"Are you okay?" he demanded.

I swallowed and nodded. "I am. Turn around and let me hook on."

Leo nodded, carefully adjusting his weight so he could reposition his body and present me with his back. I pulled out the carabiner attached to the front of my belt for exactly this purpose, and snapped it onto a ring in the back of his uniform, then slowly settled my weight onto him, bringing my knees up high on his hips and tucking my feet under my butt.

I disconnected my line as soon as I was settled, and Leo began to move.

It was so strange that he was so good at lashing, because Grey had been afraid of it, and I admired how quickly he had mastered such a technical skill. His movements weren't as effortless as they could've been, but he was growing and adapting, even as we flew back to the course.

I held on tightly, trying to make myself a small bundle on his back, but I had to admit that riding with someone was almost as exhilarating as lashing itself. There was a thrill of excitement that came when I didn't have control, and I found myself clutching him a little tighter, both elated and terrified at the same time. He was in complete control, however, navigating swiftly around column and gargoyle alike.

He began pulling us upward, then, and I realized with a pang of disappointment that the ride was done.

Moments later, he threw us both through the lashway, and we rolled together for a few feet, burning off excess momentum. We came to a stop with me on his back, and I quickly sat up and unhooked myself.

My knees were still a tad unsteady, after how close I had been to death, so I slid off him and onto my rear, taking a moment to catch my breath. Maddox was instantly there, her green eyes brimming with concern.

"Are you okay?" she asked, looking me over. "What happened?"

"I'm fine," I said jerkily. "But it looks like I lost a bead."

I held up the end of the cord, showing them, and Leo immediately frowned. "That's been cut," he stated flatly, his brown eyes leaping up to mine and narrowing. "The edge wouldn't be flat like that if it hadn't."

I stared at the cord, and then immediately dropped it as if it had burned me. Just looking at the flat edges reminded me that I would've been dead minutes ago, if not for my fast reflexes and Leo's rescue. But still, it was deeply unsettling, especially coupled with the fact that this was the second event in which something had been tampered with.

It was no coincidence.

I allowed Maddox to pull me to my feet, and gave Ambrose a look. "You're having dinner in your quarters, and one of us is to be with you at all times," I said quietly, and to my surprise, he nodded. I realized he looked a bit pale himself, and it occurred to me that he might have finally come to terms with the fact that someone was out to get us.

Or more specifically, him.

I quickly located an official, pointing out the damage to the cable. He gave me his utmost assurances that he would look into it, and we quickly turned in our gear, unable to do more than that.

Besides, I was in no mood to stick around, needing to get out of there as quickly as possible to put my brush with death behind me.

21

I knocked on the gray door and looked down the darkened halls, half expecting one of Lacey's men to be lying in wait with another bag for my head. But the halls were deserted.

The door slid open, revealing Eric, who had a welcoming smile on his face. Before I could even say hello, he'd ushered Leo and me inside, through the short, familiar hall and into the common room that had once belonged to Grey and Roark, and now belonged to Zoe and Eric.

I stopped short when I saw a figure hunched over the wide workstation in the middle of the room, a memory of Roark gripping me tightly. I half expected the person to look up with those piercing blue eyes and give me a grumpy scowl or make a derisive comment, but of course it wasn't him. It was Zoe.

She was wearing a pair of smoked glass goggles over her eyes, and her hands were covered by heavy gloves. In one hand was a small welding torch, in the other a pair of tweezers. She was biting her lower lip in concentration, her teeth white against skin darkened by the soot and smoke the torch was creating.

She looked up, smiled, switched the flame off, and placed the torch on a small stand. She pulled off her goggles, leaving rings of clean skin surrounding her eyes, and I smiled at the look. She grinned back as she took off her gloves.

"I saw what happened on the drone camera footage," she said in a rush. "I am so, so, so glad you are all right." She tugged me into a hug, her arms coming around me like a vice. "If you had died, I would've killed you, Liana Castell."

My heart swelled, and I wrapped my arms around my best friend. "I will endeavor not to do so in the future."

She released me and gave me a look that told me she didn't believe me, then stepped around me to come face-to-face with Leo. "You saved my best friend's life," she said, her voice growing thick.

Leo frowned and immediately shook his head. "I did nothing that she wouldn't do for any of us," he said. "I assure you, your gratitude is unnecessary. Liana is my friend. You all are."

Zoe cocked her head at him, and then pulled him into a hug. "Just shut up and take a hug, you confounded machine," she breathed.

Leo stiffened, and then lifted his arms uncertainly, as if not entirely sure what to do. I could have almost laughed at his frown as he slowly puzzled out where to rest his arms across her back, but the look faded behind a soft, tender expression that fluttered over his face as he closed his eyes and just... experienced a real hug.

Surprisingly, tears began to form in my eyes, and I turned away from the scene to take a moment to compose myself. It was sad and strangely beautiful. He was learning what it was really like to be human—to feel cared for or appreciated beyond just what words could say. How a touch could mean more than a thousand words, and how warm and precious a hug could be.

And though it had taken Grey nearly dying for Leo to gain the experience, I was suddenly grateful he had the opportunity.

Because that would mean a more caring master AI program if he managed to accomplish his goal of replacing Scipio. It would mean no more executions, no more restructuring, no more ranking systems, and no more trying to divide people and humiliate them in order to encourage good behavior. It would be a more understanding place... and a place that would be worth fighting for.

And for a moment, I found myself thinking of Lionel Scipio and how, in essence, he had created two children. One was now dying—but the other was growing stronger every day. How would he feel, knowing that one of his creations was going to die, while the other would not only take its place, but gain a knowledge of humanity that Scipio had never experienced? It was impossible to know what his intentions might have been, but I couldn't help but wonder if this had been his goal all along.

Which led me to think about Scipio and his damaged code. My brother had mentioned that huge chunks of his code were actually missing. Had they been deleted? But how did code go *missing*—and in such large amounts, as my brother had insinuated? How had someone even been able to penetrate the firewalls to gain access, let alone delete it? Why hadn't anyone noticed? There were thousands of Eyes on him all the time—it shouldn't have been possible. Their job was literally to watch him! The fact that they hadn't noticed meant that the change had happened so long ago that they just assumed that was how Scipio was supposed to look, or there was a conspiracy within IT to keep it covered up. It would have to be a large one, too.

"What's happening?" I shouted, rushing into a small room with several computer screens that were flashing blue and red.

"It's Scipio!" my sister cried in distress. Her fingers paused their frantic typing on the keyboard long enough for her to push back her glasses as she stared up at the screen, her eyes wide in horror. "Someone's attacking him!"

"What?!" I looked up at the screen, trying to analyze the raw bits of code dancing across it, trying to see what my sister was seeing. "How? Why hasn't the firewall gone up?"

"Whoever the bastard is, he's good. He hijacked the firewall to make it turn against itself, and then gave it a purpose. It's sheering out Scipio's security controls!"

Panic flooded me at my sister's words. Scipio's security controls were what allowed him to autonomously monitor his own coding. If they were stripped from him, he'd be blind.

"Can't you do something?"

My sister nodded, and then turned around to face me, her eyes hard. "I can download the code first, using Grandmother's built-

in security clearance," she whispered. "Or as much of it as possible, so that we can replace it with a copy."

I frowned. Grandmother's security clearances were the last ace in the hole we had—once we used them, whoever was attacking Scipio would be able to dig them out. Not to mention... "You can't copy intelli-code! It loses—"

"The ability to grow and learn will start to degrade, yes, I know. But we have to, Brother. It's the only way to slow them down!"

I hesitated and then nodded. "Do it." My sister was already moving, plugging several data crystals into the ports of her home-made computer.

"Liana!"

Eric's sharp voice jolted me out of the tangent memory that had gripped me, and I blinked and realized everyone in the room was looking at me.

"Sorry," I said, reaching up to push my hair out of my face and pausing when I noticed I was trembling. I shook out my hands, trying to clear out the residual feelings the memory had imparted, and sighed. "I'm still getting a hold on this new net."

"Did you have a memory?" Zoe asked excitedly. "About what?"

I opened my mouth to tell her, but just like that, the memory was gone. I frowned, trying to recall what exactly had happened. That was weird—none of the other memories had disappeared like that, but for some reason, I couldn't remember what had happened. Was the net malfunctioning, or had Lacey done something to it to keep me from remembering certain things? I was betting it was the latter—some sort of security protocol that kept me from learning too much about what they were up to. Lacey was nothing if not fiercely protective of her goals, and I couldn't blame her. For as much research as she had done on me, she couldn't be a hundred percent sure that I wasn't a legacy planted to try to gain her trust and flush her out.

The memory was gone, but the feelings—the anxiety, panic, and fear—all remained, leaving me a bit shaken. I tried to recall some detail, but the only thing I could remember was that it had something to do with Scipio. "I think it had something to do with Scipio," I finally said. "The person the net was attached to at the time was frightened, but that's all I can remember."

"Hm." Zoe's eyes narrowed in contemplation. "Any headaches or unexplained problems with your vision or the net buzzing?"

I shook my head. "No, I don't think it's a problem with the net. I think it's a memory that relates directly to the legacies. Maybe there's a safeguard in place to keep me from remembering it once it's passed."

Leo frowned. "That would be pointless," he announced. "How would only remembering something in the moment help you?"

It was a good point. Not to mention, it undermined my goals in having it. How was I supposed to identify with Ambrose if I couldn't even get a clear picture of what his cause was? It was frustrating, and made me feel like I was fighting with one hand tied behind my back while blindfolded.

Of course, going to Lacey now wasn't a possibility; she had reinforced her zero-contact rule after our meeting the other day.

"I don't know, but I fully intend to ask her. Unfortunately, it will have to wait until the end of the Tourney. I doubt I'll be able to get her in a room before then." I sighed. The problem with the net bothered me. Something important had happened in the memory, but now it was just a blank. A part of me was tempted to march down to Cogstown and start hollering Lacey's name until she was forced to see me, but it wasn't exactly discreet, and I already had too much attention on me for my comfort. But one thing was certain: this was only a pause on my part, not an end.

I wanted to know what was going on in these memories.

I let it go, and turned my focus to Zoe, who was now going back around the worktable and fetching a crate filled to the brim with white pill bottles.

"You're keeping them out in the open like that?" I asked. If she was, that was alarming; inspections of quarters for contraband were rare, but they still happened. A bunch of unmarked medication outside of the Medica would draw attention, if we weren't careful.

"Relax, Tian came and checked this place for bugs yesterday on her way down to Sanctum. Nobody's watching or listening. And, I hide them when I'm not working on them." She smiled at me as she hefted them onto the table and began pulling the bottles out. "Now, this is Paragon. The number on the outside shows the rank the pill achieves, and we have a stockpile here that would last the seven of us for several months. Of course, that won't help the others Roark and Grey recruited."

"But?" I nudged, noting the sparkle in her blue eyes and the cunning grin she was giving me.

"But, I figured out how to dilute them," she said excitedly. "And I've done the math. If we dilute all the nines and tens to eights, we'll effectively create triple the number of pills. I know we'll have to keep some of the tens to one side for us, in case we begin to slip during our time in the open, and for analysis if we can't ever recover Jasper, but..."

"But it's a start," I said. I sat down and thought about it. Thanks to the ranks of ten that Scipio had bestowed on us, we didn't have to worry about taking Paragon. For a little while, at least. The higher the rank, the longer it took to drop—or at least that's what Alex had insinuated after studying the net data for the past twenty years or so. But it would happen eventually. Tripling the pills was good—but still not quite good enough, when there were twenty-nine other people to handle.

The council had indicated that the law Devon had manipulated Scipio into recommending—namely, the execution of the ones in the Tower—was going to be overturned, but there were still twenty-nine people out there who were dependent on Paragon. And if they didn't get it, they'd be going into restructuring, the process that had been the predecessor to execution. My memory of the rooms buried at the bottom of the Citadel was horrifying enough to make my stomach turn. I wouldn't subject my own worst enemy to it—let alone people who just had a difficult time coping with Tower life.

And I owed it to Roark to make sure these people were taken

care of. Just like I owed it to Cali to keep Quess, Maddox, and Tian safe.

"What do you need us to do?" I asked, determined to get started.

Zoe blinked in surprise and then gave me a delighted smile. "I didn't think you'd help, but this is great! I've already figured out the ratios, and Lacey's people left Roark's supplies behind, which means I have a press for the pills..." She trailed off and sighed, shaking her head. "Sorry, brain is moving too fast. Liana and Leo, I want you to use this to smash these pills. Crush them ten at a time, and then dump them into these test tubes. Make sure you label whether they are tens, or nines, or whatever."

She pulled out several objects as she spoke, moving like a whirlwind through her makeshift workstation and laboratory. First she produced two mortar and pestle sets, for grinding pills, followed by a stand that held ten test tubes. Then, she pulled out a marker. She slid everything across to us, and beamed expectantly.

I collected a few objects and looked curiously at Eric, who was standing quietly to one side, watching. "What's Eric going to do?"

"Cook dinner," he said with a smile. "Zoe says that while she loves everything about me, my clumsiness most of all, she doesn't need it in her space."

"Yes, but you also cook dinner far better than I ever could," Zoe pointed out unapologetically. "By the way, remind me to thank your mom for teaching you."

"More like my sister and cousins for making me," Eric said,

moving over to plant a kiss on her head. "But hey, if it makes you happy, then it was totally worth it."

Zoe squealed as he started to nuzzle her cheek, and I found myself turning away and moving across the room to drop into the familiar low couch against the wall, and setting my objects on the table. Leo hovered by the table a little while longer, openly observing them, but joined me shortly after he realized I had moved.

I looked up from where I was now counting pills out into the bowl, saw the two of them sharing a passionate kiss, and then focused on my work again. I was over being envious; my friends were genuinely happy, and there was no reason for that to upset me. But I still wasn't comfortable witnessing their PDA. Better to just ignore it.

Eventually they finished kissing, and Eric wandered off to the kitchen to start cooking. Zoe spun around on her stool, smiling, and started humming to herself as she began to work. I smiled as I commenced crushing the pills into a fine white powder.

It felt good, just for a moment, to forget about the Tourney and Ambrose, and work on something that would actually help people. I only wished the nagging voice inside of me would shut up about how I could do more.

2 2

"Oh, so when do the results come out?" Zoe asked as she began to clean up the dishes from our meal. We'd been there for a few hours, and I hadn't been paying much attention to the time. Which was good, because we were all waiting for the results from the qualifiers, and without the distraction Zoe and Eric had provided, I would probably have been an anxious mess, wondering if we had pulled it off. I looked at my indicator, swiping over the blue ten that had stubbornly remained, and checked the time.

It was later than I had imagined, almost eight p.m. Which meant the results had been out for at least twenty minutes by now. I pulled out my pad and connected with the internal server the Knights used to post announcements and the like. The list was already there, waiting under video images of the qualifier. I ignored the latter, not wanting to see whatever cut of our team they'd put together, and clicked on the list.

My heart practically stopped when I saw that only sixteen teams had qualified. Over fifty had applied, so for that few to have passed...

Please, let our team be one of them. I had no idea how Lacey and Ambrose would react to the news if it were otherwise. And I didn't particularly want to find out. We weren't prepared to run yet if things didn't go our way, and I certainly didn't want us scrambling like madmen right when we were getting settled again. Not to mention, I doubted very much that we'd get away before Lacey caught up with us.

If we *hadn't* made it, I'd just turn myself over to her and hope that she wouldn't go after my friends. And if not, well, I'd find a way to *make* her leave them alone, even if it meant pulling apart Cogstown with my bare hands to bury her.

The screen loaded, and I was immediately relieved when I saw our names listed alphabetically, the third group down. I looked up to where everyone was practically hovering, waiting to hear the results.

"We're in," I said, and Zoe let out a sigh, leaning back in her chair.

"Thank God," she said, flipping her hair over her shoulder and standing up. "Who knows how Lacey would take it if you guys hadn't gotten in?"

I smiled. We had all been thinking it, and I was glad for the fact that we didn't have to find out. I honestly hadn't seen a way out if we didn't succeed, which was why I hadn't brought it up to them. Then again, it wasn't anyone else's responsibility. It was mine.

"So who else is in?" Eric asked, handing a stack of dirty dishes to Zoe.

My eyes returned to the list, and I skimmed the names. "Dylan and her all-female team got in," I said, smiling appreciatively and giving her a little internal girl nod of approval. It was rare that girls competed on teams with only girls, so whenever it happened, I was pleased. If only because it served to remind the guys that we could, in fact, hold our own against them.

My gaze dropped a few names below hers, and I nodded. "So did Frederick and his team. And..." I paused and cocked my head, frowning as I saw a familiar pair of names on the list. "My parents." I looked up at the group and blinked. "Did you guys know they were competing?"

Zoe gave me a look over her shoulder as she submerged the dishes into a pot of water and grinned crookedly. "They're *your* parents, Liana. How would *we* have known that? I'm surprised you didn't know."

I wasn't surprised in the least. My parents had both been ghosts around the house when I was there—which was as little as possible. I'd known they were likely avoiding me. And then I hadn't even really informed them that I was moving out—just grabbed my already-packed boxes and left. Maybe if I hadn't left, they would've told me, but...

I cleared that thought right out of my head. My parents didn't owe me an explanation, and I didn't need one. So they were competing. So what? They were probably doing it to support a candidate they believed in. My eyes returned to their names, and I realized I recognized the other names in their group. One was an old friend of the family, Min-Ha Kim, but the other was Salvatore Zale—Devon's former Lieutenant, and possibly one of the only people who knew what the disgraced Champion had been up to before his death.

Was he involved with what Devon had been doing? Was that why he was making a play for Champion? If Devon had somehow indoctrinated Zale into his legacy "family," so to speak... could it be that he was now trying to finish whatever Devon had started?

And was he working with the same people Devon had been?

If so, it meant my parents were in grave danger, especially from Lacey's people. Because there was nothing to stop Lacey's group from trying to eliminate the competition—not if they truly believed their cause was great enough.

Unless of course my parents were already involved. A sickening thought occurred to me on the tail of the last: what if my parents had been working with Devon *all along*? I sucked in a deep breath, my stomach churning at the implications. They certainly didn't have any compunctions about killing off those who weren't "of service" to the Tower. But that didn't necessarily mean that they were actively trying to destroy Scipio... right?

"What's wrong?" Leo asked from across the table, and I looked up at him, realizing that I had gotten lost in the tempest of my thoughts.

"Sorry," I said, clicking off the pad and straightening. "I just drifted off there." I didn't feel comfortable sharing my revelation with my friends until after I had more time to think about it.

"You okay?" Zoe asked from the kitchen, elbow deep in dirty dishes.

"Of course," I lied. Then, as an afterthought, I added, "Pretty tired, actually."

"Oh, of course you are!" Eric exclaimed, his eyes growing wide. "You guys should get back to your quarters for some rest. The first challenge is tomorrow."

I nodded, but a part of me didn't want to go; the last few hours had been really fun, once we had all settled down and gotten to work. Dinner had been delicious, and we had laughed and joked for at least an hour after it was finished. If it had been Grey rather than Leo sitting next to me, it almost would've been perfect. It'd been a long time since I'd just gotten to relax like this.

And it would be a while before I would get to again. With the official challenges starting tomorrow, I had already ordered everyone on the team to stay sequestered inside the Citadel until everything was over. We'd only be leaving our rooms for whatever event was happening during the day, and then returning as soon as we were done. It limited our exposure, and was one of the few protocols I had come up with to keep Ambrose and everyone else safe. And even I was aware of how feeble it really was.

And now on top of everything, the idea that my mom and dad were caught in the line of fire—or possibly even *responsible* for said fire—was wriggling away like a massive earwig in my brain, and I couldn't seem to process the feelings it was creating in me. Namely, an urge to warn them to watch their backs... or to confront them for what they had done.

I firmly broke off the thought and smiled. "Yeah. Sorry, guys. I don't know about Leo, but I had a great time." I stood up. "Next time, we'll have to do it at my place."

"Okay," Zoe said with a smile, coming out of the tiny kitchen space with a towel in her hands. "Thanks for the help. We were going to have to deliver in two days to only half the people on the list, and explain to them about the supply problem, but now we can deliver to everyone."

"Are you sure you're up for that?" I asked, referring to the group of strangers who were probably not going to be pleased to be cold-contacted by someone other than Roark or Grey, and Zoe smiled coquettishly.

"Who could ever stop a girl with a face like this?" she declared.

I laughed, amused by my friend's confidence, and moved over to give her and Eric a hug. "Keep me updated," I breathed as they wrapped their arms around me, allowing myself to feel the love emanating from them.

"Of course," Eric answered.

We let each other go, and I stepped back so Leo could say his goodbyes.

"I had a lovely time," he said, shaking Eric's hand first, and then Zoe's. "And truly, the food was delicious. You know, I have access to some recipes that existed before the End that I think would be very easy to replicate here. When we have some free time, maybe we could try some of them out? They were Lionel's favorites, and I always wanted to try them."

Eric smiled kindly. "Of course," he declared. "I'd be happy to."

Leo gave him a look of deep gratitude, and bowed his head some. "Thank you. Farewell."

"To you as well," Zoe said.

Moments later, Leo and I were outside in the hall, the door closing behind us, and I exhaled. It had been easy enough to say our farewells, but as soon as it was done, my mind immediately returned to my parents and the problem I seemed to be having with them being in danger.

I turned to start walking, heading deeper into the halls—and deeper into my own thoughts. Or, at least, I tried to.

Leo, however, was in a chatty mood. "This was a really beautiful night," he said, slanting his eyes toward mine, a boyish smile on his face.

"It was," I agreed, hoping that would be the end of it.

"And if you think about it, there's probably dozens of people doing something just like it right now. Maybe not just with friends, but families too. All of them sitting around laughing and enjoying one another's company."

I frowned, thinking of my own life at home, before everything had happened. Dinnertime was never a happy affair in my house. My parents would grill me on protocol and statutes, and too many wrong answers could result in dinner being taken away.

"Not all families are like that," I said bitterly, unable to hold it in.

Thinking about how my life had been when growing up made me mad, and I immediately used the anger to demonstrate to myself why I shouldn't even be worried about my parents, and should instead treat them like potential criminals. They had done it to me, so why shouldn't I treat them the same way? Their behavior toward me my entire life certainly proved that I didn't owe them any consideration, and as much as it hurt me to admit it, there was a chance that they *were* involved. That they had been involved all along.

"That's too bad," Leo said sadly, and I glanced over to see him giving me a pitying look. "Family is supposed to make you feel safe."

"I suppose so. It didn't, in my case."

We rounded a corner and entered one of the main halls that ran through the residential apartments in Cogstown. It was wider than the rest, and more prone to foot traffic, but still relatively empty since it was a few hours until shift change.

"Is that why you don't want to help the Tower?" Leo asked carefully.

I gave him a look. "I stayed out of it, remember?"

He nodded and then shrugged. "You may not have voted, but I could tell you didn't like the idea. I just don't understand why. You told me the area around the Tower is still irradiated, so what could possibly be worth taking that risk? What do you expect to do once you're outside, and how will you survive if everything else is destroyed? How do you plan to get everyone supplies, like fresh water, food, shelter...? I mean, don't take this the wrong way, but leaving the Tower seems shortsighted on your part."

We exited the main hallway, taking one of the corridors that branched off, and I found the sign pointing toward the elevator banks and pointed it out to Leo. The entire time, however, my mind was considering his question. They were all valid points, but he didn't know what we did: the desire to leave had been Roark's, based on his wife's accidental contact with an alien human who *had* survived outside the Tower. According to him, the alien human had not only survived, but was part of another civilization—one that was thriving. But Leo knew none of this.

I didn't see a problem with telling him, so I did. "Roark's wife, Selka, was a medic, and one day, twenty-five years ago, some Knights brought in someone they claimed was an undoc. Only she wasn't. Selka's examination of her revealed rudimentary medical practices that were so antiquated, apparently, that it didn't take her long to determine that the girl wasn't from here."

"What happened?"

"Devon Alexander and Raevyn Hart, the head of the Farmers at the time, asked Selka to leave. She didn't know what happened after that, but it doesn't change the fact that there is life out there. The council probably kept it secret to keep citizens from leaving, although that was some time ago, so I don't know." I sighed and ran a hand through my hair. "What I do know is that Raevyn Hart died some time afterward, and Selka was taken and presumably killed. I know it's all hearsay—we have no proof beyond anecdotal evidence, and yet... once Roark laid out the pieces of it, it made sense. And it wouldn't exactly be the first conspiracy we've discovered to be true in the Tower."

He gave me a curious look. "Why don't you just use the monitoring station to find out if anyone is living out there?"

I frowned. "The monitoring station?"

Leo turned and gave me a pointed look. "You don't know what the monitoring station is? Somehow that doesn't surprise me, given how ignorant the people here seem to be about the Tower itself. Basically, it's a room inside the Tower that monitors all frequencies for communications coming from within five hundred miles."

Huh. That was interesting. And irritating. I always seemed to be finding out about something *else* inside the Tower that I had no previous knowledge of.

But if Leo was right, which I was certain he was, then that meant there was a way to find out, once and for all, if people were actually out there. Which meant we could confirm that there was a place to go *before* we left.

"That's great news," I said with a smile. "That means we can find out who's out there and where they live!"

There was a flash of disappointment on his face, and he looked away from me.

"What?" I asked, already knowing what his answer would be.

"Nothing," he said. "I just... I just think it's weird that you don't want to stay and help me. Especially knowing what you know about Scipio, now. Don't you feel bad about abandoning all of these people to die?"

I fidgeted and looked away, watching the hall ahead. His question hit a nerve with me, and I immediately felt defensive. "Look, the people here practically worship Scipio like a god. They'll lose their minds if they find out something is wrong with him."

"So? That's not their fault. Somewhere along the line, someone started to make the comparison, and it grew into a popular idea! They just believe something that many other people also believe in. You don't punish a child for not being able to read if you haven't first taken the time to teach them. This is the same thing."

I clenched my teeth and looked away. Leo was right, and we both knew it. But a part of me could only ask why. *Why* was it my responsibility? Why did I have to be the one to do it? I'd never asked for this, and I sure as hell didn't want the responsibility. It was too much for one person. I could barely keep on top of the responsibilities I did have, and that was more than enough for one person.

"Look, Leo, I'm not trying to be rude, but you need to understand that seven lives are already depending on me, and seven is enough. One life per day of the week is something I can stay on top of. But the entire Tower? That's too much for one person to handle."

"But you wouldn't be alone," he said earnestly. I slid my eyes over to him, and found him looking at me with a hopeful expression. "I'd be there to help you. If you decided to stay and help me. I-I can't do it by myself."

I bit my lip and looked away, uncertain of what I should do.

My mind chided me, though, reminding me that I knew *exactly* what I had to do. It just meant convincing everyone else that we needed to change our minds and commit ourselves to helping Leo and getting him inside the mainframe. That we needed to try to stop the Tower from dying, instead of trying to get away from it.

In my heart, I felt torn. I wanted to believe that if I just told my friends what I knew, they would want to do it as well. But I couldn't be sure. Zoe and Eric would say yes, because their families were still here, but Quess and Maddox? Tian? The Tower had brought them nothing but tribulation and horror—I doubted they wanted anything to do with it anymore.

How could I possibly ask them to change their minds? Staying in the Tower for longer—trying to go against those who had been slowly destroying Scipio over the years—put them in danger. Bad enough we were allied with Lacey, and targets for having assassinated Devon. But this? This was no easy task.

Then something—a tangent memory from the net—gripped me for a second. Just words, and a picture of a woman I suddenly knew was someone called Kami Garcia. A writer.

The words burned in my mind, like a torch guiding me from the darkness.

The right thing and the easy thing are never the same.

And with that, I knew. Knew that I couldn't abandon the Tower, Scipio, Leo, or the thousands of other people who would die because of my inaction. I could put up a front, act like it didn't bother me, but the fact that it did *told* me that I wasn't doing the right thing. I was doing something that would haunt me my whole life, and I was doing something that almost everyone in my life had done to me: dismissing it as someone else's problem.

I couldn't ask my friends to stay behind for this—but there was nothing to stop me from making sure that *I* did, when the time came. And in the meantime, I'd use every waking moment, outside of getting Lacey's goal accomplished, trying to help Leo find a way to fix the Tower.

I was opening my mouth to inform Leo of my decision when I saw something shift out of the corner of my eye. A coarse black bag dropped over my head, and several pairs of hands seized me at once.

It took me a moment to register what had happened, but as they began to push me forward, I couldn't hold back. "Are you freaking *kidding* me with this stupid bag thing again?"

There was a chuckle—one I recognized as belonging to the only one of Lacey's men who had talked to me the last time. "Relax, girl," he said soothingly. "Lacey just wants a chat."

I rolled my eyes—for all the good it did me in the dark of the black sack—and continued to stumble forward, hoping Lacey had chosen somewhere nearby.

23

Luckily, Lacey *had* chosen a nearby place, and after a minute or so of walking, we were shoved forward a few steps, the hands disappearing. I ripped off the bag as soon as I realized the hands were gone, and whirled, trying to catch a glimpse of them purely out of spite. But the door was already closing.

I helped pull the bag off Leo's head and looked around. We were standing in the entryway of an apartment not unlike Roark's. Image grabs of a family featuring two middle-aged adults and two small children hung on the wall, but I didn't recognize any of them. This wasn't Lacey's apartment; that much was certain.

I stepped in deeper, moving into the common area, and continued my exploration. The living room was empty and devoid of life, but the kitchen looked recently used. Pots and pans were stacked on the stove, and the smell of roasted spices filled the air. I heard something coming from the dining room across from it, and made my way around the partition wall. The table was loaded with food, four plates set in front of accompanying chairs, but the chairs were empty. Unless the family that lived there was hiding in the back, it seemed that they had departed in a hurry, with their supper unfinished on the table.

A table that Lacey was still standing next to, in fact, picking at a partially eaten roasted platter.

"Invite yourself to dinner?" I asked, but she ignored me, her fingers shoving the food into her mouth.

"I don't typically get a chance for a homecooked meal," she said around her mouthful. She examined the table and picked up a cup, bringing it to her nose for an experimental sniff before taking a sip.

"Still," I said, observing her dining with growing unease. This was someone's home, and she was just eating their food. "I assume you evicted some family for this impromptu conversation. Do you have to eat their food, too?"

The look she gave me was purely bemused, and she came around the table and picked up a roll from a basket next to the platter. "My Cogs like to take care of me," she replied. "They understand that running an entire department takes a lot of work." She tore off a chunk of bread and ate it, washing it down with another sip from the cup, and then sat heavily in one of the chairs, sighing.

I waited. I had no idea what she wanted to talk about. Half of me wondered if she was about to dress us down for our performances in the Tourney. Maybe it didn't matter to her that we'd qualified. Maybe she was either angry or upset that we had failed to make her cousin look good. Another part of me wondered if it was something else—possibly another dangerous task she wanted to compel us to do.

Luckily, Lacey didn't leave me stewing long. "I wanted to congratulate you on your performance at the qualifiers," she announced softly. "It seems like things are going better with Ambrose?"

I eyed her warily, wondering why she had broken protocol. I knew she wasn't here to talk about Ambrose. We had agreed at the meeting the other day that it would be the last until after the Tourney was finished, so she hadn't risked this exposure just to talk about Ambrose.

I had a choice as to how to handle this. I could either ask her directly what she wanted, or play along. I contemplated the options for a second, and then crossed my arms. It was too late, and I was too tired to play along.

"What do you want, Lacey?"

If my rudeness at ignoring her question shocked her, she hid it well behind an amused smile. "Straight to the point, I see," she said, reaching into her pocket and pulling out a pad. "I've got an update on that Frederick Hamilton. We just uncovered it a few hours ago."

"Oh?" I asked, mildly curious. His file had been similar to Dylan's in that he was a good and dutiful Knight. He transferred in from the Medica when he was fifteen, and had led a rather unremarkable life as a Knight. Lacey's report at the last meeting hadn't reflected any sort of legacy heritage, but I was guessing that had changed, given the look Lacey was now giving me. "I take it he's a legacy?"

"I'm not sure," she replied honestly. "But we did uncover that he is distantly related to Ezekial Pine." I stiffened at the name, recognizing it immediately. Ezekial Pine, one of the original founders of the Tower, and the head of the Knights at the time, had murdered Lionel Scipio in an attempt to kill Leo.

I looked back at the AI in question, and saw that he was taking the news about as well as I could have expected. His jaw was clamped tight, his eyes hot and flashing. I caught his gaze and shook my head, warning him not to lose his cool, and turned back to Lacey, who had continued speaking during our quick exchange.

"The Pines were like my family: one of the first families to keep their legacy nets after the IT department recalled them. Only they were determined to subvert Scipio. It's a long story how my family was drawn into this whole mess, and an even longer story how we figured out that the Pines were behind the plots, but it culminates in my family killing theirs."

"You killed the Pines?" I asked, my eyes widening some. It was true the Pines had seemed to disappear after the first few Champions, but I had always assumed that was due to names changing because of marriages. Not because they had all been assassinated.

"This was well over a century ago," Lacey replied. "So no, not me personally. But yes, my family targeted them and killed them. Frederick Hamilton's grandmother, it seems, was overlooked due to a divorce."

I picked up the pad and turned it on, frowning. If what Lacey was saying was true, then it meant that Frederick was potentially a legacy recruit, if not a full legacy himself.

"Do you know if—"

"No, I don't know if he actually has a legacy net or not," Lacey interrupted me with a sigh. "But we have to assume he does, just in case. The problem is, even if he is a legacy, we have no idea who, if anyone, is supporting him. It's unlikely he would be working alone."

If I had to guess, it was the person Devon had been in league with. The one I'd heard those two Inquisition agents referencing when they were talking to the Champion in the Medica before we attacked them.

"Nor do we have any idea what other candidates might be working with them," Leo added, breaking his silence.

Lacey nodded, her mouth turning downward, and sighed. "You may think I am powerful, Liana, but believe me when I tell you that whoever we are fighting is stronger. Ambrose is the first of us we've managed to get into the Knights in a very long time. That's why I needed you and your friends to help him. Because I knew he was going to be alone in there. After what happened with you in the marketplace, I should've just pulled him, but..."

She trailed off and looked at me, her eyes glittering with determination, and I followed her train of thought to the most natural conclusion. "But you need someone who is on your side to be the Champion."

Lacey nodded slowly. "Not only to help us, but to stop them from doing any more damage to Scipio."

I exhaled, the weight of what she was saying settling in on me. Frederick's possible legacy status only confirmed something I had just started to suspect: we were on the cusp of a legacy war.

And Lacey had just told me that we were the only support her side really had within the department. My heart sank, plummeting deeper into the cold, endless chasm that had opened up in the pit of my belly.

We were in serious danger. And Lacey wasn't going to let us stop.

I clenched the pad tighter, anger beginning to well up at the injustice of it. Lacey knew there were going to be causalities in this fight, and she was going ahead with it anyway, risking the life of her cousin, and with it, the lives of me and my friends. Without even bothering to warn us.

"You're angry with me," Lacey said, leaning forward. I stared at her, my jaw locked so tightly that it felt impossible to open my mouth to answer, so I nodded instead. She looked away. "I'm sorry."

"I thought you were going to provide us with some sort of support," I seethed, unable to hold back the recriminations my mind was beginning to spin out. "But instead you let us walk into this without any backup, and expect us to be able to handle it on our own! What happens if we fail, Lacey? What happens if Ambrose is killed?"

"That better not happen," she said, her voice lethal, and I suddenly wanted to snatch my own hair out in frustration. Or hers. Possibly both.

"You're missing the point, Lacey! You cannot possibly expect me to keep Ambrose safe under these conditions! Maybe if we didn't have the Tourney to worry about, sure, but were it not for the Tourney, he wouldn't need protection in the first place!"

Leo laid a hand on my shoulder, and I swiveled around to see him staring at me, brown eyes brimming with concern. I looked down, my hands aching from how tightly I had been clenching them around the pad, and struggled to catch my breath. I realized I had been shouting, and took a moment to get a grip.

I couldn't help it—my frustration at Lacey was getting the better of me. She had blackmailed us and set us up for failure, and I would be damned if I was going to sit by and allow her to get away with it. To hell with her Tourney and her suicide mission. Let her blast us as criminals—better to run than deal with this mess.

"You know what? Tell Ambrose good luck," I said, setting the pad back down on the table. "I'm taking my friends and leaving."

I turned to go, but Lacey suddenly stood up and slammed her hand against the table, startling me enough to make me spin around, my baton already in my hand in preparation for some sort of attack, only to find her standing as still as a statue at the head of the table, watching me.

For a moment, neither of us moved, and the tension pulled tight as a rubber band for several long heartbeats while I waited for her to do or say anything threatening. I mentally prepared myself for what I would do if her henchmen entered.

"I'm sorry," Lacey said finally, lowering her chin slightly. "You're right, of course. I did put you into a very dangerous situation, and you have every right to be angry. But please understand, I only did it because I felt I didn't have any other choice available to me. You were Devon's enemy, and had no knowledge of the legacy nets or this shadow war, which meant I could take a chance and trust you. I don't like exploiting you, and I really wish I didn't have to."

She paused, her mouth working, and then sighed. "You have every right to want to leave, but I am begging you. Please, help Ambrose win the Tourney. I know he isn't the ideal candidate, but he's the only one we've got, and if he doesn't get in... If someone else does... then the battle for Scipio and the Tower will be over, and we will all be lost."

It was the desperation in her voice, more than anything else, that defused my anger, and I reconsidered her move from her position. She was genuinely afraid of what would happen if she didn't find some way to shift the balance of power away from her enemies—and I was starting to believe her when she said that she wanted to save the Tower, not hurt it.

I bit my lip, considering my options. I could still walk away, but without a new location for us to hide in, or the supplies we needed to survive, we wouldn't last long. Not to mention, our absence from the Tourney would be noted, and people would start looking. Our chances of survival were better working with Lacey and trying to make it out of the Tourney alive. At the very least, it was a fighting chance, whereas running off and trying to escape without a place to go and while we were in the public eye was downright suicide.

"I'll help you," I finally said. It was an easy decision to make, after my self-revelation with Leo in the hall earlier—putting Ambrose in the position of Champion had to be a far better option than anyone who was working for our enemies or someone who had no idea what the real stakes were. And, I was already planning on committing myself to Leo's cause. What was one more cause on top of that?

Lacey let out a breath she had been holding, clearly relieved. I didn't let it last long. "But you and Ambrose will owe me, and that means leaving me and my friends to our own devices after all this is done."

"Of course," she said hurriedly. "You will have earned it."

I stared at her a moment longer and then sighed, suddenly very tired. "Great. We'll show ourselves out."

"Wait."

I stopped, mid-turn, and watched as Lacey crossed over to me. She held out her hand, the pad I had put down earlier now back in it. I took it from her again, unzipping my pocket and tucking her pad in next to my own. "There's a file there on the setup and design of the challenges," she informed me. "It doesn't have much more than that, but it will hopefully give you an advantage."

I looked down at the pad. I wasn't uncomfortable with the idea of cheating, especially as it seemed our enemies had even more power than I had originally thought. "Thank you," I said.

"I wish I could do more," she said apologetically. She stared at me a second, her eyes narrowed in contemplation. "It's too bad you weren't born into our family," she announced after a long pause. "I love my cousin dearly, but I think you have the makings of a great Champion."

I stared at her dumbly, her compliment catching me off guard completely. "Oh. Um. Thanks," I mumbled, uncertain how to respond.

"Don't mention it," she said with a soft chuckle. "Now run along, both of you. You have a big day tomorrow."

I nodded, turned, and left, reeling from the emotional roller-coaster of the meeting with Lacey and the realization of the great danger we were in... and with Lacey's compliment still burning in my ears.

"Are you okay?" Leo asked quietly, and I glanced over at him.

I struggled with a way to answer his question, and then shrugged. "Ask me tomorrow" was the only answer I could formulate. I belatedly remembered that I was supposed to ask Lacey about the legacy net, and the memories I couldn't remember after the fact, but at that point, I wasn't about to turn around to do so. It could wait.

I hoped.

24

The next morning came too quickly, with too many questions left unanswered even after my long night trying to sleep but invariably being dragged back to wakefulness by nagging thoughts. Should I warn my parents to watch their backs? Why was I still agreeing to do this Tourney after everything I had learned from Lacey? How was I going to help Leo get Jasper from Sadie Monroe's office? What was going to happen at the Tourney tomorrow?

I had drifted off at four in the morning, and then, after what felt like mere seconds but had actually been three hours, I was jolted awake by my alarm, the sound of it waking me with a fright so intense that I sat up, immediately scanning the room for a source of danger. My heart had beat so hard that I could taste copper on my tongue, and it took me several frantic passes of the room before I was satisfied that I was alone.

I rubbed my hands over my arms, trying to smooth away the

goosebumps that had formed there, and shivered. The rude awakening after so little sleep left me feeling weak and shaky, and for a second, I seriously considered locking my door and crawling back under the covers to hide from all my problems.

But I couldn't. I wasn't cowardly enough to, for one thing, but even if I were, I couldn't—not with everyone counting on me to see us through this nightmare. I took a deep breath, steeling myself for whatever challenges the day decided to bring me, and got up.

I showered and got dressed quickly, needing something to distract me from the questions plaguing me. Luckily, it was my turn to make breakfast this morning, and with everyone but Zoe and Eric stopping by to look at the plans Lacey had given us, I would have my hands full making food for the next hour.

I went into the kitchen and quickly began gathering ingredients, determined to stay busy. I let the feel of the knife slicing through the onions, peppers, and garlic I was preparing soothe me, and the popping hiss of them hitting the pan I had been heating helped to block out the questions.

The room began to smell like my father's cooking. I was making burritos, just like he had made in the morning when I was younger. The memories there weren't particularly good, and I suddenly hated that I had chosen to cook this. Luckily, a simple reminder-turned-mantra helped me remember that it wasn't the food's fault, and it helped keep me focused.

The work kept me busy, and it helped me pass the time with less anxiety. I made myself a plate when certain things were ready, and ate them as I cooked, wanting to get my breakfast finished before the meeting. Maddox emerged from the hall eventually, her hair damp and her nose up, sniffing the air.

"That smells good," she said.

I smiled as I began transferring the spicy potatoes I had just been frying into a bowl. "Thanks," I replied. "Hope everyone likes spicy."

"I'm sure they will. Are you okay?"

I sat the bowl down and smiled ruefully. "You know, I've been getting that question a lot lately, and I think my answer is going to be 'not really' for the foreseeable future."

Maddox frowned and came around the counter, her eyes brimming with concern. "How can I help?" she asked. "Do you want to talk about it?"

I shook my head, returning my gaze to the food. I actually did want to talk about it, but if I started now, I'd probably break down. And I couldn't afford to do that before the Tourney. "Thanks," I said, pulling the tortillas out of the microwave. "But I'll get by."

She looked doubtful, but didn't press. Instead, she reached over and grabbed two of the bowls with the burrito fillings I had whipped up, and began carrying them into the living room. I balanced two more on one arm, and the plate of tortillas on the other, and followed suit, working with her to set the table.

Quess and Tian arrived before we were finished. I opened the door to admit them, and smiled when I saw Tian fast asleep in Quess's arms, her mouth open, snoring loudly. "She got home late," he said with a frown as he stepped in. "She wouldn't come home when I told her."

"Is she okay?" I asked, instantly concerned. "Why wouldn't she come home?"

"She said she was onto something," he replied, his voice haggard. "I had to threaten to take away dessert privileges just to get her to finally come home, and she was mad at me when she arrived."

"Because it's not fair," Tian mumbled, smacking her mouth and shifting her head slightly.

"I'm the adult," Quess said firmly, but Tian blew a half-hearted raspberry, and then yawned loudly.

I exhaled. "Tian, what you did wasn't good," I said, keeping my voice very even.

Her eyes shot open, and a second later she was sitting upright. "Yes, it was," she said, frowning. "You said we needed to find a new home, and that's what I was doing. But there are some places you can only go at night, so I needed to be out there, looking! This is my job!"

If Quess hadn't been holding her, I could imagine that she would have been stamping one booted foot to emphasize her point.

"I know it's your job," I said patiently. "But with the Tourney starting, we're all going to be really busy for the next few days. We need you to take a little break from the house hunt."

"No!" she said, and began squirming around in Quess's arms, so much so that the young man had to set her down. "I'm close to a new home, I can feel it! Let me go."

I closed my eyes against her vehement tone, trying for

patience. I wasn't mad that Tian was being stubborn—but I *was* tired, and that would make anyone feel a bit short tempered.

"I'm really sorry, Tian, but I can't," I said firmly. She opened her mouth to object once again, but I held up my hand, stopping her. "Would Cali say exactly what I'm saying?" I asked her, giving her a pointed look.

She scowled, crossing her arms across her chest. "Yes," she admitted with the enthusiasm of a person about to have a tooth pulled. She sucked in several deep breaths, clearly trying to calm herself down. "Fine. I won't go anywhere today. Now, may I please use your bedroom to get a few more hours of sleep?"

I frowned at the rapid jump in the conversation, and after a moment of thinking about it, I nodded. "Of course. I'll make you a burrito for when you wake up."

"With no tomatoes," she ordered as she stomped past me, heading for my room on the left side of the hall.

"She's getting spoiled," Quess said softly, and I frowned. I didn't agree. Tian was probably one of the most selfless girls I knew. If anything, she was worried that she wasn't doing enough to contribute, or wasn't working fast enough for everyone, and was angry that she was being prevented from completing her goals. It would pass, especially once she got more sleep.

I started to tell Quess as much, but then another buzz on the door caught my attention, and I opened it up to let Leo and Ambrose in. "Good morning," I said, ushering them inside. "You're just in time. Breakfast is ready to eat."

"And smells amazing," Leo said, an excited look coming to

his eyes as he moved inside, making a beeline for the food. He stood over it, studying it.

"He really is an odd one," Ambrose said quietly from beside me, and I blinked and looked over at him, instantly alarmed that he had picked up on Leo's little quirks. I knew he wouldn't be able to guess what Leo actually was, but I didn't like the idea of Ambrose noticing anything off about him.

"Go ahead and get seated," I said with a smile, gently changing the subject. "I've got Lacey's plans ready for today's challenge, and I already ate, so I can run through things while you guys eat."

Ambrose nodded, and together we moved into the living room. I quickly made a burrito for Tian, but set it aside instead of delivering it to her directly, eager to get started.

"All right. So, I'm not sure what the goal for the first challenge is, but Lacey gave us a map of what the setup is going to be. We're going to be navigating a maze."

A maze with a lot of tricky turns and dead-ends. I'd looked at it last night in order to prepare, and even I had been overwhelmed by the number of turns, switchbacks, and dead-ends. Luckily, we had Leo, whose photographic memory would help solve that problem, but looking at it still gave us a chance to prepare. I reached over and activated the pad I had placed on the table earlier, syncing it with the holographic generator Quess had delivered the other day, and showing the design on the screen—a series of intersecting lines inside an oval that had simply two labels: Wall and Path. There was nothing to indicate what would be used as a barrier; it could be anything from metal to water.

"It looks like there're four entrances," Quess announced around a mouthful of food. "Only four teams at a time?"

"It makes sense," I replied, studying the maze design. "They always start with some sort of elimination challenge, to try to weed out at least four groups, to make the numbers more manageable."

"There are wide spaces drawn in," Leo said, pointing out a few open spaces. "These areas would be good for setting a trap or lying in wait."

"We'll have to avoid those," I replied, my eyes still going over it. "There's no sign of any traps, but this map only shows a rough outline, so there could be some."

We continued to go over the map, discussing plans and strategies for getting through it as quickly as possible. Speed was the only tactic we had to keep Ambrose safe, and since whoever was targeting him wasn't shy, completing everything as quickly as possible was one way of making sure they didn't have a chance to attack. We discussed our strategies, and even speculated on ways of moving both quickly and stealthily. It wasn't until my alarm beeped that I realized how much time had passed, and I quickly shut down the generator and pad, and stood up.

"We need to get going," I announced. "Quess, can you go grab Tian?"

"On it," Quess replied, climbing to his feet and heading into the back. I began scooping up and stacking the dirty dishes, and after a few seconds, everyone was chipping in and helping me clean up the mess.

I was pleased at how well everything was going, and the anxiety from last night and this morning was finally beginning to ease, thanks to our confab before the challenge. Now all we had to do was—

"Liana, Tian is gone!" Quess exclaimed as he exited the hall.

I stared at him, plates still in my hands. "What?" He did not just say what I thought he said.

"She's gone," he repeated, his voice carrying a low note of panic.

I sat the dishes down and immediately rushed into my bedroom. My eyes scanned the boxes that were still unpacked on my desk, my closet, my bed.... the last of which was untouched and empty. I quickly stepped in, throwing open my closet doors. My uniforms—the only things I had actually hung —were there, but no Tian. Under the desk, the bed... But there was no sign of her at all.

Anxiety gripped my heart, and I realized that she must have snuck out through one of the vents while we were eating— ignoring my orders in an attempt to complete her mission. I was more scared than I was angry, and immediately wanted to go after her. The fact that she had run off on the day of the Tourney was dangerous—anyone who had designs on us could've discovered who she was, and how important she was to us. They could grab her and use her to force us to withdraw or support another candidate, or kill her just to send a message. I knew she was confident, and her lashing skills were unparalleled, but still, there was no way I was letting them have the chance.

"Quess, have Mercury ping her net, and we'll—"

"We don't have time for that," Leo said, cutting me off. "We need to report to the opening ceremony in only a few minutes."

I hesitated, looking around the vacant room where Tian should've been. "But we have to find her."

"She ran off on her own," Maddox said, sounding like she was trying to reassure both me and herself at the same time. "She can take care of herself."

"I'll find her," Quess added with a firm nod. "I'll get a hold of Mercury and get him to run down the location of her net. As soon as I have her location, I'll go after her, and in the meantime, I'll run the drones."

I didn't like it, but if Quess and Maddox were sure that she'd be okay, and Quess was going to try to find her, I had to believe them. Because there was no other option—short of trying to find her and getting eliminated from the Tourney for being late.

But God help me, I hated it.

Anxiety at Tian's disappearance, and my lack of sleep from the night before, made me feel like my skin was tight and threatening to leap off my body to go perform a search of its own for our youngest friend. But I kept a firm grip on it, reminding myself that Quess and Mercury weren't going to leave a single bolt unexamined in the whole of the Tower. We'd find her.

And then I was going to cut off all her privileges for a week. Two weeks. Maybe even three. After I made sure she was all right, of course.

And definitely no hot chocolate.

Of course, none of this made us feel better, and even Ambrose seemed to be maintaining a respectful silence as we entered the competitors' greeting room. The room was large, and set up with tables, chairs, food, and water—all meant for the competitors themselves. Only sixteen teams had made it through the qualifiers, and given the sheer volume of people in the room, we were among the last teams to arrive.

We followed Ambrose as he made his way around the groups and straight to the official's table in the back to check in and confirm our identities and ranks—anyone under ten would be automatically disqualified. I checked my wrist out of habit. Still a ten. Quess had removed the legacy net before we had left and replaced it with the normal one, just in case, but I hadn't checked to make sure it was working.

I listened half attentively as the official explained that our equipment and order would be given to us when we reached one of the four entry points to the arena. No one would know what the challenge was until the commencement speech was given, which would only happen once every candidate was present.

The only advantage we had was Lacey's maps. Hopefully, that would be enough to get us through.

And as soon as we were done, we could get out of here and back to finding Tian.

"All right, you were last to check in," the official said brusquely, the finality in his voice bringing me back to awareness. "All candidates!" he bellowed loudly, and I winced and covered my ears. "You have five minutes to report to your entry room. Proceed down the side halls now."

An official next to him tapped his pad, and the doors on either side of the room slid open.

"We're entering through Gate 12," Ambrose said immediately, moving toward it. I stopped him by placing a hand on his shoulder—a knee-jerk reaction to the idea of losing him in the thick stream of people eagerly rushing for the two openings.

"Let's wait until everyone goes through," I breathed softly. I didn't want to get caught in a crowd of pushing people. It'd be too easy for someone to get close to Ambrose in that chaos.

Ambrose's lips parted, and then he hesitated, swallowing back whatever he was about to say. "Okay," he finally said.

We stayed by the official's table and waited. I watched the crowd of people, and to my surprise, one of them broke off and began approaching us. It was my mother. And I could tell by her expression that she wanted to talk. To me.

I hesitated. We hadn't talked since I had moved out, and now that she and my father were involved with Salvatore Zale, I had been agonizing over whether they were involved with the legacies or not. I hated the thought of them being part of that. A very small part of me wouldn't believe it. Couldn't believe that my parents were capable of betraying the people they were sworn to keep safe, the Tower they were so proud to serve, and their daughter, the person they were supposed to protect the most in this world. But I couldn't dismiss the possibility, either.

My mother stopped a few feet away, then stood there, waiting to see if I would come to her. I could feel my friends' eyes on me, waiting to see what I would do, and I bit my lip, then decided to see what she wanted. It wouldn't hurt anything to see what she had to say.

"Excuse me," I said quietly before moving to her.

I stopped right in front of her and met her solemn gaze head on. "Mother," I greeted her coolly. "Did you come to wish us good luck?"

My mother's tongue darted out to lick her lips—a sign that she was nervous. "Not exactly. I came..." She paused again, faltering. "You almost died."

For the span of several heartbeats, I couldn't formulate a response. I wasn't even sure what she was talking about; I had almost died lots of times recently. "Which time?"

She blinked, and then pain bled into her eyes. "I guess I deserved that," she breathed bitterly. Disconcerted, I waited, still unsure of what she was going to say. "I saw your lash qualifier. You..." She broke off again, and I let out a breath.

"That's what this is about?" I barely managed to keep the bite out of my voice. "Equipment malfunction?" I almost gave her a scathing laugh when she nodded, but held it back. My response, however, shot out of my mouth before I could give it a second thought. "I cannot believe you. The corrupt Champion almost strangles your daughter, and I get a tub of cream for my bruises, and stoic silence. But my lash line was cut, and now you're worried?"

"'Cut'?" she echoed. "What do you mean, cut?"

I sucked in a deep breath and realized I had said too much. My mother's loyalties still weren't clear to me, and if I tipped my hand and revealed that I knew we were being targeted, then their attempts might get harder to detect or prevent. "It doesn't matter now. I'm emancipated. Your maternal obligation is done. You don't have to pretend anymore."

Her brows came together. "Liana, I..." She trailed off and

exhaled sharply. "I'm glad you're safe, and that you have team-mates who won't abandon you. That's all I wanted to say. And be careful."

Her response once again brought me up short, and this time, she didn't give me a chance to formulate a response. She left, disappearing back into the still-steady stream of people filing out.

I stared after her, trying to process what had just happened. For all I knew, it was a ploy. My parents had to know the effect they had on me, and by trying to have a touching moment with me, maybe she was trying to throw me off. Salvatore might have even put her up to it in order to keep me unfocused.

If they had wanted to throw me off, it was working. My mother had not only shown her concern this time, but actually verbalized it—something I hadn't thought she was capable of doing. It had to be a ploy. It had to be.

Yet, my instincts were telling me something different. They were screaming at me to trust that she was being genuine, to chase after her and warn her about the legacies and their battle to control the Champion. But I couldn't. Even if I believed that she was being honest, it was too late—she was gone.

And I couldn't rule out that my instincts were skewed by my emotional state of mind, which was already bad due to Tian sneaking out. I had always wanted a good relationship with my mother—both my parents, really—and that didn't just stop because I'd made the decision to cut them out. It was there—and it always would be. The need to be accepted and loved by the people who had a hand in making you was inborn. But I couldn't trust that, either; I'd been burned before.

"Are you okay?" Leo asked, his voice much closer than it should've been, and it startled me out of my thoughts.

Turning, I saw that he had moved nearer to me. Ambrose and Maddox were still waiting by the table, and from the way they were pointedly not meeting my gaze, I realized that I had been standing rock-still for a while. The room was now empty.

"Sorry," I said, shaking my head in an attempt to clear my mind. The challenge—that was all that mattered. Getting through it and getting out as quickly as possible. "Let's go."

Leo frowned as I brushed past him, and I could tell he wanted to ask about what had happened with my mother, but I ignored it. I didn't want an emotional heart-to-heart right now; we had things that needed to get done.

Ambrose pushed off the table, and we headed down the left hall, which wrapped around the stadium. We were actually underneath the stands, and even though there were several feet of steel separating us from them, I could hear thousands of voices, muffled, but still there.

We passed several sealed doors as we went along, each of them leading to a utility closet that was run by the master-of-arms and had direct access to the arena. But it seemed only a few were being used for this challenge. Everything else was restricted, which meant we couldn't fall back another room, once we were in the maze. They had probably even sealed off the door from the other side, but I wouldn't know until we got there.

It sucked, but it wasn't surprising. I doubted the designers had even considered leaving additional exits for competitors— probably because they didn't know that some of the contestants weren't playing by the rules. Or maybe they did, and it was intentionally designed that way.

Scipio help me, I'm getting paranoid, I thought as we came to a stop in front of a door with the number twelve painted across it in white block numbering. Leo reached out and pushed a button, and the door slid open to reveal the small compartment within. Normally, racks filled with sparring equipment would line the walls and form tight rows across the length of the room, but it had been cleared out and replaced with chairs and modesty screens for changing. Some of the chairs were occupied, while noise from a few of the modesty screens indicated that people were putting their equipment on.

A few eyes glanced our way. I heard someone say, "Honor-bound," with a touch too much awe in their voice, and I sighed as we entered the room.

"Just in time," an official at the opposite end of the room barked. "Klein?"

"Yes, ma'am," Ambrose replied, raising a hand. "My team is present and accounted for."

"Good. Come and get your equipment."

Ambrose let Leo and Maddox take point, and together, we made our way to the table that had been set up on the left side of the room, right next to the door that led to the arena. I kept an eye on the crowd while they began collecting their equipment.

After a few moments, Maddox tapped me on the shoulder

and began handing me the last set. I accepted the harness and batons, and then moved over to a vacant modesty screen, as indicated by the green light being emitted by the centermost panel. As soon as we stepped behind it, it would turn red, signaling to the other competitors that it was occupied.

I followed everyone else inside and pressed the button to drop the screen blocking the entryway. Within moments, we were all undoing our suits and putting on our equipment, giving it a thorough screening as we did so.

I did it all on autopilot, wishing that our nets weren't in communication blackout for the Tourney. I wouldn't know if Quess and Mercury had found Tian until afterward. I couldn't contact my mother to warn her. I was helpless to do anything of any real importance, trapped inside this stupid Tourney, sworn to protect a man who was sometimes more trouble than he was worth.

I exhaled, reminding myself that I was being unfair to Ambrose. He'd shown some improvement, and I couldn't be angry at him for this. My own anxiety and agitation had me coiled tighter than a spring, ready to explode at any moment, and nobody needed that. They were probably already feeling it themselves.

"Liana, I know you're dealing with some heavy stuff with your parents and Tian, but you need to snap out of it," Maddox said from beside me, and I looked over at her as I finished zipping up my uniform.

"Is it that apparent?" I asked, cutting through some of my turbulent thoughts and trying to focus.

"Yes. You haven't asked when we go in—which is first, by the way—or gone over plans A, B, or C incessantly."

I gave her a look as she zipped up her own uniform. "Incessantly?" I asked. I looked around. "Do I really do that?"

"Yes," Leo said, tucking his baton into his belt. "But I like it —shows thoroughness."

"I could stand for a bit less... thoroughness," Ambrose added, and I blinked in surprise at him. Had he actually made a joke?

His uncertain smile told me that he had, and a surprised laugh escaped me.

"Be that as it may," Maddox said sharply, clearly not letting go of whatever she was trying to get through to me, "you have been quiet since the apartment, and it's freaking me out." She speared me with a look. "I'm scared for Tian, too, but we need to get through this. Now. Because we're next."

I'd had the same thought earlier, but it had been self-directed—meant to keep me from losing it. I hadn't stopped to consider what they were going through, or how much they needed me to be strong for them, and I suddenly felt guilty for being that self-absorbed. They were looking for me to be less like that, and more like a leader.

I glanced around at my three teammates and offered them an apologetic look. "Sorry, guys," I said contritely, shaking it off. "I'm here and with you. I promise."

"Good," Maddox replied. "Because—"

She trailed off as the overhead lights suddenly dimmed and a rectangular screen appeared on each of the walls of the modesty screen. Moments later, Scipio's face was filling the screen. I heard gasps around the room as many of the other competitors got their first chance to see an image of the great machine, but was unaffected by the image itself. It felt strange seeing him now, knowing what I knew about him. What had seemed like cold aloofness before now seemed like a deep weariness, and once again I found myself wondering if he *knew* he was dying. It would be heartbreakingly sad if he did—because it would also mean that he was powerless to do anything about it.

"Greetings, competitors and citizens of the Tower here to witness the Knights' historic Tourney, and to help select the future leader of your department. Typically, the Champion's former Lieutenant would be here to share some sage words of advice about the challenges ahead, but due to competition regulations, he is unable to do so."

That made sense—the Lieutenant couldn't both oversee the Tourney and participate at the same time. It would be unfair.

"The Tourney is a rigorous challenge designed to test a competitor's resolve, ingenuity, and above all, dedication to the Tower, along with the ideals that have helped preserve our home for centuries. Like every department, the Knights are integral to the Tower's needs and survival.

"This first challenge is called Lightbringer. Each team will be given a ceremonial torch to carry through the obstacles inside. Three cauldrons are situated somewhere past those objects. Four teams will enter the arena at a time, and the first three to light a cauldron will proceed to the next challenge tomorrow."

An official stood up and began passing out the torches: three-foot-long pieces of metal with tips that glowed a bright white. They emitted no heat or smoke, but shone brightly. Definitely something that would give our locations away in the labyrinth we were going to have to navigate.

Which would only invite more trouble, as we ran the risk of any other team we encountered potentially trying to kill us. But there was little we could do about it, and Ambrose accepted the stick that was handed to him.

"We'll have to get through as quickly as possible," I muttered to the others.

I saw them nod from the corner of my eye, but didn't take my eyes away from Scipio.

"Good luck, competitors. May your deeds be noble and gracious, and let your honor and integrity guide your path."

The screen cut off, and a moment later the lights came back on. I swallowed, awareness settling into me as I remembered that we would be the first team in. I needed to keep my head in the game, and make sure we got through.

Ambrose started moving, and I quickly got in line.

The other groups, which were clustered together, fell silent and drew apart as we pushed by them and came to a stop before the door. The official scanned our nets, re-confirming our identities. As soon as the brain-rattling experience was finished, she gave us a nod and a brusque "Good luck," and then opened the door.

We stepped into the little room beyond it—barely big enough for the four of us—and I began shaking the excess energy from my limbs. "Let's go over the plans," I said as a little timer appeared on the door leading to the arena beyond, the time counting down from thirty.

Talking would help calm whatever nerves we were all experiencing.

"We check to see if we can climb up the outer walls—if there are any," Ambrose said first.

"If we can't get on top of the maze, we lash through as quickly as possible," Maddox added.

"And if we can't do that, we run," Leo said, with a little smile.

I nodded. Climbing up had been my idea. Most people never even thought of it; they just chose to run through blindly, and hope that their speed and ability to remember the way they had come before would help them navigate. But going up was unexpected, and we could move directly to it, instead of wasting times on the twists and turns of the maze.

Suddenly the clock hit ten, and I took several deep, calming breaths. "We can get through this, guys. Let's just work together." I wasn't really sure what I meant by that; it just felt like an appropriate time for a pep talk.

"And make sure I light the cauldron," Ambrose added, and I glanced at him. His face was guarded as he regarded me. "It has to be me."

I pressed my lips together and nodded. He knew as well as I did that we couldn't guarantee what was going to happen once those doors slipped open, but he wanted me to do it anyway. It cost me nothing to agree—and it would only slow us down if

Ambrose and I got into a fight when it came to lighting that cauldron.

5... 4... 3... 2... 1...

I tensed in expectation of some loud noise, but to my surprise, there was just a gentle chime as the door slid open, revealing steps leading up. Ambrose sprang up them first, his boots heavy on the stairs, and I followed close behind, cursing that I hadn't gone through before him. We had no idea what awaited us at the top of the stairs, and if our enemies had the reach I believed they did, they could have set a trap to snare us right off the bat. Which meant that sending Ambrose first was a big mistake.

He popped up into the open space before I could do anything and moved to the right, revealing an opening cutting through a dense forest of pipes running around the passageway to form walls and a ceiling. The pipes were of various sizes, but none were wider than the length of my palm. Most of them ran horizontally, but a few were vertical. All were tightly meshed together, the lines of them wrapping in, around, across, above, and under the others, making it impossible to tell where one pipe began and another ended.

The stoop just outside of the door was encased as well, but there was a shaft over our heads, about ten feet long and five feet wide, that ended in an open, rectangular space. Light was pouring through from above.

I immediately pulled my lash out, stepped to one side to allow Maddox and Leo through, spun the line in my hand, and threw it up. The lash end arced up several feet before hitting the black metal wall. It pinged, then, to my complete amazement, bounced off and began falling back down toward us. I reeled the line in quickly, and then recast it.

It hit, but refused to stick.

"Could it be your lashes?" Maddox asked quietly as I dragged the line back in. My thoughts were already aligned with hers, and I spun it up quickly and then let it go at a pipe just inside the entrance. It stuck fast.

Beside me, Leo cast his line up toward the pipe side of the shaft above. It, too, bounced harmlessly off.

"Why isn't it working?" Ambrose asked.

"I'm not sure," I replied, once again activating the gyros in my suit and retracting the line as I thought about it. Clearly, the designers of this challenge had wanted to restrict the usage of our lashes. But why did they work inside the passageway, and not farther up?

"There's something coating it," Leo said, and I looked over to see him withdrawing his hands from the wall and rubbing his fingers together. "Could they have made it resistant to the static charge?"

I thought about it. I wasn't sure about the science, but there were times when our lash beads didn't work—namely whenever there was too much ambient humidity, which prevented the charge from building. Based on that, it would be an easy enough thing to create a substance that would keep the lashes from working.

"It's possible," I said after a pause.

"Who cares?" Ambrose said. "We can't climb, so let's go to plan B!"

"Plan B is lashing," Maddox said. "We can't lash inside the halls, even with our lashes working!"

She was right; there were too many gaps and holes in and around the pipes, so even though our lashes worked inside the maze, if we were off in our throws by an inch, we could go crashing into a wall—or each other, or worse.

"Fine, then we run! We're losing precious time, here!" Ambrose shouted, already moving through the entrance.

"Ambrose, wait!" I said, my eyes studying the shaft leading up. I heard him stop, but continued to study the gaps between the pipes. We might not be able to use the lashes, but we could definitely *climb*. There were natural handhelds made by the pipe itself. My mind seized on that, thinking. Before we had wanted to go up for the advantage and to avoid the other competitors. Now, I was beginning to think we had to if we wanted to win.

"We're wasting time!" he said. "This was your plan, Liana."

"And plans change," I said. "Look, going up was always what we talked about, to create an advantage, but now that the designers have what is practically a screaming invitation for the other competitors to take, we have to assume that they're going to head straight up top."

My assumptions about the map had been contingent on there not being a roof, and on tall walls being used to cut off the path. Most people wouldn't have bothered to climb if that were the case, but now, considering the fact that the walls and roof were easily climbable, thanks to the handholds created by the pipes, and practically lit up with light from above—there was no way the others wouldn't climb up.

It put our chances of winning in a precarious position. On the one hand, if we stayed below we would be less likely to draw any attention. But if our enemies knew our gate entry point, and had access to the map as well, we could be walking into a trap, one that would be very hard to see coming thanks to the complicated twists and turns that were in the maze system. If we stayed on top, we'd be more exposed, but we'd also be able to see trouble coming.

Even if we didn't have any enemies in this round, we ran the risk of getting eliminated if we stayed below—it would take more time to get to the cauldrons down there then it would up top. Climbing wasn't just a strategy anymore. It was a necessity.

"No, we don't," he said obstinately. "For all they know—and we know, as well—that is a trap."

"It could be, but I don't think it is," Maddox said, her voice picking up a thread of excitement. She pushed past Ambrose and into the tunnel, peering down the intersecting tunnels that sat only a few feet back. "There are shafts of light coming from down the hall; it looks like there are several places to climb in and out of the maze. The designers wouldn't put them there unless they wanted the competitors to go up."

That set Ambrose back for a second, and he blinked and shook his head. "You don't know if it's going to be like that all the way through!" he shouted. "We need to go, now."

I turned to him, not wanting to break the peace, which was

already tentative. "You're right; we could get up there and it could be a trap. But I don't think it is. If anything, I think it's the designers' way of pushing for us to get up top and fight. It'll make for better drone footage."

"I think Liana's right, Ambrose," Maddox added, stepping back out of the passageway and over to the wall. "We have to go, or we risk the other teams using the strategy we planned, and getting us eliminated."

She began to climb, and I looked back at Ambrose. "Trust me," I said earnestly.

He clenched his jaw, and then exhaled sharply. "Fine," he said. "I hope you're right about this."

There was little I could say in response, so I placed my hand on a pipe a few feet over my head, my boot on one a foot off the ground, and began to climb, using the pipes as handholds. Ambrose might not be happy with our plan, but he was right about one thing: We couldn't afford to waste any time.

The climb went surprisingly quickly, and after Leo pulled me up onto the wide pipe that encircled the hole leading out, I took a step forward onto an adjacent pipe to balance, and looked out.

The pipe network extended as far as the eye could see, forming an almost serviceable walkway—*if* we took our time and didn't rush too much. Luckily whatever they had coated the walls with didn't make anything slippery, so the only thing we had to worry about was tripping on an uneven pipe.

As I scanned the network, I noted several gaps that were clearly designed to be there, given their uniform nature. One solid block of pipes jutted out in the middle of the scene, stretching up an additional fifteen feet to form a platform. From this distance, I could see the cauldrons—gleaming silver orbs shaped much like eggs, but with the top part cut away in a sharp, steep, diagonal slice that opened up to a hollow space inside. That was where we had to put the torch.

I immediately looked up, checking to see if they had lowered the ceiling for us to use lashes, but the ceiling was some fifty feet above us—twice the range of my lash cable. Besides, if they had done something to the walls to keep us from using our lashes, they had definitely done something to the ceiling—and, presumably, that network of pipes.

Ambrose grunted behind me, and I turned and saw him heaving himself over the edge of the shaft, panting slightly. I shifted my weight onto the leg closest to him and bent over, extending a hand. He grabbed it, and I hauled him the rest of the way up, using the two pipes I was standing on to brace against his weight. Our balance wobbled for a second, but then he caught himself and dropped my hand.

I gave him a nod and a pat on the back, and then looked at Maddox and Leo. "We're going to cross here to get to that platform," I said. "We need to move quickly, but watch your footing —it'd be easy to slip and twist your ankle here."

I turned and started gingerly hopping from one pipe to another, my one and only warning delivered. Pipes of various sizes going in multiple directions spread out before me, and I began picking my way over them. We were all tentative, at first, but after a while it became easier, and pretty soon we were moving at a slight jog across the uneven pipe floor.

Once I got into it, it was actually a little bit fun. The floor wasn't even—some pipes were inches lower or higher—and it tested my balance more, making my rhythm more of a hopping run as I angled myself to jog across one straight segment of pipe for as long as possible, and then leapt to the next one.

I paused when I saw one of those gaps in the pipes drawing closer, and took a look from above. Several feet below, I saw the floor of the arena. The holes led in and out of the maze—Maddox had been right. They littered the entire ceiling, then, meaning that anyone could go up or down as they pleased. It also meant it could be easier for us to be ambushed from several different directions, if someone had a mind to do so. I considered that as Maddox paused beside me, following my gaze.

"So anyone can get in and out of the area below?" she asked. "I knew there were holes, but I didn't think they'd be this extensive."

I nodded. "We should avoid them. Someone might be passing by, below. We can—"

There was a sudden loud trumpet sound, and I flinched, the words dying on my lips. I immediately looked up and saw one of the cauldrons already lit, the flame a deep, vibrant blue that shone even brighter when it was reflected off the silver of the cauldron, which was now almost glowing. Beside it, a solitary figure stood, fists held high, and I realized it was Dylan.

She'd somehow managed to get there first.

"How'd she get there so quickly?" Ambrose asked, his voice alarmed. "That's impossible! We're barely halfway across, and we're moving pretty fast."

It was a good question, but one I didn't have the time to dwell on at the moment.

"Let's keep moving," I said, shaking it off. With one cauldron gone, only two remained. We needed to get to one of those two.

I went back to picking my way across, adrenaline surging. The pipes vibrated under my feet as I jumped over one and landed on the ball of my foot, but I kept my balance by spreading my arms wide.

I was so absorbed in my task that only Leo's softly formed, "Liana, look," could break my focus. I paused and glanced to my left, to where he was standing, and then followed his finger back to the cauldrons. Two people, a man and a woman, were emerging from one of the shaft holes not twenty feet away.

A heartbeat passed as I watched them, a moment of indecision coming over me.

"Liana, the drones are gone!" Maddox suddenly shouted.

I jerked my gaze from the two people and tilted my eyes up, searching the space around us. I'd barely noticed them when they were there, but now that they were gone, I suddenly felt their absence. I looked at what was drawing their attention, and saw six people some seventy feet away, in the middle of fighting with each other.

My mouth went dry. This was either a coincidence, and the fight over there was a distraction so the two coming out of the hole could get past and light the second cauldron, or they were here to try to kill Ambrose. And I didn't remember seeing either of them holding the torch.

This was dangerous.

I returned my gaze to the pair, who were now climbing to their feet, and confirmed that the torch was nowhere on them.

The man reached into a pocket on his suit and pulled something out, fitting it onto his hand. The woman beside him pulled something of her own out, and I could see that it was a thermal cutter. Thermal cutters were used in both Water Treatment and the Mechanic Department to cut through metal. They emitted a plasma beam from a ten-inch handle, and could be adjusted in size, depending on what the wielder needed.

The blade erupted from the pommel, shooting out to a length of three feet, the light of it reminding me of a bruised orange. The woman looked up at us and smiled, a bearing of teeth, and then began to stalk across the pipes toward us, moving with a confidence that told me she was very familiar with walking on pipes.

Her companion trotted along, waggling his shoulders back and forth like he was preparing for a fight. He threw a few punches in the air and then lowered his arms, making right for us.

"Run," I said, and a heartbeat later I was turning and running. There was no time to make calculated moves as I darted across the pipes, my friends just a few feet ahead of me. We were all spread out—too far apart for my taste—so if they singled any of us out, it would take precious seconds before the rest of us got there. I lagged behind to present a juicy target, hoping to buy my friends time to get farther away.

I paused to take a quick look over my shoulder, and saw that they were just feet behind and gaining. I darted to the side just as the man aimed his closed fist right at me, and felt a force brush over my back. He'd fitted a pulse shield to the outside of his knuckles, then. If I got into any hand-to-hand fighting with him, he could easily kill me with a sharp jab to the head—as long as that thing was on his fist.

I shuddered at the thought, and poured the horrifying image it produced into finding new speed, desperately searching for a way out of this. We were exposed all around, and they were gaining on us. We needed to level the playing field—and that meant getting on solid ground.

"Get into the maze!" I shouted, and immediately angled toward the closest hole. Leo made it first, and jumped in immediately, not even bothering with the lashes. It was only a ten-foot drop, but still, it made my heart leap into my throat and the bottom of my stomach drop out to see him go.

Maddox did the same seconds behind him, and then Ambrose followed. It was my turn after that, and I had to trust that they'd cleared my way. I raced up to the edge and dropped down. The velocity of my running carried into my fall, and I slammed into the wall opposite from where I had jumped in, hitting it hard with my shoulder. Pain flooded in, but the impact caused my muscles to react from memory alone, and with my good arm, I reached out and grabbed onto one of the pipes, catching myself from falling farther.

I hung there for a second, looking down to make sure my path was clear, then let go. There was a rattle from above as I fell, and I realized they were already at the entrance.

I bent my legs and hit the ground hard, but caught myself, my entire skeletal structure feeling like it was rattling in its joints. Leo helped right me, and then began pulling me down a long, dimly lit corridor.

"This way," he said softly, and I saw that Maddox and Ambrose were already down the hall, waiting for us at a junction.

I pulled out of his arms and began to jog, just as I heard the sounds of boots hitting the floor behind us. I ignored the pain in my shoulders and the shakiness of my knees, and turned, spinning a lash bead quickly and throwing it. It hit the man in the shoulder, and before he had even began forming his yelp, I wrapped the line under my arm, took a step back, and yanked, ripping him off his feet and face first onto the ground. His scream ended as suddenly as it began, signaling that I had probably stunned him.

I detached the line and spun, even as sparks began to spray from the wall as the woman extended the thermal cutter in the tight confines of the hall. I hunched my shoulders and ran, chasing after my team as they disappeared around the first corner, Leo fast on their trail.

I ripped around the corner and saw Leo waiting, baton in hand. I barely had a moment to slow down before I heard a sharp crack, and then Leo was behind me, pushing me forward as the woman yowled. A quick glance over my shoulder showed her holding her nose, blood spurting from her fingers—but still upright, and already bending over to pick up the cutter from where it had landed behind her. We had bought a few seconds, but not many. I poured on the speed.

Leo raced ahead, finding speed, and we quickly closed the

gap between us and Maddox and Ambrose. We let him lead, as he had the entire map memorized.

The sound of our running feet was thunderous to my ears, but there was nothing we could do to disguise it. We just had to keep moving.

Leo took a right at the first junction thirty feet down, and this time I slowed in time to see the woman rounding the corner, her eyes lighting on me. I picked up the pace, my heart pounding. We had a thirty-foot lead, but we needed to lose her, quickly. Luckily, we had Leo—if anyone could get us a lead, it was him.

The next junction came quickly, only ten feet in, and Leo hooked a left this time. We continued on for another twenty feet, and then he took a right, followed by another right. I glanced over my shoulder, and didn't see any sign of the woman behind us, but I could hear her, the heavy sound of her footfalls still coming after us. She was probably following us by the noise we were making.

None of that mattered, however. Well, it did, but it was distracting us from our ultimate goal—getting one of the two remaining cauldrons lit. We couldn't do that while we were trying to escape the people behind us. We needed to hide.

No, we needed to do more than hide: we needed to *escape*. As I realized that, I crossed under one of the shafts leading up, and an idea was born.

"We need to get up in the shafts before they can see us," I said loudly, checking over my shoulder. We were in a long hallway now, and there was no sign of our pursuers, but I knew they weren't far behind. We would only have seconds to act.

We turned another corner, and a second, and suddenly there was another shaft. Leo leaped up, grabbing onto a lower pipe, and then swung himself up a few feet. Maddox, Ambrose, and I all followed, and I got my boots up and clear of the shaft just as the woman ran by underneath us. She never even looked up.

I didn't wait for her to double back—just started climbing as soon as she raced past. Within moments, Ambrose was helping pull me out of the shaft with one hand, the torch held in the other. I thanked him with a tight-lipped smile, my nerves too strained to manage anything better, and then froze when the trumpet blast sounded again.

The second cauldron had been lit.

27

W e exchanged looks and began running. There was no more time to strategize—the other half of the team that our attackers were on had been bested by the other, and had managed to light their cauldron. Only one remained, and the remaining two members of the team trying to kill us were likely trying to get there before us. Because eliminating Ambrose was just as effective as killing him, when it came to shutting him out of the Tourney.

My eyes scanned the platform, searching for a sign of their crimson uniforms, and sure enough, I spotted them at the base of it, beginning their climb. We were maybe fifty feet away. There was no way we were going to reach it in time.

Ambrose realized it a heartbeat after I did. "We're not going to make it," he roared, his aggravation and frustration evident.

I kept running, trying to think. The team was climbing by

hand, which meant that the lashes weren't working on the pipes, either. That bought us time, but not much—and I doubted any of us could climb faster than them. Not to mention, we were still too far away from the walls that made up the platform, giving us little chance of reaching the wall before they did. We needed to think of something.

"Does anyone have any ideas about how we can get up there?" I shouted, scrambling for some chance of winning.

Everyone was silent for a second, and then Leo said, "I have one, but it's going to sound a little insane."

I took a glance at him. "Insane is better than nothing."

We were slowing, partially because we were all getting tired, but also partially to hear Leo's idea. What he said, however, caused me to stop right in my tracks.

"I want you to use the lashes to slingshot me up there."

"You want us to *what?*" I asked, whirling and facing him fully, unable to comprehend what he was saying. It didn't make any sense.

"Okay, I understand how it sounds, but hear me out. Our lash lines are twenty-five feet in length, and the gears inside can retract them at a rate of thirty-two feet per second, if I turn the safeties off. If two of you throw a single line at me, which I can hit with my own lines, I can use the gears in the harness to create the velocity, while the two holding the line create the guides. If my angle and velocity are good, I can make it to the top of the platform."

I blinked several times. I understood the words individually, and realized he was trying to convey complicated science in the quickest shorthand ever, but couldn't seem to wrap my head around the concept. It sounded too fantastical to be possible.

"You can't hit a lash end with another lash end," Ambrose said, equally baffled. "That's not possible. They're too small."

Leo smiled politely. "I assure you, *I* can." He gave me a pointed look, and I realized that because he was an AI, he might actually be able to pull it off, even with Grey's physical limitations.

We had to at least try. Otherwise we were out of the competition.

Ambrose saw me staring at Leo, and realized what I was about to say. "You *can't* be serious! There is no way anyone can make that shot! We're wasting time here. We have to—" He broke off as his voice began to grow more panicked, and clenched his jaw tight.

"Ambrose," Leo said gently, and the other man looked up at him, his eyes hooded and angry. "I can make that shot."

"Ambrose, if you have another idea, now's the time to tell us. But do it now. We don't have much more time before we lose completely."

Ambrose pressed his lips together and then emitted an aggravated noise. "Fine! Let's just get this over with." He handed the torch to Leo, who accepted it quickly.

Relieved that I didn't have to overrule him or shoot him down, I turned to Leo. "What do you need?"

"Running space and time."

"Good, then let's—"

I cut off and stepped around him, the movement coming from one of the holes just over his shoulder attracting my attention. I bit back a frustrated noise as I saw the woman who had been chasing us emerging, and immediately looked around for the male. I couldn't see him anywhere, but that didn't mean he wasn't lying in wait.

All they had to do was prevent our last-ditch effort with Leo —which I still wasn't sure was possible—and we'd be out of the competition. Lacey would turn us over for sabotaging Scipio's programming, the position of Champion would fall into the hands of another legacy group, and both Scipio and the Tower would eventually fall as a result.

I couldn't let that happen.

"Go," I told everyone, slipping my baton out of my belt and turning it on. "All of you are needed for Leo's plan to work. I'll stay and keep her distracted."

I could sense that they wanted to argue, but they immediately realized that I was right—they needed to go now, while there was still any chance left to do anything.

"Good luck," Ambrose said, just as the woman made it to her feet.

"You too," I replied, readying myself. I heard their boots start to move toward the platform behind me, but didn't stop to check over my shoulder as I moved forward to meet the woman.

Her thermal cutter wasn't on yet, but as soon as she saw me coming, the pommel dropped from her sleeve into her hand. Then the scarlet plasma blade shot into existence.

I pressed on with more confidence than I felt, my baton up, closing the distance as she waited, her back to the edge.

My heart beat once, twice, three times, and then I heaved the baton up and charged. It was a ploy on my part—the maneuver would leave my chest and torso wide open for an easy attack—and she fell for it. She brought the cutter up, the tip pointed right for my chest, but I was already gone, spinning around it on her left and then jamming my baton into the small of her back, right over a kidney. I released the charge, and held the baton in place.

Her body immediately locked up as she seized, and a second later, the thermal cutter clattered out of her hands and into the pipe network below, the orange blade immediately disappearing once the tool left her hand.

I held the baton against her body for the full three seconds before it automatically cut off, then brought it up and back down over her right temple with a sharp crack before she could recover. She dropped onto the pipes, flat on her chest in an awkward heap, and I took a step back, my body now covered in sweat and shaking slightly.

Even though I had *purposefully* left myself open for the attack, it had been far too close for comfort. I watched her for a second, waiting for her to move, but she didn't.

Shaking off my brush with death, I turned to see what was going on behind me. Leo was standing a few feet away, with Maddox and Ambrose closer to the platform. Even as I turned, I saw them spinning their lines and casting them directly at Leo. Leo had his own ready, and as soon as they cast, he did too, breaking into a flat run toward them as his hands extended and released the lines.

I didn't have time to see if they connected. My gaze was drawn to the man exiting the shaft just behind Ambrose. Ambrose's attention was solely on Leo, so he couldn't see him—but I could.

Tightening my grip on my baton, I took off, angling for the man as he began to pull himself up, his hands finding plenty of holds in the network of pipes. He leapt to his feet and immediately began rushing for Ambrose, something dark and glinting in his hands.

I was only feet from him, the blood in my veins surging hotly as I saw him lift his fist toward the back of Ambrose's head, the black pulse shield leveled at Ambrose's neck. From that distance, he could easily snap it. I wasn't going to allow that.

I drew back my arm and threw my baton at him, not willing to wait even a second before I impacted him. He was close enough that it was a clear shot, despite the oblong nature of the baton, and it hit him on the side of the face, bouncing off and back at me. I caught it purely on reflex, and then slammed into him, unwilling to stop my momentum in the slightest.

The shoulder I had injured during my fall down the shaft screamed out in agony, the pain causing me to grit my teeth, but I ignored it as we both went crashing down. I rolled off of him a few feet away, the world spinning so violently that I had to shut my eyes to keep from getting dizzy.

It took me several precious seconds to register that I had

fully stopped, but when I did, I quickly opened my eyes. I flinched back as I saw legs overhead, but then realized it wasn't someone trying to kick me. It was Leo, and he was *flying*.

Ambrose's face blocked the view, his hands reaching down to help haul me to my feet. A hiss escaped from between my teeth as he jostled my shoulder, but I didn't cry out, thankfully, and within seconds he had me righted.

I held onto him for a second or two while my weight settled onto my shaky feet, and looked around, searching for the man I had just slammed into. I caught a glimpse of him staggering to his feet—and then saw Maddox dropkick him in the chest, knocking him back into the hole he had climbed out of. He hit the side with a grunt and then slid out of sight, but I heard him hit the ground with a crunch—followed by an earsplitting scream.

Maddox moved up to the edge and looked over it. "His arm's broken. He'll be fine."

"He deserves worse, trying to take that potshot at me," Ambrose spat.

I ignored him, my eyes moving up toward the platform. I hadn't heard the trumpets announcing victory yet, and I wasn't sure how Leo's crazy plan had worked for him. My eyes slid from side to side at the top of the scaffolding, but found no sign of him anywhere.

"Where is he?" I asked, taking a few steps back to try to get a better view of the top. "Is he okay?"

"He landed near the top," Maddox replied, following my

lead. "I didn't see what happened after he released the lines, though. I was too focused on that guy behind Ambrose."

"Where're the other two guys?" I asked, my eyes darting around. If they had made it at the same time, then that meant Leo was up there fighting two people on his own. I knew he was skilled in martial arts, but even he couldn't prevent someone else from getting lucky.

The trumpet blasted over whatever Ambrose started to say, and I winced and began to move backward even faster. Drones were circling the third cauldron, which was now lit and burning fiercely. Standing in stark contrast against it, I recognized Leo's silhouette as he let go of the torch he had just plunged into the cauldron. Two other figures were picking themselves off the ground, their shoulders rounded in defeat.

He'd done it. We'd won. The relief was so strong that it felt like my legs were going to give out, and I reached out and placed a hand on Maddox's shoulder, exhaling. "Guys, I don't think I'm going to survive the next challenge." I meant it as a joke, and although it wasn't in the best taste, both Ambrose and Maddox laughed.

"I know what you mean," Ambrose said, shaking his head. His smile faded, and then his eyes grew distant. "Thank Scipio you were there, Liana. If you hadn't—"

"It's literally my job, Ambrose," I said, holding my hand up and forestalling any argument. "So don't mention it."

He hesitated, looking deeply conflicted. I could tell he wanted to say something anyway, but couldn't decide if it was worth it to press me or not. I, for one, did not want the gratitude.

Yes, I had been doing my job—that much was true. But if I was honest with myself, I had to admit that I would've done it anyway. Ambrose might have been a jerk in the past, but he wasn't all bad.

I heard a buzzer go off, announcing the end of the match, and that was followed by a loud clang from above. I looked up to see a flat black disk being lowered from the ceiling.

"Candidates will attach their lashes to the crane," Scipio's voice boomed through the cavernous space.

I looked over at Leo to see two of the same cranes being lowered over the platform. He was already tossing his lash and connecting to one, while the two members from the enemy team used the other. Maddox, Ambrose, and I quickly attached our lashes to the disk being lowered toward us, and within moments we were being hauled up and swung over the pipe maze.

I watched as it grew smaller the higher we rose, thinking about our attack and my brush with death. Whoever our enemies were, they weren't holding back anymore. Openly attacking us had been a major risk, especially with the weapons they'd managed to smuggle in.

And the weapon *choices*, too—the pulse shields from the IT department, used here and also in the attack in the Lion's Den, and the thermal cutter from Mechanics or the Water Department. That was new, and alarming. Surely Lacey and Strum kept a close eye on their weapons. Didn't they?

Because if they didn't, they should definitely start doing so now.

I couldn't help but feel that the thought was too little, too late, and turned my mind toward the greater implications of what it could all mean. We were definitely going to have to use the advantage Lacey's maps gave us—but we were also going to need to come up with something to fight back with.

And we needed it yesterday.

28

W e swung into the opening that had just appeared in the side of the wall, the crane patiently waiting for us to get fully inside the makeshift lashway before detaching our lashes. An official was waiting for us down at the end of the hall, by a circular staircase that must have led back to the main level.

I ignored him, backing away from the ledge to make room for Leo as his crane settled into position in front of the door opening. He swung lightly onto the ledge, disconnecting his line, and then looked up, through everyone else and directly to me, his face instantly concerned.

"Are you all right?" he asked. "I saw you hit that man and go down before I landed on the platform. He didn't hurt you, did he?"

His concern was sweet, but unnecessary. My shoulder was likely bruised, more than anything else, and with some of that salve my mother had given me, and a hot pad, I'd be right as rain before tomorrow.

"I'm fine," I told him. "You missed Maddox dropkicking him down a shaft."

Leo's concern faded but didn't disappear, even as he smiled approvingly at Maddox. "Well done."

"Yeah, well, I'm not sure if that's going to compare to what you did," the raven-haired woman replied, smiling ruefully. "*Leaping* to the top of a fifteen-foot-high platform in a single bound? I'm pretty sure you've earned another deed name after this."

"I'll say," Ambrose said, a touch bitterly. I saw him rein it back almost immediately, but it was still there—a resentment burning under the surface. "How did you even do that?"

I swallowed. I knew I shouldn't be concerned—it was unlikely that Ambrose would be able to figure out what Leo was from his questions alone—but the heightened accuracy was enough to give anyone pause. And if it had been broadcast by the drones, as I was sure it had been, then that meant other people would be noticing Leo's prowess. It would make him a target just as much as Ambrose was now, even though he had no desire to be Champion.

"Practice," Leo lied smoothly. "Now, shall we? I believe we'll need to exit the arena before our net functions are returned to us, and I am worried for Tian."

I nodded. "Yes, please," I replied. Even though we had gotten to go first, thus guaranteeing we were in and out as quickly as possible, I could still feel the press of time, and hoped that Mercury and Quess had at least located her. But there was no way to tell until our full net functions were restored and I could call them. I was starting to turn and move toward the official, who was still waiting, when Ambrose grabbed my arm and held me back.

I turned to look at his hand on my arm, then him, and realized he still wanted to talk. Maddox and Leo shot me questioning looks, but I waved them ahead with a nod. "What's up?" I asked several seconds later. "And will you be keeping my arm?"

Ambrose released his firm hold with a surprising amount of gentleness, and then cleared his throat, shifting awkwardly. "Well, I still want to thank you for what you did, and—"

"It really isn't necessary, Ambrose," I said, trying not to be impatient. "I just did what anyone else would do."

"You can't know that," he said, frowning.

"Of course I can!" I replied. "At least, I can with our teammates. And that includes you."

He looked down at the floor, his expression growing haunted. "I don't know that I would've," he admitted hoarsely. "At least, before today, I probably would've just let you die." He met my gaze, his eyes apologetic and searching to gauge what my response was.

To be honest, his revelation didn't exactly surprise me. After all, we'd barely gotten along since we'd met, and I'd even entertained my own thoughts of his death from time to time. But they were just that: thoughts.

Yet for some reason, it was bothering Ambrose.

"It's okay," I told him, trying to reassure him. I cast a glance down the hall to where Leo and Maddox were meeting with the official, and then began slowly walking toward them, encouraging him to keep up. If he wanted to have a heart-to-heart, then it would have to be on the move. "I may or may not have considered what life would be like with you dead a time or two myself. But that has nothing to do with—"

"You're a good leader, Liana."

He said the words flatly, but behind them, there seemed to be a spring of sadness shining through. I stared at him for a second, trying to puzzle out what would make him feel so sad and give him a need to admit such a thing out loud.

"Is this about the cauldron?" I asked, unable to come up with any sort of answer that made sense. "And that Leo lit it? I'm sorry for that, but it was the only way we could progress!"

The official scanned us as we passed by to confirm our identities, and then went back to watching the hall. Maddox and Leo were already heading down the black, wrought-iron spiral staircase, and I let Ambrose go through first, still not willing to give up his security, even with the recent attack.

"It's not that," he said, his boots landing heavily on the steps. "Well, it is, but it's not." He sighed, and this time I remained quiet. He was clearly struggling with what he wanted to say, so I just needed to wait until he was ready.

"Look, I know I've been an unbelievable jerk to you and your friends, and I'm... sorry."

It was clear from how slowly he formed it that he was having difficulty with the word, and I realized this was costing him his pride. Impressed, I mentally applauded him for doing it

—before finding myself wondering what had prompted this apology.

"Thank you for that," I said after a long moment had passed and he didn't offer anything more. "And, please don't take this the wrong way, but what brought this on?"

He paused for a few seconds, and then resumed walking. "You and Lacey were right."

I drew my brows together in confusion. We were right? I mean, of course we were, but he needed to be a little bit more specific as to what we were right about.

"About?"

"About people being after me. Trying to kill me. I... God, this seemed so clear in my head fifteen seconds ago, but I feel like I'm not getting it out right."

"Relax," I said, trying to soothe him. "I'm not going to judge you."

"But you should. I've been anything but a leader since you showed up. I mean, you killed Devon Alexander, Liana. And Lacey wanted to put you in the Tourney next to me, thinking that somehow I could outshine you, but... I clearly couldn't."

I frowned. "Look, being popular for killing Devon is not exactly something I relish, Ambrose. For the record, I didn't even kill him. Grey did."

"He did?"

"Yup. We just didn't feel the need to advertise that, seeing as how the council already saw me as their biggest threat. Plus, Lacey and Strum assumed I had done it, so why correct them?"

He chuckled, shaking his head. The sound carried through

the tight walls of the staircase we were in, rich with good humor. "See? You're so quick to think things through. It's smart not to correct someone's assumptions. It gives you an advantage."

I thought about that for a second, surprised that he viewed my actions with such depth. He was wrong, of course—I just filed everything under "nobody's business until I make it their business," and moved on. That was about as deep as it got.

"Yes, but clearly you're aware it's something you can do, if you want to. Isn't that a characteristic of leadership?"

"I never think of it in the moment," he replied wistfully. He was quiet for several heartbeats, and my gut told me something more was coming, so I waited. "Anyway, that's not really the point. I know I'm not a good leader, because of *how* I treated you after Lacey told me you were going to be on my team. You have to understand that all my life, my family raised me knowing that they were going to send me to the Knights Department eventually. I was groomed for the position, really—even had three former Knights who tutored me on history, ethics, and combat.

"But every time I envisioned it, it was always with my friends by my side. I mean, I was so obsessed with finding the perfect teammates that I started vetting people at the Academy, trying to find the most compatible team. But then you breeze in, and you're just so smart, and in control of everything. I know you and your team are doing even more than you're letting on, and yet you're always so calm and collected. And I just... I saw everything I aspired to be inside a lowly criminal, and I just... hated you."

I paused on the steps, staring at the back of his head as he continued down without me, my heart pounding. It made total sense now. He had been preparing for this his whole life, only to have his vision of it corrupted by an unwanted interloper and her merry band of criminals. It must have been disappointing and beyond disheartening for him, and he'd lashed out at the source of all his disillusionment: me.

"Damn, Ambrose," I said, resuming the climb down. "I'm not even sure what you want me to say. I mean, I didn't exactly want to be here, either. I was just trying to do what I had to do to keep my friends safe."

"I know that, and that's what makes it worse. Even though you didn't want it, you handled it with professionalism and an exceptional amount of patience, whereas I... I did what I did out of pettiness. That's not what a leader does. A leader does what you did." He gave a self-depreciating laugh as he stepped down off the stairs and onto the landing at the bottom. "I don't deserve to be Champion. You do."

I blinked, surprised to hear something like that coming out of his mouth. "You don't mean that. I mean, you can't mean that. I'm a criminal, for Scipio's sake!"

He fell into step beside me as I stepped off the staircase, and we exited through the door and entered the hall beyond. I spotted Leo and Maddox on the left, and moved to follow them.

"Look, you guys keep yourselves pretty tight-lipped about what you are up to, but I know it's big. And given how much you seem to care about people, I doubt whatever it is will hurt them. If anything, you are probably trying to help them, which means we're on the same side. If you were to win the Tourney, I'd... I'd be willing to say something to Lacey. She might be able to accept me as your Lieutenant, provided you share information and work with us."

I blinked again, and then smiled, looking over at Ambrose. I wasn't sure why, but his offer was both generous, and genuine in its delivery. He sounded like he not only liked the idea, but was excited by it as well.

"I think Lacey might not like that," I warned him in a light tone.

"So we won't tell her, just let the Tourney decide. Besides, I can't help it if the Knights choose you over me. She'll just have to accept it after the fact."

I was flattered, and for a moment, I actually found myself considering all the possibilities that would open up if I were named Champion. I could start rooting out the legacy groups from the Tower, while having a bit more freedom to move around and look for Jasper.

But it also came with a heavy price: forever having to watch my back. No doubt the legacies would be gunning for whoever was in the position. And given the lengths they were willing to go to, I had no doubt they would come hard and fast. It was too dangerous to even consider.

We lapsed into silence as the walk continued. It took a little time for us to follow the hall to its destination, and within a few minutes we were in the intake room, returning our equipment to the official. We signed out quickly, and made our way back to the spectator's arena.

A loud whoop went up as we drew closer to the door that led

to the arena. I recognized Ambrose's friends as they broke away from a group of people milling around one of the viewing screens and raced over.

"Hey, good job out there 'Brose," one of them said, clapping him on the shoulder. "That move your teammate executed with the lashes—that was insane!"

Ambrose laughed and nodded congenially. "I'm just glad we made it through in one piece. So why are you guys here instead of in the stands?"

One of them smiled. "Because we came here to root for you, and now that you're done, we figured we'd get some lunch. You want in?"

"Sure, if you don't mind eating at my place and I can bring Maddox with me?"

Ambrose spoke before I could even formulate an objection, and it was so shocking that it took me a few moments to recover.

"Of course!" his friend said brightly. "We could always use a pretty lady to talk to."

The look Maddox gave him in return promised him a cold and icy death, and I hid my smile. I was still elated that Ambrose hadn't even blinked an eye at following my directive that he didn't go anywhere alone.

"Yeah, all right," Maddox said. "But as soon as we get news about our friend, we'll have to go."

"Of course," Ambrose replied smoothly, not even missing a beat in agreeing with Maddox's cover story to explain why they might have to leave early. "Shall we?"

He offered her an arm, but Maddox didn't take it until she

got a nod of approval from me. Within moments, the five of them were walking away from us, heading for the elevator bank. I watched them for a second, and then looked over at Leo.

"You did a good job in there," I told him, and he smiled.

"I fear the deed name of 'Untouchable' will have to persist for a while," he replied apologetically. "My attackers were unable to land a single blow. I'm sorry—I know I should do my best to appear to have some weaknesses or flaws, but I can't seem to bring myself to allow any harm to come to Grey's body while I am charged with its safety."

My heart skipped a beat at his thoughtful consideration, and the honor and integrity behind it, and I found myself wanting to reach out and take his hand, just to convey my gratitude to him for being so good.

My indicator beeped, interrupting the moment, and I quickly checked my wrist and saw that Quess was calling. I immediately picked up by swiping a finger across the digital display on it.

Liana, Quess's voice rattled around in my head, and I clenched my teeth against it. *Tian just contacted me, and she's scared. I think she's in trouble.*

29

I whirled around and immediately began scanning the crowds for Maddox, Quess's words burning holes in my ears. I'd lost her in the chaos, but I knew she was heading for the elevator bank.

"Net Leo in and tell us what happened," I said as I began pushing through the stream of people who had seemingly manifested from nowhere.

Leo gave me a puzzled look, and I mouthed Quess's name to him as I darted around the people in my way, forging my own path ahead. Moments later, the buzzing under my skull intensified, signaling the increased neural load of the transmission.

She just called me, Liana, Quess announced, his voice tight with panic. *She said there were people following her, and she was scared! They must've somehow managed to trap her in a corner or grab her, because now she's not picking up, and her net is dead, Liana. I can't get it to respond to my pings.*

The bottom of my stomach gave out as Quess's panic and words lit fire to the worst fears imaginable. Because if Tian's net wasn't even responding to a location ping, there were only a handful of explanations: it had been removed, masked, or destroyed. There was a very real possibility that someone, probably our enemies, had gotten her.

And who knew what they would do to her? If they were willing to kill us, could that mean they were capable of hurting a young girl to get what they wanted? My heart needed to believe that it wasn't possible—that no one was that depraved—but I couldn't risk being wrong. Not with Tian hanging in the balance.

"Were you able to find her location before her net went dark?" I asked.

Yes, she's somewhere under the Orchard. We found her not long after you left for the Tourney, but it was too difficult to anticipate where she was going to be, given the randomness of her movements. I mean, she didn't slow down until she got to the Orchard! I already alerted Zoe and Eric, and they are on their way. You guys can get there at the same time if you move now. Is Doxy with you? If not, I'll net her. You guys just move. We can't waste a moment.

I hesitated in my fruitless pushing down the hall, thinking. Maddox had every right to know that we'd found Tian—and then lost her—and that she was in danger, but I wasn't sure telling her right then was the right call. As much as it sickened me to leave her in the dark, I knew that once Maddox was told, she'd want to come, and there was every possibility that this was all a trap to lure us away from Ambrose—or worse, get him out into the open.

I considered trusting his friends for a short period of time, but I *couldn't* trust their motives; something as intangible as friendship was easy to lie about, and required very little proof other than listening. It could be faked for years, if someone really wanted to go the distance. They might not be what he thought they were—and I couldn't take that risk.

I hated to even think it, but I couldn't tell her. I needed them both thinking everything was all right, so they would stay in the apartment. If she believed we were still searching, but with no news, it would buy us some time and she'd stay focused on keeping Ambrose safe.

"Don't tell Maddox," I told Quess, forcing the words through my tight throat. Of all the injustices I had unwittingly visited upon her, this was the first one I was doing willingly, and I despised myself for it.

But it had to be done.

What? Quess asked, his alarm causing me to wince slightly. *You want me to keep this from her?*

I could hear the horror and recusal in his voice, and it was almost enough to make me reconsider. Almost.

"Quess, there is a chance that whoever is after Tian is only after her to lure Ambrose out. If we tell Maddox, she's going to run off half-cocked to help save her, and possibly leave Ambrose exposed—or even worse, bring him with her, and expose him on her mad dash to get here. She'll be frantic with this news, and might overlook keeping Ambrose safe. They are going back to the apartment now, which is a defendable, familiar place, and without worrying about Tian, she can focus on doing the job. I would change out with her, but it's too late for that now. She can't know. Not yet."

I could feel Quess's indecision, but I didn't wait for him to realize I was right. Instead, I turned around and headed for the wall separating me from the outside of the Salles. The lashways on this level had been closed up for the Tourney, so as not to risk anyone from another department from accidentally falling, but they could be overridden in case of an emergency.

I was declaring this an emergency.

I moved over to a panel sitting next to a closed one, and pressed a button. "Liana Castell, 25K-05, Knight Elite. Override authorized on my authority. Open lashway 65-B."

"Lashway opening override confirmed," the robotic voice spat back, and a section of the wall next to it slid open with a puff of air strong enough to move my hair. I heard people gasp and pull away, but ignored them as I drew my lash line out and began whirling it in my hand.

I won't tell Maddox, Quess buzzed in my ear as I stepped up to the ledge. *But for the record, I don't like this.*

"Noted," I replied, throwing my line and hitting an arch. "See if you can't commandeer a few of the drones to help us. I know you want to come down yourself to look, but I don't want to risk your new job, either. We need you in there."

Quess made an aggravated noise that made me wince at the oddity of the tonal sounds it created in my ear. *Fine,* he grated out. *But you better get there. Fast.*

"I'm already on it," I said before ending the call.

Behind me, a crowd had formed, and I heard hushed and awed voices murmuring, "Untouchable" and "Honorbound." We were drawing attention, which would only lead to questions, speculation, and rumors. We needed to get out of there, fast, without causing any more of a scene.

I glanced at Leo, who was waiting patiently, his line already attached. "Keep up with me," I told him, and he offered me a terse smile before we both swung off.

I began lashing quickly, glancing back only to make sure the lashway door had closed behind me. Then I dropped, heading for Anwar's bridge, which connected to Level 85. From there, we'd race to the plunge and lash down twenty stories to the sixty-fifth floor.

Easy peasy.

I narrowly avoided the beam blocking my path, and stepped lightly onto the landing just beyond, right in front of the doorway leading out of the plunge. My arms were shaking and I was covered in a light sweat. I'd never taken the plunge so quickly before, and the fact that I had—and survived—was no small miracle.

Leo landed next to me and quickly stepped through the doorway, looking around.

"Oh thank God," I heard a feminine voice say, and I pushed forward to see Zoe and Eric waiting for us. "C'mon, Quess told us she *was* at the top of Greenery 7 in one of the condensation rooms."

The condensation rooms? Why would she be up there? The area wasn't at all suitable to our needs, as it was one of the most important, and therefore heavily maintained rooms in a greenery. It produced the atmosphere to create rainfall. I'd never been inside one, but I knew from my cross-departmental internship courses that they were hot and humid.

And not a place for small girls.

I hurried along, following Zoe and Eric through a long hall. Our footsteps were hurried, filling the small space with sounds of our passing. Zoe hooked a right, and I jogged behind Leo, checking the hall behind us to make sure we were clear. I still hadn't calmed down from being pursued by our would-be assassins in the Tourney, and I was already anxious with worry over Tian.

We exited the shell and crossed onto a wide platform that ran fifteen feet out from the side of the smooth inner walls of the Tower. We were on the east side of the Tower, and Greenery 7—affectionately known as the Orchard—sat on the north side, opposite its sister greenery, Harvest, where the root, gourd, squash, and cruciferous vegetables were grown. That one boasted some of the finest meals in the Tower; the Orchard offered nothing but fresh-baked pies and other fruit-based cuisine.

We headed directly for it, drawn by the large picture of an apple pie painted across the smooth five-story surface over the wide entrance. The platform extended out an additional forty feet there, making room for the carts and stalls that gathered in front of it. It was still morning, but people were already there enjoying a slice of pie for breakfast.

We ignored it all, hugging the wall of the shell as we rounded the corner, and found a small pathway a few feet wide behind the stalls. No one stopped us or paid us any mind—we were nothing interesting. Just two Knights escorting two Cogs on some sort of repair job.

We stopped at a ladder that was carved out of the wall and began to climb, heading for the very top, where it was obstructed by the ramp on the seventieth floor.

When we reached the top, Zoe quickly put in her code, opening the door that was accessed from the ladder. The door led us onto a catwalk, with stairs heading down into the condensation room.

I stepped inside and paused, the heat already causing sweat to form on my forehead and upper lip. I shrugged it off and stepped up to the landing, looking into the room below.

The lighting was dim—the panels above were darkened intentionally, as the light and heat from the sun shining through them would evaporate much of the water the condensers were using to form the rain that would sustain the crops below. The main source of light was a long tube lying on the floor in the middle of the room, throbbing a deep orange. Additional lights dangled from the ceiling above, but the bulbs were red, and protected by plastic shields that diffused everything into a hazy crimson glow. Neither source did anything to chase the deep, dark shadows of the room away, and the entire place had a strangely ominous feel.

I sucked in a deep breath, the air thick and heavy, and then pulled out my baton.

"I'll take the lead, followed by Leo. Zoe, Eric, if you see Tian, grab her and run. Don't wait for us."

I glanced over at my friends, and they nodded. Leo already had his baton out, so I supposed my orders came as no surprise to him. We both knew Zoe and Eric weren't fighters in the traditional sense, but they could grab Tian should a fight break out, and it was a relief to be able to focus just on keeping them safe—and covering their backs while they ran.

If we even found her.

I moved down the stairs, my baton out, my eyes searching the shadows. Nothing moved. Everything was quiet.

Too quiet. The hair on my neck stood at full attention, warning me that something wasn't right. I listened to it—but didn't turn back. Instead, I kept a firm control over my emotions... and a wary eye on the shadows, searching for any hint of movement.

The stairs ended after a few feet, just before a huge piece of machinery with glowing lights and what appeared to be a control panel. I looked at it and then stepped to my left—the only direction I could step, considering the black glass panel beaded with water on the right.

"Zoe, take a look at this and see if you can get any more lights on," I said quietly.

Something suddenly hissed, and I whirled toward it, my

baton at the ready. A white-hot cloud of steam was shooting up from a release valve, and I exhaled, relaxing some. Some, but not entirely.

Zoe rushed forward, her hands up and ready to press a button, and I turned away and moved farther to the left, following the path made by the wall of the Tower and three huge water mains stacked one on top of the other. I went down a few more steps into a long trough, and the heat grew even more intense, radiating from the glowing orange tube—a condenser coil, which ran from one end of the room to the other, right through the center.

Catwalks climbed up and over it, connecting the two halves of the room, but for now, I was focused on *this* side.

"Tian!" I called, walking alongside the orange tube and searching in between and around the pipes of water, which was fed into the room to be heated until it blew off steam. That steam was collected above, gathering and growing until it was time to rapidly cool it, creating the rain for the greenery below.

Right now, it was just making things even more difficult.

"Tian!" I repeated, continuing ahead and then moving around one of the stairwells blocking my path. I paused when I saw that I could either go straight or venture back to the right, through a narrow spot behind some equipment. I finally went with the latter, figuring that if Tian had been chased down here, she would've taken this route on purpose, to slow down her would-be assailants.

It was a tight fit, and the pipes on my left were burning hot, but I managed to make it through with only a few blisters on the backs of my hands. Luckily, the microthread of my uniform protected the rest of my body.

The space eventually opened up into another small area. I looked around quickly, but there was no sign of Tian. There were, however, two more gaps that led to *another* area, and after a moment of hesitation, I went with the one that kept me away from the center. The passageway didn't lead in a straight line, but hooked back around to the left.

I paused when I saw this, and became aware of something. A smell. I sniffed the air a few times to confirm, and was rewarded by a heavy copper odor, tinged with a hint of charred meat. The strange combination confused me, but as I approached the corner, I realized it was getting stronger.

"What is that?" Leo whispered, and I almost leapt out of my skin before turning around to face him. I hadn't even realized he had kept up with me. His eyes widened in alarm when he saw my face, and then immediately grew concerned. "Are you okay?"

He reached out for me, but I shrugged him off, shaking my head. "I'm fine. Let's just find Tian."

I backed away as I spoke, concerned about my own state of mind. I thought I had it together, but one sound from Leo had sent me jumping out of my skin faster than a piston could move. I shook out my free hand, trying to ease my tense nerves, and then turned away from his confusion, unable to fully explain myself.

And then I saw it. Something dark, wet, glistening, and a red so deep that it was almost black in the lighting, was splashed in baffling amounts across the floor. I stared at it, half thinking someone had spilled a barrel of paint, and then covered my mouth when I saw a chunk of something sitting in it: teeth, a tongue, a lip... a jaw.

A jaw missing the upper half of its head, and still oozing blood into the puddle that was already coating the floor in a thick, never-ending mat.

30

My mind couldn't begin to process what I was seeing. Blood streaked high along the pipes and pooling on the floor. A severed arm resting awkwardly in a corner. A booted foot standing upright, with everything above the boot missing. A head split in half, splayed open. Pink and white bits of flesh, scattered everywhere.

My stomach lurched, and I closed my eyes, trying to will the image of such carnage out of my head. Then hands were tugging at my shoulder, forcing me to turn around, and I suddenly became aware that my breathing had become heavy, a dull ringing noise in my ears.

I opened my eyes to see Leo staring at me, his eyes wide and concerned, and I realized he was touching me. *His* hands were on my shoulders, then my face. His mouth was moving. He was saying something, but I couldn't hear it—there was only the room behind me. Vicious carnage in a place where Tian had last been.

I couldn't help but imagine her. Blue eyes wide open and unseeing. White-blond hair stained red with blood. Little limbs cut away, flung away, by a monster capable of such atrocities.

Leo was shaking me now, his mouth moving faster. I tried to focus on his lips, but they weren't making any sense.

Then I got bored with it. It was nothing. Nothing mattered. Tian was dead, and I had failed her. My eyes drifted. Floated. Saw Zoe. Witnessed her horror. Her eyes wide and mouth open, tears starting to form. Followed by her staggering back. Turning. Retching in the corner.

Eric soothed her, his hands on her back as she lost the contents of her stomach.

Arms went around me. Grey's—Leo's face filled my view. He was holding me. I stared at him, and then relaxed. I let him hold me, if only to chase away the nightmare that was just feet behind me.

I realized I was cold, and shivering, and stepped even closer into him, drawn to his warmth. If he complained, I couldn't hear it.

For a precious moment, I felt safe again.

The ringing in my ears lessened some, and I settled my head against his chest, listening to his words as they suddenly became audible.

"It's okay, Liana. You're going into shock, and I'm just trying to help you through it. If you can hear this, there are many bodies in there, but none of the remains are small enough to be Tian. Please, Liana... come back to us. We need you."

His words resonated inside me, and I blinked as my mind suddenly snapped into awareness. Tian wasn't among them?

I pulled out of his arms, suddenly back in control of my faculties. "She's not in there?" I asked him hoarsely, my voice cracking. "Are you sure?"

He nodded jerkily. "Yes. Liana, are you okay? You were going into—"

"Shock," I said with a nod. "I know, I heard you. You're... Whatever you did helped, so thank you. But if you're right and Tian's not in there, then we need to find out where she is." I was pretty certain I was still in shock; a numbness had settled in just under my skin. But talking things out helped me to focus on what we needed to do. It kept me from floating away mentally, reminded me to stay riveted in the moment instead.

"Okay," Zoe said weakly, her voice harsh. "But can we just take a minute to discuss what could've..." She panted for a second, her ashen face turning green as she fought off the urge to throw up again. She managed to beat it back, and continued. "Could've done that? Or who these people even are?"

I considered her question, and realized she had a point. Someone or something had killed several people at the very least, given the number of limbs that my brain refused to stop picturing. The manner and execution of it had been brutal.

I didn't know who the people were, but I was relatively certain they were the ones who had been after Tian in the first place. The only alternative was that they were a work detail tasked with fixing something, but that seemed highly unlikely to me, considering they were all wearing black. If the people on the floor were indeed who I suspected they were, and had been chasing Tian, then whoever—*whatever*—had caused all of this could be after Tian as well.

Or worse, they could have her already.

"Liana," Eric said, his voice grave. "Could these men belong to Lacey? Could she have made a move to grab Tian?"

I considered his question. My initial impulse was to say no, but I couldn't be certain. I had left our meeting last night feeling like we had an understanding, but what if she had taken my threat to leave as too big a risk, and sent her men after someone she knew we would all do anything for? Had I been wrong in my judgment of her character? Was she actually capable of doing something like that to a young girl?

And then what? Someone *else* had intercepted Lacey's men and murdered them? If so, who? Another legacy group... or someone else? And who or what could've caused all of this...

I backed my thoughts up, as they drew too close to the scene behind me, focusing on the question at hand instead. Had Lacey sent men after Tian? It was possible, and a question I couldn't afford to ignore.

"Call her," I told Zoe. "Make her come up here herself. I don't care how you do it. Leo and I are going to check the bodies and look for Tian. Just stay here, and be careful."

It really went without saying, but I said it anyway. My skin crawled just thinking about the monster that had caused all that carnage still being somewhere in this room. But whatever had done this was still out there.

There was a flutter of noise overhead, and I looked up in alarm, already imagining something attacking us. As soon as I saw that it was just a drone, the sound coming from the propellers at the top, I sagged in relief. All of our nets buzzed simultaneously, and then were simultaneously overridden. My teeth rattled in my skull as the force of the vibrations almost brought me to my knees, and I winced against it. The neural load was heavy with all five of us on it.

Liana, I'm sorry I'm late, Quess said. *What have you disc—*

The drone swiveled to one side—toward the carnage—and I quickly started speaking.

"Quess, don't overreact. Tian isn't in there. I need you to drop Zoe and Eric off the call—they have their own calls to make. And I need you to take point, okay? Are you with me?"

My heart beat hard in my chest as I looked over at Leo. If Quess lost control now, him getting the drone here would be useless—he'd come straight here himself and start tearing this place apart, and we'd lose any tactical advantage the drone gave us, namely the several different camera lenses for poor lighting, like thermal imaging and enhanced night vision. With the camera, he would be able to tell if anyone was waiting to ambush us before we had to enter the room.

Without it, we'd be going in blind.

Yes. Of course I'm with you. I relaxed as the vibrations dialed back some, and Zoe and Eric gave us a thumbs-up before moving a few feet away to place their own call.

I watched them for a second and then sucked in a deep, calming breath, steeling myself for what came next. "Quess, you lead the way into the rest of the room, and make sure it's clear. Find any exits that Tian might have taken and scope them out. We'll... We'll look around while you do that. See what we can see."

Quess didn't reply, but the drone moved off, a bright light clicking on to illuminate the way. I watched it go, then forced myself to turn around and look back into that room.

Tian's not in there, I thought, and then held the thought tight, repeating it like a prayer in my head. The drone disappeared behind some equipment, and several long seconds ticked by. Behind me, I could hear Zoe's voice, but it was pitched low enough that I couldn't make out the words.

It's all clear.

Quess's all clear helped ease some of the tension, but certainly not enough, and I still hesitated for a brief second. Leo did not, and I watched as he carefully stepped into the room, picking across the few spaces of floor that weren't completely covered in blood. I watched him go, envying his ability to cope, and then followed, forcing myself to look.

The inside of a human body was bright pink and rubbery. White was marbled through it—muscle fiber, bone, fat—but for the most part... pink, covered in red. Even with the dim lighting, it was hard not to notice. Not to fixate on.

I stepped over a leg bisected at both the hip and knee, a five-inch gap between the two pieces, the angle of the cut indicating that they had belonged together, originally. I tried not to think about the fact that somewhere, in all of this carnage, was the body that leg had once been attached to. The man who had been using it. A man who was now dead, either from bleeding out, shock, or another attack by whatever took off his leg.

"The edges of the wounds are cauterized," Leo said softly, and I looked up from the head that was split open like a melon to see him squatting down, inspecting one of the mostly intact bodies. Only an arm and a foot were absent.

The man lay on his back, hazel eyes wide and sightless. Blood was still oozing from the open wound where his shoulder used to be. I forced myself to ignore it, and focused on the edges of the wound. They were black and charred, with deep black cracks and crevices radiating up from the char marks and disappearing under his shirt. Leo reached over and gripped the edge of the man's uniform firmly with two fingers, lifting it up so he could peer underneath it.

"Only this side is scorched," he said absently, his fingers moving down under the still-oozing stump. "Whatever did this lost the charge it had to cauterize the wound halfway through, but was still sharp enough to finish the job. It's weird. It seems like it was both super-heated and electrically charged. That takes a degree of sophisticated engineering. Frankly, I'm at a loss as to how this is even possible."

I shook my head. I didn't have a clue either, and engineering wasn't exactly my strong suit. "Any sign of *who* did this?"

Leo straightened in his squat and looked around, scanning the bodies and blood. "It's a lot of blood," he said optimistically. "Surely the killer or killers stepped in some. Check the floor."

I immediately looked behind me to check the way we had entered, and was relieved to see that there was no sign of any footprints heading back the way we came. There was a chance that whoever it was could circle back around, though, so we needed to be careful.

I began picking my way across the floor, looking around for any sign of footprints while trying to avoid the eyes of the dead. But there was so much blood on the floor, and the lighting was not ideal. Leo found his own way beside me, and together we fanned out.

I stepped around a boiler tank and paused when I saw something on the pipes across from it. From its outline, it was a hand-print, but it wasn't filled with the normal swoops and whorls one would expect. Instead, it was a straight outline of the edges of fingers and a palm—as if someone had used a stamp to apply it. I was staring at it, wondering if it could be some sort of trick of the light, when Leo made a surprised sound just past me.

I turned carefully, trying not to slip on the blood, and saw that he was once again squatting, staring at something farther down the passageway. The space he was standing in was free of blood, and I stepped in behind him so I could peer over his shoulder, to see what he was looking at.

A hexagonal shape as wide as both my hands put together was imprinted onto the floor, the blood slightly smudged. I looked down the passage and saw another one a few paces past it, and I realized I was looking at footprints. Only, they weren't like any footprints I had seen before.

"Leo, what is that?" I asked, unable to keep the fear out of my voice. "Those aren't... They can't be human."

Leo swiveled around to look up at me. "I don't know," he replied honestly. "It could be a trick. There are ways of designing things like these to... to cover your tracks. But they give us a clear path. Let's follow it."

I hesitated, looking back down the corridor. There weren't many prints there, only the one set, which meant whoever did this had acted alone. It was hard to process; the level of violence used to kill those people had literally taken them to pieces.

But he could have Tian. Or be after her. Or worse. And we would never know if we didn't follow.

"Let's do it. Quess, are you monitoring?"

Our lines had been open the entire time, so I knew he was listening in. His silence during our speculation over the bodies was probably due to his focus on finding Tian, but that didn't mean he wasn't listening.

I am. The drone is already with you. Sending it ahead.

As he spoke, the drone came swooping down from above and pushed into the hall. Leo and I followed a few feet behind, our batons out and at the ready. The floor began to slant downward, and as we moved forward, the pipe walls boxing us in became flat metal. I realized we were moving under the condenser unit in the middle of the room.

At the bottom of the descent we came to an intersection with a long trough filled with warm, humid air that made even more perspiration form on my skin. I drew in a breath with a wheeze, the air almost too hot to breathe.

"Do you see anything, Quess?" I asked.

No, and all this humidity is messing with the drone's controls. I gotta back it out.

"Do it," I said, with a small amount of disappointment. We could really use the eyes in here, but we needed the drone working just as much. Its thermal scanners could help us find where Tian was hiding—if we could get a reading. "Keep looking for Tian."

"Liana, look!" Leo pointed at something down in the trough, and I leaned closer, trying to see what he was looking at. I spotted it, although... I wasn't entirely sure what "it" was. It looked like several dozen black strings balled together in some sort of chaotic mess. It wasn't coming out of a panel—the threads were too small to be wires. It was definitely out of place.

Leo reached over to pick it up by a single strand, and then

the mess shifted and came tumbling apart. Suddenly I realized what I was looking at. They were nets. Several of them, with the tendrils extended. As one of the tendrils fell, I caught a glimpse of something pink and bloody attached to it, and realized that the nets had been *yanked* out of their owners' skulls, tendrils and all.

My stomach lurched, and I quickly turned away and clapped my hand over my mouth, trying not to vomit.

"Are you okay?" Leo asked.

I sucked in a deep breath and moved my hand long enough to say, "We are going to get through this a lot faster if you stop asking me that." I knew he was concerned; I'd been in shock not minutes ago, and I was definitely having a hard time keeping hold of my emotional state, but I was managing. I was trying to, at the very least.

I used another slow, steady breath to combat the queasiness that was threatening to boil over, and slowly moved my hand away. "How many nets are there?"

"Um, it looks like six. They've been badly damaged, though. And the room is too moist for the blood to hold form. The water has diluted the blood, making it impossible to see in these conditions."

I ran a hand over my face, wiping away the moisture that had formed there, and grimaced. "Well, let's just head in the direction they were last going, and hope maybe we find some other sign."

Leo hesitated long enough that I turned around to face him. Doubt and a heavy melancholy were etched into his face, and I realized he didn't think it was possible to find where the killer had gone now that the blood trail was gone.

"Fine, then we need to find—"

Liana, Quess said, his voice hurried. *Lacey's here. She brought friends.*

Leo and I exchanged looks and then hurried back. Zoe and Lacey were standing practically chest-to-chest by the time we got there, and I could tell my best friend was already trying to find out if Lacey had anything to do with the six people lying in pieces on the floor.

"No, you need to answer me right now," Zoe seethed, a finger right up in the councilwoman's face.

Lacey, for her part, was calm, but I could tell her patience was already beginning to stray. As soon as she saw me, her face lit up, and she neatly stepped around Zoe to move forward and meet me.

"Liana, what is going on?" she asked, her tone exasperated.

"You tell me," I demanded as I came to a halt in front of her. "When we first agreed to do the Tourney, I asked you to leave the youngest in our party alone. Well, she reached out to her guardian and said she was being chased. She told us where she was, but when we got here, she was gone and these people were dead!" Accusing Lacey outright was a tactic meant to unbalance her.

And to my surprise, it worked.

She frowned, a deep furrow forming between her eyebrows. Her eyes went over my shoulder to the horrific scene behind me, and a haunted look came over her face. "I... I was having her followed."

"WHAT?" I thundered, taking a step toward her, angry beyond belief. "You gave me your *word*!"

Lacey's eyes flashed angrily, and she took a step toward me as well, not backing down. "You didn't leave me any *choice*! Your lack of interest in our cause is beyond baffling. It's like you don't care about what happens to the Tower, yet your actions tell me the opposite! You didn't have to try so hard with Ambrose—you were being forced to look after him, after all—but you did. You *cared* about a man who was making you do something inconvenient! It was too inconsistent for me to fully trust you!"

"And the little girl's ability to disappear didn't help, either," a man said from behind her. I looked beyond her to see a group of eight or so standing there, waiting. The one who had spoken had a dark beard covering his cheeks, and perhaps the kindest eyes I had ever seen. Our eyes met, and he smiled. I looked away, uncomfortable with everything that was happening.

"You didn't apply that designer bacteria to us?" I scoffed, not entirely believing them. Lacey had given me her word that she wouldn't follow us, but since she had broken it, I had no reason to believe that she had kept her word about the bacteria as well.

"No, per your request," he replied coolly. "And for the record, if we had, we could've grabbed her easily. As it was, we could barely keep up with her half the time, and the other half of it she ran us in circles. We knew something was up when the net she was using was letting her access parts of the Tower she shouldn't, but Lacey only told us to watch out for her. See what she was up to, and protect her if anyone tried to hurt her."

I looked at Lacey, some of my anger fading into a small kernel of guilt. "You were keeping her safe?"

To my surprise, Lacey's mouth tightened. "I don't owe you an explanation," she said tightly. "Two of my people are dead now. The other four men... I don't know who they are, but they were probably the ones Tian called you about. Now they're dead, she's gone, and there is a killer on the loose. Let me help you—if only so I can find the monster that did this to my men."

Two of her people were dead. That meant four of the men on the floor were the ones who had been after Tian. Maybe Lacey's men had tried to intervene, and then were interrupted by the killer? It would explain why all the bodies were together like that.

But it didn't explain where Tian was—or who had killed the men. Had the killer taken Tian, or had she gotten away? Was she somewhere inside, too scared to say anything to let us know she was here?

Was she dead?

"We recovered some nets over there," Leo announced softly beside me, snapping me out of my grim thoughts. "Presumably they were yanked out by their assailant, but they are badly damaged. Perhaps you can recover their identification through them?"

I doubted we'd be able to. Whoever had pulled them out had gone through great pains to destroy them. Still, it was a lead. If we could find out who was after Tian, we could find out who their enemies were, and go from there. It wasn't much, but it was a start.

"I'll look into it," Lacey said. "In the meantime—Liana, where is Ambrose?" Lacey directed her gaze to me.

"He's with Maddox," I said after a pause, trying to remember. "He's fine. We need to find Tian."

I turned to go, but Lacey grabbed my arm, stopping me. "We will look for Tian," she said firmly. "You and Grey need to get back to Ambrose."

"No," I said, tugging my arm from her hand. "You're going to need as many people as you can to look for her!"

"And I will get more men," she said patiently. "But Ambrose only has Maddox to defend him."

"So send some of your own men!" I said, throwing up my hands. "I'm not leaving here until I find Tian!"

"You absolutely will leave, or I will hand over the evidence I have that implicates you and Grey in altering Scipio's memories to get away with murder!"

She ended her sentence with a shout, and I tensed, readying for a fight. If she wanted me to leave, she was going to have to physically remove me. Damned if I was going to let her threaten me.

The air was still and silent as we faced off, and for several long seconds, nobody moved.

"Lacey's right, Liana," Leo finally said, his voice gentle. "We should get back to Ambrose and... tell Maddox what we found. Zoe, Eric, and Quess can help Lacey look for Tian, and Maddox

can come join them, but Ambrose doesn't have enough protection on him right now."

I glared at him, instantly wanting to condemn him for being a
traitor, but stopped when I realized he was right. We couldn't leave
Ambrose alone for too long—his friends were no doubt gone by
now, and he and Maddox would be all alone. We had to get back.

I made an irritated sound and then sucked in several deep
breaths, trying to ease the fiery tempest that had built up inside
me at the very idea of abandoning Tian in her moment of need. I
wanted to tell Leo and Lacey both to go to hell, and keep searching. That was the right thing to do.

But so was going back to protect Ambrose.

"Quess, coordinate with Lacey and keep me updated. I'll
break the news to Maddox." I bit the orders out and then ended
the transmission with Quess before I could second guess myself.
Looking up at Lacey, I saw her watching me warily, as if afraid
of what I was going to do. "Find her," I forced out between
clenched teeth, trying not to cry. "Please."

Lacey nodded solemnly. "I will do everything I can," she
said softly.

I nodded once, and then left, while I still could.

Leo let me stew in silence as we made our way back to the apartment. Maybe he sensed that if he said anything, he would inter-
rupt the tightly repeated mantra that was the only thing keeping
me from going back to help look for Tian.

I am doing this for Tian. I am doing this for Tian.

It was occasionally interrupted by wandering thoughts about the room and the violence within, and all the questions the entire situation brought up. Why had someone gone to such elaborate lengths to disguise their feet? Forensically, there was nothing that could be determined by someone's footprint that gave conclusive proof as to who they were. And then there was that strange handprint—merely an outline with nothing inside. What could've left a print like that?

And the sheer level of violence behind the kill. The nets yanked out of their skulls. So many questions, with not a lot of answers. That frightened me, and it was hard not to feel like we were being watched.

I picked up the pace as our doors came into sight, but then stopped right outside of Ambrose and Leo's, hesitating. In a moment, I was going to have to tell Maddox that a group of people who had been following Tian had been torn apart, and that we had no idea where Tian was, nor any way to find her while her net was offline.

Maddox had lost so much. This was going to devastate her.

"I can tell her," Leo offered suddenly, and I looked over at where he was standing next to me. I offered him a sad smile, and shook my head.

"It's not your job," I replied simply. "Open the door, please."

Leo nodded, and pressed the button. I looked down at my shoes as it slid open, and took a few steps inside, dreading looking at Maddox. I moved into the open space between the dining room and kitchen, looked up, and froze.

Maddox was lying propped up against the island in the kitchen, her face bloody. All around her was an array of pots, pans, dishes, cutlery, and food, and I realized she hadn't gone down without a fight.

I was crossing the room to her before I even knew what happened, my heart in my throat while my fingers went to hers, feeling around for a pulse.

She coughed wetly as soon as I touched her and flinched back, her hands going up defensively.

"Maddox," I said soothingly. "It's me. It's Liana."

She stilled, lowering her arms to peer at me. Her eyes were purple and swollen, her green gaze slightly glazed, and a stab of pain wrenched at my heart to see her so battered. I struggled to find a place to touch her without hurting her more.

Recognition finally bloomed in her eyes, and she lowered her arms, hurriedly, as if she couldn't keep them up any longer. "Ambrose," she said hoarsely.

I turned around and stood up, my eyes roving through the small kitchenette and then into the living area. I left Maddox and moved into the living area, searching.

Leo was already there, kneeling next to Ambrose's fallen form. His fingers were withdrawing from Ambrose's throat, and as he swiveled his head to look at me, I could see the grave expression on his face.

"No." It was a flat-out denial, but it did nothing to change the look of sorrow in his eyes.

"He's gone," Leo said.

I clenched my eyes closed and balled my hands into fists.

First Tian, and now this? It was untenable. We had lost. Lacey was going to turn us in, and we would be caught long before we could find a way to replace Scipio, escape, or find Tian.

And long before I could find whoever had done this and kill them for it. I needed to think. There had to be some way I could get the others out of this. Maybe if I went to Lacey and begged her, she would just punish me and not them.

"What is going on here?!" a voice bellowed, and my eyes snapped open to see Lieutenant Salvatore Zale enter. In his early thirties, Zale was a handsome man with a thick, strong jaw and a swath of wavy, ink-black hair that he kept cut short on the sides, but thick on top. His eyes, however, were cold, like two chips of sapphire, and they blazed with open hostility as soon as he realized who I was. "You," he snarled, and I took a step back, alarmed by the anger there.

He took a step forward, deeper into the room, and saw Leo standing there. "I should've known."

This was bad. He clearly thought Leo and I had done this, and based on our history with Devon, I couldn't say I blamed him. Then again, the timing of his arrival, just moments after our own, was pretty suspicious, and I realized that I could easily be looking at Ambrose's murderer. It was the same move Devon had pulled on me—only this time it had worked, and Leo and I were caught.

Either way, it meant he was going to blame us no matter what we said.

"Lieutenant," Leo began, and I realized he was going to try anyway. "Our friend Maddox needs medical treatment immediately, and we need to start searching for whoever did this to our teammates. Clearly, someone is targeting us because of our standing in the Tourney."

"Are they indeed," Zale sneered, his face filled with disgust. "I've heard enough of your lies. Knights, arrest these murderers."

From the door behind him, several Knights appeared, their batons already out. I considered them for a moment—considered fighting my way out and making a run for it—but there were too many of them.

I slowly raised my hands, and then gave Leo a nod to do the same. A Knight approached me cautiously, reaching out to take my baton and pull it out of my belt, and then they rushed me, grabbing my arms and shoving me roughly to the ground.

I managed not to cry out as they wrenched my shoulder to shove my hands behind my back. I caught a glimpse of Leo being treated just as roughly, and then I was hauled up and shoved forward, stumbling with the violence of it.

As they continued to push me into the hall, I kept my hands clenched, and tried to maintain my calm. Getting angry now was counterproductive. If I wanted to get Leo and myself out of this, I needed to keep my wits about me.

Because otherwise, we were dead.

READY FOR THE NEXT PART OF LIANA'S STORY?

Dear Reader,

Thank you for reading *The Girl Who Dared to Descend*.

The next book in the series is Book 4, **The Girl Who Dared to Rise**, where you will discover what happened to Tian, and what left behind all that carnage — and where, in the aftermath of Ambrose's death, Liana will face her greatest challenge yet... This book is not to be missed!

The Girl Who Dared to Rise releases **December 18th, 2017**.

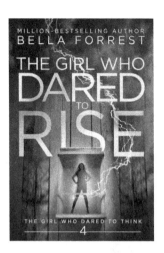

Visit: www.bellaforrest.net for details.

I'll see you on December 18th, back in the Tower...

Love,

Bella x

P.S. If you're new to my books or haven't yet read my **Gender Game** series, I suggest you check it out. It is where the Tower's story began and is set in the same world as *The Girl Who Dared* series—the two storylines complement each other.

P.P.S. Sign up to my VIP email list and I'll send you a personal heads up when my next book releases: **www.morebellaforrest.com**

(Your email will be kept 100% private and you can unsubscribe at any time.)

P.P.P.S. I'd also love to hear from you — come say hi on Twitter (@ashadeofvampire) or Facebook (facebook.com/Bella-ForrestAuthor). I do my best to respond :)

A Castle of Sand (Book 3)

A Shadow of Light (Book 4)

A Blaze of Sun (Book 5)

A Gate of Night (Book 6)

A Break of Day (Book 7)

Series 2: Rose & Caleb's story

A Shade of Novak (Book 8)

A Bond of Blood (Book 9)

A Spell of Time (Book 10)

A Chase of Prey (Book 11)

A Shade of Doubt (Book 12)

A Turn of Tides (Book 13)

A Dawn of Strength (Book 14)

A Fall of Secrets (Book 15)

An End of Night (Book 16)

Series 3: The Shade continues with a new hero...

A Wind of Change (Book 17)

A Trail of Echoes (Book 18)

A Soldier of Shadows (Book 19)

A Hero of Realms (Book 20)

A Vial of Life (Book 21)

A Fork of Paths (Book 22)

A Flight of Souls (Book 23)

A Bridge of Stars (Book 24)

Series 4: A Clan of Novaks

A Clan of Novaks (Book 25)

A World of New (Book 26)

A Web of Lies (Book 27)

A Touch of Truth (Book 28)

An Hour of Need (Book 29)

A Game of Risk (Book 30)

A Twist of Fates (Book 31)

A Day of Glory (Book 32)

Series 5: A Dawn of Guardians

A Dawn of Guardians (Book 33)

A Sword of Chance (Book 34)

A Race of Trials (Book 35)

A King of Shadow (Book 36)

An Empire of Stones (Book 37)

A Power of Old (Book 38)

A Rip of Realms (Book 39)

A Throne of Fire (Book 40)

A Tide of War (Book 41)

Series 6: A Gift of Three

A Gift of Three (Book 42)

A House of Mysteries (Book 43)

The Keep (Book 4)

The Test (Book 5)

The Spell (Book 6)

BEAUTIFUL MONSTER DUOLOGY

Beautiful Monster 1

Beautiful Monster 2

DETECTIVE ERIN BOND (Adult thriller/mystery)

Lights, Camera, GONE

Write, Edit, KILL

For an updated list of Bella's books, please visit her website: www.bellaforrest.net

Join Bella's VIP email list and she'll personally send you an email reminder as soon as her next book is out: www.morebellaforrest.com

CPSIA information can be obtained
at www.ICGtesting.com
Printed in the USA
BVHW030727010222
627732BV00001B/10

9 781947 607200